The car shuddered as a ghoul bounced on its wing, Ali tightening her grip on the wheel in a bid to keep the vehicle under control. She made little effort to avoid the deadheads – indeed, it was impossible to slalom between them, so dense was the crowd becoming – and concerned herself with ensuring the car stayed central on the road. The stiffs merely shuffled into its path like bugs collecting on the windscreen, utterly ignorant of the velocity the vehicle was moving at. The front end ploughed through a skinny naked man, who exploded like a dandelion in a strong wind, fragments washing back in the Escort's slipstream.

Hewitt was right, Gabe thought. Damn things are falling apart.

An Abaddon Books™ Publication
www.abaddonbooks.com
abaddon@rebellion.co.uk

First published in 2007 by Abaddon Books™, Rebellion Intellectual
Property Limited, The Studio, Brewer Street, Oxford, OX1 1QN, UK.

Distributed in the US and Canada by SCB Distributors.15608 South
Century New Drive, Gardena, CA 90248, USA.

10 9 8 7 6 5 4 3 2 1

Editor: Jonathan Oliver
Cover: Mark Harrison
Design: Simon Parr & Luke Preece
Marketing and PR: Keith Richardson
Creative Director and CEO: Jason Kingsley
Chief Technical Officer: Chris Kingsley

ISBN 13: 978-1-905437-13-9
ISBN 10: 1-905437-13-7
A CIP record for this book is available from the British Library

Printed in the UK by Bookmarque, Surrey

THE WORDS OF THEIR ROARING

Matthew Smith

Abaddon Books

WWW.ABADDONBOOKS.COM

For my mum and dad,
Who always knew... one day...

And for Emma,
Princess among Squaxx

Latimer spake to Ridley as fire was kindled: "Be of good cheer, Mr Ridley, and play the man. We shall this day light such a candle by God's grace in England, as I trust shall never be put out." With a bag of gunpowder around their necks, they were burned and Latimer apparently died quickly and with little pain, but Ridley burned slowly, and desired them for Christ's sake to let the fire come unto him. They heaped the faggots upon him, but it burned all his nether parts before it touched the upper, that made him leap up and down under the faggots, and often desire them to let the fire come unto him saying, "I cannot burn", and after his legs were consumed, he showed that side towards us clean, shirt and all untouched by flame.

In which pangs he laboured till one of the standers-by with his billhook pulled off the faggots above, and where he saw the fire flame up, he wrestled himself unto that side. When the flame touched the gunpowder he was seen to stir no more.

Foxe's Book of Martyrs,
16 October, 1555

PROLOGUE

Background Noise

"Did you say the stars were worlds, Tess?"

"Yes."

"All like ours?"

"I don't know; but I think so. They sometimes seem to be like the apples on our stubbard-tree. Most of them splendid and sound – a few blighted."

"Which do we live on – a splendid one or a blighted one?"

"A blighted one."

Thomas Hardy,
Tess of the D'Urbervilles

4 November 1917
Ten Miles East of Ypres, Belgium

As the soldier ran, he barely raised his eyes from the battle-scarred earth, intent on watching one foot replace the other, propelling him from danger. The rattle of gunfire had slowly faded the greater the distance he put between himself and the trenches, and the occasional mortar explosion was merely a dull thud behind him. Even so, he dared not slow his pace, despite the growing ache in his limbs. The ground was not easy to traverse; sludge becoming quagmire, plain disappearing into crater, every movement was an effort to stay upright, and to keep his boots on his feet. He had to pick his way carefully through barbed wire, sprawl in the mud if he thought he heard whisper of the enemy (and just who was that, now that he had chosen not to belong to one side or the other?). Exhaustion threatened to overwhelm him; but one notion kept him going, reassuring him as he watched his legs driving him towards that goal: escape.

Private William Steadman did not want to die.

He supposed there was a little of the childish logic in the way he kept his head down as he ran, reasoning that what he could not see would not hurt him; and rather than stop to get his bearings, he put all his effort into the act of flight itself, pointing himself in one direction and seeing where it would take him, as if he were a schoolboy released for the summer holidays. It was difficult to deny that he felt as lost and scared as if he was twelve years old, shrunken and vulnerable in an adult's uniform. But that was hardly a unique phenomenon; he'd seen his fellow soldiers – men perhaps in a civilian context he would've considered unscrupulous scoundrels and brawlers – reduced to bawling infants. Their faces had been masks of incomprehension and fear; they knew how close they were to death, how their dreams for the future, their desire to see their families again, hinged on an order.

To leave the comparative safety of the trench, cross no-man's-land and embrace the German guns was to strip a man of everything he had and was ever likely to have. And so Steadman, with his own tears icy on his cheeks, had had to listen to one of the most terrifying sounds he'd ever heard, far worse than the shriek of shrapnel cutting through the air: that of grown men crying with regret and loss. It was utterly alien and impossible to forget.

He slid his way down a bank and felt the dirt beneath him crumble. Trying to regain his balance, he increased his pace, but only succeeded in pushing himself forward and tumbling headfirst into the mud. He rolled onto his back, a part of his mind yelling at him to be back on his feet instantly, but a curious lethargy came over him, as if the earth were sapping him of strength; as if, once this close to it, it would suck him to its bosom – revenge for the damage that had been wrought on its surface. He imagined lying there, relaxing his grip on life and watching the sun and moon chase each other across the sky, his body slowly sinking into the ground, becoming part of the landscape like so many other corpses had. Every morning for the past sixteen months, he'd woken and looked out on carcasses littering the battlefield, human and animal seeding the soil. What would it be like, he wondered, to join that silent sea of the dead? To succumb to the exhaustion and close his eyes one final time? The idea stayed in his head longer than he anticipated, perversely attractive. In the last letter he'd written home, he'd said how he'd forgotten what it was like to be warm and clean, to eat and sleep in comfort, not to have the tight ball of dread lodged in his gut; those concerns would just fade away if he was to give up now, if he was to relinquish the struggle to survive...

Steadman clutched a handful of mud and brought it to his nose; it smelt rotten, diseased. It served to fuel his anger and clear his mind of any thoughts of surrender. He would not sacrifice himself for this war; it meant nothing to him. As was common with most of his comrades, he knew little of the history behind the conflict, the objectives of taking part in it, or indeed how the world will have changed once everything returned to normal. They had just been shipped over to this godforsaken hole, instructed to stand in a freezing field, point their guns in the direction of the Hun, and wait until they could be told they could go home. It was difficult to picture a more futile image than two sets of opposing forces facing each other down from opposite ends of a muddy stretch of earth, while somewhere – invisible, in another world – generals bluffed and blustered. It would be laughable, were it not for the thousands of men being thrown across the lines. Then, the stalemate became a massacre.

He held his commanders in absolute contempt. Their strategies were idiotic, their disregard for the troops who fought for them breathtaking; many was the time he had seen Allied shells landing on their own attacking battalions because the advance had been planned with so little forethought; or frightened, sobbing young lads barely out of puberty executed for refusing to go over the top, obviously incapable of holding a rifle without shaking let alone firing it. The injustice made him want to scream. He wanted to shout at the sky and pummel this sick, stinking earth. He was not some expendable, unthinking automaton they could put in front of the German bullets; as far as he was concerned, it *did* matter whether he lived or died. He thought of his parents raising him as a child, fretting when he was ill, glowing with pride when he returned from his first day at school, taking the time to show him the difference between right and wrong and the good teachings of the Lord, to be the best person he could be, and all that pain, all that effort, all that heartfelt love, blown away in an instant as he charged at the enemy and his brains splattered on the ground.

He clambered to his feet, taking deep breaths, steeling himself for the next stage of his journey. A mist was rolling in, the air chill and damp, and he assumed darkness would begin to fall within the next couple of hours. He had to find shelter if he was to last the night. He wished he'd remembered to get his watch repaired; the sky was sheathed in a thick blanket of cloud and gave nothing away, so he had little idea of the time. He didn't even know for how long he had been running; it seemed like most of the day, but he had a niggling suspicion that he hadn't covered as much ground as he hoped. The area was notoriously easy to get lost in, or to find oneself travelling in circles. He set off at a trot, intent on bedding down in the first shattered town building or abandoned farmhouse he came across.

But what exactly were his plans beyond that? He had no money, no contacts he could enlist to help him out of the country; his chance of escape seemed as slim as if he were back in the trench and awaiting that final whistle. The problem was that his desertion had been spur of the moment, a frantic bubbling of panic that eventually burst into full-blown terror. Although he had fixed bayonets in blank obedience and prepared to engage the enemy in combat, his gaze never straying to anyone on either side of him, the moment the signal came and the first soldiers went over and the shooting started, he had lost his nerve, dropped his rifle and faked injury. In the rush and confusion of men surging forward and then falling back as they were struck, he'd buried his head in his hands and played dead. As he'd willed himself to remain stationary, he could do nothing but listen to the thunderous, ear-splitting roar of the mortars, the high-pitched wail of injured men pleading for help and then cursing venomously when none arrived, and the rapid *thunk-thunk-thunk* of bullets meeting muscle and bone. When he'd opened his eyes, what was left of his regiment was several hundred yards away and he lay beneath a pile of bodies, butchered by machine-gun fire. Extricating himself slowly from the wretched heap, he'd crawled inch by inch in the opposite direction to the battle, praying silently that no one should see him and at the same time asking his Saviour to forgive his cowardice. Occasionally he would glance up, pulling corpses around him if he thought he heard anyone approaching, hating himself for his weakness. It was time consuming, arduous work, and he calmed himself through concentration, fixing his sight on some distant object, be it blasted tree or wire fence, and driving himself towards it. He was dimly aware that he was humming a hymn under his breath, a thin keening sound that suggested he was teetering on the brink of outright hysteria.

Indeed, this was insanity; he knew he had nowhere to go, knew he would be crossing dangerous terrain, knew he could give no excuse if he was discovered and was almost certainly facing court martial and the firing squad. But, he had reasoned, he had made his decision, however sudden, and should stick to the matter in hand, putting all his effort into finding a way out of this mess rather than questioning its wisdom. When he came to a secluded spot he vomited copiously, and some of the anxiety seemed to drain away with it; his mind was set, and every minute he stayed alive was a tiny triumph.

With that, he had wiped his mouth and started to run. Onward, Christian soldier, he had thought bitterly.

He had been fortunate, of that there was no doubt, that he had not been picked off by some lone sniper, and he was aware that his luck could not last for much longer. It occurred to him that maybe he had been seen by the enemy, but they had discerned in him no threat; they recognised a scared fellow human being fleeing for his life, someone who had opted out of the war, and who was not worth the trouble or the waste of ammunition. The thought gave him hope; he imagined others like him, from all sides of the conflict, congregating to wait out the hostilities. But such a haven amidst this hell, he realised, sounded fantastical.

Darkness was closing in far more quickly than he had guessed. Soon it would be pitch black, and he would be stranded out on the plain; it would be a choice of freezing to death during the night (a fire was out of the question if he was trying to avoid attention, even in the unlikely event of him finding dry tinder), or blundering on through the dark, and risk impaling himself on barbed wire or stumbling in on a German gun emplacement. Neither option appealed. He scanned the horizon for any kind of shelter, but saw nothing. He slowed his pace to a walk, his eyes roving the landscape, but the light was faltering with every step; he could barely see his hand in front of his face. Resignation and a little fear were just beginning to worry at him, to gnaw away at his resolve, when something tripped him up.

Despite himself, he yelped in alarm as he flopped to the ground and immediately swore; he knew instantly that it was a body his legs were hooked across, and more often than not where there was a body there were the remnants of an army. He glanced around quickly, certain his cry would've alerted somebody on watch, and sure enough, if he squinted, he could make out the thick seam of shadow that was a trench. But there was no sign of life. Steadman lay motionless for long minutes, waiting for anyone to emerge from the darkness, the razor-sharp wind chilling his skin and raising goosebumps. He resisted the urge to shiver, and breathed slowly, watching the thin, condensed streams dissipating in the air. But from the trench there was no movement.

Gradually, he began to edge forward, kicking his legs away from the corpse and lifting himself up onto his knees. If the trench was occupied, he thought, there had to be some kind of guard. But there was no light, no muted chatter or snores. The only explanation was that it had been overrun, the soldiers inside killed; but which side did it belong to? And could reinforcements be heading this way even as he sat here and deliberated?

Steadman turned back to the body, his hands outstretched in front of him like a blind man, feeling the contours of the uniform, his eyes aching as he concentrated in trying to see through the gloom. The design of the jacket was unfamiliar; the man seemed to have been an officer. Steadman's fingers grazed a holster and he gingerly removed the revolver, running his touch over it. It was of German issue. Clutching the gun in one hand, he lightly brushed the man's face, grimacing when his index finger disappeared into a penny-sized bullet hole in the man's forehead. It came away sticky.

At least they hadn't died by gas, he mused. It meant he wasn't in any immediate danger.

Wiping himself on the corpse's tunic, he looked back at the trench; it would be ideal to see out the night, hopefully providing him with some much-needed supplies, and it was unlikely British troops would be back this way if it had been disabled. The only problem he could foresee was a German regiment answering an injured radio operator's request for help just before he died and arriving here at daybreak. Then again, he could probably make use of one of the slain soldiers' uniforms and disguise himself amongst the dead once more.

He stood and moved to the lip of the trench, peering over cautiously; there was a dribble of light weakly spilling across the duckboards at the bottom. He returned to the German officer's body, took hold of both stiff arms and dragged it back with him, yanking it over the wire that circumscribed the trench's edge with as much strength as he could muster. The weight of the carcass made it bow in the middle, and he stepped across quickly, easing himself down into the earthwork. His eyes sought the light he had seen, and discovered it was buried beneath several corpses; faintly illuminated pale white faces stared up at him, the blood that criss-crossed their features appearing black in the darkness. He pulled them away dismissively, ignoring the lifeless thumps they made as they landed at his feet, and grasped the lamp – little more than a half-melted candle in a glass case – in his left hand before swinging it to either side of him.

"Sweet Jesus," he whispered.

It was an atrocity: the dead lay stacked like timber the length of the trench, one on top of the other. Each new sweep of the lamp brought a fresh horror, a new coupling, as soldier was piled upon soldier; they had been slaughtered like cattle in an abattoir. Steadman had thought he had witnessed every possible obscenity that man could perpetrate on his fellows, but this brought the bile rushing to his throat in an instant; there was something about the sheer scale of devastation here, all contained within the claustrophobic confines of the trench, that made him retch. That, and the noxious smell, which seemed to palpably clog the air; it was the sickly stench of matter breaking down and liquefying, yet these corpses looked as if they had only been dead several hours at the most. It wasn't as if the heat of day could have brought about such a change; it had rained steadily the past few weeks, the temperature barely a couple of degrees above zero.

He brought the back of his free right hand to cover his nose and realised he still held the gun. It seemed suddenly paltry and comically unnecessary in the face of such carnage, but he felt loath to let go of it. As he gripped it tighter, he sensed himself drawing strength from it, gaining courage. Slowly, he began to walk down the trench in search of the supplies centre, the dead pressed high to either side of him, threatening to topple over onto him at any moment and drown him in cold, white flesh. He felt a little of the wariness the Israelites must have experienced as they were led between those high, dark, roiling walls of the Red Sea with nothing but their faith to protect them.

Steadman tried to keep his eyes on the ground, using the lamp to guide himself past outstretched limbs that he would've otherwise stumbled over, but the lure to raise the light and gaze upon the ravaged soldiers' features was too great. A ghoulish curiosity, he supposed. The sight was appalling, but he kept returning to it, testing his endurance the way the tongue endlessly probes a painful tooth; agonising yet irresistible. Even so, when he did glance up, many of the dead no longer had recognisable features; their faces were indistinct, pulpy masses as if they'd been shot at close range. Others were eviscerated, evidently bayoneted repeatedly. He shook his head, ashamed to call himself human, refusing to align himself with a species that could commit such heinous acts of barbarism.

Why had they been so systematically slaughtered, and with such an obviously bloodthirsty callousness, he wondered. If this was the result of some mania, why then take the time to stack the bodies as if for a funeral pyre?

The smell was beginning to make him feel dizzy, and every time he closed his eyes gory images assailed him. His legs cried out for rest, and his throat for water. He was on the verge of collapse when the lamp illuminated the opening to some kind of officers' structure ahead, judging by the map table standing outside it. He sighed with relief and increased his pace towards it. There was a tarpaulin hanging across the entrance acting as a makeshift door, and Steadman hoped it would provide adequate shelter, not only to shield him from the cold but also remove from view, at least temporarily, the horrors of the trench: out of sight, if not mind. He covered the last few yards at speed and stumbled inside, pulling the sheeting closed behind him.

The first thing that caught his eye was the bed in the corner, half-hidden in shadow; he couldn't remember the last time he'd felt the caress of a pillow. He looked around the dark room quickly, taking in the large table, the surface of which was scattered with the remains of a meal, a couple of chairs, the stove, the walls plastered with maps and directives. He crossed to the table, placed the lamp and the revolver upon it, picked up a jug three quarters full of water, and took a long swig; it tasted rusty, but he drained it to the last drop. Then, he searched for scraps of food on the plates, shovelling hard pieces of bread into his mouth and chewing appreciatively before slumping exhaustedly into a chair.

Steadman sat unmoving for what seemed a very long

time, too spent to think cohesively. Finally, he ran his hands over his face, his fingers rasping against his unshaven chin, and realised he was trembling. He felt hollow and scared; he would need a miracle to get out of this situation. He tried to reason through the consequences of today's actions and plan what he should do next, but his mind would not stay still for a moment; it fluttered, startled, from one scenario to another and would not allow him to concentrate. He assumed it was tiredness; his eyelids were beginning to droop as sleep crept up on him, and he was just considering whether to attempt to get the furnace going before burying himself beneath the bedclothes when he heard a soft mewling coming from the far corner.

He froze, unsure whether he had imagined it, deciding it could possibly be a combination of the wind and his fatigued senses. But then it came again, louder, undoubtedly human. It sounded like someone in considerable distress. He inched his hands across to the lamp and pistol and simultaneously rose to his feet, taking cautious steps around the table. There was a shape on the floor, silhouetted in the blackness. He shuffled closer and crouched down, lifting the lantern to see clearly.

Lying with his back to the wall was a British soldier, his familiar uniform soaked with blood. His eyes, rolling wide in their sockets like a beast aware of its impending death, squinted at the sudden light and tried to turn his head to face it. As he did so, Steadman saw the extent of the man's appalling injuries: a portion of the right side of his skull was missing, a cavernous red hole where his ear should have been, fragments of bone and clumps of hair standing at right angles. There was a vermilion halo sprayed on the wall behind him. Between his legs were three kerosene cans.

The soldier kept attempting to open his mouth to speak, but only made the soft, piteous cry that Steadman had heard. The man's eyes were moving wildly as if panic-stricken, his head shaking from side to side. Steadman got the impression that he was trying to communicate something, or maybe to warn him, but it wasn't until the man raised his right hand that had otherwise been hidden beneath his body and revealed the gun that was still clutched in it that he realised the horrific truth: the soldier had done this to himself. It had meant to be a suicide, but something had gone wrong, for it had left him mortally wounded and more than likely out of his mind in pain and shock. He pointed at the doorway and pulled the trigger repeatedly, grunting with each effort as the hammer slammed down on empty chambers. Presumably he'd tried to use the last bullet on himself.

"Can you hear me? Can you understand?" Steadman started to say, but faltered, realising it was pointless.

He muttered an oath under his breath, unable to comprehend. He felt dislocated, as if in his escape he had torn through a veil and discovered madness existing alongside him. He wanted to ask him what had happened here, what had terrified him to the point of trying to take his own life, but the soldier was obviously beyond rational thought; indeed, it was remarkable that he was still alive at all. But it left Steadman with a dilemma; he was loath to leave him in this state and prolong his suffering, but didn't know if he possessed the courage to finish what the man had started. The latter was the merciful option (there was nothing a medic could do for him now), but he wasn't sure he could reconcile that fact with his faith. In all his twenty-five years on the planet, he had never killed anything higher up the food chain than a bluebottle.

Odd, he mused, that with all the mass murder going on around him, thousands of men dying in seconds to capture a few feet of ground, he should balk at one act of kindness.

The soldier started to wail louder, and Steadman thought he caught the semblance of actual words beneath it; surprised, he moved closer, straining to hear.

"... they... they *come*..." he gurgled, waving the gun in front of him. "... they know you're here..."

"Who? The Germans?"

If the man heard the question, he gave no indication. "... burn... should've *burned*..." His voice descended into a groan.

Steadman was puzzled for a moment, then glanced down at the kerosene cans and flashed back to the corpses piled outside.

... *as if for a funeral pyre...*

... *burn...*

"Mother of God," he said quietly. Understanding gradually began to dawn, and with it came a tingle of fear; had this soldier been left here to destroy the remains? But to what end? To cover up a war crime? Or to make absolutely sure they were truly dead? For some reason he hadn't been able to go through with it – what had he seen that suicide was the only way out?

There was a scrabbling from beyond the doorway, a sound that turned Steadman's bowels to water. The dying soldier suddenly became animated, shaking and crying ever more violently. Steadman stood and backed away, his eyes fixed on the tarpaulin-covered entrance. He tried to reason that it could be rats scurrying amongst the bodies, but couldn't even convince himself. He felt his breaths becoming shorter, his scalp prickle with sweat despite the chill. The revolver was slippery in his hand.

A low moan echoed outside; and then the sheeting bulged as if something was pushing against it, looking for a way in. Steadman attempted to swallow, the inside of his mouth like sandpaper, and raised the gun. He sensed a breeze brush against his face, but had seen nothing come through the doorway; he moved nearer, peering into the gloom.

"Show yourself," he demanded, his voice cracking; then yelled in fright as something grabbed his leg. He staggered, glanced down and recoiled in disgust: the upper half of a German soldier's torso was crawling across the floor, one hand clutched around his ankle. In its wake, like a snail's trail, it left a glistening smear of blood, painted there by the entrails emerging from its rapidly evacuating stomach cavity. Its head was upturned, its eyes glazed, its mouth open and emitting a tiny wail from the back of its throat. Immobilised with shock, Steadman could do nothing but stare as the creature puts its lips to his trouser leg and attempt to bite through it.

Blinking himself out of his paralysis, he roared in revulsion, kicked out at it and managed to loosen its grip; he stepped away and without thinking fired the gun, catching it in the shoulder. The impact knocked it back, but it was clearly still alive; it struggled to right itself like a turtle flipped onto its shell. Steadman moved closer in horrified fascination, raising the revolver for a better shot, then caught himself before he could pull the trigger. He'd never killed anything before, either on two legs or four, and yet here he was prepared to act without pause; this creature, as his mind had fixedly called it, was still a man. He had survived horrendous injuries, either through enormous willpower or some quirk of physiology that enabled the heart to still beat even as the veins and arteries spurted into empty air, and, like the

British soldier, could not be long for this world. Did that give him the right to help usher him towards death?

The German was crawling in his direction once more. Clearly, despite the pain he must be in, he was not going to give up on Steadman as his objective. Steadman allowed him to draw closer, and dropped to his haunches.

"I cannot help you," he enunciated, wishing he could recall what little of the language he knew. He shook his head, holding up his hands. *"Nicht... gut..."*

The man didn't seem to understand, or even to hear him. Still he approached, whimpering like a whipped dog, his insides rasping against the wooden floor. He grasped Steadman's boot and started gnawing on it as if it were a bone; Steadman could feel teeth attempting to penetrate the leather. Tears sprang in his eyes; he knew now that this was not one man desperately clinging onto life despite the ravages of his injuries. This was something else entirely, something beyond any kind of reasoning. He was no longer human, but the product of something... unholy. He shook himself free of the man's clutches, put the revolver to the back of his skull and squeezed his eyes shut at the same time as he squeezed the trigger. He winced at the bang, thinking: forgive me.

When he opened his eyes, the man was finally motionless, the contents of his head spread out in a parabola around him. Steadman shivered uncontrollably, the gun trembling before him. He could not stay in this charnel pit a moment longer; better he took his chances on the battlefield or in a military cell than spend the night amongst this horror.

He moved towards the doorway, glancing back at the British soldier when he heard him cry out. "I'm sorry," he said, turning his head away.

Steadman pulled back the tarpaulin and bit down on a

scream: the trench was alive. Where there was once dead stacked upon dead, shadows now shifted and slithered, a familiar wail carrying on the wind. He saw arms and hands clawing themselves free like the freshly buried rising from their graves. Dark figures wobbled as they stood and grew accustomed to their newfound resurrection; some were missing appendages, some emptied viscera at their feet the moment they were upright, but it didn't take them long for their heads to turn in his direction. He could see them sense him, almost as if they were sniffing the air and hearing the beat of a warm, living heart. They began to shuffle forward, tripping over one another, the trench a tangle of grasping limbs.

Steadman did not hesitate. He rushed back to the soldier, grabbed the kerosene cans and began to splash fuel through the entranceway at the approaching creatures. When all three cans were empty, he flung the lantern into the throng.

Instantly, the dark confines of the trench became an explosion of light. The first of the figures were immediately immolated, man-sized candles awkwardly stumbling into those behind, the touch allowing the fire to spread. Thick black smoke began billowing into the air, and soon it was impossible to distinguish between the shapes being devoured by the wall of flame. For a moment, Steadman felt a small spark of hope; the inferno seemed to have halted them. But mere seconds later he saw that they were still coming, implacable and relentless, that ever-present moaning barely rising an octave. The ones at the front were shrivelled husks, turning to ash before his eyes, but they were replaced by others, unconcernedly treading on their fallen comrades as they surged forwards.

Steadman let loose a cry of frustration and fired at the nearest creature, blowing a puff of soot from its arm.

There was no way out. He checked the chambers of the revolver and found he had three bullets left. That was at least some comfort.

He walked over to the British soldier and knelt beside him. He knew what Steadman intended and nodded slightly, his eyes pleading. Steadman embraced him and placed the gun barrel under his chin, offering a silent prayer before firing.

He sat down next to the body and surveyed the room, littered with the dead. His faith had instructed him that life was to be preserved at all costs – but that had been shattered. Death was preferable to the parody of life these creatures exhibited.

They were beginning to come through the doorway, shadows dancing on the walls as the flames flickered. They bumped into the table and chairs and bed, trying to find their way around, igniting fires as they did so.

He put the revolver in his mouth, tasting the oil. Funny: he had refused to be sacrificed to the war, made the choice of life over death, and yet here he was preparing to offer himself up to Purgatory. This seemed the lesser of two evils; whatever those things were – and the Army was aware of them, that was plainly evident – he guessed that if they took him, he would end up in a far, far worse place. Better this way; better a sinner than a victim of the Devil's works.

Steadman turned his head and looked up at a map of Europe on the wall, which was starting to smoulder and blacken as the creatures brushed past. Maybe this is the Apocalypse, he thought as his finger tightened on the trigger. Maybe this is the beginning of the end.

If they're the future... God help the living.

PART ONE

A Sound Like Breaking Glass

Cruell and sodaine, hast thou since
Purpled thy naile, in blood of innocence?

John Donne,
The Flea

Now

CHAPTER ONE

The head didn't so much explode when hit by the bullet as deflate, a fat sack of gas puckering like an emptied balloon, haloed by a blossoming cloud of dust and powdered shards of ancient bone.

"Fuckin' things are rotten," Hewitt muttered. "See the way it burst like a goddamned watermelon?"

Gabe grunted a reply, chambering another round. He put his eye to the infrared sight and swept the street, their vantage point from atop the multi-storey car park offering a decent view of the shadowy thoroughfare beneath them. Dark figures were stumbling in the blood-red gloom of the eyepiece, hunched silhouettes shuffling aimlessly from one side of the road to the other. They seemed unperturbed by the shot that had rung out seconds earlier, or the fact that the skull of one of their brethren had vanished in a puff of miasmic residue, what was left below the neck keeling over like a felled tree. They stepped over him – or, rather, through him, snagging their feet on his form if they wandered too close – barely aware the body was even there. Gabe moved the rifle in tiny increments, following the path of each figure, trying to gauge the numbers, his crosshairs alighting on one for several moments before drifting across to its nearest companion.

"Well?" he heard Hewitt ask. "How many you reckon?"

"About two dozen in the street," he answered quietly, continuing his vigil. "Seem fairly spread out. Can't see too many nooks and crannies to hold any nasty surprises."

He felt Hewitt shift up onto his knees beside him and once more peer into his night-vision binoculars. It was enough for Gabe to finally take his eye from the rifle-sight and irritably study his colleague. The kid annoyed him for numerous reasons – he was excitable but lacked the experience to put that enthusiasm to good use, he wasted ammo, and he had a sarcastic streak, a trait Gabe found particularly ignoble – but it never failed to particularly rankle him that Hewitt would often ask his opinion then double-check it for himself immediately afterwards. Gabe guessed the kid was trying to assume he had some kind of say in the decision-making process, rather than being the extra pair of hands he undoubtedly was, useful only for the inevitable donkey work. If it weren't for the bountiful haul they were expecting, Gabe would quite happily go on one of these missions alone. He could certainly do without having to converse with the little idiot. But he kept these niggles to himself, chiefly because Flowers seemed fond of the kid – Hewitt was, after all, eager to please and would go out of his way to find favour in the boss man's eyes, looking to weasel his way up the hierarchy. You had to watch what you said sometimes, in case a version of the truth spilled back to the wrong people.

"Yeah," Hewitt drawled with an infuriating note of authority to his voice that sounded alien coming out of his mouth. "Two dozen looks about right to me too." He turned to Gabe. "Where's the store?"

"Right at the end, in a little square offset from the main street."

"Shit." He looked anxiously again through the binoculars.

Gabe tried to stop the smile that creased his lips, but nothing could prevent it. He turned his head away so the kid wouldn't catch sight of it. "I think we can take 'em. Four-man team shouldn't have any trouble."

"What about the way back? We're gonna be weighed down—"

"I'll keep you covered, don't worry," Gabe said, admonishing himself for the patronising tone that had snuck in. He glanced at the man and woman silently crouched against one of the car park's concrete pillars behind them. "Ali, Davis – there's no other way round, so we'll be going straight through. Stay sharp. Standard routine; pick your targets and don't panic, okay?"

"Can't we use the motor?" the man – Davis – asked.

"Road's fucked," Hewitt interjected.

"What he said," Gabe continued. "It's blocked with debris, and we can't risk cracking an axle. We'll drive up as far as we can go, then we'll have to be quick on our toes. Ali, you'll have to stay with the vehicle. Keep the engine running; let us know if the situation develops. I don't want to come out of there and find someone's stolen our ride."

The woman nodded. "You think there's others like us in the area?"

"Not in the immediate vicinity – deadheads are too concentrated – but our gunshots are gonna be heard by pockets of survivors, no question of that. Anything pops up that ain't maggoty, you give us a squawk."

Davis clicked the safety off on his snubnose. "This had better be worth it."

"Michaelson's info hasn't let us down yet," Gabe said, swinging his rifle onto his shoulder as he stood. "Come on, let's hop to it."

They scampered through the heavy silence of the abandoned car park, their feet tapping quietly against the cold grey ground. Lights still burned in fluorescent tubes positioned on the ceiling, powered by a forgotten generator left rumbling untended in the bowels of the building, giving the vast open space surrounding them a stark, flat glare. A few vehicles were dotted around this level, some of them with their doors hanging wide as if the occupants had fled in a great hurry. Rancid bags of food bulged from the open hatchback of a nearby Fiat, a black cloud of flies rising from it as they passed, settling in their wake. Tyre marks and oil splatters streaked the floor, and something darker and textured was sprayed up against a ticket machine. A fading crimson handprint neatly filled one of the reinforced glass panels of a door that led to the stairwell, the wood beneath it splintered as if repeatedly kicked.

Gabe led the others through the concrete expanse, gluing themselves to the walls where they could, avoiding the impenetrable shadows of the stairs or the lift shaft till they came in sight of his armoured Escort. He tossed the keys to Ali and motioned for her to start it up, then scanned the pools of fluorescent light diminishing into the distance. The emptiness was unnerving. If he concentrated, beyond the silence he could hear the moans drifting on the still air. In truth, they were always there, a white-noise hum you tried to tune out. It was a permanent aural backdrop, like mordant birdsong.

But all the birds are gone, he thought not for the first time, cocking his head and looking out at the starless night, and the skies and treetops and roofs of the city will never echo with their sound again.

The vehicle barked into life, the roar of Ali revving the accelerator rebounding off the concrete walls. The noise would undoubtedly attract some attention, but the stiffs were going to know they were amongst them soon enough anyway. Davis yanked open the rear door behind the driver's seat and folded himself in; Hewitt sparked up a cigarette and clambered in the other side, positioning his shotgun through the window. Gabe stood for a moment beside the rumbling car, listening to its timbre, holding a palm against the vibrating roof, confident that the engine was turning over smoothly, careful to discern there were no wheezy splutters emerging from the exhaust pipe. He'd briefly and inexpertly serviced the car himself only a few days before, but he had to make sure they could rely on their ride. London was no longer a town that you wanted to travel by foot if you could help it.

Satisfied, he swung into the bucket seat beside Ali and strapped himself in. The interior was refitted to provide the maximum protection, the tubular bars of a roll cage strengthening the shell if the Escort were to flip. Outside, front and rear windscreens were covered with a thick wire mesh that didn't particularly aid visibility but were a lifesaver when it came to force of numbers attempting entry. Similarly, the side panelling and roof were reinforced with steel plates capable of withstanding a high-speed impact. It meant the vehicle had the rather undignified appearance of a hammered-together metal box, but previous excursions had proved both its reliability and durability; many a time Gabe had ploughed it through a dozen-strong crowd of stiffs with barely a dent on the bodywork, their grasping fingers unable to find purchase, grave-brittle bones snapping when struck. It wasn't quite a tank – though Hewitt had badgered him often enough (not entirely jokingly) for some kind of mortar cannon to be operated through the sunroof – but it suited its purpose.

Ali guided the car past the raised exit barriers, the attendant booths long deserted, and onto the slip road. Gabe repeated the route to her, noting a handful of shambling figures detaching themselves from the twilight. The vehicle was like a beacon to them, its sound and movement awakening their interest – the only living thing, in all likelihood, for a radius of a couple of miles. He heard Hewitt working the slide on the shotgun behind him, and glanced in the wing-mirror to see him lean out slightly, flicking the dog-end of his cigarette at the nearest zombs.

"I don't want you taking any unnecessary potshots, Hewitt," Gabe warned him. "Conserve your ammo."

"Yeah, yeah," Hewitt murmured in reply, resting the barrel on the window frame.

Gabe turned in his seat to face the kid, but the younger man refused to meet his gaze, instead concentrating furiously on the darkened buildings passing by. Davis clearly caught the tension between the two, though said nothing.

"I'm serious," Gabe remarked. "There are far, far too many of the things for us to gun down every one indiscriminately, and it's just a waste of resources we can't afford to squander. This isn't a duck-shoot. You choose your targets and you make them count, understand?"

"I said I heard you, O'Connell," the kid answered, glaring at Gabe finally. "I have done this once or twice before, you know. Christ, I can handle it."

"I know you've done it before." Gabe softened his tone, returning to face the front. "I'm just saying: don't leave yourself open."

"Main street's coming up on the left," Ali said quietly.

"OK, we'll only be able to get a couple of hundred yards down it before we'll have to bail out."

The dead were emerging in increasing numbers, their hungered, soul-black groans growing in volume. They staggered from shadowy shopfronts and doorways, stumbling off the pavement and onto the road, what little senses still chiming in their grey-green skulls alerting them to the proximity of warm flesh. They made half-hearted attempts at reaching out to the car as it sped past them, their cries developing a note of angry disappointment. Gabe watched them in the mirror attempt a stiff-legged pursuit, arms held out in front of them, pushing past one another with an eagerness that seemed at odds with their barely functioning bodies. *They only come alive at the prospect of food*, he thought, *and right now we're their movable feast.*

"Fuckers," Hewitt murmured from the back, grimacing at the throng with an unconcealed hatred.

Ali slowed the Escort slightly to take the turn onto the main road, wrenching hard on the steering wheel. The tyres span on something on the tarmac and lost their purchase, the vehicle's rear fishtailing, and for a moment the car was skidding, the sharp screech of rubber drowning out the cries of the dead. The woman pumped the brake and steered into the slide, bringing the car to a juddering halt; thrusting it into gear, she stomped on the accelerator and the vehicle lunged forward, powering down the high street. Watching her from the corner of his eye, Gabe noticed that Ali hadn't even broken a sweat, her face a mask of grim determination. A small, morose woman in her forties, an ex-wife of one of Flowers' button men, she was one of the best drivers in the boss man's predictably male-dominated outfit and had characteristically proven her worth with little flamboyance or showy technique. Even Hewitt held his tongue when piloted by her, confident in her hands.

"What was it?" Gabe asked over his shoulder.

"Roadkill, I think," Davis answered, peering out of the back window at a red pulpy residue the car had just skidded through. "Something splattered across the highway."

"Remains of the day," Hewitt remarked, snorting back a laugh. "Somebody ended up zombie supper."

"Enough of that," Gabe snapped, trying to keep the tension from his voice. "Concentrate on the job in hand."

The hordes of dead were becoming more clotted as they sped forward, a clawing, mewling mass that shambled towards the Escort as one. The longest deceased were merely desiccated skeletons clothed in a tissue-thin brown veil of rank flesh, their eyes shrivelled back into their sockets, their crooked limbs flapping independently of the torso as if the muscle and bone within had perished; the freshest corpses had recognisable features, the skin grey and taut, their fatal wounds often readily apparent. They were young and old, male and female, of all races, from every level of the social strata. Death was the great leveller, no question of that, Gabe mused. There was no distinction between them anymore, nothing to separate this mob into individual entities: a paunchy bald man in a torn business suit lurched beside a teenager in motorcycle leathers with a scarlet-raw face, and a grandmother still clothed in her burial shroud and caked in the undertaker's make-up. They paid no heed to each other, each seemingly oblivious to their neighbour and indeed the numbers of their kin surrounding them; locked inside their own private resurrection, all they wanted, all they hungered for, was the living, driven by an insatiable craving their brains could not possibly fathom.

The car shuddered as a ghoul bounced off its wing, Ali tightening her grip on the wheel in a bid to keep the vehicle under control. She made little effort to avoid the deadheads – indeed, it was impossible to slalom between them, so dense was the crowd becoming – and concerned herself with ensuring the car stayed central on the road.

The stiffs merely shuffled into its path like bugs collecting on the windscreen, utterly ignorant of the velocity the vehicle was moving at. The front end ploughed through a skinny naked man, who exploded like a dandelion in a strong wind, fragments washing back in the Escort's slipstream.

Hewitt was right, Gabe thought. *Damn things are falling apart.*

"Don't think I can go much further," Ali yelled above the *thump-thump-thump* of the dead rebounding off the bodywork or fists slamming down on the steel panelling. The car's suspension started to bounce as it rolled over cadavers and rubble. Several blackened vehicles lay on their sides on the pavement ahead, or poking half out of shattered shop windows. A bus leaned precariously against a wall, displaying its undercarriage.

"OK, this is the end of the line, guys," Gabe shouted, tearing free his seat belt. "Hewitt, Davis – create a circumference, then follow me." He turned to the woman. "Ali, once they start following us, that'll take the heat off you. Turn the car around, keep her running. We're not back in ten minutes, get out of here."

"Good luck."

Gabe smiled. "Piece of cake."

Hewitt was the first out, simultaneously throwing open the door and discharging his shotgun at the nearest knot of ghouls; the blast punched through them as if he had hurled a grenade, flinging a handful backwards and, in one case, bisecting another at the waist. He worked the slide and fired again, popping a number of heads with a single shell, then used the butt to club the skull of a zombie in a stained traffic warden's uniform that dared to venture too close. *Goddamn*, he thought, *that felt satisfying.*

Davis appeared on the other side of the Escort and sprayed the dead with a burst from his sub-machine gun, raking them with bullets that tore through their empty, papery carcasses. They folded like wheat before a thresher. He pulled his snubnose from the waistband of his jeans with his left hand and snapped off half a dozen deft, accurate headshots, silencing the prone, moaning zombies forever.

Gabe clambered from the car, put his rifle to his shoulder and marched forward, firing with each step, taking down a ghoul at a time. He didn't break his stride but swung his gun smoothly from left to right, choosing each target quickly and calmly. His breathing was shallow and composed, his actions clinical, unhurried; he simply switched off that part of his brain that whispered just how close he was to being eaten alive, a hair's breadth away from having his entrails devoured before his very eyes.

It was a tightrope-walk act, a death-defying (*un*death-defying?) feat, acknowledging the physical danger he was in but reaching an inner equilibrium that would not surrender to it. He had lived and fought in this land of the dead for long enough to adapt to it and meet its challenges accordingly. Nothing would faze him, he didn't think, not ever again; not even the bizarre sight of two undead schoolgirls – little more than fifteen, he guessed, when they had resurrected – stuttering towards him, white blouses slathered in blood, tights and sneakers shredded, a forearm wound on one of them open to the bone and suppurating, the cheek of the other swollen with blowfly. He felt an undeniable tingle of sadness as he watched them stagger, groans emerging from their still lungs, their misted eyes fixed unshakably on him; but the pause was only momentary as he dropped both to the ground with a couple of neat holes drilled in their foreheads.

"Let's go," Gabe shouted, satisfied that they had cleared enough breathing space. "Move."

"You sure you know the way?" Hewitt demanded.

"Just follow me."

The three of them ran. Each man had flares tucked into his belt, and they would light one at regular intervals and drop it to the ground as they progressed, creating a landing strip for them to move through. The ghouls feared fire for some reason – a primeval terror that apparently still functioned in their putrid cerebella – and the burning torches made them pause. Gabe was in the lead, his rifle held against his chest, swatting away any stiffs that came within two feet of him, trying to limit his ammo usage. It didn't take much effort to knock the walking dead to the ground, their reactions and balance dulled by entropy – if you were quick on your feet and kept your wits about you, you could embark on short trips like this with the minimum of hindrance – and right now all he considered them to be was an annoyance to be avoided rather than an enemy that needed destroying. Maybe the day would come when the living would take to the streets and attempt to wipe out the zombies, but there were too many of them at the moment for such an undertaking to be practical. It would require an organised army to perform the necessary cull, and even the government and military had seemingly lost all pretence of containing the situation. All that was left was for guys like Flowers, and no doubt many others, to seize the opportunities that the world now presented them with, and make a killing.

He cast an eye over his shoulder to check his colleagues were still behind him. Davis followed, arms outstretched, his snubnose in one hand and his machine-gun in the other, turning his head left and right as he made sure the ghouls were kept at bay, occasionally firing a short burst into the throng. He was a big man, over six foot and wide around the midriff, his physique made even bulkier by the body armour he wore over his chest. It was supposedly one more layer of defence for the dead to tear through if you ever found yourself compromised, but Gabe considered such garments restricting when speed was of the essence. He presumed Davis had purloined the vest from his former occupation as a cop – along with what seemed half his station's armoury – and the skills he brought to Flowers' organisation made him a valuable member of the team. It took Harry a while to trust having an ex-policeman in the outfit, Gabe remembered, but these days notions of law and criminality were redundant, brushed aside by a common foe to be united against. Davis kept himself to himself mostly, no doubt ruminating on the strange path fate had chosen for him, and perhaps a touch ashamed too.

Hewitt was bringing up the rear, keeping watch on the ragged bunches of the dead that were regrouping in the trio's wake and starting to lurch after them. So far the kid's notoriously itchy trigger-finger seemed to be under control, but Gabe didn't expect it to last long. Hewitt had too much to prove, a wild and unpredictable element that could put them all in danger if it wasn't stamped on soon. He thought following orders was somehow beneath him, and that being a loose cannon was an endearing quality. Barely in his twenties, he was a youngster that had graduated from teenage gangs and petty thievery to armed robbery overnight, and hadn't had the time to mature. He had a ruthless streak, which admittedly to some was an asset, and appeared to genuinely loathe the deadheads, though Gabe wondered if he truly saw much distinction between them and the living. Certainly, he knew the kid disliked and resented him and would supplant his command any chance he could.

The street they ran down had once been a busy retail area, alive even at the twilight hours with taxis and shoppers, light flooding across the paving stones from glittery window displays. Now, it was like a smudgy stain, bereft of all colour; the stores that lined the thoroughfare were dark, gutted holes that merged with the night. From the glow cast by the flares, Gabe could see the outlines of mannequins slumped against the spiderwebbed glass, the grey flicker of TVs tuned to long-dead channels broadcasting static twenty-four hours a day, the liquefying mass of fruit and vegetables left to rot from discarded crates.

He spotted the turning for the square they needed, and turned to Davis. "Over there," he said, pointing with the barrel of his rifle. The road came to an abrupt end, giving way to a pedestrianised section, and a gap opened in the shopfronts. Gabe motioned with his head for them to follow and doubled his speed towards it.

Upon entering the cul-de-sac, he saw their destination immediately, tucked away in the corner of the narrow faux-Elizabethan square with its dark-beamed boutiques and coffee outlets. How Michaelson had managed to find it was a mystery – unless you knew it was here, it could easily evade the attention of the casual passer-by. Running his eyes over the exterior of the building, Gabe guessed that it hadn't been touched since its owners had fled, which was a minor miracle.

Their scout had certainly earned his commission, he thought with a smile, as he appraised the gold script upon the black sign above the door: HENDERSON & SON, JEWELLERS.

The other two men caught up with him. "OK, Davis, I want you on lookout," he ordered, glancing at them. "Hewitt, with me. This shouldn't take us more than five minutes."

Without a word, the former policeman passed the kid the two empty holdalls then positioned himself beneath the awning of a pizza restaurant, resting his machine-gun on a metal dining table. Gabe led Hewitt to the jeweller's entrance and tried the door – locked. Discerning nothing beyond the glass, he swung his rifle-butt and smashed the panelling, immediately setting off a shrieking siren that bathed the area in a blue pulsating light. Hewitt stepped out from the doorway and levelled his shotgun at the alarm several feet above them, blowing it off the wall. The strident wail was cut dead, devolving into an oscilloscope whine as pieces of the plastic casing clattered to the ground around them.

Hewitt shrugged as he returned to Gabe. "Might as well hear ourselves think."

The older man knocked the shards of glass free and stepped into the darkened shop. He fished into his pocket and pulled out a flashlight, sweeping its beam over the cases containing rings, necklaces, brooches and watches. The interior of the store was small, with just a counter and till at the far end, and a solid wooden door leading to a back room. Gabe strode over to it, but that too was bolted.

"OK, we haven't got the time to be graceful about this," Gabe muttered. "Grab as much as you can." He yanked a crowbar from his bag and shattered the nearest cabinet, silver and gold chains spilling out into his hands. There was a crash behind him as Hewitt did the same, tipping an entire display of pendants into the bag he had spread on the carpet. The two men worked quickly and efficiently, not stopping to separate diamonds from crystal but pouring them all haphazardly into the holdalls, occasionally casting a glance to Davis outside as he sporadically let rip with a burst of automatic fire. The groans of the dead seemed to be growing closer.

"You nearly finished there?" Gabe asked, zipping up one of the holdalls. He picked it up briefly to test its weight, wincing as his muscles strained, then wandered over to the till, breaking it open with a couple of blows from the crowbar. He pocketed a few hundred pounds in cash.

"Almost," Hewitt muttered, shaking a box of signet rings into his bag. He crouched, sifting a hand through the loot, then looked up at his companion. "What the fuck are we doing this for anyway?"

Gabe sighed. "We haven't got the time for this—"

"I mean, look at us – robbing a jewellery store like it fucking *means* anything any more." He held up a handful of necklaces. "All of this, it's worthless... pointless. The best we can do with it is melt it down into more slugs to put through their rotten fucking heads."

"Harry knows what he's doing."

"Does he? Seems to me we should be out there stomping on a few zombie skulls, making a concerted effort to be putting the bastards below ground where they should be, rather than stealing shit that's got no fucking value anymore—"

"You think this situation is going to last?" Gabe threw his arms up, impatient now. "You think the deadheads are going to be around forever? They're falling apart, you said so yourself. It's a plague, it's running its natural course, and the world adapts around it and learns to evolve. A fucking meteor wiped out the dinosaurs and the balance of the planet shifted, but it set off in a new direction. That's what Flowers sees is going to happen – the zombies are going to pass on and we're going to have to put ourselves back together again. And he's going to be in a position to be top of the heap." He kicked a jingling tangle of gold chains towards the kid. "And this stuff... yes, it means nothing now, but in five, ten years Harry's going to emerge as the richest, most powerful man in the city and everyone's going to have to barter with him for a slice."

Hewitt looked sullen. Gabe motioned to him to pick up his bag. "Come on, let's move. We're running out of time." He unhooked his two-way from his belt and spoke into it. "Ali, how's it going?"

"Few creeps trying to get in, but most followed you," the crackly voice responded. "Feel like a sitting duck out here. I think they're getting agitated."

"Understood. We'll be with you in a couple of minutes."

Gabe locked stares with Hewitt for a moment, then strode past him out of the shop, swinging his holdall onto his shoulder, shifting its weight until it felt comfortable. Davis raised his eyebrows and nodded towards the bodies of a half-dozen ghouls lying in the mouth of the square. More were trying to navigate past their fallen cousins.

"OK," Gabe murmured wearily. "Lock and load."

Hewitt emerged from the jeweller's, two bags strapped across his back, chambering shells into his shotgun. He barely acknowledged the other two men, merely walked towards the stiffs that were shuffling nearer, pumping the slide-action. "Come on, you fuckers," he called. "Who's first?"

Gabe shook his head. What was it like to feel young?

CHAPTER TWO

They drove in silence out of central London's narrowly clustered maze of streets, a tangible sense of relief flooding through the interior of the car as the roads became wider, the buildings sparser, and they headed into the outskirts. Davis and Hewitt sat in the back reloading their weapons, the former breathing a little hard, Gabe noticed. He hoped it was merely the weight of the body armour coupled with the frantic return to the vehicle that was the cause of his exhaustion, but he'd caught, out of the corner of his eye, the former policeman wiping his brow with a trembling hand, and wondered if the pressures of their situation were starting to catch up with him. Gabe had seen it happen to sterner stuff than Davis, and you could never predict how those nearing breakdown could affect future outings like tonight's.

If the last few years had taught him anything – if the plague had taught humanity anything – it was the importance of reliance on comrades, on knowing there's somebody with you to cover your back. Strange that it should be a crisis of this magnitude to deliver such a lesson, but its simplicity did not diminish its truth – operate as a tight unit, and you'll survive. Allow it to unravel a touch and you put everybody's lives at risk.

For all Flowers' failings – and he pushed those in his organisation hard in his pursuit of power, there was no question of that – Harry understood that a machine could only perform at its best if the individual parts were all working together. One loose screw could bring it crashing down, as previous experience has shown. Gabe mused that he would have to have a word with the boss about Davis, maybe recommend him for evaluation with the docs. Better to catch these things early.

He supposed he ought to have a whisper too about Hewitt's increasing belligerence and refusal to toe the line, but knew he would think better of it once they reached base. The idiot found favour in Flowers' court for some reason, and Gabe would undoubtedly be seen as making waves if he criticised Hewitt's conduct, no matter how obliquely. He couldn't quite ascertain what it was that Harry saw in the kid, but he clearly sparked something in him – some nascent paternal feelings, perhaps – that brought forth the highly rare qualities of indulgence and forgiveness from the old man. Flowers evidently looked upon him as quasi-family. Judging by Hewitt's outburst in the jeweller's, the appreciation was hardly mutual; the youngster clearly saw Harry's scheme as a sign that their employer was losing it, and probably spent many an evening dreaming what he would do with the outfit if it had him at its head. Flowers had seen off leadership challenges before, but this one could strike him close and deep if it wasn't nipped in the bud. Trouble was always brewing, Gabe thought, rubbing the bridge of his nose.

The zombies were less of a nuisance once they got out of the city, scattered mostly in groups of fours and fives in parks and residential districts, staggering between the privet hedges seeking living flesh to feast upon. Another primal instinct that seemed to be still blipping in their brains was a herding nature: the stiffs appeared to be naturally aware that, with supplies so close to hand, most human survivors were found hiding in the big concrete tangles of the major conurbations ('cemeteries', Gabe had heard one wit dub these overrun metropolises). Therefore, concentrated numbers of the dead gravitated there like predators drawn to a watering hole, hoping to chance upon something warm and tender, leaving the sprawling suburbs relatively empty and easier to traverse.

Ali guided the Escort with little effort through the smouldering, garbage-strewn streets of Catford and Bromley, casually avoiding the few cadavers that stumbled into their path. Watching the deserted semi-detached houses pass by – front doors standing wide open, children's toys left scattered in gardens, the odd splash of red on a window – Gabe felt tears prick his eyes. He pinched them closed for a moment. The dark, charnel terrors of the city he could cope with (he had long been inured to the day-to-day bloodshed by now) but it was the quiet reminders of life before the dead rose that tugged at his heart. What was once comforting familiarity now looked like a blackened shell with all the life, all the goodness, ripped out of it. These routes through suburbia never failed to affect him in this way, but while he could stem the tears from flowing he couldn't turn off his emotions entirely. Everything he'd taken for granted, everything normal, now looked alien without the context of the people who'd once lived here. They'd breathed life into it, and without them it merely became a place fit for the dead.

He'd like to think that what he told Hewitt earlier was true; that this was a phase they were travelling through, a footnote in history. He imagined the fourteenth-century peasants sprouting boils and seeing entire towns and villages decimated thought much the same about the Black Death – that their situation was surely going to get better, that this couldn't be the end for mankind. They had been facing species extinction, to be wiped from the surface of the earth, and humanity, resilient as ever, crawled through it, clinging tenaciously to life as it always had. Now it was staring down into the abyss once more, and the optimistic embraced the notion that there had to be an escape. Flowers was one such idealist, fervently having faith that it was only a matter of time before society would start to rebuild itself (of course, Harry had his own ideas of what that society would be, including instating him as its lord and master).

"All outbreaks have a shelf-life," he'd told Gabe once. "They ravage through an unprepared populace, laying waste to everything they touch. But they also consume themselves eventually, all that energy and greed directed inwards."

Gabe had thought that much the same could be said about humanity.

Flowers was waiting for the virus to burn itself out, when it could no longer sustain the corpses it had reanimated. Gabe wanted to believe that would happen, and he couldn't deny there were signs that the zombies were disintegrating – the bacteria that bubbled away inside each ghoul's cranium, that had awakened its motor functions, was no match for time and tide, after all. But could things ever really return to what they had once been? Could these homes ever be filled again without being a pale imitation of the life they had once contained? He wondered if he'd grown so used to the emptiness that the sight of people walking freely again might seem equally unreal, a simulacrum of civilization recreated from memory but with its soul indelibly bruised.

The streetlamps and boxy buildings of the suburbs faded away as the car picked its way through the Kent countryside. Gabe marvelled at the way nature still ran its course, unaware of the cataclysmic events that had taken place around it. If it wasn't for the quiet – even in the densest of forests, it was rare to hear birdsong – out here it was possible to believe that nothing was wrong. The woodlands and emerald fields were mostly untainted by the dead, though the odd lost shambling figure could sometimes be discerned on a remote path, looking from a distance as dangerous as a rambler. Even then, any ghouls you encountered within these environs had more than likely been released by a local farm for sport rather than being on the prowl; it had become a popular country pastime to take potshots at captured deadheads, occasionally even riding them down. Flowers had aspirations to get in with the horsy set, and had been on several of these hunts, though Gabe guessed that as a quarry they offered little challenge and not much of a satisfying kill. As with any of these shindigs, it was a social gathering with a touch of carnage thrown in. Harry had told him – typically eyes a-gleam like it was a barometer of a man of his stature – that one of the squires that had invited him for such a get-together had scores of stiffs locked in a converted stable, ready for whenever his friends fancied some target practice of a weekend. The resurrected had been rounded up in the city and carted back in cattle trucks.

This kind of attitude was symptomatic of the way some had adapted to living with the dead, Gabe thought as Ali turned the Escort off the winding lane and onto a narrow, conifer-lined track. Once the initial shock had dissipated, once it became clear that the authorities were not going to be able to solve it – indeed, once it was apparent that there was no authority left at all – people resorted to different methods of coping with the crisis. The immediate, predictable response for many was to go on a looting rampage, positively embracing the breakdown of order, reverting to turn-of-the-century outlaws; a few survived this way, living on the road, smashing and grabbing what they could, but most underestimated the numbers of the dead that were growing daily, and especially did not take them seriously as a threat. Stupidity was the chief cause of death within the first few months. For your average Joe, once they realised that there was nowhere to run to, that the plague was everywhere, they hunkered down like refugees in a war-torn state, waiting for somebody to tell them what to do. They were still there now, years later, living in tribes in cellars and boarded-up tenements, scrabbling for scraps, still hoping to be rescued.

But for a few, he mused, as the track widened, the foliage cleared and the vehicle slowly approached the gates of Flowers' mansion, it's been a matter of staying in control. The ruling elite has always tackled disaster in its own fashion, far removed from the epicentre, and the emergence of the undead had been no different for them than any other form of social unrest. They used it for their own advantage, whether for recreation – in the case of the ghoul hunts, and any manner of unsavoury antics the aristocrats got up to within their lodges – or for consolidating their already powerful position. For Harry, it was the latter; once he saw past the ravenous zombies, the outbreak was a fortuitous means to an end. He'd always lived outside governmental authority anyway, and so the breakdown of the police and the strictures of the law courts were to him of little consequence; on the contrary, their collapse was to be rejoiced.

"What," he'd say, sweeping his arms about his opulent study, "I'm supposed to be crying because I don't have to pay tax anymore? That there's no longer some snoop from Customs and Excise investigating my affairs? That I'm going to miss my phones being tapped?"

Flowers viewed it as a golden opportunity, ripe for the plucking. His regular business shrank once the plague took hold – he gradually lost contact with his associates overseas, as Russia, Syria, Pakistan and the

US all seemingly suffered similar fates, descending into chaos, and unsurprisingly the takings from his clubs and bars went through the floor in the space of twenty-four hours – but the boss man had always prided himself on seeing the bigger picture. He had no need for profit in the interim, and money was as worthless as the paper it was printed on. So he drew himself back, planned out his strategy and prepared for his own personal and financial resurrection once the virus was played out. He built himself a regular army to protect him and enforce his will, sent scouts into the city to uncover vital supplies, had scientists kidnapped from Ministry of Defence laboratories to conduct research into the epidemic to gain an understanding of how to destroy the dead more efficiently. This was a chance that had been handed to him, and he couldn't afford to fuck it up; never, in his twenty years as head of his firm, could he imagine a time when he might be able to legitimately call the whole of London his domain. What had once been carved up by various crimelords all angling for more territory was now there for the taking in its entirety, and he was determined it was going to be his. And of course, with the capital established, he could spread his tentacles north, east, west and south, engulf a country that had fallen into anarchy. Whenever Harry talked about such an eventuality with Gabe, he hugged himself, his excitement contagious.

"The possibilities," he would whisper, "the possibilities that have been presented to me..."

As Ali pulled up to the main gates, a guard opened a padlocked door set into the chainlink fence and strode across, a flashlight bobbing in hand, an M16 weighted in the other. He stopped at the passenger side, Gabe rolling down the window to greet him.

"Patricks."

"Hey, O'Connell," the guard replied, shining the light into the car. "Any problems?"

"No, went fine." Gabe winced at the glare of the torch. Patricks crouched and swept it left and right, pausing momentarily to rest the beam on each occupant's face, then gave the outside of the vehicle a casual perusal. "Stiffs seem to be falling apart more than ever."

The other man nodded curtly. "Tell me about it. Couple got through the perimeter out by the woods earlier on." He blithely motioned behind him to the dense wall of shadow to the rear of the great house. "Tripped a landmine and the remains been stinking out the gardens ever since. Poor old Sanderson has been burying that shit since sundown. Even the dogs won't touch it."

"Can't say I blame them. They've been known to refuse Barrett's fried breakfasts."

Patricks barked a laugh in agreement. "Oh, by the way, the old man wants to see you. Said you were to call in on him when you got back."

He slapped the Escort's roof and indicated for them to continue. He slung his rifle over his shoulder, unhooked a two-way from his belt, and spoke briefly into it. Seconds later, the gates swung open. Gabe gave the guard the thumbs-up, and Ali edged the car through the opening and onto the main driveway, tyres crunching on the gravel that curled round in a semi-circle to the front of the mansion. Almost immediately, the gates clanged shut as soon as they were through.

Positioned just inside them on either side of the driveway were two sentry posts, an armed guard stationed on each, equipped with infrared nightsights and high-calibre automatic weapons. The lawns that surrounded the house were a cat's cradle of tripwires – themselves interspersed with warning signs for the benefit of the living – triggering small bundles of dynamite. The perimeter fence could be electrified if necessary, and dog-handlers patrolled its length constantly, the animals particularly good at sniffing out approaching ghouls. It was the most well-defended building that Gabe had seen since the advent of the outbreak, and that included governmental offices: one of the many testaments to Harry's organisational skills as well as his wealth.

The mansion's ivy-choked eighteenth-century facade belied the modern interior, Flowers having gutted much of the original fixtures and fittings to make way for the operations centre he required: libraries and studies were stripped to accommodate research labs, armouries and workshops. For an old geezer, he didn't seem to care for tradition or nostalgia; business in his opinion was all about staying one step ahead. To that end he was something of a gadget freak, and loved to drop in on the tech-boys, who would regale him with their latest developments.

Ali pulled the car up alongside several others outside the garages. Gabe stepped out and opened the boot, removing the holdalls and passing them to Davis and Hewitt, who appeared at his side.

"I'm going to see what Harry wants," he told the two men. "Take that lot down to the treasury. And make sure you get an inventory, OK?" Gabe locked stares with Hewitt, who grumpily spun away and trudged towards the house, before turning his attention to the ex-cop. "Keep an eye on him," he murmured. "Ensure everything's tagged and bagged." Davis nodded his assent and followed his colleague.

Gabe turned to see Ali emerge from the vehicle; she locked it up and threw him the keys. He smiled in gratitude, but her hangdog expression didn't change.

"There's about a quarter tank in there," she told him. "Might want to fill her up, in case you need to get somewhere in a hurry."

"I'll do it in the morning, thanks."

"You worried about him?" she asked, leaning against the side of the Escort and nodding towards the small figure of Hewitt climbing the stone steps to the front door.

"I guess. A bit." He shrugged. "He's too reckless, and doesn't account for the consequences. I think he sees this all as one big videogame."

"He'll never listen to advice. Take that from someone who's raised a pair of teenage boys." Gabe vaguely remembered her mentioning her children before, but had always refrained from enquiring what had happened to them. "The only time he'll take stock of his actions is if he puts himself in danger. If he nearly gets himself killed, then you might see a different side to him."

"Wishful thinking," he replied, half joking.

"Could be the best lesson he'll ever get," she answered, and strolled away towards the garages, leaving Gabe wondering exactly what kind of mother she'd been.

He nodded to the two bored-looking guys standing guard just inside the entrance, and made his way through the stone-flagged reception hall, a cavernous space dominated by the huge carpeted staircase that swept up to the first floor. Despite the lateness of the hour, sounds of activity still echoed from the many corridors branching off the foyer; indeed, the headquarters of Flowers' outfit never really slept, the men working in shifts on various tasks, from the upkeep of the house to zombie procurement. Harry himself only caught a few zeds when it was unavoidable, feeling that he'd be missing something important otherwise. Gabe considered dropping in on the kitchen after he'd reported to the boss, which ticked over twenty-four seven for the benefit of those toiling through the night. He could do with a cup of tea and a chance to put his feet up; it was easy to forget how important these simple pleasures were when you spent much of your time putting bullets through the heads of decaying cadavers.

He spotted a familiar face emerge from one of antechambers, twirling a dog lead in his hand.

"Yo, Hendricks," Gabe called, smiling. "Taking your lady friend out tonight?"

"Oh yes," he replied, glancing down at the chain with affection. "A chance to get away from you animals and spend an evening with someone a tad more civilised."

"I'm sure her conversation's a blast."

"Ella listens, that's the main thing. It's an underrated quality."

Ella was his tawny German Shepherd, one of the handful of dogs kept in the kennels for patrol purposes. Hendricks had a particular affinity with all of them, but she was his favourite, and she was remarkably well trained. Affable and docile for much of the time, as soon as she caught whiff of a Returner her wolfen nature emerged. It surprised Gabe to learn that even the dogs hated the ghouls, without even knowing what they truly were, which made the stiffs something quite unique – a common enemy that bonded man and beast.

"You want to try it some time, O'Connell," he continued. "You don't know how refreshing it is just to have a quiet few moments, just enjoying each other's company."

"Hey, sounds beautiful. Me, I think I'll stick with the human race."

"That's always been your problem: misplaced loyalty."

"Talking of which, you seen the old man tonight?"

"Yeah, he's with the boffins," Hendricks answered, swinging the lead towards an annexe behind the staircase. "Ashberry's there too. Harry seems quite excited about something the colonel picked up on the airwaves."

"No shit?"

"You know how he is; always got some bit between his teeth. Listen, I hear the call of the wild, so I better go."

"Don't want to keep your canine chums waiting."

"Fuck you, you're just jealous," he said, laughing as he headed towards the front gardens.

Gabe strode down the dark, bare passage towards the lab complex, smiling to himself. He'd known Hendricks since he first joined Flowers' organisation and he hadn't changed in that time; a big, soft-hearted lug of a man, perhaps too generous of spirit for a professional thief and enforcer. He was defiantly old school, a generation and world away from the likes of Hewitt, and took no pleasure in violence, using it as a last resort and only under the specific orders of the boss. He was a natural to be in charge of the dogs, and seemed to genuinely prefer their company to that of his colleagues. Gabe often wondered what had led him to falling in with Harry and choosing a life outside the law when he appeared to exhibit none of the qualities one would expect, but Hendricks would not be drawn, merely stating that it was impossible for anyone to predict where they will end up. Instead he would turn the questioning onto Gabe, asking whether he could explain what *he* was doing being part of the firm, and Gabe could only shake his head, unable to answer. It was a bizarre situation to be in, but ever since the outbreak he'd known he'd made the right choice. If he hadn't joined the outfit, he'd no doubt be just another survivor at best, scratching out an existence amongst the ruins.

The corridor opened out into the research facility, and he spotted Flowers and Colonel Ashberry watching the scientists through an observation window. Beyond the glass was the lab area, where a number of whitecoats were flitting between half a dozen morgue slabs upon which zombie subjects were strapped. Gabe paused in the doorway and cleared his throat. The two men glanced over their shoulders and raised their eyebrows in recognition, Harry immediately returning his gaze to the work being done before him.

"Gabriel, my boy," his employer said. "All back in one piece?"

"Safe and sound," Gabe replied, walking forward, nodding a greeting to the military man. "We didn't encounter any problems."

"What about Michaelson's info? Was it accurate?"

"On the money, so to speak. Store hadn't been touched since the deadheads rose. I think we came away with between fifty and hundred k's worth of merchandise."

Harry finally turned to face him. "Impressive." The boss was an imposing figure in the flesh; lean and wiry with a grizzled, sandblasted complexion and a few white hairs still fighting the good fight on his crown. The watery blue eyes that peered out from the craggy folds of his face, however, indicated the intelligence that lay within that pensionable frame. Once you found yourself fixed in their glare, it seemed he was capable of sensing the slightest untruth. His mood too was never easy to judge at any given time, and that kept those around him nervous, a wrong-footedness he often used to his advantage. Gabe had never seen anyone who could switch from a beaming smile to a look of murderous rage with nary an expression in between. "But then you've always been one of my best thieves, Gabriel."

"I just go where I'm pointed."

"Indeed. What have you stolen for me over the years – guns? Money? Computer equipment? You've even kidnapped the odd rival, if memory serves."

"On your orders."

"Without question. But my point remains that you can be relied upon to get the job done with the minimum of fuss." Without taking his eyes off Gabe, Flowers motioned towards the lab with a swift nod of the head. "Do you ever consider yourself a remote-control creature, O'Connell?"

Gabe flicked his gaze through the glass then back to his boss. "You mean, do I think I'm not much better than them? One of the mindless majority?"

Harry's face bisected into a grin. "I'm pulling your chain, boy. Of course you're working towards the greater good, like everybody here. But similarly, they," he tapped the partition with a knuckle, "could be useful to us, could be directed by us."

"We're trying to ascertain how the virus is working on the cadavers," Ashberry piped up. He was a stiff-backed, humourless goon in his forties that had decided, without a great deal of prevarication, to abandon his middle-ranking post amongst the governmental forces and defect to Flowers' outfit. The colonel believed that the power base had shifted to those with the vision to take back the city – in other words, Harry. Ashberry's military knowledge had proved invaluable in planning operations and procuring weaponry from army installations. He clearly hoped that if the old man's coup ever came off, he could grab himself a slice of the action and claim a position that his previous career had never afforded him. Gabe was sceptical that Harry would ever be that grateful; he could see the uniformed prick being hung out to dry once his usefulness had expired. "We have a theory that the bacteria is evolving inside the brain, slowly changing how the zombies behave. Their instincts are becoming less random, and they're showing signs of memory retention."

By 'we', he meant the small team of researchers that had been removed at gunpoint from the secret MoD labs – the details of their whereabouts provided by Ashberry – and forced to work for Flowers. They were essentially doing the same work, but the difference was they were unable to leave the mansion and their findings were to be delivered directly to the boss. Gabe watched a whitecoat peel the top of a skull off a still-struggling stiff, careful to keep the organ inside intact. It was a horrorshow in there, a mix of butchery and experimentation that he couldn't stomach for long. Harry, naturally, seemed to revel in it.

"If we could determine how the virus controls the dead," the colonel continued, "then there's a chance we could modify it ourselves, get it to fire up some of the neural connections that enable speech, the understanding of language, the basic implementation of tools. And most importantly, make them not want to eat us."

"Turn them into your puppets, you mean," Gabe said.

"Oh, Gabriel," Flowers murmured, "much more than that. We're giving life back to these poor wretches. Why do you think they moan and cry so? They hate their condition, hate what they've become, jealous of the sound of beating hearts and the touch of warm breath. They consume us to try to claw it back, to feel blood rushing in their veins once more. But it always leaves them unsatisfied."

Gabe felt that had more to do with the fact that the

dead's digestive tracts were unable to process what they ate, but bit his tongue. Harry was evidently in a poetic mood tonight. "And of course, unzombiefying makes them much less of a threat when it comes to taking London."

"Better to win round enemies than tackle them head-on, that's always been my motto."

Gabe could think of more than one occasion when he'd done just the opposite.

"Our problem," Ashberry said, trying to steer the conversation back to the matter at hand, "has been isolating the virus from the brain samples we're examining. Once it gets into the nervous system, it embeds itself totally, essentially taking over the host. It's hard to see where what was once human ends and the thing the disease has turned it into begins."

"What these backroom boys need is untainted cultures of the original virus to work from," Flowers said. "By reverse-engineering that, they might be able to get somewhere. And we've just had a stroke of rather good luck."

"Which is?"

"I was monitoring a line of encrypted military radio traffic earlier," the colonel told him. "Government forces are transporting a portion of their stock from their stronghold at St Thomas' Hospital to an MoD complex beneath Westminster. Obviously, they're desperately trying to look for an antidote too – but they want to find a way of defeating the plague and make the zombies fall down dead permanently, rather than our solution, which is to turn them into something else."

"So what do you want me to do?" Gabe asked, knowing the answer even as the words left his lips.

"Why, you're going to do what you do best, son," Harry said, putting an arm round the younger man's shoulders. "You're going to hijack it."

CHAPTER THREE

17.32 pm

Gabe knocked gently on the door but entered without waiting for an answer. He didn't acknowledge the other occupant in the room at first, merely took a dining chair from beside the fireplace and carried it over to the bay window overlooking the gardens. He positioned it next to the woman in the armchair, silently staring out at Flowers' manicured greenery, equally unresponsive to her guest. Gabe sat down and gazed out on the lawns below for several hushed moments, the gloom of evening stealing in and sapping the light from the afternoon. Beyond the treetops at the far end of his employer's estate, blue-black clouds massed threatening a downpour, hearkening the approaching darkness. Already, shadows were gathering in the room, and when he turned finally to face her it was difficult to discern her expression; her profile was partially obscured by a heavy blonde fringe. She was propped against several cushions, and although her eyes were open she was utterly motionless.

"Anna," he said, his voice catching in his throat. He felt uncomfortable breaking the quiet, and his words felt strange leaving his lips and inhabiting this place. A clock ticked in the background, spacing out the seconds. "Anna, I just thought I'd come say hello. I haven't had a chance to see you recently."

No reply; indeed, if it wasn't for the slightest twitch in her pupils as they remained fixed on the view through the glass it would be impossible to tell if she was conscious.

"I hope you've been keeping well," Gabe persevered. "I'm sure you're being well looked after, but if there's ever anything you need, you know you only have to ask and I'll do everything I can to help. You know that, don't you?" With the question hanging in the air between them unanswered, he tried another tack and followed her gaze to the gardens. "I must've said it before, but you do have a beautiful outlook to wake up to every morning. Especially at this time of year. The splashes of bright yellows and mauves, the scent of honeysuckle... Harry sure does have green fingers."

Smiling despite himself, his expression froze when her head turned suddenly and she looked at him. There was no emotion behind her smooth, pale face; no anger, or longing, or disgust, just an achingly perfect mask framed by her blonde ringlets. Her skin was soft and delicate, but painfully lacking in colour; even her lips were drained of blood. An observer standing at a distance might suggest that she was wearing foundation, so uniform was her whiteness, but Gabe knew that there wasn't a touch of make-up on her. Her ice-blue eyes were all the more startling for the contrast to her complexion, as sharp and flawless as a spring morning; he could not gaze into those twin shards for long without his own orbs pricking with a desire to hold, comfort and protect her. They looked instantly sad and knowing, innocent and troubled.

"Anna?" he started, aware that the volume of his voice had dropped even further, now little more than a whisper.

"What do you want from me?" she said tremulously, her stare unwavering. "What do you think I can give you?"

At first he couldn't reply, as the accusation rang in his head. What possible recompense could he offer her for what she had lost? As ever, the suggestion nagged at the back of his mind that his interest in her well-being was as much a salve to his guilt as it was a natural wish to watch over her. At best it meant he could rest easy in his bed, satisfied that he had at least made the effort. The fact that there had been no visible improvement in her condition for the past five years was clearly evidence that his guardianship made no difference. Yet still he made these visits, attempting to engage her in conversation, but rarely waking her from her daze. Perhaps she was torturing him, conscious of him squirming beneath her cool gaze, aware that as long as she was withdrawn from him, she was forever beyond his reach... If it was punishment, did he deserve any less?

"Anna... you don't have to give me anything, other than to accept that all I want is the best for you," he finally said. "I'm not here to demand or cajole anything out of you. I just want you to know that I'm always here for you."

"You're looking for forgiveness; that's what you're after, isn't it?" He flinched at the flecks of spite that flew in his direction. She turned her head away from him, as if to dismiss his presence. "Don't you understand nothing can change what has happened? Not your words, not your actions, and not your honourable intentions. What's done is done and we're trapped in the consequences."

"I'm trying to help us all move on—"

"What for? Where is there to move to?" Any emotion that had blossomed in her words now drained away, replaced by an inaudible murmur. "The time for living is over."

"Gabriel."

He turned to see Flowers standing in the doorway, then glanced back at Anna; she had retreated back into herself, her eyes hooded, her breathing shallow. He inched his hand out to rest it upon her forearm, but it hovered a few inches above her before he pulled it back. Gabe quietly got to his feet and walked over to his boss, who nodded for him to leave the room, pulling the door shut after him.

"What did you talk to her about?"

"Nothing," the younger man replied. "Just offering my support, like always."

"She seemed upset."

Gabe shook his head. "She refuses to open up. I want her to progress past the state she's in. I want to help her to develop. But it's like she's... locked."

"Son, you know her condition. Even the bods in the lab are struggling to understand her psychological mindset. You think you can get her to snap out of it?"

"What's the alternative?" He could feel his anger rising. "Keep her shut away in there like a pet? Like one of your caged test subjects?"

Harry's expression darkened. "Anna will stay with me at my discretion, and I'll treat her as I see fit. Don't overstep the mark, boy, or you'll find your little visits curtailed indefinitely. You'll have to make your heartfelt confessions to somebody else."

Gabe clenched his fists and stared at the floor, saying nothing.

"Assemble your team," Flowers ordered, striding away from him down the corridor, "and let's focus on the here and now."

An hour later, Gabe led his squad in a two-vehicle convoy down the mansion's driveway and through the gates. Before it passed out of sight, he glanced back at the house in his rear-view mirror and saw a solitary figure watching from a second-floor window. For a moment, he thought he saw it move, as if reaching out to the glass; but seconds later it was lost to shadow.

19.46 pm

As far as Eric Richards was concerned, when he was behind the wheel of a vehicle, he was solely in charge. It was his dominion. He'd been a contract driver for St Thomas' for the past twenty-seven years and once a man occupies this kind of position for such a length of time – or so Richards liked to believe – he could be expected to exude a certain authority and command a little respect. He'd bowed before others with a similar weight of experience in their chosen fields – the medical staff he'd dealt with briefly, the admin office he'd answered to – and wouldn't have dreamt of telling them how to do a job they'd been performing perfectly well, and often for several decades. So it was that, considering his history, having first been employed as a porter in 1959 and moved sideways into transporting supplies, he felt he had the right to assume he could occupy a level of efficient autonomy. And up until recently, that had indeed been the case.

But when the dead rose, all boundaries shifted irrevocably, and Richards was someone who liked the comforting structure of routine and the knowledge of his place in the scheme of things. He'd been working when he received a call from his wife Doreen that the news was reporting cases of mass hysteria and murder taking place all across the country. It was impossible not to be aware that something was going on, with his colleagues' blasted mobile phones chirruping every few minutes, but he'd underestimated just how widespread the crisis was. TV reports and newspapers were always blowing up situations into full-blown catastrophes, then forgetting about them the following week to focus on another scandal, so when she first spoke to him, her voice breathless with worry, he'd calmed her with platitudes and told her to take such stories with a pinch of salt. They lived in Blackheath, for heaven's sake; very little of consequence affected them in the heart of suburbia. Doreen had been persuaded to view it all with a healthy degree of scepticism – drug addicts on a rampage on a council estate, no doubt, or maybe some kind of sickness brought on by an outbreak of food poisoning – and when he said goodbye she sounded halfway convinced. He'd returned to his duties, trying to brush off the uneasy pall that had settled over him, but word was snowballing through the hospital that something was definitely very wrong.

News filtered back that Casualty was being inundated with patients – those suffering from bite wounds, mainly, complaining of being set upon by complete strangers in the street – and that numbers were rising. Richards had always prided himself on his pragmatism and his ability to stand firm when others around him were flustered, but even he couldn't dismiss the sense that they were being catapulted towards a major disaster. He'd borrowed one of the other driver's mobiles to ring Doreen. After half a dozen failed calls, the network jammed solid, he ran to a nearby phone box and tried once more. She'd answered after it had rung for a full two minutes, sounding distant and distracted, claiming she and their fourteen-year-old son Max – sent home from school as news began to spread – had been hiding upstairs because somebody had battered on the front door attempting entry. He'd told her to stay where they were and that he'd come get them. Those were his final words to her. Richards never saw or spoke to his wife or son again.

His efforts to return home were thwarted at every turn; roads snaking out of London were rammed with traffic, and the police started closing off areas considered dangerous. He abandoned his car at one point, seeing if he could perhaps make it there on foot, but every route he took saw him turned away by an official, who refused to listen to his pleas. A policeman advised him against travelling alone, and that he should seek the safety of a well-lit, well-fortified building, adding that the army was being consulted on containing the out-of-control individuals. Richards had trudged back to St Thomas', not knowing where else to go, the radio offering similar recommendations that citizens should find shelter with others in libraries, sports centres, churches, shopping malls and office complexes to ride out the coming storm. Public transport was grinding to a halt as train and underground operators abandoned their posts. All around him was chaos. He had never witnessed panic before, not in its purest form; as a child in the Blitz, every adult had seemed so reserved and resolute, waiting patiently in the Anderson shelters for the Luftwaffe to finish their night's work and then returning in the morning to pick up the pieces. Walking the city streets back to the hospital, crowds surged in every direction, equally lost and hopeless, shouting and screaming as they barged past each other, sheer fear etched on their faces. None of them, as far as he was aware, had even seen what it was that had ignited such anarchy, but the terror passed between them like a viral agent, spreading to all it touched. The monster didn't even have to raise its ugly head, and still its victims tore themselves apart to escape its approach.

He'd helped out where he could at the hospital, keeping himself busy in an effort to force from his mind the image of Doreen and Max cowering in the master bedroom, waiting for rescue. He consoled himself that it surely had to be a temporary situation, that the trouble would pass. The radio said as much, its resident experts speculating that once the armed forces entered the fray everything would be brought under control. That was until the broadcast stations went dead and they lost all contact with what was going on in the outside world. Richards felt as if he were adrift, cut off from his former life; the daily routines that he relied upon, everything he trusted and founded his beliefs upon, had fallen apart before him and he didn't have anything else left to hold on to.

Then the full horror hit, when the doctors tending the injured discovered that those bitten by the assailants became infected with their madness. A wave of violence washed through Casualty with a shocking suddenness, the corridors echoing with the cries of nurses as the bedridden abruptly rose and began to attack their carers. Richards hadn't believed the stories he was hearing from those fleeing the scene; that the bite victims had actually died, that their breath and pulse had ceased, that no brain activity could be detected, before their terrifying resurrection moments later. And the maniacs weren't merely lashing out indiscriminately, they were tearing chunks from those they could overpower, consuming the flesh with an unholy relish. Other patients – the elderly and infirm, those plugged into drips and heart monitors – could only watch helpless as the killers rounded on them too. Richards had listened to these reports, shaking his head, unwilling to accept each fresh tale of atrocity.

He plunged into the mêlée, intent on helping where he could, but was faced with a slaughterhouse, bodies littering the wards, the shiny floor now slick with blood and viscera. One of those touched by the insanity – a bearded man in a trench coat, a large portion of meat missing from his neck – dropped the flap of crimson matter he was gnawing on and staggered towards him, a moan issuing from the back of his ravaged throat. Richards grabbed a fire extinguisher without hesitation and stove in the degenerate's skull, before retreating to the bright safety of the car park.

Army and police arrived within minutes, setting up a perimeter around the hospital's entrances, allowing none of the murderers to escape. They also corralled the survivors away from the building, telling them not to go near it until they pronounced it safe. Richards sensed St Thomas' had become strategically important for some reason, or why else would the authorities be so quick to come to their aid? Armed flak-jacketed soldiers strode into the reception area, and seconds later bursts of automatic gunfire and the dull thud of explosions ripped through the walls. He overheard an officer asking an administrator where the mortuary was, and then relaying the directions into a walkie-talkie.

For several long hours, two to three hundred staff stood in the hospital grounds behind a cordon of police, waiting for someone to explain what was going on. Eventually, a ruffled soldier emerged and nodded at his captain, and the lawmen relaxed their position. A smart, severe-looking woman Richards didn't recognise – one of St Thomas' directors, he guessed – seized the initiative and demanded to know the truth. A sergeant stepped forward and, with remarkable honesty and brusqueness, replied that an escaped virus had brought the dead back to life, with cannibalistic tendencies. Infection was passed on through the saliva of the undead, and those bitten would inevitably suffer cardiac arrest and join their ranks. They could only be stopped by destroying the brain, be it either by bullet or blunt instrument. Richards had glanced at those around him as they tried to assimilate this information, their incredulity tempered by the inescapable events of the day. Many began to weep. How could they argue against what they had seen with their own eyes? He himself didn't know what to feel, a cold, heavy rock in his chest where his heart used to be.

The sergeant went on to say that the plague wasn't just localised but spreading throughout the country, and a state of national emergency had been declared. The military needed to assume command of St Thomas' as a base of operations, and was requesting that all hospital staff remain to assist them. He warned them that right now the city was a no-go zone, and that they would be better served by staying put. Richards looked at the machine guns that each soldier carried and came to the conclusion that they weren't going to be letting anyone go anywhere. So under the supervision of the soldiers, the remaining workers returned to the deathly silent wards and began the slow, laborious process of removing the corpses, or at least clearing them to the fully stocked mortuaries so makeshift control centres could be established. The hours that Richards spent carrying cadavers indelibly seared images in his mind that he would take to his grave; both the victims of the Returners – looking like they'd been set upon by wild animals – and the remnants of the ghouls themselves, riddled with bullets, chilled his blood. Each new room held a particular horror. They found a few survivors hiding in locked linen cupboards and offices, only now summoning up the courage to put their heads around the door, but for the most part the corridors were carpeted with a red morass of bodies. Noting many of the wounds on the dead, Richards suspected the military had purged the entire building with little distinction between zombies and patients; any injured were similarly blasted in the head without a second thought.

The strangest discovery was in the morgues themselves, where the catalogued cadavers that had been residing in the drawers – the DOAs from the previous few days, the flatliners – had attempted to punch their way through their steel coffins upon their resurrection. Fist-sized gouges were visible in the metal as they'd been torn open from the inside. Each slab had to be pulled out with an armed soldier standing close by, ready to put a round through the carcass within if it had somehow missed the cull.

Toiling day and night, the authorities gradually reshaped the hospital into a research base; military personnel used the wards as barracks while escorted Ministry of Defence scientists began to arrive in batches to conduct experiments on the dead they'd kept aside. Richards could not sleep for thinking of his wife, but news brought in from the outside was not good; the city was a mess, lawlessness running rampant as the plague spread with frightening rapidity. With communications failing daily, there was no way he could get word to see if she was out of harm's reach. The military posted a permanent guard, as much to stop those inside from straying as to protect them; staff were effectively warned that they would not be allowed to leave the facility. Thus Richards found himself employed on what became, over the following months, a government outpost, receiving his instructions from the captain in charge. Many of his colleagues voiced their disapproval at the military suddenly assuming command of what had been a civilian organisation, but short of staring down the barrel of a service revolver there was nothing much they could do about it. It was clear that this wasn't an isolated case; the authorities were struggling to maintain control across the country, and if it meant the boys with the guns were running the show, then everybody else had better fall in behind them.

It was errands such as tonight's delivery that Richards was tasked with: driving a truckload of medical samples to another of the MoD complexes across town. It wasn't a million miles away from the job he'd had in his previous life – that regular existence in which he'd been embedded seemed centuries ago – but it was now shorn of any shred of independence. He was accompanied in his cab by a Sergeant Perrington, who ordered him at what speed he should drive, the directions he should take, and constantly advised on what safety tips he should adhere to. Richards found it utterly demeaning for a man of his years but was as powerless as a prisoner. There were half a dozen armed guards riding in the back with the cargo, and an army van was tailgating his vehicle. In fact, the only reason they bothered to use him at all, rather than have a squaddie drive the supplies, was because he knew best how to handle the truck's temperamental gears and spongy clutch.

They were crossing Westminster Bridge when he first caught sight of something in his headlamps. He glanced in his wing mirror, and checked that the escort was still following; in fact, it was so close that if he stopped suddenly it could rear-end him. If that were the case, he would have to flare his brake lights and warn them. It was raining lightly, a sprinkle of drops peppering the windscreen, so he scraped the wipers once against the glass to get a better view, peering out into the night, the headlights casting a pool of illumination onto the road ahead. The edge of their limit just brushed against a silhouette that was jogging towards the truck, its outline barely discernible from the surrounding blackness. He could sense Perrington looking at him questioningly.

"What is it?" the sergeant asked.

"Not sure. I think there's somebody out there."

Perrington leaned forward. "A stiff?"

Richards shook his head. "I don't think so. It's moving towards us too fast. I think he's alive." He expected the army man to respond to that but there was no reply. "You want me to stop?"

"Keep going."

"But he might be in trouble—"

"You keep going," Perrington ordered sternly. "We stop for no one."

As the truck progressed across the bridge, the figure emerged into the light: he was indeed one of the living, and he looked terrified. He was little more than a teenager, probably barely into his twenties, and he was sprinting towards the truck, his arms waving in the air in an effort to get them to slow down. The rain had plastered his hair to his forehead, and Richards could even see the puffs of condensed breath blown out with each exhalation. The kid was exhausted, as if he'd been running a great distance.

"He's scared about something," the driver remarked. "I don't think he's going to take no for an answer."

"He'll soon get out of the way when he realises we aren't stopping."

"What if he's warning us about something? Could be the road's blocked."

"Then we'll find out for ourselves."

"You think that's wise?" Richards started, then fell silent for a second. "Oh shit." He tapped the brake, hearing the van behind him screech as the tyres skidded on the wet tarmac.

"What the hell are you doing?" Perrington snapped, momentarily ignoring his two-way, which barked into life on his lap as the other driver demanded to know what was going on. "I gave you an explicit order not to slow down."

"Look!" the older man yelled and lifted one hand from the wheel to point. The truck was still moving, but now coasting to a halt. The runner saw the vehicle had altered its speed, and dropped his arms, casting a glance over his shoulder, his gaze resting on the same sight that Richards was focusing his attention on.

Shuffling into the truck's beams of light was a gaggle of Returners, at least thirty in number. They shambled forwards, the kid their object of interest, their groans echoing amidst the metal stanchions of the bridge.

"Goddammit," Perrington breathed. "Put your foot down. We can go through them."

"We can't leave him here."

"I'm not going to tell you again. Now bloody drive!"

"The hell with you. Some of us are still human," Richards snarled and stomped on the brake, bringing the vehicle to a stop. Before the sergeant could lean across and grab him, he tore open his door and stepped down onto the road. The chill evening air cut through his cotton jacket and rain glued his shirt to his chest. Out here the sounds of the approaching dead carried further, their footsteps dragging along the ground in unison, the moans seemingly coming from every direction, reflecting off the surface of the Thames below them. The youngster marched quickly over to him, gulping in deep lungfuls.

"Thank Christ," he said quietly, putting a hand on Richards' shoulder as he bent double to recover. "I thought I wasn't going to make it..."

"It's OK. You'll be all right. You'll be safe now." The driver turned at the sound of boots on tarmac, and saw a handful of squaddies take up a position at the head of the truck, sighting their rifles on the throng of ghouls that were growing nearer. There was now perhaps only a hundred or so yards between them.

"Clear a path for us," Perrington instructed his men from the passenger seat, glaring at Richards. "Since we've lost our momentum, we'll have to thin them down a bit so we can plough through."

The guns barked rapidly as each soldier selected his target and fired, the deadheads at the front dropping face down with each impact, brains squirting out of their skulls. Their kin behind them hardly reacted, merely took their place and walked into the wall of bullets without a glimmer of fear or understanding. The bodies stacked up almost instantly.

"Sarge?" a voice called out. "Something weird here..."

"What do you mean?"

"Fuckin' pusbags are muzzled. Every one of 'em."

Richards looked back at the kid, puzzled, his mouth dropping open as the youngster yanked an automatic from his belt, hidden beneath his shirt.

"Game's over for you, old man," Hewitt said with a smile as he put a slug between the driver's eyes.

19.49 pm

Gabe ordered his team to move in immediately, with the intention of overpowering the soldiers while they were still dealing with the gaggle of deadheads. The half-dozen triggers jumped out of the Bedford van they'd been tooling up in and began to move across the bridge, the van coasting slowly alongside them, providing cover. Time was of the essence; it wouldn't take long for the military to deal with the stiffs, and they had the advantage of numbers and superior firepower. If Gabe's squad were to have a chance of pulling off the hijack successfully, it would mean attacking when their opponents were otherwise engaged. He clicked the safety off on his pistol and followed the others.

As he reached the scattered remains of the zombie distraction lying in a tangle on the road, he fleetingly looked at the bridles that were wrapped around their jaws. It was a ruse that he'd adopted on several occasions in the past, and he had found it was an effective means of instilling panic in the enemy. They rarely saw that the mouths had been clamped shut before it was too late. Even so, despite the muzzles, there was always a lack of volunteers to play the 'victim'. Gabe had made sure that Hewitt had drawn the short straw, a result that the kid had responded to furiously, but the older man had felt this was just the brush with danger that could encourage a little responsibility in the youngster.

The rattle of gunfire echoed through the still night air, ear-splittingly loud. The army men had formed a cordon around the truck and were shooting at will; the last of the ghouls were now only a few feet away, but a handful of the military had switched their attention to the bushwhackers. One of Flowers' enforcers – a bear of a man named Duvall – let rip with a full automatic, punching holes in the lorry's windshield and passenger door. Each time the squaddies cowered from the rapid-fire assault, the team advanced, tightening the circle, forcing them to retreat. Gabe scanned the haze of smoke for Hewitt, who should've infiltrated their defence, and spotted him putting his gun to the back of a soldier's head and pulling the trigger at point-blank range. He'd told each of them he wanted the minimum of casualties, with deaths acceptable only as a last resort, but the kid was drilling humans without compunction.

Gabe began to jog over towards him to pull him back before the whole operation became a slaughter. He stopped when he caught sight of what was behind the truck: a military escort vehicle that was unloading armoured-up soldiers but not deploying them, remaining hidden at the rear. Gabe guessed the strategy; they were drawing the hijackers forward, giving a false impression of defeat, before doubling their defence. The robbers needed to even the playing field a touch.

He signalled to Hanner, who had a small grenade-launcher holstered across his back, and pointed over the truck, indicating to drop the explosive behind it. It would scatter the reinforcements and hopefully disorientate them enough for his squad to surge ahead. Hanner nodded, unslung the weapon and sighted the necessary angle. But moments before the grenade powered from the barrel, a bullet slammed into his shoulder, pushing him backwards, his finger squeezing instinctively on the trigger. It threw his aim off, the missile ricocheted against a bridge stanchion and fell short, hitting the truck's bonnet and igniting its engine. The front of the vehicle exploded in a ball of orange flame, pulsing out a wave of heat that knocked Gabe to his knees. Others were flung sideways, some toppling into the icy waters of the Thames below. Seconds later, the petrol tank blew, and the blast was deafening, throwing the lorry upwards a couple of metres as everyone within its radius shielded their faces from the white-hot blaze. Gabe's ears rang as he woozily watched fire lick the starlit sky.

19.52 pm

They heard the noise even in the depths. It vibrated through the water, accompanied by a rapid succession of loud splashes. There was not enough rational thought left in their core cerebella to assimilate what the sound indicated, or its cause; but one instinct that still reverberated within them was that when the silence was broken, it meant life was close by, and where there was life there was flesh. It had been a theory that had been proven right time after time, to the point where they sought out the living through some primitive radar rather than by any other kind of recognition.

They were crossing the riverbed, their hungry search forever unfulfilled. Fluid flowed in and out of their still lungs with the ebb of the tide, their already cold skin untouched by the immense chill. Their surroundings meant nothing to them, just terrain to travel. But once they heard the sounds, they suddenly had direction. As one, they turned and waded through the silt and darkness towards the bank, the crackle above them leading them like a beacon.

19.55 pm

"Oh Christ."

The words snapped Gabe free from his trance. He shook his head, trying to reboot his senses. Everything was as it had been a minute before: the truck was still burning in the middle of the road, and the injured were crawling away from it, clothes and limbs blackened. The odd burst of gunfire still erupted now and then as each side tried to take advantage of the confusion, but Gabe – hunched against the bridge wall – was trying to hear what somebody was shouting about. Duvall was looking out beyond the thoroughfare and pointing. Gabe followed his gaze and attempted, by the light of the flames, to make sense of the black shapes that were emerging from the water. There were hundreds of them, dripping silhouettes that rose from the deep and were shuffling up a causeway towards the bridge. Realisation slapped him seconds later. All he could think was: *The dead are coming. We've awoken the dead.*

"We gotta get out of here," Duvall yelled. "We can't fight that number. Abandon the operation."

Gabe nodded slowly, and began to call for his team to retreat. The soldiers had spotted the zombies coming their way by now too and had all but stopped firing, watching with horror as the shambling dregs of the river came ever closer.

"Move it," Gabe cried. "Grab what injured you can and go."

They stumbled backwards away from the truck towards their own vehicles. Gabe made a vain effort to count how many of the squad were missing, but couldn't keep track. He looked around for Hewitt, who must've been near the lorry when it went up, but couldn't see him. He began to run, knowing that personal survival was now imperative.

Then the bullet caught him in the leg.

He gasped with shock, and collapsed onto his front, grit stinging his hands and face. It had come from behind, and passed through his calf, shattering the bone. Agony lanced up his knee and thigh as he felt his trouser filling with blood, but even so he tried to crawl, desperate to get away. He kept hoping that one of his comrades would spot him and drag him to safety, but nobody seemed to be around. He tried to scream, but couldn't find the voice.

His leg was numb now, and every movement was torture. He slid, inch after painful inch, refusing to give up. He didn't want to die at the hands of the dead; he couldn't accept such a fate. He felt for his gun, but it had gone. Desperation clawed at his mind to escape, but fatigue and blood loss were swamping his muscles, slowing him to a standstill.

He closed his eyes, an image of Anna framed against the window his last thought before he lost consciousness.

CHAPTER FOUR

The river glittered with the early-morning rays of the sun as the Mondeo pulled onto Westminster Bridge and parked several feet away from the smouldering ruins of the military truck. Two men stepped out of the car and walked up to the sooty, skeletal shell, giving cursory glances to the mass of bodies lying the length of the road. One of them stopped and pulled a semi-automatic from his shoulder holster, turning his gaze back and forth as he kept watch, flipping open a pair of shades from his shirt pocket to protect his eyes from the glare coming off the water. The other sauntered slowly around the burned-out vehicle, peering into the cab and the remains of the truck bed, occasionally nudging a charred piece of chassis with his toe. He stood for long moments staring at the wreck with his hands on his hips as if lost in thought, or studying it as though it were about to reveal some great mystery.

Eventually he strode back to his companion, pausing to kneel next to a Returner corpse and examining its wounds: much of the right side of its head was missing, its jellied contents sprayed across the tarmac. He straightened and crossed to a uniformed body, the torso peppered with bullet holes, and lifted its right arm: the fingers and thumb of that hand had been gnawed off, recently enough for the stumps to be still weeping. The man put his own digits to the soldier's cheek, gauging by his skin temperature how long he'd been dead, and put the time scale at about eleven hours. He guessed the victim had died of his gunshot injuries before a passing maggotshit had sensed enough warmth in the cadaver to munch down on. Once a body went cold, the zombies paid no attention, hence the reason they never tried to eat each other. It had been theorised that if the stiffs caught a human and began to consume him alive, they would feed for about an hour or two before their hot lunch cooled off and they lost interest. By that point, the meal had been so disassembled that resurrection was impossible; in fact, uninterrupted they would probably be down to the bone marrow at that stage. The man wondered briefly why soldier-boy here hadn't got up and walked, but then saw the small neat hole in his temple. That would do it, he concluded.

He stood and gingerly hopped over the corpses to the bridge wall, looking out across the Thames, the light wind ruffling the river, wavelets lapping against the embankment. He tugged a mobile from his jacket pocket and swiftly dialled. The voice at the other end answered with a brusque acknowledgement.

"Well?"

"It's a mess. Truck's a barbecue, nothing to be salvaged from that. Complete write-off. And we're talking sheer carnage here – must be close to forty bodies, both deadheads and living. Well, they *were* living."

"Any of them ours?"

"Yeah, I recognise a couple. Collins and Stokes are here, looks like they took a few hits to the head each. How many we missing all told?"

"Five, including O'Connell."

"Nah, there's no sign of the others. Could've resurrected, I suppose, and staggered off – either that or done a runner." He leaned out over the parapet, peering down at the river's surface. "Or they went for a dip," he added.

"The rest are... what? Army?"

"Yep, standard government troops. Put up quite a fight by the looks of things." He paused. "There's something else, Harry. The kid was right; there was a second vehicle. There're tyre marks behind the truck as if they sped away in a goddamn hurry. Could've taken some captives, I guess."

There was silence for a moment, then Flowers said: "Put Hewitt on, Patricks."

The man held out his phone to his companion. "He wants to talk to you."

Hewitt shouldered his gun and retrieved the handset. "Harry."

"Son, I want to make sure you've got your story straight." The boss sounded remarkably old and weary to his ears, the most vulnerable he'd ever heard him. Maybe it was a trick of the line's tinny timbre, but it was as if Flowers was reeling from a blow he had taken himself. "You saw O'Connell go down?"

"I saw what I saw. After it all went to shit, things got fucked up. The truck exploded and knocked me to the ground, but it also sent the army assholes running. They had reinforcements in this escort SUV that had been tailgating the target vehicle, and that started reversing the fuck out of there. Once I got my wind back, I attempted to carry on with the objective but then the earth just opened up and spat out every deadfuck from here to creation." Hewitt paced backwards and forwards with the rhythm of his account of the night's events. "I heard O'Connell tell everyone to get the hell out of there, and I headed towards him but he went down, took a hit. Seconds later, he was surrounded by uniforms. The smoke that was coming off the wreck was enough to allow me to sneak past 'em and hook up with what remained of the team."

"But you didn't see them finish O'Connell off?"

"Nope. There was gunfire, but that was the army boys taking care of the stiffs."

"So you think he's still alive? And that they took him with them?"

"If O'Connell had made it out of there in one piece, he would've been in contact with you one way or another, even if he was holed up somewhere, bleeding out. So, yeah, I think the government fucks have got him."

There was no immediate reply to that. All Hewitt could hear was Flowers breathing into the receiver as he mulled over what he had been told. He lifted his sunglasses onto his forehead and rolled his eyes at Patricks, switching the mobile to his other hand. How many times did the old fart need telling? Him and the other survivors had been up all night debriefing Harry and that long streak of piss traitor Ashberry on what happened; they were fucked off that they'd come away without the sample, but they hit the roof at the suggestion that one of their own was now in the custody of the military. It especially didn't look good when the guy that was meant to be leading the hijack was the one that fell into the hands of the enemy. O'Connell was one of the boss's right-hand men, had been with him since before the outbreak. That right now he could be sitting in some army compound singing about Flowers' set-up was giving the old geezer heart palpitations. He would've probably been less upset if they'd returned with O'Connell's eviscerated liver and told him that was all that was left after he got jumped by a gang of deadheads.

"OK," Hewitt's employer said at last with a heavy sigh. "We've got to accept he's a liability, and could compromise everything. If he's decided to change sides, then I want him found and I want him fed to a fucking pusbrain, feet first. If he's their prisoner, well... same rules apply. Can't take the risk on them getting any info out of him." A sense of resolve came back into Flowers' voice, in contrast to how pitiful he'd sounded a moment ago. "I want to you to find him, son. You and Patricks scour the damn city if you have to, but just seek him out and eliminate him before he causes us any more problems. Don't come back unless you got his balls for a brooch, you understand me?"

"Gotcha. Terminate with extreme prejudice."

The phone went dead. Hewitt flipped it shut and handed back to the other man with a smile.

"Well," he said, sliding the shades back into position. "Now things are getting interesting..."

Gabe flickered open his sleep-crusted eyelids, waited for the swirling to settle down, and watched a dull green ceiling coalesce into focus. He traced the cracks that ran along its surface as his fuzzy memory cranked into gear and he tried to remember where he was and what had happened to him. It took several seconds for him to recollect the events leading up to him passing out, and with the realisation came the ache. It started behind his knee and travelled up his leg, a fresh pain slotting into place as each new image of the battle on the bridge blossomed in his mind like a slideshow beamed into his skull. He reached out instinctively to clutch at his injury and shock cut through his agonised haze when he discovered that his arms were tightly strapped to the bed he was lying upon.

He woke up fast. He was dressed in just a T-shirt and jeans, the right leg cut away around the shin and calf to accommodate the bandage woven around it, and he could feel dried blood gluing the hairs of his thigh together. Predictably, he'd been stripped of anything else that he'd had on him. Gabe looked down at his bonds – knotted lengths of white linen – and tested their strength, his muscles straining against them, but they were firmly secured to the bed's frame. Adjusting his position to gain a better view of his surroundings brought a sharp stab of pain to his spine, and he slumped back prone, wondering how long he'd been unconscious and hog-tied like this. Every part of him seemed to be on fire, from top to toe.

He cast a wary gaze around him; it looked like a hospital ward or dormitory. Five other beds were lined against the opposite side of the room, all empty, the sheets flattened as if they hadn't been visited in many a month. It appeared he was the only occupant, but judging by the cleanliness of the floor and the bare walls he couldn't say he was surprised; this didn't look like a place where one could convalesce and regain one's health. It had a fatal air about it, a suggestion that the dying would be left here to see out their final moments. The plaster was grimy, darkened in spots, and the linoleum discoloured by a mixture of scuffed footprints, dirt and ancient body-fluids. A couple of fluorescent tubes were fitted to the ceiling, but they looked as if they had long since burned out, now grey and lifeless.

It sparked a memory in him, of awaking in a hospital after the bike accident, shivering with pain. The déjà vu was almost as insidious as the ache in his bones.

Following his initial confusion, it took Gabe a few minutes for the truth to sink in that he had survived. The memory of his legs collapsing out from under him burned brightly in his head, and the desperation of his attempted crawl to safety stuck bitterly in his throat. Tears formed in his eyes as the terror he had experienced for those fleeting seconds resurfaced. It can't have lasted any time at all, but for those few elongated moments the urge to live had never been more powerful, and the thought of falling victim to the ghouls – to see them stumble closer, to feel their cold dead hands clasp on his limbs, to smell their fetid stench as their teeth bit down on his skin – instilled in him a palpable fear. He shivered, the delayed after-effects of his narrow brush with being eaten alive bubbling up inside him as each horrific eventuality and permutation played across his imagination.

But he had escaped, he told himself, trying to bring the anxiety under control; or at least, he had been ushered out of immediate danger by persons unknown. Surveying his environs again, he felt it was safe to assume that this wasn't one of Harry's safe houses, and that he wasn't being kept here solely to recuperate. He had to have been retrieved by the troops before they evacuated the area – they had that second vehicle, he dimly remembered – and bundled back to a government complex. But for what reason would they want him alive, and, indeed, fix up his leg so he could be mobile again? Looters and bandits, especially those that preyed on military convoys, were given short shrift, and it wasn't that long after the outbreak took hold that a shoot-to-kill policy was imposed. Soldiers were notoriously merciless in handing out summary executions, and under other circumstances the military wouldn't have cared less if he'd ended up passing through a zombie's digestive tract. No, they had to have a reason for taking him and keeping him here; he had to have something they wanted. But what? Information?

The prospect gave him chills again, but not so much at the thought of what they could do to him as to what Harry's reaction was going to be once he realised that Gabe was in enemy hands. He'd become a compromise to the organisation. Flowers prided himself on a closely knit outfit, and would not accept security lapses, plugging (in every sense of the word) anything that threatened to destabilise his set-up. Gabe had worked for his employer for many years, and had been privy to the old man's numerous dealings. For Gabe to be captured by the opposition was a major embarrassment. Gabe could envision Harry making the equation, of tallying up his loyalty and friendship and weighing it against the trouble this predicament could cause him... but who was he kidding? The old man would decide Gabe's fate without a second thought.

Funny, he mused. For a moment there he'd been reassuring himself that he was still alive, that he'd made it through intact, when all along he was a dead man walking. His die had been cast the second that he fell, and it was just a matter of waiting now before the bullet caught up with him.

Multiple footsteps were approaching, he realised, as their *tap-tap-tap* resounded in the corridor beyond the room, growing louder as they came closer. There was a jangle of keys, the door was unlocked, and a pair of uniforms, rifles slung over their shoulders, entered, fixing him with a blank glare. Then a suit and a whitecoat emerged between the two and marched up to the bedside, the doc twisting his head to study Gabe's face intently. He reached out and pulled Gabe's eyes open wide with the fingers of one hand, retrieving a pen light from his breast pocket with the other and shining it into his pupils. Meanwhile, the suit wandered round to the foot of the bed, fiddling with his shirt cuffs.

"How are you feeling? Any concussion? Double vision?" the whitecoat asked, clicking the light off.

Gabe shook his head. "Leg's killing me."

"Painkillers have worn off. We'll give you some more

presently." His gaze flickered to the knotted linen tying Gabe's arms to the bed frame, and turned his attention to the suit. "Are the restraints necessary? They're probably interfering with his blood supply."

The government man raised his eyebrows, then nodded to the squaddies to go ahead and untie them. "OK. I think our friend here isn't stupid enough to try anything with an armed guard in the room."

Once they were free, Gabe brought his arms up to his chest and rubbed them, getting the circulation moving again. "So who are you?" he asked.

"The name's Fletchley," the suit replied. "I work for the Home Office. Or at least I did. I suppose it's a moot point whether such a thing still exists anymore." He motioned to the doctor, a leathery-faced, harried-looking old soak with sprigs of grey hair erupting from a bulbous nose. "That's Dr Hillman. He patched up your leg."

"Yeah, remind me to thank whichever arsehole it was that shot me when my back was turned."

"Rules of engagement, Mr O'Connell," Fletchley replied with a sigh. "The military has every right to protect government property. Even so, none of my troops can verify that they were the ones that fired upon you as your motley crew fled. That you fell into our lap is a bonus, I won't deny that."

Gabe's brow furrowed. "Well, if one of your boys didn't—"

"Who knows? Perhaps a stray round caught you at one unlucky moment. But at the time we were more concerned with evacuating the area." Fletchley stuck his hands in his pockets and looked down at the thief. The civil servant had a surprisingly youthful air, although he had to be in his late forties; his face was thin and rosy-cheeked, the pale skin seemed almost papery, his thatch of brown hair equally fine and insubstantial. Judging by his build housed within the dark woollen suit, he was slender and narrow-shouldered. "You may or may not have ascertained by now that the sample you were after was being transported in the back-up van. The truck you quite spectacularly destroyed was a decoy, intended to draw the fire of anyone attempting such an escapade. We should've guessed Harry Flowers' move into the medical arena would be typically heavy-handed."

Gabe flinched at the mention of his boss's name, dropping his gaze away from the Home Office man.

"Mr O'Connell," Fletchley said softly, "we know who you are and who you work for. Mr Flowers has been a thorn in our side for quite some time – redirecting arms supplies, kidnapping government scientists, conducting organised looting expeditions... His methodology is really quite impressive, if he'd used it for the common good instead of building his own power base. And let's face it, that what this is about, isn't it? Harry wants to take on the entire city."

Gabe didn't reply, opting instead to study the cuts that criss-crossed his palms, tracing them with his fingers.

Fletchley exhaled wearily. "I'm growing short on patience, O'Connell, and time is not on our side. We are not going to stand by and see Flowers attempt a coup. Do you honestly think that if your boss achieves his aim and takes control of the city that matters will improve? Do you think he has the best interests of those that have managed to survive through this at heart? If Flowers wiped every zombie from every corner of London, the regime that he would put in place would be just as dangerous and just as restrictive. Society may be destabilised at the moment, but it will be nothing compared to the lawlessness that will break out in his wake, because there are those that will not sit quietly and accept Flowers as their ruler. The capital will descend into tribalism and all-out warfare... and at its heart, a grasping, power-hungry dictator using his position to exploit those below him."

"You're telling me you prefer the deadfucks?"

"I'm telling you that Flowers will simply replace them with something a lot worse. What, for example, did he tell you he had in mind for the virus culture he wanted you to steal?" When Gabe refused to answer, Fletchley leaned forward and pressed down on his calf, causing him to hiss in pain. Hillman started to say something, but was silenced by a glare from the civil servant. "My tolerance towards your attitude is rapidly coming to an end," he continued. "Perhaps a few days without morphine will loosen your tongue?"

Gabe locked stares with Fletchley, feeling the throb in his leg muscle subside. He swallowed, knowing they could do what they liked to him, could keep him in a perpetual state of agony if it suited them. And did he owe Harry any loyalty anyway? If the gang lord was going to put the whack on him no matter what he said, what did it gain him by refusing to reveal his plans? Chances were these government pricks knew a lot more about Flowers' intentions than he did.

"Harry was seeking a way to make the stiffs more docile," he said finally. "He reckoned if they adapted the virus, they could turn them into non-cannibals, make them more... civilised, I suppose. That way his organisation could take to the streets without any opposition."

"That's what he told you, is it?" Fletchley looked amused.

"Well, yeah." Gabe was instantly suspicious. "He had his scientists working on it."

The suit laughed. "Those scientists – which, may I

remind you, Flowers had removed from Ministry of Defence research bases – have been getting word back to us through primitive radio relay. From what they say, your boss isn't interested in curing the plague – at least, not all of it. According to them, he's planning on keeping a regular private army of flesh-eaters back for his own use."

"Say that again?"

"I'd guess you'd call them his elite bodyguard. Flowers doesn't want to get rid of the zombies entirely, not when he can use them for his own purposes. I imagine you could get someone to do whatever you wanted with a pack of slavering Returners on a leash that need constant feeding. And we all know that the dead get restless if they don't eat for long periods, so I shudder to think what he's going to be using for pet treats."

Gabe laid his head back on the pillow, wondering if this could possibly be true. Could Flowers be that ruthless, maintaining his own battalion of undead enforcers to support his reign? And to keep them supplied with human meat... was he going to have his own farm, cultivating men and women like livestock, all so he could rule London unapposed?

Fletchley pulled up a chair and sat beside the bed. "You don't have to believe me, of course, but I think you realise that there's no cause for me to lie. I want Flowers stopped; it's as simple as that. There are many reasons, but it all comes down to the fact that he's a serious menace that cannot go unchecked."

"Why are you telling me this? Why are you keeping me here? If you know so much about what he's planning, what use am I to you?"

"It's not so much what you know, Mr O'Connell, it's what you can do for us. We have need of your skills.

Naturally, once your leg's healed and we inevitably let you out of here to fulfil this task, there's nothing to stop you running back to your boss. But we both know you'd be returning to the lion's den. The moment you fell into our clutches, you were marked for execution. I know all too well how Flowers' paranoid kind work. But as a result, you are now free of obligation, offering allegiance to no one."

"So by that token, why should I do anything for you?"

"Well, quite. I mean, apart from repaying the care and attention that Dr Hillman here has lavished on you," Fletchley shared a brief grin with the medic, "there's the opportunity to do something worthwhile with your life, Mr O'Connell. What we're asking you to be involved with could turn the plague around forever and save thousands of lives. You've been in Flowers' employ for many years, I know, and no doubt you've seen that as your sole interest, your world. But now's the chance to do something for the greater good, to help others rather than support one man's greed. To step outside Harry Flowers' shadow." The government man leaned closer. "You must've lost loved ones since the outbreak, Gabriel. Don't you want to redeem yourself in their eyes?"

Gabe didn't answer. He stared at the cracked ceiling, but all he could see was the outline of the woman at the window.

CHAPTER FIVE

The same two soldiers that had arrived with Fletchley that first time he had regained consciousness came for him again almost a week later, by which point he found he could put a not-insubstantial amount of pressure on his injured leg, and the doc had decreased his painkiller dosage. He was sitting on the edge of the bed exercising the muscle when they marched through the doors and instructed him to go with them. Although he hissed as he limped along a series of dreary corridors between the two squaddies – perhaps acting a little more pained than was strictly necessary, slowing their journey out of simple bloody-mindedness and taking a perverse pleasure at being a nuisance – he made a note of the building he was passing through, trying to gauge where they were situated. What had looked like a hospital ward upon awaking was clearly now merely a medical wing, amounting to little more than a couple of rooms in the whole complex. The office architecture he was entering now – with its walls of metal cabinets, file boxes piled high, and computer terminals covering every surface, rats' nests of cables strewn across the dull brown carpet – told him that this was some kind of government bunker that had been in existence, in all probability, since the 1970s. Most likely, the authorities thought they would escape down here in the eventuality of a nuclear conflict. Few, if any, would have believed that the end of the world would've been brought about by a zombie plague.

It seemed to be very understaffed. The scale of the mess was drowning the dozen or so clerks he saw tapping away at keyboards or juggling ring binders and ledgers, the exact purpose of their work a mystery. It was as if somebody hadn't told them that the world outside had changed, and they were blithely carrying on, balancing books, chasing up invoices, sorting through correspondence. There was something quite comically surreal about watching them potter between desks like accountants, refusing to believe that the apocalypse had already arrived.

The reams of paper stacked up on the floor and crammed into cupboards looked like the last remnants of the human race. He tried to catch a glimpse of what was written on them as he was hurried past, and merely saw a jumble of figures, addresses and names. He got the impression they were census reports and electoral registers, dating back over the last six or seven decades. Quite what they were doing here, or what use they could ever be in the current circumstances, he couldn't fathom. It was as if the record on every man, woman and child in the country had been inexpertly stuffed into the nearest available storage facility once the undead situation had quickly spun out of control. For what reason, he mused: as a list of the missing? Almost certainly sixty per cent of the people transcribed on these printouts were no longer living. Who was ever going to read or process this information? And what could they ever do with it? As he eyed each shelf, bowing under the weight of bulging folders, he had the inescapable morbid sense that this was intended to be some kind of mausoleum of mankind, a memorial – not etched in stone but immortalised in documentation. No epitaph, he thought, just the facts of who we were and that we were once here. Gabe didn't know which was the more chilling: the idea that he was walking through his species' history, or that his fellow Homo sapiens were dumb enough to consider that this really mattered anymore.

The lead trooper halted at a door and rapped upon it, ushering Gabe through when he heard a response.

Fletchley was sitting on the other side of a desk – itself a landslide of reports, photographs and stationery – and signalled to the thief to pull up a chair. Fletchley glanced at the soldiers and they withdrew, leaving the two men alone in the office. Gabe briefly gave the room the once-over, unsurprised to see yet more sheaves of paperwork poking from overfilled suspension files. It took him a couple of seconds to note that there was no window – the dim light came courtesy of a bare bulb hanging above his head – and he determined that this complex was definitely below ground. The one object of note in the room was a vast map of London pinned to the wall, virtually covering it vertically from skirting board to ceiling. There were drawing pins and coloured stickers spiralling across it.

Fletchley noticed his momentary interest in the map and motioned towards it. "We're tracking the movements of the Returners," he said. "Trying to distinguish a feeding pattern, seeing if we can pre-empt their grazing routine."

"They go where the meat is," Gabe replied. "I would've thought that was obvious."

"Not necessarily. True, they'll zone in on the living if they sense them in their vicinity, but they're not simply ambling about anymore, hoping to stumble upon a meal. They're remembering where they've fed before, learning how to navigate themselves around the city to find the best spots."

Gabe looked back at the map. "You've witnessed this?"

"Oh yes. Or rather, our backroom boys have. They've released electronically tagged dead back onto the streets and monitored their journeys through radar. They've seen them coming back to the same feeding grounds time after time, even returning here, where they were set free, aware that living are in the area. The information is staying with them, you see, and they're acting upon it. It's cognition. They're thinking."

"It's instinct, surely. The same instinct that keeps them upright on two feet, that makes them scared of fire, that leads them to hunt in packs. They're driven by motor functions. Any animal with half a brain develops a knowledge of where the food is if it follows its nose enough times."

Fletchley sat back, clicking the end of his pen distractedly. "They're animals, certainly, demonstrating as they do a low-level intelligence. I don't think they can really be called 'zombies' anymore, not in the classical sense. They're not just reanimated cadavers. They're showing signs of skill development, of memory retention, of recognition. They're no longer monsters of folklore, but could possibly be classified as a new sub-species."

"Classified," Gabe repeated, opening his arms wide to take in the room. "That about sums this place up. What are you doing here, Fletchley? Cataloguing? Archiving? Filing fascinating data like that while the world consumes itself?"

The government man abruptly stood and walked around his desk, seating himself upon an uncluttered corner directly in front of the thief. He continued to tap the pen into the palm of his left hand. "You think all this is... folly?"

"I think you're clinging on to bureaucracy despite the fact that there isn't the authority to support it anymore. What usefulness do these records hold? Who's ever going to care enough to dig them out again? Everything's changed, in case you haven't noticed; the slate's been wiped clean. All that came before might as well be ancient history, 'cause it has no bearing on what we're facing here and now."

"You don't believe that."

"Don't I?" A vision of Anna swirled in Gabe's head and he struggled to mentally swat it away. "That'll be why I work for Harry Flowers, then." *Worked*, he admonished himself.

"Ah yes, Mr Flowers. The man who would be king. You think he's the future?"

"I think that he will decide where the city goes over the next few years. All power has shifted to him. While you and the rest of the pencil pushers have squirreled yourselves away down here, building a nest from the detritus of what you once had, he's been taking London apart piece by piece. And there's nothing you can do about it."

"So you say." Fletchley paused, rolling the pen between his hands. "Mr O'Connell, where you and I differ is that what you see as detritus, I see as a reminder of what civilisation used to be. When society used to be built on rules and regulations and communal living, rather than the outlaw, self-interested way of doing things that now seems to be the norm. And this, all this," he picked up a selection of loose pages from his desk and sprinkled them onto Gabe's lap, "is what I'm fighting for. It tells me that I'm not a looter or a criminal thug, stealing and murdering my way to the top. It tells me that I'm not something that destroys what it can't have, and devours what it can with an insatiable appetite. What it does tell me is that I'm a civilised human being, capable of rising above the common beasts."

Gabe said nothing, brushing the documents to the floor.

"Let me remind you of something," Fletchley continued. "We captured you in the process of attempting to hijack a government vehicle. It was within our rights under martial law to have you executed. Instead, you were brought here, your injury was tended to, and you're seated before me with very little threat to your person. On the other hand, your employer – the man you reckon will lead the citizens out of the wreckage, and who will make sure no doubt that they will bow before him – has more than likely put a mark on your head to stop you spilling his secrets. If you were to return to his organisation, you would get a bullet in the back of the skull before you even got up the driveway. Now tell me: which sounds like the side of the angels to you?"

"All the same, I think I still trust Harry more, even if he does want me dead. At least it's a black and white relationship."

The civil servant's mouth creased into a strained smile. "I would've assumed we were past the question of trust. If it makes you feel any better, I can make my personal opinion of you quite plain: I think you're a waste of space, O'Connell. I think you, Flowers and the rest of your lawless fraternity have taken advantage of others your whole life–"

"You know *nothing* about me–"

"–and since the outbreak, you've exploited human suffering and the breakdown of order to further your own aims. You care for nothing or no one in the pursuit of wealth and power. You're a user, O'Connell, a parasite, and under any other circumstances I wouldn't place the slightest value upon you. But the situation we find ourselves in calls for strange bedfellows. To be quite blunt, we wish to make use of you."

"What, a parasite like me?"

"I'm simply making my intentions clear. We need someone on the ground that can pass through the underworld unhindered, someone without the taint of authority. And of course someone who has considerable experience in the art of thievery."

"So you want me to steal for you? That's not taking advantage of others then?"

Fletchley rocked forward off the desk and onto his feet, walking over to the map. He turned back to Gabe, tapping a marked area with the tip of his pen. "Not in this case. Not when it's stealing from a criminal. You've heard presumably of Resurrection Alley, and the uses to which the dead are put there?"

The younger man nodded, frowning.

The civil servant gazed at the image of the capital before him. "There've been... rumours of what Andrei Vassily is keeping inside the settlement. We have limited intelligence gatherers around the city, alerting us to the latest developments, and word repeatedly comes back: Vassily has something. It's never been verified, but it's been mentioned by too many disparate sources for us not to take it seriously. Bottom line, the word is that he is in possession of a truly self-aware Returner. Possibly the first we have knowledge of in the country."

"A smart deadhead?" Gabe said, struggling to follow where his role fitted into this. "Where did it come from?"

"Your guess is as good as mine, if indeed the reports are true. Quite what he's doing with it is another question; keeping him warm during the cold winter evenings, for all I know. But its presence, if it exists, cannot be ignored; it might be the most important and decisive find since the plague took hold. A chance to turn the contagion around."

"You've lost me."

"The virus is changing, Flowers and his scientists are right about that. It's evolving, adapting the ghouls for its own ends; they're growing smarter as it works on their higher brain functions, allowing them to recognise elements from their pre-dead state – names, objects, places." Fletchley tapped the map again. "The feeding patterns tell us just how far they've come. They're still flesh-eaters, and unable to comprehend much beyond that basic need; but a self-aware Returner is the best evidence we have that a zombie is capable of rational thought. The bacterium within it must've developed at a phenomenal rate. We need to take a look at it."

"Hold on, you want me to hijack a *stiff*?"

"Of course not. But we need a blood sample." Fletchley locked stares with Gabe. "I told you that this opportunity could save thousands of lives, that it would be for the greater good. If we could learn to duplicate the virus in that advanced form, it's possible we could reverse the effects of the zombiefication process, halt the spread of the infection."

Gabe thought of Anna sitting in her chair in the silent room, looking out over Harry's gardens. There was an absence at the heart of her he had never been able to touch: not yet. "You could turn people back to who they were? From before, I mean?"

The government man shrugged and shook his head. "It's impossible to say. I doubt we could help some – the effects of mortification would've been too great. But others, those that have resurrected more recently, we could perhaps return a semblance of cognition to. At the very least, give them a new diet. But it's a chance we can't afford not to take. At the risk of sounding melodramatic, it might well be mankind's best hope."

"Sentiments like that don't mean much to somebody like Andrei Vassily," Gabe murmured.

"Nor Harry Flowers, not if there's influence to be wielded or money to be made. But maybe they strike a chord with you."

"You mean a wanted lowlife with nothing left to lose?"

"Exactly."

It was the smells that were his guide through the streets. Down here, amongst the ruins, there were no directions to aid him on his journey. Thus he relied on his other senses to lead him in his descent from the main West End arterial thoroughfares into the narrow alleys and dank, deserted squares. Such was the quiet, he cocked his head at the distant clatter of movement or the suggestion of a faint zombie moan carried on the breeze; his palate was sharpened to recognise a change in the air, taste the sour ashes of a hidden brazier crackling somewhere; but it was the scents that were his beacon, the sweetness of roasting meat underscored by the tang of corruption, the sour stink of bodies pressed together. In an environment where cadavers lay discarded with as much dignity as rubbish bags heaped in a skip, the surroundings rapidly grew ripe with decay, and it took a finely tuned nose to separate the stench of death from that of life. Not unlike the ghouls, he sensed the proximity of his own kind by following a feeling of warmth generated by the beating of many hearts.

Gabe stepped warily down subway steps, aware that his progress was unquestionably being monitored by those that he sought. CCTV cameras hooked up at the subway's entrance had their pictures rerouted to give the Alley warning of who was approaching. The fact that he had been able to advance so far unhindered was a positive sign that his presence wasn't unwelcome. Even so, he would be wise to remain cautious, he told himself, because anything was possible with these people. He strode through the underpass unhurriedly, his footsteps echoing disconcertingly loud in the enclosed space, the yellow fluorescents set in the walls barely illuminating the grimy, refuse-sodden floor ahead. He concentrated on the sulphur gleam of the streetlights beckoning him at the end of the tunnel, refusing to pause or glance over his shoulder. He knew he had to look like he belonged here, that he wasn't a stranger sent to stir trouble, and was more than a thrill-seeking tourist; rather, that he knew the score of what it was to cross into the underworld. Of course, if they were aware of who it was that had sent him on this errand, his entry would've been denied before he got within several hundred feet of the place.

Gabe exited the subway, and got his first glimpse of Resurrection Alley, its gated threshold strung between the mighty pillars of a flyover support. Apart from the one guarded doorway, there was no other opportunity to gain entrance, its chain link fence tucked snug on either side against the sheer revetments that were impossible to climb. In its own downmarket way, its security was on a par with Harry's mansion. The storm fences had been extended to the underpass steps, so as one ascended it was into a steel-mesh corridor that channelled the visitor towards the Alley's gate.

The fences were essential; out here in the wild, barren plains of the capital it was zombie country. A good two-dozen deadheads battered themselves against the barriers, trying to gnaw their way through. Once they saw – or, more accurately, sensed – Gabe emerge, they shook the wire frenziedly and attempted to force their fingers beyond the divide. It was initially shocking to be so close to the ghouls, separated by mere inches, and their excited groans at his arrival hit him like a roar after the solitude of his journey here. Once he became accustomed to their presence, he made sure he walked directly down the centre of the passage, careful not to drift too close to their grasping hands and ceaseless jaws; but despite trying to keep his demeanour cool and collected, he couldn't help looking worriedly at the fences as they shook with the furious flesh-crazed craving of the dead. They didn't seem strong enough to keep them at bay.

As he approached, he marvelled at the scale of the settlement – dwarfed itself by the vast cement expanse of the motorway above – and the organisation that it had taken to establish itself deep in the middle of nowhere. It was some distance from the nearest cluster of stores that still contained supplies; it seemed at the mercy of the elements, the cold concrete landscape offering little respite; and running the gauntlet of deadheads every time you arrived or departed was, in Gabe's eyes, an unnecessary risk. But he had heard that this was the way its inhabitants liked it, far from the more populated areas of London, apparently embracing their marginalised position. It made daily existence into some kind of extreme sport, riding on the cusp of danger. And more pertinently, it removed Resurrection Alley from the immediate clutches of the authorities that might try to impose some kind of order on the place.

Out here, it operated under its own rules; and that was the primary temptation for so many of its clientele, willing to make the trip to see and experience for themselves the distractions for which the Alley was renowned. It reputedly offered anything that the punter was willing to pay for, would accede to the basest desires, and asked little questions if the money was right; and it found there were plenty who were looking for such a paradise, so many in fact that Vassily and his lieutenants had the luxury of picking and choosing who they would allow within its walls. Those whose overheated lusts suggested instability could be easily refused entry, and while simple sightseers were treated with disdain, they were considered rich pickings ripe for fleecing. All of which led to its growing reputation of exclusivity – and of course the more people were denied access the more they wanted to taste its forbidden fruits for themselves. The place had become a modern legend, an intersection of fact and fiction. The stories that Gabe had heard from those that had returned from a day or two's partying within the Alley were almost fantastical. He had been there only once before, acting as superfluous back-up when Harry decided to pay Vassily a goodwill visit about three years ago. As it was, Gabe got to see little of the reputed entertainment; he and the five-strong other triggermen were housed in a nondescript office and fed coffee and cigarettes while Flowers and Vassily chewed the fat. Presumably, since they weren't parting with any cash, the Alley was a closed shop.

Harry tolerated the Alley, allowed it to operate independently and not pay him any tithe, which was possibly down to the fact that Flowers had a history with Andrei's old man, Goran. They had been rivals back in the day, and Andrei was still oblivious to the truth behind his father's death. Harry wanted it kept that way for the time being. Thus, the two bosses existed in a forced atmosphere of bonhomie, fully aware that the other would one day want to expand their empire. Flowers knew that when London was his, it would mean that the Alley would fall finally under his remit; the inevitable war would be bloody and hard-fought, but his control had to be total. He wouldn't brook small islands within the city escaping his rule. It would be absolute or nothing.

Gabe sidled up to the entrance, wondering if he would be recognised as one of Flowers' men. There was no reason why his face should've been indelibly printed on the memories of the guards after all that time, and he'd never met Andrei in person, who had come back from abroad to take over his father's business when he died. But even if they did make him he had resolved to come clean and just tell them that he'd broken free from his former employer, which was certainly no lie. Whether they'd go for it or not was another matter. The guy on the other side of the chain link gate was eyeing him suspiciously – Gabe supposed that most revellers visited the Alley as a group rather than turning up on their own – and was absent-mindedly running his forefinger along the stock of the pump-action shotgun he held down at his side.

"How's it going?" Gabe greeted him with as much forced jollity as he could muster.

The guard nodded a reply. He was black, with a thin moustache and a bandanna wrapped around a bald head. He had had a three-quarter chewed apple in the other hand, which he threw to one side. "You lookin' for something?"

"Been looking for this place, my friend. I heard the Alley was the place to go."

"Is that right? You realise not anyone can jus' stroll in here."

"What, is it a 'if the face fits' kind of deal?" When the man didn't answer, merely studied him intently, Gabe shrugged dispiritedly. "There I was kinda thinking that this was somewhere where I might find myself a good time. Few drinks, bit of gambling..." The guard remained unmoved. "I got money," Gabe added, with an exaggeratedly naive delve into his pockets.

The shotgun twitched and Gabe froze. "You come here on your own?" the guard asked, motioning with the weapon for him to keep his hands where he could see them.

"Yep. Truth of the matter is, I've been travelling down from the north, kinda looking for a bolthole to call my own, if you see what I mean. Guy I met, fellow drifter, he told me about this place, said that it was a regular Disneyland in Stiff City. Thought I owed it to myself to kick loose for a while and have some fun."

The guard didn't look convinced, but he glanced up at the CCTV camera that was positioned on the other side of the fence. Someone was watching him, Gabe guessed, trying to discern if he was trouble. He hoped that his 'just arrived in the city' spiel would be enough to get them salivating at how much of his cash they could get him to part with. The man's mobile phone burbled and he spoke briefly into it, then started ramming free bolts and unlocked the gate, beckoning Gabe across the threshold before securing it again.

"OK, arms out," the man said, placing the shotgun as his feet. He patted Gabe down quickly and desultorily, finding nothing, though he took the liberty of removing a couple of twenty-pound notes from Gabe's wallet. "Call it a gate fee," he said, winking. "Go on then. Your promised land awaits."

Gabe smiled, as if he wasn't quite sure what he was letting himself in for. But his expression disappeared as soon as his back was turned and he strode into the crowds of Resurrection Alley, conscious not only of the rasp of the miniature revolver taped just below his ankle, but also of the syringe pressing against his foot inside his left boot.

As Gabe threaded his way through the Alley's evening clientele, with every step – his leg had adequately recovered enough for him to disguise his limp so that it didn't draw attention – he tried to rationalise who he was doing this for. Certainly not Fletchley; despite the civil servant's disarming candour, an inbuilt distrust of suits stopped him from taking the ministerial lackey at his word. He liked to believe that the man had the nation's interests at heart, but the speed with which the government had lost control suggested that this might be just a face-saving damage limitation exercise. Also, he had heard on the grapevine that more than a handful of senior members of the cabinet (including possibly the Premier himself) had fallen victim to the plague, and were locked in a secure establishment in the eventuality that a cure was found.

There was perhaps an element of wanting to put a spoke in Flowers' plans – especially given the worrying revelations of what Harry intended to do with the city once it was his – but in the main he told himself his altruism just extended to two people: himself and Anna. He'd made a promise to help her; it was principally why he'd chosen to stay in Flowers' outfit. If he could help snap her out of her fugue state – surely Fletchley would make her a priority case for treatment, as a favour returned, if they could somehow pry her away from Harry's grasp – then it offered something he'd been perhaps losing sight of over the years: hope. The civil servant had been right;

he had lived for too long in Flowers' shadow, bending to his will, the gang lord's limitless ambition chipping away at his sense of moral duty. What was the point in helping pave the way for his former employer's brave new world if it helped no one? Indeed, if it put in place a situation that was even worse? It was time he took control for himself, and put his own plans in motion.

The Alley's boulevards were stained red from the spluttering neon on the buildings lining each side, advertising their contents. The majority of them were spit n' sawdust live shows: deadfuck baiting, shooting galleries or strip joints. Naked, mostly female, zombs writhed in windows, chained to poles, muzzles strapped over their mouths, advertising the entertainment within. Their dull eyes stared out at the crowds pausing to watch. Supposedly their frantic straining against their bonds was meant to be erotic, but to Gabe's eyes it looked desperate and so far removed from what he found attractive that he struggled to imagine how any of these slack-jawed fun-seekers were willing to pay to go into some back room and make out with a hosed-down and tethered ghoul, all its teeth and nails removed, its veins pumped full of formaldehyde and its skin slathered in that shit that undertakers used to make sure nothing came off mid-coitus. It amazed him how people would so quickly turn to something that in any other circumstances they would find utterly abhorrent. Social codes abandoned, they embraced a regression to animalistic urges.

Slipping through the throng, he was continuously accosted by enthusiastic barkers, championing each establishment's delights – hunting parties, with prizes for the most undead bagged; wrestling matches, the combatants armed with nothing but their bare fists against a trio of stiffs; bars with dissections performed every hour.

It was stimulation overload, a descent into a De Sadeian hell. For the enterprising pornographer or club owner, the rise of the dead had given them an underclass they could exploit without fear of recrimination; that could be broken and abused until they fell apart and were replaced. Anyone looking to unwind or let off a little steam could, for a fee, get themselves a Returner to beat on for an hour or so, safe in the knowledge that they weren't battering anything that experienced pain, or was even breathing. As long as it wasn't a recognisable family member that was up on stage being fed into a mincer before a baying audience – and it could happen; once a victim resurrected it was fair game for the Alley's entertainment, no matter what they once were in their previous existence – visitors were happy to use the pusbags for whatever dark designs they saw fit.

Gabe knew that Vassily would be keeping this smart zombie of his out of public view, and that he would have to arrange a meet with the settlement's leader, if he was going to get close to it at all. He recalled that one of Andrei's lieutenants ran the security on a cage-fighting dive on the central strip; perhaps he could get word through that way. He headed off in search of it, determinedly doing his best to ignore the brightly lit windows, and the horrors that they displayed for sale.

"That him?"

"No question. Always knew that fucker had nine lives."

"What's he doing here?"

"Hiding out, maybe. More likely he's looking to get in with Vassily's mob."

"Shit, this could be awkward. Harry's not going to want to bring a war to the Alley."

"Fuck it, get on the phone, tell Flowers we found him. We'll let him call the shots."

CHAPTER SIX

It was the noise that hit him as soon as he entered. Upon stepping through the door, Gabe had to squint against the club's gloom, its sole illumination the spotlights beaming their paltry glow upon the cage set up in the middle of the interior. Everything beyond their reach was a mass of heaving shadow; but once his eyes became accustomed to the darkness he could judge by the silhouettes of the crowd that the venue was packed. The blue smoke that drifted ethereally beneath the rafters added to the slow, thick air that made the room feel stagnant and claustrophobic. He could discern little of the clientele that were pressing forward to get a better view of the action that was taking place inside the steel ring at the centre, but the roar of cheers, shouts and curses was deafening. From this distance, with the neglected bar just to his right, he could see little of what the mob was baying for but he could discern, between the cries, the crunch of bone splintering and the rattle of the cage as bodies were thrown against it. Each punch was punctuated by another eruption from the audience.

Gabe sidled over to the barman leaning on the counter. He raised his eyebrows at the thief's approach, and Gabe nodded a greeting, ordering a beer. The barman withdrew one from a wheezing cooler cabinet powered, Gabe noted, by a small rumbling generator tucked away in a corner; cables snaked away from it up the walls and across the beams, providing the electricity for what seemed the whole building. It lent the bar the faintest stench of kerosene, and when he took a swig from the bottle it tasted like the lager had been brewed from something similar. He swilled it around his mouth, summoning the courage to swallow, but threw some coins onto the counter top instead, waiting until the barman's concentration was fixed on retrieving the money before spitting the beer onto the floor. His tongue felt as if someone had scoured it with a wire brush. He chanced a look at the bottle, but there was no label on it. No wonder the crowd was so rowdy, he thought; they've probably been sent half-mad through alcohol poisoning.

He leaned forward as the man was counting up the pennies. "Does Jackson still work here? Bryan Jackson? I heard he was chief of security." Gabe had to shout at the top of his voice even though there was barely a foot between them. Evidently, whomever the audience was rooting for had pulled off something pretty spectacular because the applause went through the roof.

The barman glanced up at him then down again, not catching his eye for more than a second. "You a friend of Bryan's?"

Gabe nodded. "Know him from way back. Used to run with his crew when I was younger." He played with the bottle to give the impression he hadn't forgotten about it while at the same time deliberately not putting it anywhere near his lips. "Been travelling down from the north, trying to find friends that I've lost contact with. Last time I spoke to him I thought he'd said he was working at the Alley."

"What did you say your name was?"

"I didn't. It's O'Connell."

"Bryan's kinda busy right now," the barman replied, gesturing to the crowd. "As you can see, we get a full house on fight nights and there's always a chance that some bozo is going to get a temper on him. The sec team usually have their hands full when the match is over. But his office is over there, on the far side." He pointed across the room towards the impenetrable murk beyond the cage. "Perhaps you can catch him there, when he's taking a break."

Gabe thanked him, picked up his bottle and started to ease his way through the throng. He didn't think it was possible but the cacophony substantially increased the closer he got to the epicentre of the club and the nearer he drew to the fence-encircled pit. The slap of flesh meeting flesh on the other side of the steel mesh reverberated in his head, and the watching mob pressing in against him moved as one body, pogoing with excitement, raising their fists in the air, yelling with triumph or anger. It was unquestionably mostly men in the audience, and they appeared to feed off each other's energy, vicariously channelling the violence from the act they were watching into bellowing approval. It was impossible to distinguish any actual words amongst the chants and jeers; it melded into a wall of sound that each added to with every full-throated roar. Gabe moved through the undulating, gesticulating mass carefully, picking his route with caution, knowing that if he upset just one component of this seething organism, it would turn its aggressive focus inwards and spill into a ruck. It wasn't difficult to detect the barely suppressed savagery in the spectators; its stink hung in the air mixed with the cigarette smoke, a bouquet of terrifying primal brutality, sweat and the ever-present undercurrent of rotting meat.

A space cleared before him and Gabe could at last view the cage-fight unobstructed. The human grappler was bare-chested and sheathed in perspiration, dark blood splattered across his torso and arms, though Gabe guessed that it wasn't his own. The man was wearing a Mexican wrestler-style hooded mask that completely shielded his features, but the weight of his frame put his age at somewhere in his mid-forties. Gabe wondered how long he had been taking part in bouts like this; he reminded the thief of a circus strongman or fairground boxer, long gone to seed, and performing humiliating acts of strength and endurance for a paying public.

He was without weapons, but he had long metal cuffs around each wrist, both with a hooked blade on the underside. From the look of the four Returners he was locked in the cage with, it seemed that was all the arsenal he needed: they were falling apart before him, one of their arms was already lying on the crimson-flecked straw that covered the floor of the pit. Their gullets were open black wounds, from which their moans echoed through their severed vocal cords, and it looked as if their grey-green skulls were only staying atop their spinal columns by the flimsiest thread. Jagged cuts criss-crossed their faces and limbs, laying them open to yellow bone; and yet still they came for him, hungry and relentless. They weren't chained to anything, which surprised Gabe; he had seen fights like this before where the ghouls were on a leash, which only extended so far, giving the living opponent a sliver of an advantage should the maggotbrain be particularly feisty. Here, no such help was required. The moment a zombie came within grasping distance, the wrestler easily sidestepped its approach and brought down his forearm, the blade slicing through the tissue-thin skin in an instant.

It became apparent that he was playing with them to a certain degree. He could've finished them off within moments with a handful of judicious swipes to the brain, but he was dragging out their demise for the maximum entertainment, trimming pieces off them with the skill of a butcher. He used the ghouls for comedy value, pushing one in front into its fellows and watching them tumble like a troupe of clowns; then, as another would try to right itself, he would stamp on its gnarled hand, the dry, sharp snapping of brittle digits accompanied by another bellow of admiration from the crowd.

Eventually, Gabe detected the show beginning to wrap up; the wavering cadavers looked like they'd stumbled through a jet engine – chunks of their bodies were missing in a jigsaw-style effect – and were barely offering any resistance. The audience was growing restless, demanding a spectacular climax, and the wrestler whetted their bloodlust with a denouement worthy of one experienced at performing before the public: he spun, hooking his right leg around the nearest Returner's waist so that it was pulled nearer, then lashed out with both arms beneath the zomb's chin, severing its head completely. There was little blood, and the remains collapsed to the floor like a felled tree, the skull following after with an eggshell crack as it hit the ground.

The crowd approved, starting a chant that the fighter attempted to execute his finishing moves to, slashing open the last three ghouls to every beat of the rhythm. They each followed the fate of the first, necks split asunder, until the man stood in the middle of the cage, blood-slicked and victorious, viscera curled at his feet, his arms held above his head, pumping his fists to the throng's adoration. Those at the front of the mass surged forward and grabbed hold of the bars, rattling them with angry exultation. Their desire to see violence meted out was satisfied, and now it was exploding outwards, directionless. Gabe could understand now why the barman said the security team had their hands full; it would take all their efforts to quell such a riled mob. Minor scuffles began to break out in the thick of the crowd, and he took the opportunity to remove himself from the danger zone. He edged well away from the trouble, backing up against the far wall where he'd been told Jackson's office was situated, just as the bouncers moved in armed with short black saps, seemingly ungluing themselves from the shadows.

They handled the situation with efficient brutality, ushering those that didn't want their own heads broken to vacate the premises. Most of the clientele were on their way out the door without having to be asked, eager to find the next live show, or have a go at something similar themselves, their appetites for destruction piqued. That was the chief attraction of Resurrection Alley: the fun never stopped. You could move from club to bar to gambling den to whorehouse to Grand Guignol theatre and find some new atrocity to keep you amused and occupied while the industrial-strength booze and pills, purchased from the tiny but dedicated band of dealers, went to work on your nervous system. It was amazing how quickly such a state of insobriety and tolerance towards the most inhuman acts imaginable could become the norm. Those that defended their actions perpetrated whilst holidaying in the Alley would more often than not merely claim they were letting off steam; but what that didn't account for was the rage that such relaxation unleashed. It was like seeing mankind sloughing off its daily face in a bid to enjoy itself, and in the process unveiling the hideous dark heart of what it actually was.

Those scrappers that were too enthused by the bout they'd just witnessed and who were continuing to tussle with their neighbours were given short shrift; the security guards struck the ringleaders across their temples, rendering them instantly unconscious. Once more than half a dozen were lying prone on the bar's floor, then the fight went out of the rest, and they held up their hands in surrender, retreating towards the exit. The last to leave were instructed to pick up those that were out cold and to carry them outside; what happened to them after that was not the venue's concern. It was a disclaimer of the Alley that anyone partying within its walls did so at their own risk; while it was prepared to put on the entertainment, it wasn't going to sweep up the mess afterwards, and Andrei Vassily had given his men carte blanche to act with extreme prejudice whenever they saw fit. While anything was possible here, that didn't necessarily assign the punter any consumer rights.

As the dazed and contrite spectators staggered into the street, Gabe noted the wrestler unlock the cage door and step out. Shorn of his audience, he looked smaller somehow, almost deflated. He was taking deep breaths, stretching his muscles, rolling his head and massaging the back of his neck as he trudged with the gait of the deeply weary towards the security office. He was about to lift his mask free – he had unpeeled it as far as just below his nose revealing a stubbly chin and jowls – when he spotted the younger man leaning against the wall in the gloom. He paused, pulling the disguise back in place, studying Gabe with watery eyes, then nodded. Gabe returned the greeting, and the man passed through into the room beyond, shoulders slouched like someone who was slowly dying inside.

"Place is closed, pal, in case you hadn't noticed," a voice said close to Gabe's ear. He turned and saw one of the bouncers twirling his sap next to him. "Next show is in a couple of hours. Suggest y'hop it."

"I wanted a word with Jackson. He around?"

"Bryan?" The man looked surprised, then swivelled and called out across the room. "Bryan! Guy here looking for you."

"Yeah? I know you?" The broad-shouldered, bearded figure that approached hadn't changed since Gabe had last seen him. His dark eyes set deep in a fleshy face were as impossible to gauge as ever, and it looked like he'd added to the enormous tattoo that spread across his torso, a snake's head emerging from his shirt collar to nestle at his throat.

"Gabriel O'Connell."

He squinted as he rolled the name around his head, pupils disappearing in the pronounced skin folds like black buttons in dough. "Rings a bell..." He pointed a stubby finger. "You one of Flowers' men?"

"*Was*. Me and the boss man had something of a falling out."

"Yeah, I recognise you now. You were one of his triggers last time he paid a visit. Thought you were supposed to be his capo?"

"Like I said, situation's changed," Gabe replied, shrugging, wondering how Harry truly saw their relationship. There was no denying that the old geezer was grateful for what Gabe had done for him the night they lost Anna; but at the same time Harry held him personally responsible for the events that had unfolded, using his guilt as a means to manipulate his loyalty. He could've had Gabe killed back then too, for what he did, but kept him on, knowing he could use him. So Flowers probably hadn't given it a second thought when he at last signed Gabe's death warrant; as far as he was concerned it was another traitorous ex-employee who was going to get what he deserved.

Jackson stepped closer, uncomfortably so; there was only a foot or so between them. Gabe had to look up to maintain eye contact, the security man being a head taller. "So, what, you decided to do a runner? Or you thought Andrei might offer you a better deal?" He smiled crookedly. "Or did Flowers throw you out like a discarded bitch when you'd served your purpose?"

"If you think I might be a threat to your position as Andrei's number one benchwarmer, then don't worry," Gabe answered, unwavering. "I'm not about to fly in and boot you out of the nest. Truth is, I've got a proposition for your boss that I'd like to take to him personally, if you're amenable."

Jackson laughed, loud and abrupt. "I bet you have. Y'know, I seem to remember you being this polite when we were pointing guns at one another. Trouble is, O'Connell, what makes you think I'm going to let you see him? All I've got is your word that you've severed links with Harry. Maybe you're out to demonstrate your loyalty to him by getting close to his biggest rival."

"You think I'd come here on an assassination run and announce myself to all and sundry? Do you think I'd make a fucking *appointment*? Credit me with a little intelligence. Fact is, I've come here showing Andrei and yourself nothing but respect, and it would be nice if it was reciprocated. From what I remember of Andrei, he's a stickler for manners." That shut the fat bastard up, Gabe thought, watching Jackson chew his lower lip. "I'd like to speak to him because I have a plan that could be advantageous to him and his whole organisation, that could challenge Harry's power base."

"So you *are* switching sides?"

"I'm not going to lie to you, Jackson: Flowers and me are history. And, as I'm sure you know, no one walks away from his set-up – it's either the Life or fed to the deadheads. There's nothing in between. So my still breathing is a major upset to Harry, and he would like nothing more than to shut me up permanently. I, on the other hand, would like to remove him from my back, equally permanently. Andrei's the only one with the guts and the resources to do that, and the man best placed in the city to inherit Harry's territory if what I'm going to suggest to him pays off. I think he will be interested to at least hear what I've got to say."

"Andrei doesn't usually grant an audience with underlings," Jackson said hesitantly. "If you ain't on his level, then he ain't interested." The security man was conflicted, Gabe could tell; he liked to build up this barrier around his boss, make it seem like anyone who wanted to get close to Vassily would have to negotiate with him first, but the fact was he didn't have either the authority or the chutzpah to come to decisions like this on the hoof. If Jackson were to have him thrown out of the Alley, there was nothing Gabe could do about it; but Gabe was relying on the fact that there would be a niggling part of the enforcer's mind that would be telling him he could be dismissing an opportunity that Andrei might've grabbed hold of if he was aware of it. And if his boss learned later that he never got to hear this proposition because Jackson took it upon himself to act on his behalf, then his employment could be cut short very quickly indeed. Basically, it came down to the fact that, for all his meat-headed bluster, Jackson couldn't disguise his fear of responsibility; he was someone that, despite his position of trust, always liked to defer upwards.

"Look, just put my case to him, tell him what I told you, that's all I'm asking," Gabe said reasonably. "If he's willing to hear me out, fine. If he listens, then tells me to get the fuck out of here, then that's cool, I'll walk, no problem. But give him the choice, if nothing else."

Jackson breathed heavily through his nose, his already lined brow furrowed further, and the snake's head tattoo flexed with the rise and fall of his chest. His gimlet eyes remained fixed on Gabe as he fished into his back pocket and pulled out his mobile; without looking at it he thumbed a button and held it up to his ear. "Gull, it's Jackson," he murmured seconds later. "Andrei with you?" He listened to the reply, then said: "Got something here that Andrei might want to be aware of. A messenger, of sorts." He paused. "No, I think he's going to want to hear this for himself. Don't worry, he'll be fully prepped." He muttered an affirmative, then flipped the phone shut. "Got your five minutes," he said sullenly. "I'll take you over there now."

"Appreciate it."

"Gonna have to pat you down—"

"No need," Gabe replied, lifting his leg and sliding his fingers into his boot, tearing free the tiny pistol, and holding it out handle-first. "That's what I'm packing." Jackson glared at it, then at him. Gabe gave a half smile. "Thought I'd go into this with the best intentions. Safety's on."

The security guard snatched it from him. "You know full well that the Alley is a weapons-free zone. And yet you didn't declare it to the guy at the gate?"

"Guess I forgot. You can see what a peashooter it is."

Jackson tightened his grip around the gun, and leaned closer to Gabe. "Don't make me regret this," he snarled. Then he motioned with his head for the thief to follow.

Jackson led him to a jeep parked outside the club, told him to climb in, then cautiously steered it through the heaving boulevards of the settlement towards the imposing warehouse-style building that housed Vassily's inner quarters. Drawing nearer, Gabe could see that the place was teeming with triggermen. Going by the tooled-up muscle that were posted at every entrance, any attempt to take Andrei head-on was doomed to failure, and Gabe would find attempting to infiltrate the complex to steal a few moments with this self-aware zombie (if indeed it even existed) a very difficult task. His best bet was going to be to somehow lose his escort whilst inside its walls, and worry about getting out later. His head was filled with diversions – fire, flood, electrical fault – that he could instigate to draw the guards' attention away from his escape. But right now, the matter at hand was determining if the creature was anything more than hearsay.

The jeep slew to a halt before a pair of heavy iron doors, an Uzi-wielding goon wandering over from his station to investigate. Jackson waved him away, and instructed Gabe to stick close as he punched in a security code on the keypad set into the brickwork. The lock sprung open with a heavy clunk. He pushed one of the doors open wide enough for them to slip through, then let it clang back into position behind them. They were in a bare stone corridor, and Jackson strode forward towards a set of curving white painted steps at the far end, the thief scurrying to keep up. As he began to climb, Gabe couldn't help but contrast the puritanical sparseness of Vassily's headquarters to the opulence of Harry's mansion. It was as if the head of Resurrection Alley was trying to distance himself from the degenerate entertainment through which he made his money. Punish himself, even. There was little here to suggest that this was the home of a powerful gang lord, so lacking was it in signs of wealth, or any kinds of comfort. He knew Andrei lacked much of Flowers' brutish ruthlessness – he was a second-generation mobster, unused to waging wars – but this seemed as much like a monastery as it did a fortress, a place where there was only room for cold functionality. It was odd that at the heart of the Alley's wild decadence stood this quiet stone island, in which rested its king.

The stairs stopped at a wooden door and Jackson rapped on it, turning the heavy brass handle without waiting for an answer. Inside were the first signs that this was a home as well as a castle; a carpet covered the floor, drapes and paintings adorned the walls. A couple of buttonmen were lounging on a leather sofa, machine guns resting casually on their laps, and they stood when the two of them entered, looking at Gabe quizzically.

"So who's this?" the taller, craggy-faced one asked with blunt disdain.

"Hey, Gull," Jackson greeted him. "This is O'Connell, the messenger I mentioned. Used to be one of Flowers' enforcers."

"No shit?"

"Said he wanted to have a word with Andrei, something that would be to his advantage."

Gull pulled an expression that suggested he was very far from being impressed. The second guy was hefting his weapon with excessive theatricality. "Got our own stoolie, have we?"

"You managed to have a word?"

"Garvey's in there with Andrei," Gull said, lazily motioning towards an adjoining door. He turned his attention to Gabe. "He's prepared to give you a few minutes, so keep it quick. He's not keen on timewasters." He looked back at Jackson. "You searched him?"

"He surrendered the only gun he had."

The thief surreptitiously pressed his foot against the syringe in his boot, checking it was still in place.

"OK. Take him through, Jackson."

Gabe followed the other man into the antechamber, decorated in a similar fashion to the outer office, though an expansive bookcase lined one wall. Andrei Vassily was sitting in an armchair, his tan suit immaculate, his legs crossed, fingers steepled under his chin. He was in his early forties, and there was a composed look of serenity to his dark features, as if his every act was fluid and unhurried, economical but perfectly judged. To his right stood a severe-looking woman in a business suit, thin to the point of reptilian.

"Mr Vassily," Jackson began, "this is—"

"I know who he is," Andrei replied, his voice soft, a hint of an East European accent. Gabe evidently failed to conceal his surprise because the older man nodded faintly. "Oh yes, I recognised you as one of Harry's when you arrived. I told the man at the gate to let you in. So what happened between you and your former employer?"

"I... screwed up, and he's cut me adrift from the organisation."

"And no doubt you're now a loose end that he wishes to tie up. What brings you here? Looking for a new job?"

Gabe shook his head. "Partly a warning, partly a proposition. Mr Vassily, I'm sure you don't need me to tell you that Harry's looking to expand his empire over the next year. He wants London, all of it, and the impasse that has existed between the two of you for so long is going to be tested. Make no mistake, when the time comes he will take the Alley by any means necessary, and right now he's working on the means to control the city. He's going to turn the deadheads to his advantage, create an obedient army from them."

Andrei raised his eyebrows. "Harry always did see the big picture."

"Flowers has got his scientists working on the virus, trying to adapt it for such an application. They're making progress, but slowly. They don't have what you've got."

"Which is what?"

"A self-aware Returner."

"Is that right?" Vassily exchanged a look with the woman at his side.

"Or so the rumour goes. Since cutting ties with Harry I've hooked up with an ex-government boffin, studying the plague independently, and he's developing a serum that can boost the intelligence of the dead. With the right resources and contacts, he could produce it on a massive scale. A blood sample from a ghoul whose consciousness has evolved to such a degree would advance his research enormously. I felt, Mr Vassily, that you would see the advantages in entering into such a business opportunity."

"And we would... what? Forge an army of our own?"

"Better to do it before Flowers gains the upper hand. If you can stay ahead of him—"

"Yeah, that's always been my problem," a voice said behind Gabe. He felt a coldness lodge in his chest as he turned towards its source, his legs growing suddenly weak. "I'm always lagging behind."

Harry Flowers sauntered into the room, Hewitt at his left shoulder, a couple of other boys from the house behind him. He fixed Gabe with an icy grin.

"Long time no see, son."

CHAPTER SEVEN

For a moment, Gabe could do nothing but stand there and stare back at his former boss. The office, Andrei Vassily, Jackson and the rest, slid away off the periphery of his vision. It was only for the briefest of seconds, but within that fraction of time all he saw was Flowers' face studying him with a mixture of hatred and unconcealed mirth. That sensation of stasis seemed to encompass the pair of them, as if they were two museum exhibits eyeing one another from either side of a display case. He blinked and the rest of the world came racing back into focus. He cleared his throat, realising that he'd been holding his breath.

"Harry."

"Hello, Gabriel," the old man remarked, as if he were tipping his hat to a neighbour he saw every morning. Gabe could detect little malice in his voice. "We'd been wondering where you'd got to."

"The... the hijack was a bust," Gabe said slowly, aware that excuses would make no difference but unable to think of anything else to say. He was damned if he was going to apologise to him, and he promised himself that he wouldn't beg. He wouldn't spend his last few minutes on earth on his knees. "Everything got fucked up. The target got destroyed, we unwittingly riled an army of pusbags that were beneath the river, we didn't have any choice but to retreat. Government pricks caught me as I tried to make it back to the motor."

Did he imagine it, or did he see the slightest beginnings of a smirk twitch at the corner of Hewitt's mouth? He shouldn't have been surprised that the kid was enjoying his predicament – no doubt promotion had been offered to Gabe's soon-to-be-vacant position in the outfit – but there was something about the way he was standing there, a bastard full to bursting with bad news, and struggling to contain himself. It was somehow agonisingly predictable that he had survived that night on the bridge, scurrying vermin-like to safety.

"Please," Harry said, looking pained, holding up a hand. "Let's not rake over the past. Mr Hewitt's given me a full account of the operation's failure. Such eventualities, while tiresome, are par for the course. What's less acceptable is a security lapse."

"Harry, for what's it's worth, I told them nothing. They know plenty about you already."

"These are your new paymasters, I take it?"

"I work for no one. Not anymore."

"Oh, I would like to believe that, Gabriel, honestly I would," Flowers replied flamboyantly, taking a step or two towards him. "It gives me no pleasure to be standing here before you like this. You were one of my most trusted aides, and you were a good little thief. You were an *asset*, boy." He reached out and grabbed Gabe's chin hard between thumb and forefinger. "But don't insult my intelligence by telling me that the authorities simply let you go without asking for nothing in return. The fact that you're simply still alive indicates that you bargained your way out of their custody. And lo and behold you turn up at the Alley, seeking to curry favour with Andrei."

The younger man couldn't answer, his jaw held firmly in place by Harry's solid grip, but he glared back, refusing to look away from the gang lord's blazing eyes.

"Didn't take much for you to turn traitor, did it?" Flowers spat, wrenching his hand away.

"Just circumstances," Gabe said. "Ask Ashberry. That's how anyone ends up becoming involved with an old arsehole like you."

Harry pulled an ancient snubnose Colt from his trouser belt and without hesitation shot Gabe in the belly. The roar of the gun's detonation in the enclosed space of the office was deafening, a clap of thunder that caught everyone by surprise. Gabe staggered, crumpling onto his backside, his hands clutching at his wound, trying to stem the blood that pumped between his fingers. White-hot pain encircled his torso as if a flaming vice had been tightened around him, and stars danced in his vision. He chanced a look at the entry point, then glanced away. His palms were sticky and a deep shade of crimson.

"Don't worry, Mr O'Connell," Harry said, standing over him. "You won't die yet. Gutshot will take a while to bleed out. It'll poison your organs and starve your brain of oxygen, but you'll be conscious enough for what I've got planned for you."

"I don't remember agreeing to you perforating your mark on my property," Gabe heard Vassily protest, the words floating down to him as if he was listening to the exchange underwater. "I said I'd give you the guy, I didn't say you could redecorate my office with him."

"Sorry, Andrei. Temper got the better of me."

"Mr Vassily, sir, with respect: what the hell is going on?" Jackson asked. "You knew O'Connell was coming to see you?"

"Harry had asked that we keep an eye out for him; that's why I approved his entry into the Alley, and let those looking for him know that he was in the area. Sorry I didn't keep you informed, Jackson, but I thought the least number of personnel that knew the less likely he would get spooked and make a run for it."

"I am grateful, Andrei," Harry said, his voice now amiable. "I'll reimburse you for the inconvenience. I just need one more favour."

"Which is?"

"Where do you keep this super-smart maggotbrain of yours?"

Gabe felt himself being lifted off the floor, the movement sending new paroxysms of pain through his body. He kept his right arm wrapped tightly around his midriff, though he could sense the loss of blood was already beginning to take its toll. His head felt heavy and woozy, his eyesight blurry, and shivers ran the course of his skin. Each fresh exhalation was an effort, the air raspy in his throat, and his heart was pounding irregularly, like it was slowly winding down, gradually starved of power. However, despite his state, he willed himself to stay alert to what was going on around him, concentrating furiously on the others' words.

Vassily had seemed initially reluctant to lead Harry to this self-aware zombie of his, evidently regarding his pet as his alone and not for display to others. But Flowers seemed to have cut some deal with the Alley boss that would make it worth his while. Indeed, Andrei's co-operation in Gabe's capture was apparently to be rewarded with a hefty fee – though whether it was in territory, manpower or loot, was impossible to discern – and Harry was willing to increase his offer to make this extra allowance. At first, Gabe couldn't fathom why his former employer was so adamant in gaining access to the ghoul – normally Harry couldn't stand being near deadheads – but when Flowers started mentioning Hewitt in the same breath and having made the kid a 'promise', Gabe realised what the old man was up to, and what his own fate was going to be.

Since humanity had learned to live with the dead, the worst fate imaginable had become to be consumed alive by the Returners; it was considered more noble to take your own life and that of those around you rather than end your days as a meal for a ravening pack of rotting cadavers. There was a sense of violation to the death – of falling victim to an unstoppable frenzied lust – that most would not bear contemplate suffering. Consequently, it was not unknown for this appalling demise to be instrumental in punishing the guilty, particularly amongst the criminal community. In the past it would have been a burial in a concrete casket, or a kneecapping. These days, new situations call for fresh solutions, and many was the embezzler, turncoat or loose cannon that had been thrown to the undead, even fed to them piece by piece. It was horrific to watch; but the threat was usually strong enough to keep even the dimmest element of the underworld in line.

Now, Gabe realised that was what Harry had in store for him; not a couple of bullets casually unloaded into the back of his skull, but a slow, lingering execution, a warning to his other lieutenants about what happens when you attempt to cross him. A bubble of panic exploded in the fear centre of his brain, and he summoned up what reserves of strength he still had in an attempt to wrest himself free from his captors, but it was useless. Vassily's goons – Gull and the younger man – held him secure as they moved through an adjoining door, down a set of steps and into a bare concrete space, apparently a section of what had once been the warehouse that hadn't been converted into the office complex. What looked like a false wall or a partition ran across the length of the room, and when Vassily strode over to a bank of switches and flipped one, the divider separated and its two halves disappeared into the stone walls at either side, revealing the wide, smooth expanse of a mirrored viewing screen, a steel door set next to it.

Gabe was pushed forward, closer to the two-way mirror, and Andrei, Harry and the rest followed. For a moment, there was just blackness on the other side of the screen, and they simply gazed at their own reflections; then Andrei snapped a wall switch and the fluorescents flickered into life, illuminating a room on the other side of the divide that wasn't dissimilar to the one they were in. A cold, grey concrete area, with little concession to decoration. There was furniture in this room, however – a tatty armchair stood in one corner, with a small coffee table before it, on which stood an ancient portable television, an antenna perched on top. A battered VCR sat beside the TV, a small hillock of cassettes piled upon it. Nearer the viewing window was a larger table, with a couple of wooden chairs tucked beneath it; seated motionless at one of these chairs was Andrei's intelligent zombie, its arms resting on the table surface like a mannequin that had been positioned to approximate someone waiting to be served dinner. Its eye sockets were empty, but as light flooded the room it cocked its head sideways in tiny, incremental movements. It was impossible to deny that that creature was aware that its environment had changed, and it was reacting to the shift – something Gabe had never witnessed in a Returner before.

Physically, it had seen better days: it was in an advanced state of putrefaction, and its charcoal-black body had been reduced to little more than a deep-fried skeleton. Its hairless head appeared too big for its flimsy frame, and every time it was jerkily turned it wobbled as if not securely tethered. The shrunken sockets were pits of absolute shadow, and the lips had shrivelled away to give it a permanent rictus grin. It took Gabe a few seconds to realise that the ghoul had been dressed in a jacket – and presumably trousers too, though they were hidden by the lip of the table – which hung loosely about its emaciated torso and had become stained in God-knew-what bodily excretions. The effect was bizarre, as if someone had attempted to construct a picture of normalcy when the truth was the very far from that.

"Christ," Gabe heard Harry mutter. "How long have you kept that thing here, Andrei?"

"Many years," Vassily replied quietly. "Many years." He leaned forward and pushed a button on the wall next to a speakerphone. "Can you hear me? Nod if you can." His voice echoed on the other side of the screen, and the zombie's attention perked up to the sound of it; it raised its gaze to the speaker, determining where the words had come from. Then it dropped its head forward in the unmistakable approximation of a nod, and lifted its right hand in acknowledgement.

"Jesus," Hewitt said. "Just what the fuck *is* that thing?"

Vassily glared at him. "It's learning, is what it is. It's working out how to be human again. By my reckoning, it's about two-thirds of the way there."

"Fuckin' abomination needs a slug put through its skull if it wants me to accept it."

"That's enough," Flowers snapped, shooting the kid a warning glance. He turned back to Andrei. "You're teaching it?"

Vassily nodded, watching the ghoul trace a pattern on the table's surface with a shredded finger. "At first, I noticed it using its memory through repetition. Y'know, remembering when to expect me when I came to visit, training itself to behave if it was to receive a reward, the same way any domesticated animal will do with its master. But there was more to it – it started to adopt human tropes, signals, mannerisms, like it was beginning to recall little flashes of what it had been pre-death. A hand on my arm in a gesture of friendship, an attempt at my name... it was as if the virus was instructing it how to be alive."

"It was still a flesh-eater, though."

"Yes. Still is, in fact. Can't seem to override that motor function yet, though it mainly consumes offal from the kitchens. It doesn't need it to survive, of course – stomach organs have long since atrophied anyway – but it gets restless if it doesn't feed after a while, and won't concentrate. That's what the videotapes are there for; I've been trying to develop its language and recognition skills. They're parenting guides, really, but are quite good in the circumstances. Nevertheless, it's still too dangerous not to be kept on a chain."

"How did you come by it in the first place?" Harry asked.

Vassily didn't reply at first. "I found him at his place of death. I've no idea why he should be so special, why the virus should be evolving so quickly and advancing his state of awareness. Maybe it's the age... maybe they're all like this and the bacteria just needs time to work on them..."

"So are we feeding O'Connell to this fuckin' thing or what?" Hewitt enquired testily, looking at Flowers. The old man nodded gravely, and signalled to Vassily.

The Alley boss spoke into the intercom again. "Stand away from the door. Do you understand?"

The ghoul moaned softly, and the chair it was sitting on suddenly screeched against the stone-tiled floor as it staggered to its feet, its stick-thin arms supporting its weight against the tabletop. It straightened and stiff-leggedly swivelled and stumbled towards the rear of the room, stopping close to the TV and waiting for its next instruction. It was clear it had done this many times before, and was following a routine pattern.

"Jesus..." Hewitt breathed again. None of them had ever seen a deadhead perform like this, responding to orders, seemingly fully cognitive of what Vassily was telling it.

Andrei motioned to Jackson, who stepped forward and pulled down on the door's heavy locking handle. It clunked open with a finality that sent a chill travelling down Gabe's spine.

"I never thought it would come to this, son," Flowers said regretfully. "I had high hopes for you. But you leave me no choice."

"Harry," Gabe choked out, the spreading coldness from his belly wound worming its way across his torso and seizing his throat, leaving him unable to swallow. Every word was an effort, dredged spluttering from the depths of his chest. "Don't do this... I told them nothing, you know that..."

"Put him in," Flowers said, and Jackson shoved open the door and pushed Gabe inside. He tumbled to his knees, putting out a hand to cushion his fall, jarring it against the cold floor, and squeezed his eyes shut momentarily at the sound of the door being slammed shut behind him.

When he opened them, the first thing he saw were the deep red stains ingrained in the stone; wide circular splashes that had dried from scarlet to maroon. He guessed that they had been there for quite some time, and that Vassily hadn't been entirely truthful about what he'd been feeding this pet ghoul of his. He was certain that offal wouldn't leave that arterial spray.

The deadhead itself had noticed his arrival and was shuffling towards him. Gabe scooted backwards, the small of his back hitting the wall a couple of feet later; he looked around him, trying to find something that could aid his escape, but the room was solidly built. It was square and plain, with no other exit save the thick steel door that he'd been dragged through, and that would be impenetrable from this side. He looked towards the mirrored screen and wondered how strong it was; could it withstand one of the chairs being thrown at it? Even if he succeeded in breaking through, there would be no way out, with Harry and his goons keeping guard; but perhaps he could force one of them to open fire and end Flowers' little execution a touch prematurely. He snorted a desperate laugh; when the best of his options was a quick death, he knew he'd reached the end of the road. Still, he didn't see why he should make things easy for the old man.

The zombie staggered closer, a thin whine issuing from its ever-grinning mouth, and Gabe realised that he had to make a choice – if he went for the window, he would only have one chance and it would leave him open for the Returner to grab hold of him. If he didn't, perhaps he could concentrate on evading its clutches, or even try fending it off. But how long could he keep that up, he asked himself. He was growing faint from loss of blood, and would only be delaying the inevitable. He made his decision in a second.

Pulling his legs under him, he pushed himself up against the wall until he was standing. He took a couple of painful breaths, keeping one eye on the advancing ghoul, then sprang forward, covering the space between the door and the table in three giant strides. He hooked his left hand around the chair's topmost slat, lifted it, spun and flung it with all the strength he could muster at the viewing screen. It arced in the air and hit the glass dead centre with a dull thud, bouncing back half the distance it had flown to crash to the ground.

The window was unmarked.

Gabe was too exhausted to react. He turned to face the deadhead that was reaching out for him. Its hands clutched at his shirt, and at such proximity he gagged from its rank smell. Its jaws opened like a creaking hinge.

Then it stopped.

Impossibly, its eyeless visage was regarding him, seeing him despite the lack of organs. Its skeletal hands brushed over his features, as if it was reading him through touch, and something was igniting a flame of recognition within its dormant memory. Then it began to whine again, louder this time, growing in power, becoming a cry. At first it was just noise, a banshee wail; but it soon coalesced into a word that Gabe had to struggle to believe he was hearing.

"Fllooooowwwwaarrrrzzzzzz..."

It *knew* him. The creature knew and remembered him, through association with Harry. How he had no idea, or indeed what enabled this zombie to possess the powers of cognition. But something had sparked it off, and it stood there roaring the name of his former boss in his face.

The deadhead momentarily transfixed, Gabe seized the advantage and delved into his boot retrieving the syringe. Flicking off the plastic cap, he held it like a dagger in his right hand and stabbed it forcefully into the side of the ghoul's liquescent skull. Virtually the entire length of the hypodermic disappeared into its head, and its cry abruptly stopped, as if a switch had been thrown. He pulled it free, expecting the zombie to instantly collapse, but the thing suddenly grasped his left arm and took a bite, tearing the flesh and muscle from his bicep, blood spurting from the limb in a fountain. Gabe yelled in agony and brought the syringe down on its head repeatedly until it finally sank to the floor, and was motionless.

Gabe fell to his knees, lengthening shadows stealing into the edges of his vision, and turned as the door was wrenched open, Vassily tearing through with Harry close behind, staring at the inert corpse lying next to him.

"Why did he call your name?" Vassily was screaming. "Why did my father call your name?" His accent grew thicker in his anger.

His father, Gabe considered woozily. That thing was his *father*? Goran Vassily, the kingpin whose demise Harry was responsible for? The club fire? Mother of Christ, it remembered him from its pre-death...

"Andrei—" Flowers began.

Vassily pulled an automatic from inside his jacket and pointed it at the ganglord. "What the fuck did you do to my father that he would remember your name like that?"

"Andrei, put the damn gun down."

"If you had something to do with his death, if that's why he said your name, I swear to fucking Christ you will not walk out of this room."

"Andrei, don't make threats you can't back up..."

"You think I couldn't take you down? You think I'm fucking scared of Harry Flowers?"

Vassily's questions went unanswered, for a moment later a bullet exploded through his neck. He gurgled, clutching at his ravaged throat, then crumpled into a heap on the floor. Before anyone could react, Jackson and the rest of the Alley boss's men were rapidly mown down; it was only once the firing had stopped that it became clear that Hewitt was the shooter.

"Better that we get our retaliation in first," he said.

Harry nodded slowly. "Unfortunate turn of events, but nothing that can't be salvaged. Get in touch with the boys back at the mansion, tell them to get tooled up. We're taking charge of the Alley." He spotted Gabe bleeding and crossed over to him. "And you... Jesus, you're a regular troublemaker, aren't you? If you think you're getting a bullet in the head and a safe passage out of this world, think again. Welcome to purgatory, son."

"H-Harry..." Gabe whispered.

Flowers leaned forward. "Keep it brief."

"Fuck you," the younger man said and plunged the syringe into the old man's calf. He bellowed in pain and staggered backwards, the hypodermic still protruding from his leg. As a couple of his men went forward to tend to him, Hewitt marched up to Gabe and pointed his gun above his heart.

"Just fuckin' die," he snarled and pulled the trigger, darkness exploding across the thief's mind.

PART TWO

Swan Song

I am the enemy you killed, my friend.
I knew you in this dark: for so you frowned
Yesterday through me as you jabbed and killed.
I parried; but my hands were loath and cold.

Wilfred Owen,
Strange Meeting

Five Years Earlier

CHAPTER EIGHT

It was a city that Gabe had lived in most of his life and had a grudging respect for, but even he couldn't deny that London showed an ugly face in summer. All its sprawling, overcrowded, soot-smeared qualities seemed to swell with the heat. Where what was once bearable in the sharp weeks of winter – its inhabitants barricaded against the bitter wind and driving sleet by thick coats and scarves as they walked its streets – became a claustrophobic, stinking concrete furnace as soon as the sun began to beat down on the baking tarmac. Perhaps it was because its citizens relaxed a touch and loosened their protective clothing, showed a little of themselves to the unforgiving metropolis. For London, it was the merciless season; everything became exacerbated – strained relationships, the stink of pollution, the heaving pavements choked with visitors and workers alike – as if a noose was being drawn tight around its walls for three sweaty months before it slackened off and the city settled back into a more natural rhythm of life once again.

It could be seen everywhere, Gabe thought, as he pedalled down Buckingham Palace Road towards Victoria Station, from the architecture to the citizens sweltering within. It could be witnessed in the firework explosions of red and orange light as a dying sun reflected off the office buildings' glass surfaces, and in the distant edifice of Canary Wharf's pyramidal tower steaming into an azure sky. It could be discerned in the blossoming patches of perspiration on the back of businessmen's shirts, and in their red-faced, squinting demeanour as they hurried to catch their cramped trains, unyielding leather shoes tramping hard down on scorched flagstones, jackets tucked over arms, ties unravelled, collars unbuttoned, air scratchy at the back of their throats. It could be felt as the grime slicked on bare arms and faces – a combination of dirt, moisture and insect residue – to the point where one had to scrub the taint of London off once one escaped its environs. It could be heard in the constant snarl of traffic and the strident accompanying blare of anger as tempers flared, drivers boiling inside their automobiles; and it could be smelled in the sickly patchwork of odours that rose from the depths of the city, of unwashed bodies crushed together, of what was once fresh growing sour in the heat of day. If the metropolis was an organism, then in summer it was an exhausted beast, irritable and grubby, floundering as it cooked in its own juices.

Gabe knew what it was like to be stifled in one of those office complexes, a paltry portable electric fan perched atop a nearby filing cabinet cooling the film of sweat on his skin, doing nothing to ease the pressure that would make his forehead throb. After a short stint in the army (whose strict embrace he'd been forced into after his raucous teenage years hotwiring cars) he'd jobbed for a lengthy period at a small local newspaper, chasing advertising and compiling the copy for the listings section – tedious, unsatisfactory work, in which he spent much of his day yearning to just up and walk out the door, never to return – and he could still remember the discomfort of stagnant afternoons, sheaves of paper gluing themselves to his damp hands and fatigue weighing down on him like a lead weight. His colleagues were mostly middle-aged hacks, filling time before their inevitable early retirement, regaling him with tales of when they had a career on Fleet Street, of tyrannical editors and marathon drinking sessions, a hint of self-pity that they were reduced to filing stories on OAP charity walkathons.

Gabe had usually found them likeable coves, but the heat didn't agree with them; they stewed and flustered, muttering to themselves, and contributed to the musty atmosphere in which the air felt like it had been trapped in a tomb. He longed to open a window, but the old soaks complained of the traffic noise and fumes emanating from Pentonville Road below. The building in which they worked had stood there since the 1950s, a stone's throw from King's Cross, and little had been done to modernise the place in the intervening decades; the walls were cracked and spattered with encroaching mould, the carpet was worn through to the floorboards, and the weak ceiling lights gave everything a dull sepia tone. Fill it with perspiring, cantankerous boozers and it was wont to turn a little ripe.

He knew he had to get out before he became preserved in the others' ale breath and cigarette ash; he would be discovered decades later petrified, chipped free and put on display. He was never returning to military life, that much was certain; although his superiors had cast a blind eye to his petty criminal past, one tour of Afghanistan was enough. He had supposed he ought to seek out an opportunity at a more modern place of work – one with air-con and bright, open spaces – but for some reason he couldn't summon the enthusiasm. He'd seen such offices on his travels to and from home – the smokers clustered outside in the street, huddled together like the remnants of a species slowly facing extinction, the reception areas with the elongated sofas and modern art – and their sterility repelled him. It worried him that maybe his extended proximity to the journalistic lags he kept company with had somehow inured him to such luxuries as a workstation that wasn't fragranced like an ashtray or fixtures and fittings that hadn't been beset by damp; but every time he stepped inside one of those silver skyscrapers, he found them soul-destroying and lacking personality. He didn't know when this transformation had taken place, but it was apparent that he'd been mentally conditioned to be incapable of working in such surroundings without wishing to start scrawling across the tasteful abstracts that adorned the walls. He tried to beat this programming to the best of his ability, diligently attending job interviews with the necessary can-do attitude. The people he spoke to, however, he found were either smug and impolite suits, or braying Sloane Square refugees that raised his hackles with each strangulated vowel. Gabe would walk out of the revolving glass doors firm in the belief that he belonged to a different tribe to these cretins; and indeed he had to wonder if there was life beyond the nicotine-stained domain of the newspaper.

In the end, fate came along and lent a hand: the paper folded suddenly and with little fanfare. For the hacks, it meant extended leisure time, and they greeted the news of the office's closure with unconcealed glee. For Gabe, however, at twenty-four, he couldn't afford to be so blasé. His qualifications were mediocre, and he felt many might be reticent about employing a former soldier, especially one that had had brushes with the law. Even so, the newspaper job, for all its shortcomings, had been enough to cast doubt on whether he was cut out to sit at a desk all day, tapping away at a keyboard, all life passing him by outside. He felt jaded with white-collar work, and the thought of spending more summers suffocating in an open-plan oven, shuffling files, filled him with dread.

It had been his flatmate that had posited the solution. They had been throwing possible career routes between each other – based on Gabe's nebulous ideas of how he wanted to make a living that didn't involve some kind of corporate infrastructure – when Tom suggested a cycle courier. Gabe assimilated the notion and ticked off its advantages: it was outdoor work, it involved little contact with colleagues, it had a built-in fitness regime, and there was a pure simplicity to the job that appealed. He even owned his own bike, and growing up in the city had afforded him an almost encyclopaedic knowledge of London's thoroughfares that could be put to his advantage. The more he mulled the possibility, the more he could see that this could be his way to escape the stifling office environment, and use his love of the capital to work for him rather than be swallowed by its oppressive sprawl.

He visited some local firms and eventually signed up. Within days he was pleased to discover that his instincts had been right, and the job gave him just the satisfaction that he craved. The sheer volume of traffic that he had to contend with had been an initial shock, but once he got the hang of making his presence known on the roads, forcing motorists to acknowledge that he was there, then it became a breeze. The freedom felt exhilarating, and he got to see the metropolis in a whole new light, a hidden London of back alleys and secret squares, centuries of history overlapping in forgotten corners far from the public gaze.

Despite the marvels that the city still clutched to her bosom and that he continued to uncover on his journeys, Gabe reflected, it never looked its best in the middle of July. A little of its beauty was tarnished as it wilted under the heat, but he was glad to be witnessing it out here rather than viewing it through an office window, a position he'd been in for close to a year now.

He shuttled across into Belgrave Square, and headed towards Hyde Park Corner, squeezing down the tight back roads of Knightsbridge, pedalling hard. He piloted his bike down Wilton Place, a car approaching in the other direction allowing him to pass. He powered forward, keen not to keep it waiting.

When the Audi swung out suddenly from its parking slot on the left-hand side of the street, Gabe barely had time to brake – and consequently slammed into its wing at full speed.

Hospital at first was a nightmare glimpsed through waking moments. He was told later – when he had been capable of processing the information – that he had been severely concussed (in addition to three fractured ribs, a broken nose and extensive facial bruising). But at the time Gabe flittered in and out of consciousness, snatching only handfuls of sobriety. He found it difficult to differentiate between the world inside his head and that of his bedridden condition; or rather it was hard to choose which was worse. When he was asleep, plunged into a sea of shadow in which he seemed to be constantly rushing forward, as if caught in a slipstream or surrendering to the inexorable pull of a current. Sometimes the darkness dissolved enough for him to discern that he was racing along the city streets, his body floating only a few feet from the tarmac. A vague thought would always pop into his dream-self's mind that he was on a collision course, that unless he fought the power that controlled him, he was going to smash into an obstacle that was undoubtedly going to be standing in his way. It started as a suggestion, an irrational feeling that bubbled out of nowhere, but it would quickly blossom into panic and an incontrovertible sense of certainty that he was racing towards disaster. The city appeared abandoned as he raced through it – amorphous, indistinct buildings on either side, roads empty of life – but without question, somewhere, there was trouble waiting to hit him head-on.

He never discovered it. The fear would build in tandem with his velocity to such a degree that he would surface into consciousness with a gasp, as if he had dived into himself and was returning for air. But his waking episodes were no respite; the heat and chaos in the ward day and night left him unable to relax, and any movement he attempted made him aware of his injuries. His body seemed to ache right down to the bone. The doctors kept him doped up, so his notion of reality was woozy at best, and he had few visitors to help anchor him to the everyday; his mother was living somewhere in Europe with her new husband, and his father was infirm, cared for by a nurse of his own back in Cork. With no siblings, the only face he could lucidly recognise was that of his flatmate Tom, whose sporadic trips to see him were as irregular as Gabe's sleep patterns. The combination of the drugs and fatigue would inevitably propel him towards unconsciousness again, a journey he vainly fought, terrified of once more flying through London with no notion of where he was going, or possibly finally meeting what was waiting for him at that moment of impact he knew was unavoidable.

Over the following weeks, his confused mind stabilised and his lucid periods lengthened. His memories of the accident slowly returned, and if he closed his eyes he could visualise the front wheel of his bike buckling against the driver's door of the Audi, throwing him forward and across its bonnet. The recollection of his head bouncing off the windscreen – did it shatter? He couldn't remember hearing the sound of breaking glass; all that filled his ears was the screech of brakes and the scrape of metal on metal – made him gingerly run his fingertips over his puffy face. The skin was tender to the touch, and a lump the size of a golf ball had risen above his right eyebrow. He asked a nurse for a mirror, because the contours of his face no longer felt familiar, and the reflection that stared back at him confirmed it; he barely recognised himself. He'd been assured that the injuries would heal eventually, and that the swelling would go down given time, but even so the red-raw damage and the changes it had wrought on his appearance shocked him. His nose swathed in bandages, his lips split where his teeth had pierced them, purple-black bruises running in parallel with his jawline, he felt like he'd been battered into a different shape, moulded and created anew with all the attendant pain that such a process entails. He wouldn't be the same, he knew, no matter how well he recovered; already he considered what he looked like before the accident to be the face of somebody else.

It proved true enough the moment he left the hospital, his bones sufficiently knitted together. The trip back to his flat was one fraught with anxiety as the noise and relentlessness of the traffic caused him to visibly cringe, despite Tom's reassurances. Gabe tried to remain calm, aware that a mere month ago he'd been whizzing through these very streets on his bike with nothing to protect him but a helmet and a shoulder bag, but now the idea seemed inconceivable. It was as if he were viewing the city through different eyes, seeing potential dangers at every turn. He dug his fingers into the passenger seat of his flatmate's Mini as it rounded a corner and braked at a crossing, expecting a phantom vehicle to thunder into their path any second. Tom told him that he had spoken to the doctor before they had released Gabe, and he had mentioned that a victim of such a serious accident was very likely to exhibit symptoms of something approaching post-traumatic stress, and that it was perfectly natural for him to be fretful once he returned to the real world. But it would pass as soon as he got his strength back and grew more confident.

For Gabe, that day seemed a long time coming. Ensconced within the walls of his flat, he found himself lacking the courage to venture outside, and the more time he spent inside on his own – Tom working long shifts at a bar in the West End – the more he found comfort in seclusion. Rather than facing down his fear, he embraced it and let it control him, ensuring that his daily routine was subservient to it. The courier company he worked for regularly got in touch, asking when he felt ready to return to work, and he fobbed them off with excuses, claiming he still needed time to recover. In truth, he was physically back to normal bar a few scars and tender patches, but in his head the thought of braving London's roads once more filled him with panic. He relived the accident again and again in his dreams, awaking sweating at the moment of impact and with a hard cluster of pain at his temple. Eventually, his boss telephoned him to apologetically let him go, saying that without any end to his convalescence in sight they couldn't afford to keep him on their books any longer. He was unemployed once more, and felt in no fit state to do anything about it.

As soon as Tom learned that Gabe was out of a job, he sat down with his flatmate for a crisis talk.

"Mate, we gotta do something or we're going to be out on our ear. There's no way I can manage on my wage alone, and I doubt your income support is going to add much. You've got to get yourself out there."

"I know, I know," Gabe replied, conscious of the fact that there was no situation that couldn't be made worse by having a little guilt thrown into the mix. "I don't want to put us both in the lurch, of course I don't. It's just... I'm scared of going out there. I'm on edge, thinking something is going to happen. My stomach knots, I can't breathe, feel nauseous..."

"It's a panic attack. The doc said you could expect them. But you can't afford to let them run your life. It's like you're caught in a loop – the more you stay in here, agonising over what's going to happen to you if you step outside the flat, the more the anxiety spreads. You're feeding it by not coming to terms with it. If you went out on those streets and became accustomed to them once again, you'd find that the fear would lessen. It's what you don't know – it's what you're imagining is out there – that's causing this apprehension."

"I wish it was as easy as that..."

"It's the only way forward, mate," Tom replied, a hint of exasperation entering his voice. "Otherwise it's going to explode into full-blown agoraphobia, and you'll be bunkered away in here for the rest of your life. You're, what? Twenty-five? You're going to imprison yourself for the next sixty years, is that it? Unless you're prepared to give in to it, you've gotta be strong and fight it."

They sat in silence, Gabe listening to the hum of traffic filtering through the window, acting as an additional taunt to Tom's words. He knew his friend was right, and wished he possessed the resolve to act upon the advice. He admonished himself for being weak and pathetic. Was he really going to let this fear get the better of him? Was he really going to sacrifice his life to it? Otherwise, what difference would it have made if his guts had been splattered under the tyres of that Audi? Survival had given him a choice – either he grasped the chance with both hands or he just upped and surrendered right now.

"It's something only you can do, Gabe," Tom said.

"Of course, I'll help you in any way I can, but I can't make you take the first step. That's your responsibility." He sighed. "The other alternative is that you work from home. You know, tele-sales, or something. But whatever you decide, we've reached crunch-point, mate. We're in deep shit unless we take action now."

Gabe agreed that it was time he got busy rebuilding his life, and promised that he would take charge of the situation; the implication being that he would finally face up to his fear of London's streets. But when it came to it, he found picking up the telephone to enquire about finding work cold-calling and selling kitchens the easy option. He hated himself even as he listened to the saleswoman's explanations of what the job entailed and the techniques of keeping the potential customer on the line. It seemed he had taken several long strides backwards, placing himself in employment that he despised and shackled once more to the mundane grind of monotonous, dismal toil. He put the telephone receiver down, having accepted the numerous conditions, and slumped in an armchair, feeling wretched.

As it turned out, the work proved to be more stultifying than even he could stand, and at last gave him the incentive to get him through the front door. The countless hang-ups and insults thrown at him as he initiated his spiel were the final straw, and as he sat staring at the living-room wall, a disconnected tone buzzing in his ear, he realised that nothing that was out there on the roads could possibly be any worse than this. Indeed, if this stuttering circle of a half-life was all he had to look forward to, a little danger would come as welcome relief. He flung the phone to the floor, and strode out into the street before the fear-centre of his brain could stop him.

He walked, without much regard to a direction or

purpose, simply putting distance between him and the flat that he'd entombed himself within for weeks on end. Despite the familiar surge of sickness and the growing pounding in his head, as trucks roared past and sirens wailed, he didn't halt his progress; rather, he rode the anxiety out, staying above the wave and letting it carry him forward rather than disappearing beneath it. Breathing deeply, with each step he found himself surfing on something else too, something he hadn't felt since he'd been in uniform: adrenaline. He was terrified, but in contrast to his self-inflicted exile, there was a joy to his terror. It gave him an edge he had forgotten existed. He walked for hours, perversely enjoying the thrill he got from punishing his panicking senses. He was living again, he decided triumphantly.

When Gabe informed Tom that he wanted to return to traversing the city's arteries, his flatmate commended him on his courage but warned that perhaps getting back on a bike would make him feel a touch too vulnerable at such an early stage. He suggested a compromise to ease his way back into the ebb and flow of the capital's heart.

"Fact is, there's a sniff of a job at work," he said slowly. "Not in the bar itself, but working for the guy that owns it. Several of his boys come in to drink there, and they've mentioned on more than one occasion that he's after a new full-time driver."

"A chauffeur-type job, you mean?"

"Pretty much. The geezer's after someone who knows the city like the back of his hand, and let's face it, Gabe, that's your forte. If you're going to work to your strengths, then this could be an ideal opportunity. And at the risk of sounding like some pop-psychologist, it's going to be good therapy for you, getting you confident about being on the roads again."

Gabe mulled it over. Piloting some rich creep around all day didn't have the same appeal or sense of freedom that cycling afforded him, but he could see it would work as a stepping-stone to regaining his self-assurance. Plus the prospect of visiting the many corners of London again was always an attraction. "What's he like, this boss?"

Tom shrugged. "Rarely comes in to the bar. Seen him once, I think; seemed sound to me. Gary the manager deals with him, and they get on OK. He owns clubs all over, so I'd imagine he's proper loaded. You're interested then?"

Gabe nodded.

"Cool, OK, I'll put in a word with Gary, see if you can get a meet with the boss." Tom smiled. "Good to see you back on your feet, mate."

"Yeah, feels good to me too," Gabe replied. "Oh, by the way, what's this bloke's name? The boss-guy?"

"It's Flowers. Harry Flowers."

CHAPTER NINE

The jet-black limo wound its way through the tight lanes of the Oxfordshire countryside, incongruous amongst the fields of maize and rapeseed and the thinly populated farmhouses that dotted the landscape. Any motorists that passed it couldn't help but cast an eye over it and briefly wonder its business or destination, the fact plainly evident that the occupants were not local. The windows were mirrored, so they offered no clue as to the nature of those within the car, but its size and ostentation suggested it clearly wasn't a commuter or tourist. It could possibly be lost, a few observers mused, but it had come so far out into the country that it could only be here by design rather than accident.

If a villager caught sight of it as it passed through the four or five cottage hamlets that represented suburbia out in this rural expanse, then there was a glimmer of recognition; they'd seen vehicles of this ilk drive past their homes before on irregular occasions over the past two or three decades. Sometimes they had police escorts, a couple of motorbike cops stationed nose and tail, but mostly these dark limousines came alone, driver and passengers always obscured. However, anyone that had lived around here for any substantial length of time knew full well where these particular travellers were heading, and could even hazard a guess as to their occupation. Few, though, that had been born and raised in the area had ever gone near the place to which they were undoubtedly journeying – indeed, getting anywhere near it was nigh-on impossible – and while it was nestled away in secluded woodland, of interest only to those that were aware of its existence, its presence cast a pall over the surroundings. They did not know what was done there, or to what purpose these visitors made their periodic trips, but there was little argument that much good would ever come of it.

The car turned off the main road through a gap in the hedgerow onto a narrow track that was bisected by a metal gate a few feet later. The vehicle slowed, and the driver's window slid down, a hand emerging clutching an ID card, holding it up to an infra-red sensor that was positioned on the gate post. There was a click and the barrier shuddered open, allowing enough time for the limo to pass before locking itself closed again. The car bounced along the dusty, furrowed track, thick foliage pressing in on either side; occasionally, the man seated in the back seat noted, razor wire could be glimpsed between the trees, ten-feet high mesh fences that were strung with warning signs and keep-out notices. They completely encompassed the six acres of private land the limo was travelling across, ensuring that the curious public were kept at a sufficient distance.

It didn't always entirely dissuade those that were determined to gain access to the facility. Over the years there had been a small handful of security breaches by anti-government protestors and troublemakers (and even the odd broadsheet journalist), all trying to pierce the veil of secrecy that was necessary to allow the compound's work to continue. None of them had succeeded in getting within a hundred feet of the laboratories, unprepared for the number of armed guards that patrolled the grounds at regular intervals. Out in these deep, dark woods – as intruders were repeatedly told with the intention of scaring them out of their nosy habits – it was very easy for someone to vanish without trace, and those trespassing on Ministry of Defence property could be shot without warning. The strict new measures that had been introduced to defend the country against terrorism enabled government buildings to protect themselves with maximum force, a handy tool at their disposal. Nobody had been killed yet trying to break into the research centre, fortunately; but, as with most things, it was probably only a matter of time. A ruling party keen to be seen cracking down on those that threatened homeland security, an increasingly paranoid nation and an unruly section of the populace that insisted on sticking its beak into matters that didn't concern them was a volatile combination. Put them together and it spelt BOOM.

The man couldn't understand why there were those so insistent on broadcasting the country's defence secrets in the first place; the work that was being developed at this research centre was in Britain's interests, enabling her to protect herself against her many enemies. God knew, they needed all the edge they could get in an ever-unstable planet. Rogue leaders and power-hungry tyrants were ten a penny, always strutting before the world stage, swinging their dicks. Half were big-headed buffoons, admittedly, that posed minimal threat, as long as there were departments monitoring their movements; if they just stuck to torturing their own people and blowing their nation's assets on building monuments to their vast egos, then it kept them occupied and out of the world's hair.

But it was once they started having designs on expanding their empire and instigating pan-global hatred that they become a nuisance, a bracket that the remaining fifty per cent fell into. These were the foes that needed removing for the safety of international stability, and more often than not it was a process that was conducted well out of the media's spotlight. Wars never ended, despite what was released to the public. That was what few not in governmental office understood; surrenders were accepted, deals were signed, coalition forces claimed victory, but the fighting never ceased. It was a necessary fact of the political landscape that conflicts carried on past the point of the official end to hostilities to make sure the peace remained rooted, weeding out intransigents that could pose problems in the future. The warlords that Britain and the rest of the civilised world were in eternal opposition to were like cockroaches – stamp on one and a dozen more escape into the cracks. Thus, safeguarding the nation's position in the global community was an unending battle, one in which they needed the very latest technological developments at their disposal on the frontline; and creating such weapons required research far from the public's gaze, as much for their own safety as anything else, in secret MoD complexes.

Places such as this one, the man mused, as the car slowed before a checkpoint. Officially, it was called Monkhill; it had been established not long after the Second World War, very much at Churchill's behest – a man who knew that victory wasn't just achieved, it was *maintained* – and was one of several dotted around the country charged with building upon the military's arms reserves to tackle the new faces that enemies of democracy wore in the twenty-first century.

A guard with a clipboard strode from the booth beside the barrier and tapped on the driver's window. A fellow soldier remained on watch, a rifle held against his chest, his eyes roving over the vehicle. It was strictly a formality – the car carried an HM government seal on its windscreen and its registration would've been verified by the CCTV cameras that had tracked its progress from the road – but the security here was as stringent as the man had ever encountered. A lunatic with thirty pounds of

Semtex strapped to his chest was more likely to be able to board a passenger jet than a rambler was to accidentally stray onto the facility's grounds.

The driver buzzed his window down. "Peter Sedgworth MP," he said, reaching across to the dashboard and retrieving a sheaf of paper, passing it to the guard. "He has an appointment with Doctor Gannon."

The soldier scanned the document, then affixed it to his clipboard, unhooking a pen from his fatigues' breast pocket and scribbling something upon it. He nodded, then said: "Wait there." He motioned with his head for his companion to join him and together they walked slowly around the car, scooting to their knees to check beneath the chassis. Sedgworth watched their movements impassively from the other side of the mirrored glass, the fingers of his left hand tapping an impatient rhythm on the briefcase on his lap. The driver was asked to pop the bonnet open so the engine could be examined, before being instructed to unlock the boot.

"Excuse me a moment, Minister," he muttered and clambered out. Sedgworth heard the boot yawn open behind him and felt the weight of the vehicle shift. He sighed and found his eyes running over the correspondence from Gannon that he'd been clutching for much of the journey from London. The doctor was uncharacteristically excited about developments they'd been making in a biological agent that he had insinuated could prove revolutionary in cutting the level of military casualties. He didn't go into much detail – was it a medical antidote? A compound that augmented a trooper's abilities? – but the scientific blather and optimistic rhetoric had pricked the Defence Minister's interest enough for him to come investigate it for himself.

In the decade or so that the two men had worked together, Sedgworth's experience of Gannon was that he wasn't one for waxing lyrical about the research centre's achievements, or promising unrealistic targets – indeed, the dour Scot had tested his patience on more than one occasion by failing to deliver new weaponry past the prototype stage, claiming that they were either unworkable or dangerous to the wielder. Several defence contracts had been lost because Gannon was a stickler for perfection, which hadn't made him many friends in Parliament. More than a few of Sedgworth's governmental colleagues had suggested that it was time the good doctor was retired for a younger replacement more amenable to rubber-stamping valuable army projects; but the Defence Minister had stuck by him because he could still pull moments of eclectic genius out of the bag. As long as he continued to demonstrate the forward thinking that had made him internationally renowned, Gannon still had a place in the department.

Which meant his enthusiasm for the current endeavour was well worth witnessing first-hand, if it was as boundary breaking as he claimed in his reports. In fact, the doctor's results couldn't have come at a better time for Sedgworth; with the various conflicts in the Middle East and central Europe dragging on year after year, and the British forces increasingly tied up in peacekeeping roles that were meant to last no more than the initial twelve-month period – they'd since ballooned into three times that – he was under substantial pressure from the PM to find a way to limit the numbers of soldiers heading overseas. Or at least make their job easier. Television footage of Union Jack-draped coffins being offloaded at military airfields was not the kind of publicity the Government needed, and it was an image that the voters were guaranteed to remember come election day. Sedgworth had been instructed to find a way to run the Army more efficiently, and preferably cut the casualty rate. As the PM told him, every war widow that was created was effectively a cross on the opposition's ballot paper. Quite how he was supposed to achieve this was unclear, short of withdrawing the troops from the crisis zones – his budget was stretched as it was. But the old man had been copping heat from all sides of the House and from the media over the mess the UK's forces were mired in, and had demanded that action be taken to stem the tide of bodies that were returning to these shores.

Gannon's breakthrough, therefore, could be the answer that would save his skin, Sedgworth believed, running his eyes over the documents before him once more as the boot was slammed shut and the driver clambered back into the front seat. The guards raised the barrier, and waved the car forward. The Defence Minister didn't claim to understand what the doctor was telling him in his letters, but if it meant he wouldn't be handing in his resignation in six months' time, then he was going to get behind it all the way. This could possibly resurrect his political career.

The limo parked before the facility's glass doors, and Sedgworth strode through the reception area, stopping momentarily to have his briefcase X-rayed and himself patted down by a soldier. Gannon was waiting for him, leaning nonchalantly by the lifts, arms folded, and the politician raised his eyebrows at him in greeting as the woman behind the reception desk handed him a visitor's badge. He wandered over to the doctor, looking down momentarily to affix the plastic tag to his suit lapel.

"Minister," Gannon said by way of acknowledgement, terse as ever.

"Come on, Robert," Sedgworth replied, offering his hand, which the scientist shook. "It's Peter. Let's not stand on ceremony."

Gannon shrugged. "It's that kind of place. Enough rules and regulations to make you forget you're human. You'll have had the intimate probing, then?"

"Checked and double-checked, right down to my approved governmental underwear. Nobody could ever accuse security of being lax here."

"Aye, we run a tight ship, all right." He pressed the lift's call button. "Come on, I'll take you down to the labs. That's where all the fun stuff happens."

Sedgworth studied the doctor as he stood gazing up at the lights above the lift doors indicating its ascent. He was in his early fifties, but carried himself as if he were fifteen years younger; he had a tendency to slouch, which reminded the politician of his own teenage son, and coupled with his surly demeanour there was something comically grumpy about the man. He was thin and wiry, and a good five inches shorter than the MP, with a shock of black curly hair atop an angular head. Despite his position as chief research officer at Monkhill, he looked and acted as if he were the student intern, scuffing his trainer-bedecked feet through the lab corridors with his hands in his pockets, scowling at colleagues whose theories he frequently and arrogantly dismissed without a second thought. It was easy to see why he put so many powerful people's backs up. Once they realised that multi-million pound corporate decisions could rest on the say-so of this scruffbag, they wondered if somebody in the department wasn't having a joke. But while he clearly didn't pay much attention to his appearance, his weapons research work was exacting; every attention to detail that wasn't apparent in his attire was there in his experiments and conclusions, precise and often inspired.

The lift doors slid open and the two men entered, Gannon jabbing a button for one of the sub-levels.

"Did you have a good journey?" he asked, casting a glance at the minister.

"Oh yes. Well, as good as could be expected, getting out of London."

The scientist smiled thinly. "You don't like leaving the city, then?"

"Not if I can help it. I've got nothing against the country, it's just... I don't care for all that scenery. It makes me nervous. Too open."

Gannon chuckled. "Spoken like a true metropolitan. Never happier than when you're no more than five feet away from a black cab and a Starbucks." He leant against the elevator wall. "I appreciate you braving the heart of darkness today, though, Peter. Out here in the wild frontier."

"I had to come and see for myself what you were getting so excited about." Sedgworth lifted up his briefcase and slapped it jovially. "Your reports were so enthusiastic, as if you were anticipating big things from this latest project."

The scientist wobbled his head, as if he wasn't inclined to agree. "It's early days. I shouldn't have got your hopes up that I would have a solution waiting for you. The fundamentals are in place, it's just a matter of fine-tuning to the point where it's workable. It could go either way at the moment, but I'm cautiously optimistic."

The minister smiled to shield his disappointment. "I've been intrigued by the progress you said you'd been making in cutting troop casualties. You didn't go into much detail. What is it, some kind of amphetamine variant that boosts the soldier's resilience?"

"You'll see for yourself soon enough," the doctor replied cryptically. The lift shuddered to a halt and the doors parted, revealing a gloomy, bare-concrete corridor. Gannon gestured for the politician to step ahead of him, and the two men wandered down the passageway, Sedgworth's Italian brogues clicking loudly on the flagstone floor. There was a chill in the air, as if they'd emerged into some underground cavern, and the minister involuntarily shivered, goosebumps rising on the back of his neck.

Gannon noticed the government man pulling his suit jacket around him. "Yeah, sorry about the temperature," he said. "We find it helps with the work we're doing. You get used to it after a while. Let me tell you, you really wouldn't want this place to be an oven."

"Oh? Why's that?"

"It'd turn ripe in hours. You'll get the idea when you see what we're doing in the labs."

They walked further into the bowels of the research facility, windows set in the walls on either side revealing white-coated scientists peering into microscopes and sitting before computers. Sedgworth caught sight of a crimson smear on the front of one of their tunics, as if the person had come straight from an abattoir. He hesitated, watching the medic in question inject a solution into something strapped to a gurney, hidden by the worktable.

"Are you doing animal testing here?" the politician asked. "I thought it was agreed that animal subjects were only to be used in experiments expressly approved by myself?" It was one of the few issues he felt strongly about, and had pledged when he took office to substantially reduce the amount of weapons testing on living creatures. It had won him the looney-tune liberal vote and the derision of his more cynical colleagues, but it was a belief he was proud to have remained reasonably consistent on.

"No. Nothing... living," Gannon replied. He stopped and faced the minister, chewing his lip and clearly choosing his words carefully. "You asked us to find ways of cutting army casualties, something which isn't easy to anticipate. There's no way we can foresee what a soldier will face on the battlefield, or the conditions they will have to fight under. No amount of protective garments will protect an individual in certain situations, when death can come in so many forms. And the human body will take only so much damage before it becomes irreparable and medical technology can no longer assist it."

"I thought you were looking at performance-enhancing drugs? Augmenting a trooper's strength and stamina?"

"It's a route we went down, I admit," Gannon said, nodding. "But again it comes down to the body's inability to handle the demands that we're asking to place upon it. We were attempting to limit the subject's need for fuel and sleep coupled with a steroidal muscle-growth programme. We tried surgical procedures too, adjusting eyesight and hearing as well as certain... cerebral tweaks."

"Christ," Sedgworth exclaimed. "You're telling me you were looking into cutting into their *heads*? What were you hoping to prove?"

The scientist looked at the politician levelly. "We thought perhaps hormones could be modulated, turning the emotions on and off like a tap. Increase anger, decrease the level of fear flooding the brain." He tapped his temple. "Maybe even find a way to instil logical thinking, encourage the subject to think rationally in the heat of conflict."

"It wasn't successful, I take it?"

Gannon shook his head. "As I said, the human body couldn't handle it. The drugs were unreliable and the level of steroids required to boost the soldier's musculature would have sent them crazy. We delivered preliminary samples to a local barracks – nothing life-threatening, just mild prototypes to see if they noticed any improvement in performance – and the reports we got back were that the regiment complained of headaches, nausea, muscle strain and dizziness. The compound was trying to work on them, I think, but it was taking every cell in a direction it didn't want to go... or at least every cell didn't have the ability to expand beyond its means. There's a lot of potential locked up in our bodies, Minister, it's just that we're too fragile to explore it fully."

"So where do we go from here? From what you've just said, you make it sound like we should replace the armed forces with robots – logical, fearless, without need for food or sleep..."

"...and disposable. I agree that would be the ideal solution. But it's prohibitively expensive. Unfortunately, a flesh-and-blood soldier's life is right now significantly less costly than that of his or her cybernetic counterpart. But that's the thinking we began to pursue – if we couldn't substantially alter a subject's make-up to protect them, the only other way of reducing casualties was to send a proxy in their stead."

"A proxy?"

"A substitute. An army that was eminently expendable, that a country could lose in great numbers without the pressure of consequences."

Sedgworth frowned. "I don't see what you're getting at, Rob."

"Follow me." Gannon turned and headed towards a

door at the end of the corridor. He laid his hand upon the handle and paused, glancing back at the politician as if he were about to add something, then thought better of it. Instead he walked into the darkened room beyond, the government man a couple of steps behind. Despite his proximity, he lost sight of the doctor for a moment, such was the gloom within; the only light available was that spilling into the room from outside, a source that was shut off when the door was closed behind him. He saw the outline of Gannon's white coat move amongst the tenebrous shadow, but could not discern any other detail in the space around him.

"Robert?" the minister asked querulously.

"I'm going to flip the lights on," a whispered reply came from somewhere to his left. "I'm going to ask you not to make too much noise. The test subject I have in here is quite easily distressed."

"Test subject? I thought —" His words died in his mouth when the fluorescents flickered into life above him and he could at last see what was in the room with him.

It reminded him of a dungeon – the walls and floor were bare grey stone, with no windows or furniture – and manacled to the far wall was what at first appeared to be a human being. It was dressed in military fatigues, and so Sedgworth assumed it to be one of the guards that had volunteered for a drugs trial. He certainly sounded as if he was doped up, emitting a mournful groan and straining at his bonds, his arms chained above his head. But as the minister stepped closer, he noticed macabre details about the figure. His face was sallow, blue-green skin stretched over the skull; his eyes were clouded, and the way he moved his head suggested he could barely see, and that rather he was sensing that others were in the room by scent or some internal radar; and the nearer the politician got to the man, the more he became aware of the stench that was emanating from him. He smelt... rotten. Sedgworth opened his mouth to say something to Gannon, but the doctor interrupted him.

"Don't move any closer," he warned. "You'll get him riled up. He might not be able to grab you, but could still give you a bite if you're not careful."

The minister automatically retreated a few paces. "Is he being kept prisoner?"

"Of a sort. As I said, he's a test subject, but he's restrained for our protection."

"What in God's name have you done to him? He looks like he's... decaying."

"He is, though in our defence that was nothing to do with us. Nothing we can do to stop entropy." Gannon smiled as if at a private joke. "What we gave him was *life*."

Sedgworth glanced at the scientist as if he was mad. "Are you telling me this man was dead?"

"Three weeks ago, he was shipped back to the UK with fatal abdominal injuries. Car bomb in Baghdad. He had died instantly, and had no close family to miss him. Not long after we took receipt of his corpse, we injected it with a serum we've been working on, just at the base of the neck. Five hours after that he got up and walked."

The politician's mouth was hanging open, alternately studying Gannon and the moaning figure, struggling to be free of his cuffs. "Wait, wait, back up... where did you get the authority to commandeer the deceased?"

"That's kind of on a need-to-know basis."

"I think I bloody need to know," Sedgworth snarled.

Gannon shrugged. "It starts with your boss, and trickles down from there."

The government man's mouth snapped shut. The PM

had evidently been putting wheels in motion over his head. "This... this is the grand scheme that could save our armed forces?" he said, gesturing around him.

"It's the ideal solution. They don't tire or feel pain, can survive numerous injuries as long as the brain remains intact, and resurrection seems to bring an enhanced aggression. They go for anyone." He nodded to the undead soldier. "He took a chunk out of my assistant's hand before he could be strapped down."

"They? You've got more of them?"

"We're monitoring several subjects. About a dozen, to be exact."

Sedgworth shook his head. "It's obscene, like something out of *Frankenstein*. How on earth can you imagine that the public will go for this? I mean, we're talking zombies here, for Christ's sake."

"We try to avoid the 'Z' word, Minister. It suggests voodoo. These are motorised cadavers; simply shells for the HS-03 virus that is putting their neurons back together. As for Joe Public, what makes you think they need to be told anything?"

The politician didn't reply. He turned and watched the dead man standing a few feet from him. It was grinding its jaw, drool falling from its black lips. "Is he conscious?" he asked finally.

"Barely. Next to no language skills or coordination. At the moment, it's pure instinct – it walks and tries to feed, which is redundant since it doesn't require the energy or the sustenance anymore. But we're working on it, see if we can kick-start its development."

Sedgworth strode towards the door. "This is insane," he muttered. "I cannot condone these experiments. Don't the dead deserve any respect anymore?"

"The dead are a resource, just like any other," Gannon

answered, following the politician out of the room, flicking the lights off as he left and shutting the door behind him. The creature's cries drifted softly through the partition. "Or would you rather the country sacrificed more troops?"

Sedgworth rounded on him. "You're a doctor, Robert. You're meant to preserve life, not play with it. When did that change?"

"I *am* preserving life," the scientist replied angrily. "I'm trying to save the lives of every serviceman and woman currently operating in a war zone. I'm trying to create an army that can work for *us*." He dropped his head and exhaled wearily. "Anyway, what makes you think this is the first time that medical science has been put to use in this way? Others have been here before; in fact, their blueprints have proved most helpful."

"What others?"

"The German High Command, for a start. They thought they could claim Europe with their own special division in World War One. They called it *Totenkrieg*..."

CHAPTER TEN

"You're Gabriel?"

The voice came from the open doorway. Gabe looked up to see the shadowed outline of a man filling the frame, a pair of bodyguards hovering over each shoulder. He walked into the living room, clasping a cup of tea in his hands, the light from the expansive picture window finally revealing his features: a grizzled, sinewy character, with a fuzzy white crew cut atop his head. Clad in a tan linen suit and a white shirt open at the neck, he moved unhurriedly to an armchair opposite the sofa upon which Gabe was nervously perched. The two guards had followed him through the door and closed it behind them, standing sentinel before the threshold.

"That's right. Pleased to meet you, Mr Flowers." The younger man instantly rose and proffered his hand. Flowers glanced down at it, turned slightly to place his cup and saucer on a small table beside the chair, and then shook it, his grip firm. He released Gabe and dropped back into his seat, motioning for his guest to do the same.

"Gabriel... It's a name you don't hear very often these days."

"My father is from Cork."

"Ah. You're of good Catholic stock, I take it?"

"Well, not really. He lapsed not long after meeting my mother, much to the disappointment of my grandparents. I think my name may have been some kind of appeasement."

Flowers nodded slowly, his piercing blue eyes studying Gabe. "And are you religious at all, Mr O'Connell?" he asked.

"Nah. I think I lost any semblance of faith the moment

I hit puberty. Didn't see how a loving God could justify all that teenage angst. That, and the spots, obviously."

Flowers smiled. "You're an atheist then?"

"Technically, though that always sounds so final. Let's just say I'm hedging my bets." He swallowed, watching as the older man took a sip from his teacup. "And yourself?" he enquired, hoping it wasn't too personal a question to ask a potential employer.

"I went to church every Sunday with my wife, years ago," Flowers replied, casting his eyes downwards to regard the contents of his cup. "But after she died, it felt like a... charade. An empty gesture. A pointless display of supplication towards a higher authority that I no longer respected." He was silent for a moment. "But I've always been interested in the power that those houses of God wield; there's no denying that, whatever your belief, the strength of faith is invested in their walls. You can feel it as soon as you enter one." He drained the teacup and set it back on its saucer. "That's my principle interest, Mr O'Connell – power; its acquisition and the most effective way to exert it." Flowers gestured around him. "You like the house?"

Gabe nodded, though he had seen little of its interior beyond the entrance hall and this lounge into which he had been ushered. Rather, he was wondering how the conversation had taken such a bizarre turn so early. He had been warned that Harry Flowers could be a touch eccentric, and if he was honest he had found the prospect refreshing, a throwback to the characters he used to work with on the local newspaper. But what clearly separated them from the sixty-year-old seated across from him now was the sheer level of influence and purpose that Flowers exuded; this was no harmless old codger, prone to flights of fancy, but a sharp entrepreneur whose digressions had an agenda of their own. Anything he said, he said for a reason. He had gathered that much just from a few minutes in his company, and from reading between the lines of what he had been told about Flowers by the lieutenants that had brought Gabe to this point.

Three days earlier, his flatmate Tom had instructed him to come to the bar on a Friday night, when one of Flowers' crew was guaranteed to be dropping by. Upon arriving Gabe was directed towards a dimly lit corner table, where he stood before a rotund, besuited figure cradling a gin and tonic. The man gave him the once-over and asked – prior to introducing himself or indulging in any conversational niceties – why he wanted to work for Harry Flowers. For such a forthright question, Gabe was initially stumped. He had expected a degree of small talk ahead of the crux of their business, and the immediate answer that he was desperate for the money seemed unwise. Instead, he replied that his knowledge of the city would make him an asset to Mr Flowers' organisation, and that if Flowers was looking for a good driver, then no one handled London's roads better than he. The man considered this response, then said that Gabe had come recommended (a commendation he suspected Tom had a hand in), and that he had been assigned by Mr Flowers to size up such suitable candidates before the boss called them in for a chat. His demeanour warming, he invited Gabe to sit and drink with him, informing him that his name was Childs, and that he had worked for Flowers for over ten years.

The younger man listened with polite interest as Childs gave him a potted history of his employer's dealings – a successful import/export company at the age of thirty, a move into property just as the boom-time hit, and the establishment of his line of clubs and bars – that painted the picture of a self-made millionaire. The reverence with which Childs spoke Flowers' name suggested a loyalty that Gabe had never experienced himself. He'd struggled with authority in the past, disliked being part of a team; but clearly being part of Flowers' outfit was a way of life. When he mentioned the man's obvious fondness for his boss, he didn't appear embarrassed.

"Harry's straight down the line," he said, a zealot's gleam in his eye. "He won't hesitate to tell you what's on his mind, but you'll find his honesty and fairness refreshing. There's no bullshit, nothing underhand. If you do well, he lets you know; if you fuck up, he'll kick your arse. It can be a little strange at first, true – 'cause he always lets you know what he's thinking, he has a tendency to go off at a tangent, so you have to be on the ball to keep up with him. Other times, you just have to go with it. But his attitude has got him where he is today, and it's enabled him to gather together a workforce that's proud to be at his right hand."

Gabe came away impressed with the dedication that Flowers evidently instilled in his employees, and when he got the call twenty-four hours later that the boss-man wanted to see him at his Essex mansion, he wondered if some of Childs' enthusiasm had rubbed off; he hadn't even met Flowers and already he felt honoured to be summoned into his presence. A car had arrived this morning to transport him there, and throughout the journey he was regaled with tales of Harry's business acumen by the driver and his escort – one of Childs' assistants called Hendricks, a dog-loving giant, who yapped about his kennels incessantly – their allegiance equally strong. The more he heard about him, the more Flowers was taking on an almost legendary status, a mythic name spoken in hushed, devoted tones, whose vast reputation preceded him. Despite, or perhaps because of, Childs' allusion to his boss's unconventional thought processes – "You need three brains just to catch up with him" – Gabe was looking forward to finally greeting the man in the flesh. When they swung round in front of the huge house and parked in its shadow, he was struck suddenly with the realisation of just how rich and important this guy was.

Now, under Flowers' gaze, sunlight streaming through the window, the trees in the grounds beyond bowing as they were tussled by a growing breeze, he could sense the power that the man had spoken of moments before, and the impression that he released it like a vapour wherever he went, an aura of tough, uncompromising authority. No wonder it was his guiding obsession to attain more; he wanted to build upon what he had, and consolidate his air of absolute control.

"The house is beautiful," Gabe replied.

"It's my church," Flowers said flatly. "It's where I operate from. I have many properties situated around the city – indeed, around the country – but this is where I'm strongest. This is my home."

"This is where you do your business from?"

"Mainly. I've reached that degree of wealth that fortunately renders the workplace obsolete, and have enough staff that I can delegate the day-to-day toil to. But I still need to put in an appearance in my various operations, just to make sure things are running smoothly. I like to think I'm a hands-on kind of boss." Flowers smiled again, though Gabe noted it barely touched his eyes, which remained as uncomfortably focused on him as always. "Hence the need for a driver. My average day can consist of a fair amount of shuttling back and forth, and I need someone that can take me from A to B with calm assurance. London's roads can be... taxing."

Gabe nodded, the screen inside his mind replaying in startling close-up the moment he ricocheted off the bonnet of the Audi and slammed into the tarmac.

"You came with a glowing reference, Mr O'Connell," Flowers said, cocking his head to one side and studying his subject. "It could of course be just as easy for myself to use one of my existing employees as a chauffeur. But other tasks demand their attention most of the time; and it appeals to me to be driven by someone with a genuine love for the city. You worked as a courier previously, I understand?"

"Before my accident, yes."

"So you feel you know the capital?"

"Whatever face the city shows, I think I've seen it."

Flowers exchanged a glance with one the guards standing before the door, a sense of amusement creasing his lips. "The city has many secrets, that's true," he said, returning his gaze to his guest. "And should you work for me, you will be privy to some of them."

Gabe expected him to expound further, but a mobile phone started ringing. Flowers reached into his jacket pocket and retrieved the device, answering it and listening intently. A minute or so later he clicked it shut and abruptly got to his feet, indicating their meeting was at an end. Gabe hastily stood, shaking his hand once more, though this time Flowers was the first to initiate the gesture. "My associates will be in touch."

"I've got my CV here, if you want it," Gabe replied quickly, patting the bag slung over his shoulder. "Or if there's any other documents you'd like to check—"

"That won't be necessary, Mr O'Connell. I've seen all I need to. Now, if you'll excuse me, I have business to attend to." He nodded a curt goodbye and turned to the door, the men opening it for him. He disappeared through without another word, the guards following, haunting his every move. They closed the door behind them.

Gabe stood in the suddenly hushed room, the sound of a ticking clock on the mantelpiece filling his ears, feeling strangely abandoned and listless, as if all the energy had suddenly been sucked from the air. He only snapped back into focus when Hendricks entered seconds later and told him he'd give him a lift back home.

He got the call from Childs a couple of days later to inform him that the job was his. He had expected to feel pleased, but his elation was oddly muted; he got the impression this decision had been made possibly even before Flowers had laid eyes upon him, that the old man had been toying with him slightly. His interview had been an attempt for the boss to see how Gabe handled himself face to face, and whether he could be intimidated easily. He assumed he had passed the test, though remained unsure why such a performance was required for such a straightforward role, and wondered if it boded well for his future relationship with his employer. Harry Flowers evidently liked to play games with power, as well as shop for it.

He pressed Tom for information on what he knew about the man, but his flatmate claimed ignorance, repeating his claims that he had had no dealings with him, and that even his superior – Gary, the bar manager – mostly spoke to just Flowers' underlings. Tom did admit that he had heavily championed Gabe for the job, partly because he felt it would be good for him to get back out on the roads, and partly because they were financially desperate. The money Flowers was offering, and the immediacy of the work, was not to be sniffed at. Gabe knew what he was implying: that after Tom's efforts to secure him this work, and with a substantial regular wage laid before him, he would be foolish – not to mention potentially homeless and friendless – if he didn't accept the offer. Once that was taken into consideration, he buried his reservations and spoke to Childs, telling him he would gladly fill the position.

However, he wasn't naive enough to believe that Flowers was entirely on the level, and his first few days working for the man confirmed it. Although his import companies and clubs were legitimate enough on the surface – or to a degree to keep the police from his door, at least – he was evidently not beyond stooping to intimidation to claw more of his precious power. Much of Gabe's initial work seemed to be driving Flowers and a cadre of his lieutenants to backwater businesses and wholesale outlets in the East End and waiting outside while they disappeared into the buildings for a couple of hours. Although he was instructed to stay within the car – a gleaming Jag that he was more than happy to get behind the wheel of – and therefore saw nothing of the transactions taking place inside, when his colleagues returned he occasionally caught glimpses of crimson spots on white cuffs, or a film of sweat on a few of the men's foreheads. He knew enough not to ask questions, and Flowers never revealed what had gone on, but was probably all too aware that Gabe had his suspicions.

Gabe knew that the moment the suggestion of criminal activity reared its head, the smart thing would be to get out of the outfit immediately. But the fact was that there was much about the job that he enjoyed, not least the frisson of excitement at being part of an enterprise that operated on the fringes of the law, a throwback to his wild youth. He grew to like the camaraderie between Flowers' employees, a closely knit group that watched out for one another, bonded by a disregard for conventional authority, and he appreciated the shared glory of being associated with the boss himself. Every time he piloted Flowers through the streets of London he could feel the instinctive respect that the man garnered from those around him. Perhaps there was a touch of fear there too – Flowers often remarked that nothing put people in their place quite like a fearsome reputation – but that seemed more attributed to the facade that Harry liked to project rather than any genuine malice on his part. Indeed, the greater the length of time Gabe spent in his employer's company, the more he realised he was becoming like Childs, Hendricks and the rest – drawn into Harry Flowers' inescapable orbit, he found the strength of personality there arresting. He was funny, clever and remarkably honest for one who spent much of his time concealing his dealings from those that would subject them to scrutiny. He had a temper on him, but the nuclear blast of his anger lasted only as long as the time it took for the person on the other end of his wrath to get the message before it was whipped out of sight again. He felt at times like a surrogate father, affectionately lording it over his unruly family, paternally responsible for his charges, and Gabe wondered if the absence of his own family, the loneliness of his convalescence as he recovered from his accident, brought this into even sharper relief. As long as he was part of Flowers' outfit, then someone would always have his back.

As the weeks elongated into months, Gabe became slowly but surely inured to the surreptitious side of the boss-man's custom, perhaps a little more easily than he expected. He was never asked to be involved, and Flowers clearly appreciated his unquestioning attitude. Even so, it wasn't as if this was the only sphere in which he conducted business. Indeed, there were relatively few of these clandestine meetings amongst the daily routine. Gabe would drive him to lunches with overseas manufacturers, distribution heads and other such mundane facets of his empire, and in the evenings there were appearances at charity parties and club openings, where he would rub shoulders with minor actors and musicians, many hankering for his patronage. He appeared extraordinarily well connected. When Gabe opened the Jag's rear door and Flowers emerged, he transformed from the shady operator into the popular philanthropist; and by extension Gabe got a taste of the glamour and fame, if only at a distance.

Such benefits were enough to make his position with Flowers a tenable one, but there was a further element that piqued his interest even more and ensured his renewed enthusiasm for the job. Every alternate Wednesday, Harry instructed Gabe to take him – strangely, always using one of the other pool cars rather than his regular Jag – to a flat in Vauxhall, into which he would disappear for almost exactly an hour. He always went alone, smelling strongly of aftershave, and entered and departed empty-handed. He would say next to nothing about the nature of these visits, and often the journey back from the apartment was a silent one, Flowers broodily glaring through one of the car's side windows. Gabe never attempted any enquiries, knowing from his boss's mood that such questioning would not go down well, but posited a theory in his head that the flat housed a mistress that Harry was courting, and had been for some time. He had not mentioned any women in his life since the death of his wife, but all the evidence – the scent, the spring with which he left the car, the gloom in which he returned – pointed to a doomed affair of some sort.

After driving Flowers to several of these assignations, the mystery nagged at Gabe; probably more than it should. What business was it of his if Harry got his bi-weekly jollies with some old flame? The routine despondency with which he returned to the car suggested the relationship had been dragging on over a fairly lengthy period, and the driver imagined the unseen lover as being of a similar age to Flowers; a wrinkly gangster's moll kept in affluent seclusion. It really was nothing to do with him and not worth musing on, he reminded himself, and he wouldn't have thought anymore of it if he had not seen the face at the window.

Gabe didn't know why he looked up when he did; usually he was still sitting behind the wheel when Flowers reappeared, but on that bright Wednesday he was leaning against the bonnet of the parked car, enjoying the warmth of the sun's rays. He heard the front door slam and saw his boss heading towards him across the forecourt; stepping back to duck into the vehicle, his eyes flickered momentarily upwards at the building's frontage and he caught sight of the young woman gazing down at him. He knew instantly that this was the subject of Harry's visits. Even from that distance, he could see a resemblance in the narrowness of her cheeks and the dazzling blue eyes. It was not a bed-partner he was spending time with – it was a relation, and, in all probability, his daughter. They locked stares for long seconds before she vanished behind the curtains, and Gabe was left with an indescribable ache at her absence. He snapped from his reverie when he realised that Harry had almost reached him, and tried to put her from his mind for the journey back to the mansion. He made no mention to his employer at having seen the woman, and Flowers – being typically morose – did not indulge in conversation.

But Gabe found it difficult to erase the face from his memory; there was something so sad and heartbreaking about the cast of her features that he kept returning to it. He studied it from what he could recollect – the long blonde hair hanging to her shoulders, the pale white skin, the small teeth visible behind the purse of her lips – and tried to analyse why this woman looked so caged and lonely. For all he knew, she could be married with half a dozen rugrats under her belt; but her demeanour suggested otherwise. She appeared afraid, and her father's trips to see her – for Flowers had to be her parent, there was no question of that, the more he compared the two – did nothing to assuage that fear; indeed, it possibly even heightened it.

Gabe looked forward to each trip to south London and a chanced glimpse of the mystery woman, and though he never saw her as clearly on subsequent visits he could always discern her outline hovering at the curtains' edge, like a spirit trapped behind glass. Flowers appeared not to notice Gabe's eyes constantly drifting to the same window, but that was hardly surprising; he was becoming increasingly distracted. Gossip amongst the men suggested that an old rival of Harry's had started moving in on their territory – Goran Vassily, a kingpin from eastern Europe, who had carved out a chunk of property north of the Thames, and with whom Flowers had a volatile relationship. Vassily was making challenges to Harry's power base: customers were being stolen, profits slashed, insults traded. Flowers was said to be livid, and he spent more and more time at the mansion, issuing directives to combat this threat. As a result, the journeys to Vauxhall dried up, and Gabe was left haunted by her image.

He had considered asking some of the others in Harry's employ whether they knew anything about her, but discarded the idea, worried that word might get back to the old man, who would no doubt take a very dim view of his chauffeur poking his nose in other people's personal matters. He wasn't sure who he could trust amongst the ranks; who would keep their mouths shut and who would find his casual curiosity suspicious.

Suddenly, Gabe made an unconscious decision before the rational side of him could oppose it: he would go see her without Flowers' knowledge. It was a risky strategy, and one that seemed to fly in the face of common sense, but he didn't think he'd be able to put that face from his mind until he'd made an attempt to help her. He recognised a vulnerability that he himself had struggled to overcome following his accident, and saw in those pained features a desire to escape the claustrophobic confines of her dwelling, if only she wasn't so scared of what lay beyond. As someone who had suffered similar circumstances, Gabe felt he was in a useful position to give her whatever aid she required. To minimise the amount of deceit required, he chose a day when he needed to take the Jag in for a service, and could legitimately escape Harry's gaze, though in truth the boss was so preoccupied with this enemy organisation muscling in on his operations that Gabe doubted he would be even missed. Every morning seemed to bring with it some fresh tale of disrespect and a growing sense of events escalating: a small fire in a club bathroom; shots fired outside several bars; an increased police presence acting on anonymous tip-offs.

He drove over to the apartment block not knowing what he was going to say, and stood before the list of residents next to the exterior door, his mind still blank.

There was only one woman's name marked, and that read Anna Randolph, Flat 4. His hand, acting independently, reached out and pressed the button adjacent to it.

A reply came seconds later out of the speaker. "Yes?"

"Ms Randolph?" Gabe exhaled and took a leap of faith. "I work for your father. Mr Flowers."

The silence stretched interminably. Finally: "And?"

"And he hasn't been able to make it for a few weeks, so I... I came in his stead. To see how you were."

More silence. "Who are you?"

"My name's Gabriel O'Connell. As I said, I work for Harry."

"Look up for a moment."

"Huh?"

"Just look up."

He did as he was told, seeing instantly the CCTV camera positioned just under the roof of the porch. He looked straight into its flat black eye.

"You're the driver, aren't you?" came a crackly voice from the intercom. "The one who brings him."

"That's right."

"And he doesn't know you're here, does he?"

"Well, I..." Gabe stuttered. "I thought..."

"Push the door." A buzzer sounded and the lock snapped free. Gabe paused for a moment, cast a glance behind him, then entered, jogging up the short flight of stairs to the first landing. Number four was opposite the stairwell. He rapped on its door, which was opened by the woman from the window. She was shorter than he imagined, in her early twenties, and wore a black vest top and grey sweatpants. She beckoned for him to enter, and ushered him into the living room, a chaotic sprawl of discarded clothes, magazines, CDs, books and unwashed mugs.

"Sorry to disturb you like this," he began.

"If Harry knew you were here," she answered, sitting on a sofa arm, one leg folded under the other, "he'd have you strung up. I'm presuming you know the risk you're taking?"

"To be honest, I'm not sure myself what I'm doing here. Why'd you let me in?"

"I'd see you looking up at my window when you'd come to collect Dad. You have a trustworthy face, I guess. Somehow I wasn't entirely surprised you turned up at my door."

He nodded slightly. "I wanted to talk to you. You seemed lonely and... I don't know, a bit trapped, I suppose." He ran a hand through his hair. "I don't make a habit of this, I have to say. Turning up at stranger's doors for a chat, I mean."

"You must have been sure, though. As I said, Harry will feed you your balls if he finds out you've been here."

"I know. It felt like something I had to get out of my system. If I didn't... I would've been haunted by what I didn't do because I didn't have the nerve." She was studying him, clearly a family trait. "Why does he keep you here?"

"For my protection. Dad's made a fair few enemies over the years, so he thought it better I didn't stay at the mansion. Hence me taking on mother's maiden name too. But it suits me, being as far away from him as I can. If he would let me, I'd escape to the other side of world."

"I got the impression that the two of you don't have a happy relationship."

"My father's an animal, and the fact that he acts the popular businessman somehow makes it even worse. If he was a simple thug that didn't know any better, I might have some semblance of respect for him; but he's very exacting in how he inflicts pain. If something stands in the way of getting what he wants then he won't hesitate to destroy it."

The vehemence of her words took him aback. She must've noticed his shock because her tone softened. "Look, clear some of that stuff off the chair and sit down. You look like you're waiting for a bus."

Gabe picked up a stack of unironed T-shirts and placed them on the carpet. Seating himself, he took in his surroundings: there was clutter everywhere, spilling from cupboards and off shelves, though there was a comforting homeliness to it. There was no sense of ostentation. The furniture was evidently several decades old, and an extensive album collection was lying in piles around a tatty stereo player held together by duct tape. It didn't look like she had much use for her father's wealth. He noticed there were no photographs of Flowers perched amongst the bric-a-brac, only a woman he took to be Anna's mother; the two of them were smiling out of many of the picture frames.

"Is that why you didn't tell me to get lost?" he asked. "Because having me here would upset him?"

"Partly," she conceded. "I do like making things as difficult for him as I can. He deserves it."

"What on earth do the two of you talk about when he comes to visit?"

"Not a lot. It's mostly just him apologising, and asking for forgiveness. Me, I'm just counting the hours till he goes."

"Forgiveness? For what?"

She sighed. "Long story."

"That's kind of why I'm here," he said, smiling. "Anything you want to get off your chest, I'm willing to listen."

She paused as she picked at a nail. "Suffice to say, I used

to see this guy that was friends with the wrong crowd. Dad made sure he left town and didn't come back."

"More enemies?"

She nodded. "Of a sort." She looked up at him, the same piercing blue eyes as her father boring into him. "Do you want a cup of tea?"

He smiled and replied that he would, and when she returned with two steaming mugs they chatted comfortably about their pasts. Gabe told her about soldiering overseas and the scenes he witnessed there, and the accident and the terror he'd experienced at leaving the safety of his home. Anna sympathised, telling him that Flowers had instilled in her at an early age a dread of straying from his side, informing her that there were all manner of bad people who could do her harm. She realised in her late teens, after he'd hounded her mother to death, that he was the one she needed to be afraid of. But even so, he wouldn't let her go, refusing to keep her at anything more than arm's length.

Gabe felt an assurance with Anna that put him at his ease, bonded by their similar experiences of living with fear, and though he was conscious of the time that was slipping away as he sat inside this Vauxhall flat watching the shapes her mouth made as she spoke, it was good to be in her company. With each anecdote, she was clearly relishing a chance to relate to someone, having broken free of Flowers' control. She told him about bands that she liked, playing song after song, scattering CDs in an arc around her as she searched through her collection, and reeled off novels that he should be reading. It was like he had suddenly tapped into the reservoir of her interests, and it came bubbling to the surface.

"You got any kids?" she asked him after he'd told her a little about his own family.

"No, none. I've never been in a steady enough relationship."

"I had one once, with the guy from the wrong crowd. A baby boy. Dad insisted I give him up for adoption, said I wasn't in a fit state to cope." She was studying an album sleeve, running her eyes over it sadly.

"I'm sorry to hear that."

"Post-natal depression." She looked over at him. "I'd like to see him again, though, one day. He'd be a proper little lad by now."

Eventually, he told her he had to go, but would like to return, if that was OK with her. She told him it was, as long as he was careful. He should never underestimate Harry, she said. Gabe promised he would take every precaution, and true to his word he came back a week later, and then another seven days after that, and then twice more the following month.

Unaware that on each occasion he was being closely watched.

The first inkling that something was wrong came when his mobile rang at 3.30 in the morning. At first he was content to let it run to voicemail, but it didn't stop; somebody was calling his number repeatedly. Rousing himself from sleep, Gabe sleepily glanced at the display and saw Flowers' name. A chill ran down his spine, and all notion of fatigue left him instantly. He answered it warily.

There was no greeting. "They've got her," Harry whispered, hard and precise, the anger vibrant within each word. "They've got her because of *you*."

CHAPTER ELEVEN

Dr Jenny Cranfield leaned back from her desk, her head throbbing. She removed her glasses and rubbed the bridge of her nose as she reread the last paragraph she had written on the monitor screen, then stood from her chair, arching her back. She had been hunched over her workstation for the best part of the morning, and her neck felt as stiff as the corpse on the gurney behind her. She reached up and squeezed the nape and her shoulders, the muscles tense beneath her touch, though her efforts were limited with only one good hand at her disposal. She looked down at the left, the appendage swathed in bandages, and once more attempted to flex it, but the cramping pain returned to travel up her arm. It was like a dead weight, as if the tendons within had frozen; she fought the urge to slam it against the wall, just to give it back some sensation.

Jenny tugged open a drawer and rooted amongst the detritus to retrieve a packet of paracetamol, then wandered over to the sink. She swallowed two of the tablets, and leant under the running tap to wash them down. As she wiped her mouth, her gaze returned to her injured limb; she was certain the fatigue and her body's tenderness were in some way connected to the bite she had received. She'd been checked out by one of her colleagues straight after the incident, who had cleaned and dressed her wound before giving her a couple of jabs, mostly as a precautionary measure. He'd said he could detect nothing untoward and had taken a blood sample to put her mind at rest, but she remained convinced the wound was infected. Who knew what diseases that test subject could possibly be carrying?

Gannon had assured her that the corpse had been sterilised before the experimentation began, but even then, he had admitted, post-resurrection the virus hadn't halted the cadaver's necrosis – flesh and muscle were continuing to rot as bacteria set to work upon the dead tissue. That had certainly popped his little balloon; what use would the military have for a platoon of these things if they were falling apart? He had convinced himself that they could still be deployed for limited periods, though he was plainly disappointed with the results, blindly hoping that HS-03 would suddenly pull a miracle out of the bag. Still, she reasoned, it wouldn't be the first time that the British Army had been sent out with substandard equipment.

She didn't know how long the project was destined to last anyway. By all accounts, the Minister was less than impressed and determined to shut it down, though Gannon characteristically remained optimistic that he could make the politician see sense. She wasn't sure if the politician didn't have a point. In twelve years of researching and engineering toxins and bio-weapons for the MoD, this had crossed the line from genuinely working in the best interests of the country's defence to ghoulish frivolity. Gannon was a brilliant scientist – one of the top minds in the UK – but he must've recognised that this was going to be a hard sell, and she now thought that he was persevering with it out of sheer obstinacy. If the media ever got the merest sniff of the work that was being conducted here, they were going to crucify him – and undoubtedly Sedgworth too, no matter what plausible denials he could muster – and tar him with the familiar accusations of playing God. For once, Jenny was inclined to agree; this mockery of the dead had no place in a nation's arsenal, even if it did save troops' lives. What could they possibly claim to be battling *for*, sending out a squad of reanimated cadavers to fight on their behalf? Freedom? Democracy? Peace? They who had enslaved their own dead? Who, in whatever corner of the globe, would consider that *civilised*?

And there was the aggression factor, something that had taken them all by surprise. Gannon's theorising had suggested that once HS-03 got to work on primary functions of the brain – triggering movement and the most basic awareness of its surroundings – it would render the motorised corpse entirely open to direction, allowing them to input orders and place it completely within their control. But the virus had taken hold on the cerebellum's centre and developed it in a totally unexpected direction; along with the motor-control and rudimentary behaviour patterns came an uncontrollable violence. It was as if it had awoken the brain's most primal root, reverting the subject back to an animalistic state.

In the case of Corporal Littleton – or HS-03/ref.4176, to give him his official title – within minutes of getting up and walking, he (*it*, she admonished herself, she had to remember to refer to them as impersonal objects; they were no longer human beings, displayed no intelligent life-signs, and exhibited similarly no personality; they were simply dead sacks of meat) appeared threatened by the scientists' presence and lashed out. Even then, it wasn't clear how the corpse had managed to ascertain that there were people in the room – there were four of them: Gannon, herself, and McKendrick and Horton – since it didn't appear to have had his sight fully restored. The pupils were filmy, and the way it moved its head seemed to indicate that it was using some other sensory perception to gain understanding of its environment. Likewise, sound and smell must've been equally undeveloped, if they were indeed working at all. But there was no denying it was immediately aware of their proximity, for it staggered towards them in a stiff-legged gait, gnarled fingers reaching out. As they all backed away, Gannon whispered that perhaps it was looking to feel whether they were of the same species to reassure itself; reading their physiognomy like a blind man runs his fingers over Braille. It clattered into them and Jenny put out her left hand to restrain it, a mistake she instantly regretted.

Its advance was not borne out of a need for kin recognition, but hunger. It grasped her wrist and bowed its head as if for a romantic peck, but instead bit down on the fleshy part of her palm, ripping away a fat inch of skin and muscle with a savage twist. Jenny screamed, white-hot pain lancing through her forearm, watching, unbelieving, as blood pumped in a crimson mini-fountain from her ravaged hand and hit the floor in heavy splats that blossomed into rusty explosions on the tiles. The cadaver stood before them, still holding her in a vice-like grip, and slowly began to chew, red trickles coating its chin, stark against the pale white of its face. It exhibited no semblance of pleasure in the act, its features as blank as if it were still lying on the slab, as if this was something it was directed to do by an inner instinct. Indeed, it exuded the disinterested air of a baby suckling upon a teat, unconcerned by the method by which it obtained its food, only that its belly was being filled.

Gannon and the others were paralysed for mere seconds, but those moments seemed as if time had slowed to a crawl; they stared, frozen, at the ragged bite-mark on Jenny's hand, which was by now slick with blood. It was only when the corpse ducked forward once more to take one of her fingers between its teeth that they finally sprang into action. They seized its arms and wrestled it back, forcing it to relinquish its hold of her wrist. Once she was free, she sank to her knees, sobbing, clasping her wounded limb to her chest, already feeling a stiffness stealing its way up her arm. She shrugged off her white coat and wrapped it around the injury, stemming the flow of vermilion fluid from her already pallid hand.

Once the cadaver was distracted from its meal, it fixed its attention on the three scientists that were trying to pin it down; apparently, its greed was indiscriminate. It lunged for them too, jaw snapping, grasping for anything it could catch hold of. For one tense moment, it grabbed Horton's shirt and yanked him forward, its maw opening wide to take a chunk out of his neck, but Gannon punched it hard in the temple. It evidently did little to hurt it, but blindsided it enough for them to consolidate their grip on its arms. They yelled at Jenny to hit the security alarm, and she woozily found her feet to slam her fist down on the red button encased on the wall.

Within seconds, half a dozen armed personnel filled the room, Gannon repeatedly instructing them not to shoot. Instead he got one of them to pass him a pair of binds to secure the creature's hands behind its back, another to hogtie its feet together, then fashioned a makeshift muzzle from a broken-in-half broom handle jammed between its teeth. Only once he was confident that it was fully incapacitated and that it posed no additional threat did he indicate to his colleagues that they could back away from it. They stood in a semi-circle, breathing heavily, looking down at the cadaver wriggling like a bug trapped for a school kid's project, its teeth cracking against the broom handle, sliding out of grey gums. The security guards in particular were a little taken aback by what they were witnessing; they were generally not privy to the nature of the experiments that were conducted within the labs, and had next to no knowledge of Gannon's resurrection serum. Possibly keeping them in the dark like that was a wise move, Jenny had mused; many of them were ex-military, and if they knew where HS-03/ref.4176 had come from, what it had been in life, they might not have been so quick to come to Gannon's aid.

Instead, he'd reassured them that the subject was merely being tested for increased levels of adrenaline, and its pallor and mania were side effects of the drugs they were prescribing. She could tell they didn't believe him for a second, but since they could not formulate an explanation for themselves, they seemed to grudgingly accept it. Gannon was told that for a security breach of this kind – and especially since a member of staff had been wounded (all eyes had turned towards her then, her deathly white face and arms pockmarked with maroon stains) – a report would have to be kicked upstairs. Gannon had readily agreed, eager to usher them out of the room, fully aware that the MoD bods would clamp down on it and make sure no details ever emerged outside of Monkhill.

While he and Horton had dragged their bound creature off to a quieter area where it could be monitored safely, McKendrick had led her to the infirmary and treated her injury. McKendrick was a relatively recent addition to the team, having transferred over from an outpost north of Sydney, and was a cautious, introspective young man. As he carefully wrapped the bandages around her hand, she asked him if he thought what they were doing was a step too far.

"I don't like it," he'd said. "But I doubt it'll stay like this for long."

"What do you mean?"

"This," he groped for the right expression, "walking army of the dead that's supposedly going to fight for us. It's not going to happen. The public, the politicians, they're not going to stand for it. But what it could prove to be is a starting point, a catalyst for a whole new take on the problem. The idea of using reanimated cadavers will mutate into something else, something more workable, and we'll take the best bits from what we learned with HS-03 and use them in a different direction."

"Gannon seems keen on his pet ghouls."

McKendrick snorted a laugh. "I think he actually fancies himself as a Junior Frankenstein. But it's his pride that, for the moment, won't let him see past his zombies."

"Don't let him hear you use the Z word."

"He kids himself that the HS-03 subjects are in the best interests of the country, but the fact is he just wants to be like the criminal mastermind from the horror movies, controlling them all. What's that one about the dead working down a Cornish tin mine?"

"I don't know," Jenny replied, looking down at her bandaged limb. "Those sort of films aren't really my cup of tea."

"Well, that's what Gannon would have them doing, if he had his way." He paused. "But it'll change. He'll recognise the serum's limitations, and it'll spark off some new theories and we'll start working on... I don't know, combating organ failure or bolstering a soldier's immune system." He paused again. "Things can't stay the way they are." He finished binding her wound. "Best I could do. You'll probably have some scarring."

As Jenny stood in the lab, head still throbbing despite the tablets, she tentatively pressed her fingers against the linen-wrapped flesh of her hand; it felt rigid and unmoving, as it if were calcifying. She was beginning to worry at what kind of infection had spread into her system, and considered taking herself off to A&E at the local hospital. Gannon would hit the roof if he found out; once the Casualty docs started asking questions, it could bring down all sorts of unwanted heat on the facility. If Monkhill had a cardinal rule, it was *containment* – the neighbours had no reason to know the research that was being conducted on the premises, and if problems arose, they were to be dealt with inside its walls. Once it entered the public domain, there was no way of controlling the snowballing of information. All the same, she was aware that she was gradually feeling worse – her legs seemed wobbly, and her eyelids were growing heavy – and decided she should readmit herself to the infirmary, and let them sort it out. She was in no fit state to work.

She pushed herself away from the worktop edge and headed towards the door, immediately sensing a rushing wave of nausea pass through her. She staggered and clattered into her chair, coughing bile into the back of her throat, putting out her good hand to steady herself. It made contact with the gurney upon which the cadaver lay, strapped and muzzled, it's searching eyes swivelling in their sockets at her sudden proximity. It was the fourth or fifth test subject to have been injected with HS-03 – a John Doe that had been commandeered from a military hospital – and its stomach cavity had been surgically emptied to gauge the effect of hunger upon its actions. The edges of its belly were pinned open, and several feet of intestine had been removed and curled into a large stainless steel dish to the side. All that remained of its digestive tract was a russet-brown hole surrounded by muscle and fat, and yet it had attempted to feed whenever she had gone near it, its teeth champing, its head struggling to get closer to her. It was clearly not looking to sustain itself, since it no longer had the organs that required the nourishment, but was instead simply gorging itself on the primal act of consuming meat, directed by the virus working on its brain.

Jenny leaned against the gurney, gazing down at its naked form, sweat now prickling her brow, and suddenly, barely thinking, she reached forward and untied the muzzle. Instantly, it issued a groan and moved its jaw in a bovine manner, trying to chew on anything it could reach. Its arms strained against the bonds, and its dissected abdomen tore a little with the movement, the skin splitting as far up as the ribcage and down to the pubic bone, red sheaths of muscle visible beneath the yellowish skin.

Jenny held out her right hand above its mouth, and the corpse snapped at it, like a pet offered a treat. Its head pushed higher, its neck wrenching with the effort, but she kept the limb safely out of its reach, the fingers several inches from its clacking teeth. Then, she replaced the offered titbit, proffering her injured left hand. The result was what she feared: the creature showed no interest, its head sinking back onto the stretcher, exhibiting none of the excitement it had showed seconds ago. She waved it closer still, but there was no response. She stepped back from the gurney, breathing heavily, her mind racing at the implications; the dead subjects were stimulated by the presence of living flesh, seeking to feed upon it. The fact that it didn't react to the wounded limb suggested that the cadaver couldn't sense a pulse. As far as it was concerned, her left hand was as a dead as it was.

She had to get help, she instructed herself. A necrosis had spread from the bite and was in the process of killing all the cells in her lower arm, no doubt coursing through her body as she stood there, passing on its taint. The thought made her feel sick again, and light-headed. She stumbled forward, leaving the corpse mewling behind her, and focused on getting out the door, taking no more than half a dozen steps before a paralysing coldness arced through her, punching the breath out of her and draining all the strength from her legs. Jenny dropped to her knees, bringing her hands to her chest; she felt as if her lungs were crystallising, seizing up. She gasped, clawing for air, aware of her muscles shaking. She was dying, she realised, and she didn't have the energy to cry for help. Her body was riddled with the bacteria, and it was shutting everything down, organ after organ, like light switches being flipped one by one. She curled into a ball, visualising the virus racing through her, changing her from the inside out, blood cells laid waste by the nuclear blast of its wake. A growing darkness was stealing into her head, and an agonizing swell of pain blossomed throughout her being. Her mouth was frozen into a savage rictus grimace by the time her heart stopped half an hour later.

Twenty minutes after that, her mouth started moving again.

Gannon was tinkering with a cadaver's brain when he first heard the alarms. He was trying to reverse-engineer the serum, or at least tweak the affect it had on the organ's central core, reducing the resurrected corpses' predatory, cannibalistic tendencies (but they *weren't* cannibals, he told himself; their desire for human flesh was not an interspecies act, since they were no longer of the same genus). The speed with which HS-03 took hold of those it was administered to had been expected. After all, it had been artificially constructed based on the HIV, cancer and influenza models – tenacious, aggressive viruses that took no time at all in disabling a victim, riddling its cells, destroying the immune system and adapting the subject for its own use. And, indeed, part of his interest in creating HS-03 from the ground up was to monitor what the bacteria actually wanted to do. To the observer, for example, cancer has no other purpose but to destroy; but to understand it, the scientist had to look at it from the virus's point of view – what did it seek to gain from corrupting its host? Could it possibly see itself as an instrument of change, developing a fully functioning body into something else? The question was, what was that change initiating? In the case of HS-03, it was using the dead as a blank slate, hot-wiring their neurons and kick-starting them into life – but a life dictated by the virus and what it wanted.

Gannon couldn't fathom why it was instigating this primal hunger, especially since it had been proven that the need for food was purely superficial. It was almost as if the bacteria was unlocking and accessing the latent memories still trapped within the cadavers' heads, the root instincts that were as much the legacy of mankind's stone-age ancestors as the nub of their prehensile tails. It was reawakening them, channelling them.

When they first discovered this hunger for flesh, Gannon had hoped that it could be fine-tuned into an additional weapon, something extra in their biological arsenal. Not only would they be fearless and indefatigable, but this army would consume what it destroyed, like a plague of locusts sweeping through the enemy ranks. But he soon realised that their cravings were indiscriminate and impossible to control; his colleagues too were uneasy with this side effect of HS-03, especially after Dr Cranfield was assaulted and bitten. Bringing the dead back to life had tested their scientific moralities to the limit, but honing them as carnivorous attack dogs was something else entirely. More than a handful had protested and refused to go near what they called the 'ghouls'. Gannon had argued that they were being emotive, and basing their opinions on what they may have seen in late-night movies, but he knew the writing was on the wall for the project. Sedgworth would never greenlight it, not as it stood; he wouldn't want to be known as the minister that unleashed the flesh-crazed undead on the world. That was the sort of thing that history would judge a man by.

The politician had tried to remain unmoved by what Gannon had told him about *Totenkrieg*, but the doctor could detect that the Minister was secretly shocked that something like this had been attempted before. Or, more likely, the fact that the powers-that-be on the home front had deemed the scheme worthy of stealing from the Germans once the war was over. It never really got beyond the planning stage with them either; they'd only ever developed one platoon, and the viral prototype had been crudely manufactured. He wondered if they too had had control issues with the resurrected, unprepared for what they had let loose.

He had a skull open before him, the flap of scalp peeled back like the lid of a tin can, and was probing the dull-grey organ within, dissecting choice segments for examination and testing. What had become immediately evident was that, while the resurrected could survive any amount of tissue damage and limb removal (they had undergone a barrage of weapons' fire trials), brain injury cancelled their ticket for good. Clearly, once HS-03's activation point was destroyed, either by bullet or blunt trauma, it lost its hold over the corpse. As soon as he'd drilled into this particular head, the subject had gone still. He wondered if the virus survived beyond the host shutting down. He wanted to chart its growth and development, to see if it could be limited somehow; if he could stunt its spread, perhaps he could curtail the cadavers' carnivorous instincts.

Gannon slid a sliver of brain matter under the microscope and was adjusting the magnification when he heard the dull popping of a gun being fired somewhere further down the facility's corridor. He looked up instantly, cocking an ear and wondering if he could have imagined it. His query was answered straight away; it came again in a short burst, this time followed by shouting that was growing louder as if the cries were coming closer. A moment's silence, then the alarm sounded, a strident wail that got him moving.

He strode out of his lab and into the corridor, white coat twisting in his wake, only to confront a scene from a nightmare. A security guard was edging backwards, a pistol gripped in both hands, attention fixed on the figure stumbling towards him. It took a Gannon a second to realise that it was Jenny Cranfield. The lower half of her face was coated in blood, and her hands, even the bandaged one, were crimson, as if she'd dipped them in a pot of paint. She stumbled stiff-legged, barely aware of her surroundings, and it wasn't until his eyes travelled to the floor that he saw the two bodies lying motionless just behind her, their throats torn open. It was Horton, and his assistant, Petley. They looked like they'd been savaged by an animal.

"What the fuck's up with her?" the guard said as he came level with Gannon, gun still held out in front of him.

"What happened?"

"Heard screams coming from one of the labs down there. She was fucking ripping into them, eating their throats out. I thought it was a practical joke at first. I mean, I know what you guys have got down here, what with the fucking dead boys and all. Thought it was just a load of fake blood and a bunch of bored docs trying to wind me up. But there's something up with her eyes, I saw it as soon as she turned round, and she went for me as soon as she knew I was there. I saw too that the guys were properly goners, there was no mistaking that."

"I heard shooting."

"I had no choice. I gave her a warning, said I was licensed to protect the facility, but she kept coming. I put a couple of rounds in her shoulder to push her back, and when that didn't stop her I aimed for her chest. She should've gone down, but it was like she barely even noticed. Is she fucking high on something?"

Gannon now saw the red holes on Jenny's lab coat and blouse where she'd taken the hits; the blood had bloomed in flowery explosions on the white material. But she seemed unconcerned by the injuries, continuing her advance. He shook his head in disbelief, not wanting to admit to what he was seeing. She'd been infected, it was the only explanation. The bite she'd received on the hand must've passed on the virus – did it travel in the saliva? – and effectively killed her, then brought her back with the same characteristics as the test subjects.

My God, he thought, if it can spread like this, we have to contain it.

"Jenny," he called out over the blare of the alarm,

hoping that some vestige of her intelligence still remained. "Jenny, can you understand me? It's Robert."

She gave no indication that she could even hear him, her blind eyes sweeping the corridor as she stumbled forward. They were running out of space to back into.

"Aim for the head," Gannon murmured.

"What?"

"Shoot her in the head," he hissed. "It's the only way to stop her."

Just at that moment, the lift doors opened and a security team poured out, alerted by the triggered alarm. They jogged towards the scene of carnage, semi-automatics held down by their sides, and paused beside the two bodies. Their arrival caused Jenny to halt and half-turn, sensing their presence. The team leader seemed unsure of who he should be directing his warnings at, but once he caught sight of the ragged, gore-flecked woman, he raised his gun.

"Don't make another move," he shouted.

"You have to shoot her in the head," Gannon yelled. "She's infected. There's nothing else you can do to stop her. Kill her." Then, as an afterthought: "She's already dead anyway."

"What the hell are you talking about?" the squad leader replied, not taking his eyes off Jenny, who staggered vaguely in his direction.

"She's infected with a virus that she'll pass on to you if you allow her to get close. She'll kill you, believe me."

"Doctor Cranfield," the other man said, directing his attention to the swaying figure, "I'm not taking any chances. Do not move. We'll try to help you. But don't come any nearer."

Jenny paid the words no heed. She moaned quietly, and continued to totter forward.

"Damn it, this is your last chance," he started, when a hand shot out and fastened on his ankle. He yelped, looking down to see one of the bodies – one of the scientists with the gouged throats, who couldn't possibly be still alive – pulling himself forward and taking a bite out of his right calf, tearing a thick chunk of flesh from his leg, stringy sections of muscle trailing from the wound. He screamed and overbalanced, his finger tightening on his semi-automatic's trigger; bullets blasted through the windows of a nearby lab and exploded the vials and test tubes inside. He hit the floor to find his attacker crawling over him, hands tearing at his uniform. His colleagues instantly rushed to his aid, four of them pulling at the scientist, unaware that the other corpse was getting to his feet behind them.

The thing that used to be Horton grabbed one of the guards by the head so hard a finger pierced an eye socket and wrenched it backwards, simultaneously taking a mouthful from his shoulder. The others turned, shocked, momentarily slackening their grip on the figure assaulting their superior; it was enough for the scientist to wriggle free and chew a lip free from his victim's face. The team leader had his gun trapped under him, but brought it up enough to fire several shots into the man's belly. He didn't even flinch.

By this point, Jenny had reached the fray. One of the security guards spotted her and brought his weapon to bear, shooting her in the torso half a dozen times.

"In the fucking *head*," Gannon bellowed.

The guard raised his aim and fired, the back of Jenny's skull exploding in a vermilion shower, shattering one of the lab windows behind her. She dropped to her knees, then collapsed sideways.

"Give me your gun," Gannon instructed to the man

standing beside him, who – stunned – passed it to him without question. The doctor ran toward the melee. Another of the team was wrestling with Horton, fending him off as he snapped his teeth ravenously, while Petley was being lifted to give the gunman enough room to take a shot. Gannon didn't hesitate: he placed the barrel against the side of Horton's head and fired, brain matter painting the wall and sprinkling the guard's face. Then he turned and helped them pull Petley away from his meal, just enough to stick a gun in his mouth and empty his skull. Gannon felt a slick, warm mass wash against his skin as the corpse slid to the floor.

He sagged against the wall. For a moment, all he heard was the wailing of the alarm offset by the choked groans of the injured, and when he put a hand to his forehead it came away wet and bloody. Shakily, he got to his feet and strode over to a telephone mounted near the lifts, grabbing the receiver that connected the labs with the front desk.

"This is Doctor Gannon. We have an emergency – quarantine restrictions are to be put in place immediately. Nobody goes anywhere without my say-so. Inform the ministry we need clean-up and medical staff here *right now*."

He gazed back at the carnage, hoping that they could do enough to lock it down. But in truth, unbeknownst to the doctor, the end of the world had already begun.

CHAPTER TWELVE

The gun felt cold and heavy in his hands. Gabe stared at the semi-automatic laid across his upturned palms, its dark surface slick and glinting dully, his fingers curling around the butt and trigger guard. He hadn't handled one since his days in the army, promised himself he never would again. He looked up at Flowers questioningly, the older man standing before him, his face a blank mask of rage. They were in the mansion's hallway, a large contingent of Flowers' workforce massing like an army preparing for war. They were slotting revolvers into their waistbands, or concealing pump-action shotguns beneath long heavy coats.

"Harry... I can't..."

"No excuses. Since you're responsible for the situation, you're going to help resolve it; and everyone's going in armed. If you're unfamiliar with the weapon, then I suggest you learn pretty damn quick. We're moving out now."

"Harry," Gabe replied, trying to keep his voice level, "you've always kept me removed from the blunt end of your business dealings, and I've appreciated that. I got the impression you felt that there was no need to involve me; if nothing else for the reason that you knew how unhelpful I'd be. I was employed as a driver, and that's as far as my responsibilities went"

Flowers stepped closer until they were merely inches apart. "Everyone is going in armed," he spat in a slow, menacing monotone. "And you want to talk about responsibility? I employed you to follow my orders, to take me where I directed, to keep your mouth shut and know your place. Do what I ask and we'll get along famously, isn't that what I told you when you first joined? A fairly simple code to live by, I would've thought. But evidently it wasn't enough for you – you felt you also had the right to go behind my back and meddle in matters that didn't concern you. Putting my daughter's life in danger also fell into your responsibilities, did it?"

"Of course I never meant—"

"Answer the question."

Gabe gripped the gun tighter. "No. I know I was not employed to look after Anna."

Flowers lunged forward, grabbing the younger man by his jacket lapels and slamming him against the wall. The small knot of enforcers standing behind Harry visibly flinched, taken aback by the speed of the attack. "Don't you *dare* say her fucking name," Flowers roared. "Not after what you've done. She was safe there, none of my enemies knew where she was. But once you started making your little journeys, anyone keeping the mansion under observation and following you could deduce that someone important was living in that flat. Your idiocy could see my child murdered, and you talk of looking *after* her?"

"I'm sorry, I didn't think. But I believed she needed help, someone to talk to."

"She had *me*. She had her *father*." Flowers pushed Gabe back further, his balled fists pressing against the younger man's chest, just below his throat. "You pompous little shit, who the fuck do you think you are? What, you see yourself as some white knight riding in to save her? All you've done is delivered her to the very people that could do her the most harm. And in the same breath as talking about coming to her aid, you're trying to weasel out of getting her back. If it's anyone's responsibility that she's returned here safely, it's yours, so don't tell me you don't want to get involved. Your actions made sure you were involved whether you like it or not."

Gabe couldn't argue with this. He desperately wanted to save Anna from whatever trouble she may be in, and with each passing moment – Flowers hissing bile in his face, pushing him harder into the wall – he felt his resolve strengthening and a determination flourishing, and he was damned if he was going to be painted as the sole villain.

"You know what, Harry?" he said. "You're right. I have a duty to help get her back. But I want to make this clear: I'm doing this for *her*, as a friend. This has nothing to do with helping you in your hostile activities. Because, let's be truthful about this – it's because of *you* that she was taken. She's merely a weak link to get to you, a pawn in your empire building. You see everyone around you as a viable commodity, and now they have something of yours to barter with. So slap me around and shout in my face all you like, but let's not forget it's your business that's put Anna in this position."

Flowers face crumpled into a slack glare of hatred as if the tension that had been restraining him was released for a moment, and he swung a fist back. Gabe used the sudden relaxation of his grip to bring his arms up and knock the old man's other hand away, dodging the punch that whistled past his jaw and cracked the plaster behind him. He hefted the gun and placed the barrel between Harry's eyes, aware that other weapons were instantly being raised in his direction.

"I'm not gonna take your bullshit, boss," he murmured as Flowers lifted his gaze to the semi-automatic resting against his forehead, a fleeting glimmer of worry replaced by a sardonic smile.

"You've got some balls, I'll give you that much,

O'Connell," he said, taking a step back and swatting the gun to one side. "But if you want to take a shot, you need to flick the safety off first. Remember that for next time."

They moved out ten minutes later: four long, sleek cars moving swiftly in the early hours of the morning. Ironically, given his job within the outfit, Gabe was not asked to drive. Instead, he was seated in the back of the second vehicle, sandwiched between five triggermen. Harry rode in the lead car, but whether he was deliberately keeping his distance and felt threatened being in Gabe's proximity, the younger man couldn't tell.

His employer had treated being held at gunpoint as little more than a gag, an admirable display of verve, and had been disarmingly flippant about what had happened. Perhaps the fury he'd displayed had been purposely intended to invite that reaction and show what Gabe was made of? Or possibly Flowers never believed that his driver had the guts to pull the trigger in the end.Either way, Gabe felt he should be counting his blessings that he hadn't had his legs broken for that little stunt. Thinking back, it seemed like he'd lost all sense of rationality – the idea of pointing a loaded gun (or at least he assumed it was loaded; what if Flowers wanted his revenge by sending him in with an empty hand cannon?) to someone's head would've been alien to him merely a few days ago. But something was altering inside him, a growing vigour, that he put down to the considerable influence of those that he worked with. He felt an increasing need to prove himself and the belief that change could be wrought through a greater strength. That show of muscle – these four cars of tooled-up gunmen, bent on intimidation – was what was going to get Anna back, not negotiation or compromise.

He glanced at his neighbours. He wanted to feel part of this payback, that he wasn't just along for the ride. He caught Hendricks' eye. "These enemies of Harry's – who are they?"

"Crew that have been moving in from north London over the past couple of decades. Started out in Willesden, Kilburn, and been slowly making their way south. Been putting the frighteners on landlords and club owners, chancing their arm at protection rackets, and running the local pimps out of town. They got their fingers in the trafficking business – drugs and girls – and have undercut all the dealers with cheap shit. They're from Eastern Europe originally, I think, and are importing sixteen year olds from Slovakia, their colons stuffed with smack."

"And now they've reached Harry's territory?"

"Their head guy – Vassily – is an old rival of Harry's. One of his contemporaries. His mob has tried to broker with Harry, tried to persuade him to share. 'Course, Harry wasn't having any of it. He told them to piss off back to the arse-end of the Balkans before he put a boot under them. They didn't, and have been trying to chip away at his set-up ever since."

"I'm surprised Flowers hasn't taken this step before," Gabe said, motioning to the other men on either side of them.

"He has, or at least he's issued ultimatums. But the thing is, war is bad for the status quo. It just brings the heat down on you, and exposes business dealings to the authorities that you'd rather were kept out of sight. Actual engagement with the enemy is the last resort. But they've got less to lose than us, and they know it. They're still operating on the fringes of the underworld and are difficult to pin down, while Harry's got a reputation to consider. They're scavengers, provoking organisations into outright conflict and then stealing what crumbs they can in the aftermath."

The vehicles headed into the outskirts of the city, the roads virtually deserted at this hour apart from haulage lorries and coaches, and cleaning trucks scouring the gutters. The pavements too were empty of pedestrians save those that had made shop doorways their home. The night had the strange luminous quality that comes before the onset of dawn, a grey misty taint to the darkness that was beaded by the sodium smears of the street lights. None of the men in the car seemed tired, despite the hour. It was as if they had been preparing for this moment, and were ready to go to war as soon as the order was given.

"So where are we going to find them?" Gabe asked.

"Little bird on the Met has told us that a club in Ladbroke Grove is their HQ. Far as we know, they're unaware we've got this information."

"You think that's where they've taken Anna?"

Hendricks studied him for a second. "It's the only place we know where they could've gone," he replied finally. "They don't want her particularly, they just want to use her as a bargaining chip to get Harry to start cutting them a slice of his manor's action. So far Harry hasn't shown a weakness that they've been able to exploit, but tonight they're holding a trump card. Our only hope is that they don't expect him to come to them like this, mob-handed. They're banking on him seeking to appease them, not matching them strength for strength. It's a risky strategy, of course – Anna's life is at stake." He paused, then said: "You've really put him in a delicate situation."

Gabe nodded slowly. "I know."

Hendricks turned to face him. "This relationship with his daughter, it compromises an awful lot. We're going to have be very careful going in. What did you think you were doing?"

"She was a mystery, a face at the window. She looked like she needed a friend. I felt like I wouldn't be able to relax until I spoke to her, until I... solved the mystery." Gabe smiled ruefully. "I think I underestimated even that. She wasn't going to open up that easily."

"But was it worth it? You've incurred Harry's wrath, put his kid in the hands of the enemy, potentially undermined his power base if tonight doesn't go his way. If she gets hurt, it's going to get even worse, and I wouldn't want to be in your shoes. All this 'cause you couldn't leave things alone."

"If I knew that I was putting her in danger, then of course I would've stayed away. I'm not so selfish that I would purposely put her in the firing line. I thought I was giving her company. I never imagined that it would have consequences of this magnitude."

"Well, that's all it takes, son," Hendricks answered, peering out through the glass at the empty London streets. "One act and the repercussions ripple outwards. Everyone gets caught in them." The car started to slow, pulling in to the kerb. "Looks like we're here."

It came to a halt behind the lead vehicle, out of which Flowers' men were already unfolding themselves, the old man included. They stood on the pavement, casting glances up and down the road, pulling their coats around them, before fixing their attention on the building opposite. Gabe alighted from his own car and followed their gaze: it was an innocuous frontage to a club, little more than a narrow doorway squeezed between a motorbike dealership and a snooker hall. There was no name announcing itself above the entrance.

Harry nodded at his men, then motioned for them to follow. They strode across the street as one body, as if part of the darkness had suddenly come alive and was sweeping towards a specific destination. Flowers reached the threshold and a bouncer – shaven headed, bulky, biker's beard – emerged from the shadows just inside, blocking the passage. The thud of music could be heard drifting up from some cavernous place below them.

"Help you, gents?" he said.

"Here to see Goran," Harry replied, already trying to move past. "I imagine he's expecting us."

The doorman took a cursory look at the fifteen-strong gathering stood before the club and shook his head. "I don't think so." There was a slight accent to his voice that meant each word was clipped.

"Oh, you don't think so?" Harry asked and pulled his snubnose from his belt with one movement, then shot him in the kneecap. The bouncer went down like a felled tree, the crack of the gun muffled by the noise emanating from inside. When the guy started to yell – a mixture of pain and a call for help, Gabe guessed – the old man struck him against the bridge of the nose with the flat of the revolver. He went quiet then. "Don't see much point in being subtle about this," Flowers murmured, then added: "Gandry, Miller – stay on the door. No one gets past you, understand? Oh, and disable the alarm system, phone line and the CCTV cameras."

The two men nodded. Flowers beckoned for the rest to come with him into the bowels of the building. They walked down a short corridor, the music growing louder, past a ticket booth, the woman inside watching them nervously, slipping off her stool and backing away when Hendricks halted and rested his gun barrel against the grille. He raised his eyebrows and instructed her to lace her hands above her head and not to move a muscle. There were four more security personnel loitering in this area who jumped to their feet the moment that Harry strode into view, and who hit the ground just as quickly when he put a bullet through each of their thighs. They mutely rolled on their backs, their groans swallowed by the thumping bass.

"Stick them in there with her," Harry said to another three of his men, motioning to the booth, "and keep an eye on them. Any trouble, start working your way through their limbs." He turned to the rest. "I want this place locked down. We're in charge now – any nosy bastard starts poking around, asking questions or wants to leave, make an example of him. The last thing I want is a 999 call going out. From now until the moment we leave, this building is under *our* control. Once we get to the dancefloor level," he swept a hand towards the steep stairs that disappeared into a swirl of magenta and emerald lights, flickering to the pulse of the music, "you're going to spread yourselves amongst the crowd and contain it. The bouncers are going to notice you, but make your weapons known to them. If you can, take them out of commission altogether. From what I understand, Vassily's office is on the other side, next to the DJ booth. I'll be heading over there, and I want to make sure there's not going to be a riot getting in my way. OK?" His question was answered with silent confirmation. "OK. Let's go."

The remaining ten, with Harry at the head, picked their way down the steps and into the club proper. It was a horseshoe-shaped room, ringed by a bar on a raised area around which stood tables and stools. In the centre was the dancefloor itself. It was a dark mass of moving bodies. The roving lights would occasionally capture a face or an arm held aloft, but then they would be gone again, reduced to silhouette. There were more figures standing around the rim watching and drinking, but none seemed to have paid the new arrivals any heed. Flowers nodded and made a casual gesture with his hand, motioning left and right, and portions of the group peeled off, zeroing in on the bulky shadows that were undoubtedly the security staff, wordlessly encircling the space. The old man beckoned for Gabe to come with him and they pushed their way into the crowd, gathering glances from quizzical clubbers, who parted without question for the two men who weaved their way through them, seemingly oblivious to the music. Something about their demeanour told the dancers not to get in their way.

To the right of the stage that the pounding sound system was built upon was a door marked AUTHORISED PERSONNEL ONLY and Flowers headed towards it, looking back only once over his shoulder to confirm that Gabe was still behind him, and that the gyrating mob was concealing their progress. He put a shoulder to the door and shoved his way in, Gabe following closely in his wake.

After the darkness of the dancefloor, the fluorescent-bathed corridor on the other side caused them to squint momentarily, and the noise level reduced instantly to a low-level throb. To the left and a few feet ahead was a large open section, containing a desk, computer and several filing cabinets. A man was leaning against a worktop with his back to them, writing hurriedly on a document.

"You get those orders sorted?" he called, without looking around.

When there was no response, he cocked an eye over

his shoulder, frowned, then his eyes widened when Harry walked towards him, gun pointed at the man's face. He turned fully, dropping the pen.

"Where is she?" Flowers growled.

"Who the fuck are you?" the man spat, bravado failing to disguise his fear. "What are you talking about?"

"Unwise," Flowers said, and smacked him once in the temple with the revolver handle. The man gasped and staggered, blood trickling down his forehead from a gash. "Stall me again and I'll put a bullet through your eye. Last time: where is she?"

The man locked stares with Harry, red drips coursing off his eyebrow. "Goran's got her... in the back." He nodded behind him.

"I hope for your sake no one's touched her."

"She's still in one piece. Just about." He smiled. "For how long, though, I couldn't say. Once Goran finds Papa's here he might reach the limit of his benevolence."

"If he knows anything about me, then he'd have to be insane. Or suicidal."

"Funny. Your daughter said something similar about you—"

The man jerked as Flowers fired a bullet into his skull, collapsing into a heap at the old man's feet. Gabe jumped, the roar of the gun blast resonating in the spacious office. Harry didn't even pause, merely strode further down the corridor. The building this far back looked skeletal, as if it had been left half finished; exposed beams and wiring ran across the ceiling, and the bare floor and walls were plain concrete. There was little need to be surreptitious – Harry had all but announced himself, and a pair of Vashsily's goons stepped forward ahead of their boss, who lingered beside a sofa. Anna was seated upon it, seemingly unharmed, her wrists and ankles unbound. She didn't appear scared, more resigned, as if this situation was inevitable.

"Nice place you've got here, Goran," Flowers said. "Love what you've done with it."

"You know I've never indulged in ostentation like you, Harry," Vassily replied. He was of a similar age to Flowers, and cut from the same cloth: a weathered exterior that bore the weight of a lifetime's experience.

"That why you're so keen to get your hands on what I've got? Envious?"

"I don't want everything, Harry. I just think a little competition could excite our profits a tad. We've known each other for so long, we've tolerated each other for decades now, we're in danger of growing stagnant and complacent. It never hurts to give the natural process of things a shove."

"So kidnapping's progress, is it?"

Vassily smiled. "Ah, you're just pissed you didn't get there first. Unfortunately for you, my son is abroad."

"I'd say that *he* was the fortunate one. This way, he doesn't get to see me execute his old man."

Vassily's triggermen bristled, their guns raised, and Gabe felt his grip tightening around his semi-automatic. His gaze kept returning to Anna, but she – deliberately, he thought – studiously avoided making eye contact. He turned his attention instead to the exchange between the two bosses, trying to remain sensitive to the shifting levels of tension.

"Don't take it so personally, Harry," Vassily was saying. "It's all about gaining the advantage in this business, is it not? You have my word that not a hair on her pretty head has been harmed, and if we're all amicable, there's no reason why we won't all come away with what we want."

"You think I'm here to negotiate?"

"I don't see how you're in a position not to."

"Because there's over a dozen of my men stationed around your club right now, and all it takes is one word from me and they'll burn it and everyone inside to the fucking ground."

"You're not that ruthless. You were never one for collateral damage."

"Let's just say you've caught me in a particularly bad mood."

Vassily paused, looking first at Flowers, then at Anna and back again. "You'd commit mass murder for her sake? You'd kill innocent people rather than lose an inch of territory?"

"I'd slaughter you all because you involved my daughter. My terms are simple: return her now, and maybe I'll be lenient."

"Quite the family man these days, aren't you, Harry? It must've been hard losing your wife. What was it – an accidental overdose? Or at least, that was the official line." Gabe caught the sudden glance Anna gave her father. "I can imagine that must've strengthened the bond between you and your little girl."

"Goran, you're about five seconds away from meeting your maker," Flowers replied, anger flooding his voice, "so I suggest you shut the fuck up and tell your boys to lower their cannons."

Vassily continued speaking as if he hadn't heard. "Which makes what you did to her," he nodded at Flowers' daughter, "so particularly... callous."

Anna stood suddenly, glaring questioningly at her father, who glanced at her for the first time since they'd arrived. Vassily's two enforcers shifted their position, unsure at this development, keeping an eye on both of them. Gabe's thumb found the safety catch and eased it slowly off.

"Don't listen to him," Flowers said dismissively.

"What are you talking about?" Anna demanded of her captor.

"Oh, I'm sure it's just rumour and innuendo, my dear," Vassily said with mock modesty. "One of those stories you hear on the grapevine that knocks you back and makes you realise whether you really know a person."

"Goran—" Flowers snarled.

Anna: "Tell me."

Vassily faced her. "Your own child, Anna. The baby boy you gave birth to. Harry convinced you to put him up for adoption; took advantage of your fragile state as you suffered a particularly nasty period of post-natal depression. He claimed he didn't like the crew the father ran with, thought it would compromise his position. And while this may have certainly been the case – the guy was dropped off a flyover eight months later – the truth is that he always feared having an heir, a grandson that could prove a threat to him. That could undermine his power. So he took... pre-emptive action."

Gabe followed this exchange feeling like an eavesdropper on a family argument. He watched Anna's face intently. This was clearly news to her, and something suggested her world was about to be swept out from under her feet. Tears were welling in her eyes.

"He took your son, Anna," Vassily continued, "and he murdered him. Smothered him in his own blanket. Even if he put him up for adoption, there was always the fear that he would come to discover his heritage, and seek to claim it. This way, he could sleep easy."

Anna turned to Flowers, her cheeks glistening. "*Why? How could you do this?*"

"Anna, please..."

"You're not denying it, are you?"

Flowers looked more vulnerable than Gabe had ever seen him. "Sweetheart, I've tortured myself every day and night since, and I'll go to hell for it. Sleep easy? I will never, ever forgive myself for what I did, and I've tried to make it up to you. But there are no excuses."

"I don't understand how you could be so heartless," Anna sobbed. "Why did you do it?"

"Your child... was a weak link I couldn't control." Harry sniffed back his own tears. "I was wrong, I know. I should've embraced the life he brought, I should've let it steer me. But then... change was bad. I couldn't accept it."

"And there was me thinking you weren't open to negotiation," Vassily snickered.

Flowers glared at the other man, fury burning in his red-rimmed eyes. "You fucker." He raised his gun, but in that instant Vassily pulled Anna close and tugged free a revolver of his own from beneath his jacket, holding it to her waist.

"I don't think so, Harry," he said. "I realise this has all been very traumatic for the pair of you, but there's still a few more truths to be hammered home. It's time you recognised that you're in no position to refuse me anything. It's time we ought to discuss how we divide your empire."

"Never."

"I'm sorry, there was me believing you had a choice in the matter." He nudged the barrel harder into her body, though Anna looked as if she barely noticed it. She stared at her feet, numb with shock. Gabe licked his dry lips, eyes flicking between each of the people in the sparse room, head buzzing with adrenaline. "You've already destroyed whatever relationship you had with your daughter, don't go one step further and have her blood on your hands too."

"I won't give you anything." His gun remained where it was, unwavering.

Vassily shook his head. "What makes you think you've got the strength to deny me?"

Flowers didn't reply. A second later he fired, the bullet slamming into Anna's chest, knocking her to one side. Vassily was momentarily stunned as he looked down to see the hole in his midriff where the slug had passed through his hostage and penetrated him. Flowers fired again, pumping a further four rounds into the man's midriff. Vassily's goons returned fire, blasting Harry in the arm and stomach, dropping him to the ground.

"Harry!" Gabe shouted, swinging his own weapon to bear and pulling the trigger. The recoil punched hard into his hand, and his first shots went wild, but he was standing at close enough distance to lower his angle and the two men took hits in the cheek and neck. They went down, spritzing blood.

He hurried across to Anna and felt her pulse; it was there but weak. He turned to see Flowers crawling across towards them, painting a wide crimson streak in his wake.

"Harry, she needs an ambulance urgently. I don't know if she's going to make it."

"No," he whispered. "She comes back with us... back to the house... get the boys down here."

Gabe didn't move. "She could die. You might have killed your daughter."

Flowers rolled onto his back. "Had to show... no weaknesses." He coughed. "Tell the boys... light the fuses. We burn this place down...." He closed his eyes.

"Harry?"

"Bring it all down," he murmured, then lost consciousness.

CHAPTER THIRTEEN

It spread with frightening speed. Despite Gannon's successful attempts at getting the facility immediately locked down and ordering in MoD medics garbed in full hazard suits, he hadn't reckoned on HS-03's microbes travelling in the air. All previous experiments with the virus had seen it carried within a liquid, whether it be the serum in which it was injected into the test subjects, its transportation through the blood supply, or – so he theorised – passed from carrier to victim via the saliva, which entered the circulatory system from the bite wound. He had believed that contagion would require full-body contact, and some degree of penetration, similar to HIV, and as such any threat to the general public could be limited. If they isolated the dead and those that had received injuries, then there was no chance of it going beyond the compound. But he had underestimated the tenacity of the virus. Once the security guard's bullets had ripped through the lab, test tubes and containment vessels were shattered, and the bacteria escaped into the ventilation shafts, blown beyond the research centre's walls in a matter of seconds. Although he would not learn of the breach for several hours, there was little Gannon could've done to stop it, and indeed the facility was permeated with HS-03 by the time he came off the phone to the emergency services.

It had no effect on the living, and there was nothing in the air to suggest its presence. As far as he and his team were concerned, the damaged samples merely represented a loss of six months' work, and he assumed that the virus expired the moment its solution came apart. He directed those that hadn't been evacuated to the upper levels to wear breathing apparatus as a precautionary measure, just in case there was the risk of any chemical vapours from the wrecked lab, but in reality the virus had been passing through their lungs long before they donned their gas masks.

Gannon wanted to keep the resurrected that still remained for further study, but his colleagues – naturally upset at what had happened to Jenny Cranfield, Horton and Petley – pressured him into destroying them before there were any more casualties. They were obviously too dangerous to be moved elsewhere. Reluctantly, he went from subject to subject – there was just over ten of them left now – and slid a scalpel into the base of their skulls. They went immediately limp as all brain activity abruptly ceased.

He was sad to see so much research and experimentation being brought to a close with such finality, although a cruel, clinical part of his mind reminded him that a handful of walking dead were already brewing in the shape of the guards who had received bites in the melee. They were currently lying on gurneys out in the corridor, their injuries being treated as best they could in the circumstances. Gannon had refused requests from the medics to airlift them out of the compound to somewhere where they could receive better care, stating quietly – well out of earshot of the patients – that they were highly infectious. He didn't mention the fact that they were as good as dead, and when he instructed that their legs and arms were to be strapped he claimed that previous victims had been prone to seizure and psychotic episodes.

Exhausted, Gannon found a chair and gave himself five minutes rest. The events of the past couple of hours had passed with the inexorable unravelling of a nightmare, unstoppable and unreal – everything had leapt out of control so quickly, it now seemed absurd that he'd proudly shown Sedgworth these very labs only a few days before, confident that the HS-03 project could work. The Minister was no doubt aware of the failure that had resulted in three scientists' deaths (technically, Gannon supposed, at *his* hand) and an inquiry was going to be instigated. It wouldn't be public, of course, and the families of the deceased would be rigorously compensated to buy their silence, but there was no question that Gannon was for the high jump. Sedgworth himself could lose his position, and he wouldn't fall without taking a few with him.

The scientist closed his eyes wearily, but in his head he was faced with the bloodied vision of Jenny Cranfield staggering towards him, stiff and jerky, seeking him out through his warmth. Moments before she had been a living woman – intelligent, good-natured, conscientious – and because of what he had created she had been transformed into this creature, a horrible shadow of what she'd been in life. That was what was so painful – that she was still recognisably Jenny, someone he'd conversed with on a daily basis, but she no longer held any memories or traits that made her human. All this thing that had assumed her form wanted to do was kill and feed. It had subsumed all her civility and dignity, and made her in death something less than an animal. And *he* was responsible.

Cries from the injured forced him to open his eyes, and he stood, arching his back before heading towards them. He wondered if he would ever be able to come to terms with the consequences of what he had let loose here. The one crumb of comfort he clutched at was that at least HS-03 hadn't escaped into the wider world – the death toll could've been much, much higher.

As with any outbreak, the reports were scattered at first, small snapshots of terror and chaos that began to connect across the country with rapid speed.

A congregation gathered for a funeral service in Banbury were stunned into silence when loud thumps began to emerge from the casket; thinking impossibly that the person inside could somehow still be alive – an eighty-five-year-old grandfather, who'd died of pneumonia – half a dozen of the mourners had wrenched free the coffin lid, only to be confronted by a frenzied apparition that immediately sat up and tore his nephew's windpipe out with his hands.

In Wiltshire, four boys that had snuck into woodland near their homes with a copy of *Penthouse* purloined from one of the quartet's older brothers stood in fear as a groaning figure stumbled towards them, the needle from the heroin injection that had killed him still hanging from the crook of his arm. They had dropped the magazine and fled, their story dismissed as high spirits, until the first of the news items came on TV that evening.

On the Dorset coast, the crew of a fishing trawler lost at sea emerged from the water and shambled up the beach, blue and bloated from the days they'd spent drifting with the tide, and attacked anyone that approached them. Eight were consumed within an hour.

A surgeon fell into the corridor in a London hospital, his nose and half his lower jaw missing, when the body he was conducting an autopsy on had suddenly grabbed him. Moments after his appearance, the corpse itself had followed him out, still chewing on what it had ripped off. Those that had witnessed this later told authorities that they could hear rattling coming from the drawers in the mortuary.

And so it went, the violence spiralling with every passing minute. HS-03 seemed to be flexing its muscles too, growing stronger as it weaved its way amongst the populace. Those that received a bite but managed to flee from the ghouls took less than twelve hours to succumb to the fatal symptoms, resurrecting a scant fifteen minutes later. It was just enough time for the victims to seek solace with loved ones or descend upon a casualty ward before they themselves wreaked bloody havoc, doubling, tripling, the infection rate. Even those that had been partially devoured were on their feet eventually – or at least what remained of them. The dead evidently grew tired of their meals once they went cold, and would stumble off in search of something warmer.

The police were stretched thin from the outset. What started as vague bulletins of national unrest became a situation that was impossible to contain. Even when the army was drafted in, even when direct orders were issued to shoot all hostiles on sight (it didn't take them long to recognise that a bullet in the brain stopped the corpses instantly), the cops and the soldiers were unused to being asked to fire on unarmed women and children, and often made the mistake of trying to reason with the creatures. Despite repeated assurances that these things were no longer human, many believed that they could try to awaken latent memories of the dead's past life and corral them by non-lethal means. It didn't work. The ghouls would not be halted by words alone. They were implacable, remorseless, utterly mindless, and it was averaged later that the military lost a man every five minutes to an overwhelming enemy that was completely alien to notions of humanity and compassion.

Panic gripped the public as virulently as the infection itself. Roads were jammed with refugees fleeing the cities, the rail network and other services ground to a standstill as employees deserted their posts, and flights out of the country were cancelled when overseas airports started refusing to accept UK arrivals. Every nation around the globe closed down its borders, walling themselves in, cutting themselves off from their neighbours. It was rumoured that HS-03 snuck abroad despite these precautions, that – whether the bacteria survived being blown across the Channel or an infected traveller slipped through the net – it was rampaging across the Continent equally as fast; as far east as Russia, some said. By then it made little difference since the United Kingdom was losing all contact with former allies, even after the UN's appeal for aid. All the member states were frightened of the virus spreading, and as a consequence left the UK to fend for itself. For the citizens themselves, there was nowhere for them to go, no matter how far they ran.

Order broke down simultaneously. Although some banded together in anti-Returner squads – a priest had first coined the term in a TV interview, presumably as a non-pejorative, non-superstitious name for the phenomenon, and it stuck – to aid the authorities, many took the ensuing anarchy as a carte blanche to indulge in acts of criminality. Looting was rife, murder and rape commonplace; some seemed to have forgotten the dead were there at all. As lawlessness took hold, the streets became no-go areas, and survivors locked themselves away in shelters and communes, waiting for the news that it was safe to emerge.

In the meantime, the inheritors of this new land wandered their territory, driven by an insatiable hunger.

Flowers' car sped away from the conflagration, the burning club lighting up the encroaching dawn. His men had given enough warning, Gabe hoped, for all those inside to have escaped before they snapped open the gas pipes and left the burning rags to set it off. Whether any of Vassily's enforcers made it was another question; he didn't see any amongst the frantic crowd that poured through the front doors. He expected that Harry didn't want word getting back as to who was responsible for the blaze.

The old man was drifting in and out of consciousness, sometimes lucid – thanking Gabe for his assistance – sometimes mumbling nonsensically under his breath. He had refused to be taken to hospital, stating that the mansion had adequate medical facilities to care for both him and Anna.

They were in danger of losing her, Gabe knew, as he constantly checked her pulse. Her skin was cold, and her heartbeat had slowed dramatically. She was so still and quiet he kept thinking that she had slipped away, but occasionally her eyelids would flutter open to fix him with a curious gaze before closing again. Something was keeping her hovering on the brink of death, fixed in a half-life stasis. He made a silent assurance to her that he wouldn't leave her side.

He had contemplated overruling Flowers' demands and getting her to a doctor, but as they sped out of the city it became clear that they shouldn't hang around. The radio was full of weird reports of some kind of mass disturbance, and that hospitals all over the country were being deluged with victims of those running riot. Ambulances and other emergency vehicles rocketed past, sirens blaring.

Gabe didn't know what was going on, but they had

worries of their own to take care of. He watched the sun rise over the London skyline as they left it behind, wondering what the new day was going to bring.

PART THREE

Living With the Dead

My God! My God! Look not so fierce on me!

Christopher Marlowe,
Dr Faustus

PART THREE

Living with the Land

Fifteen Years Later

CHAPTER FOURTEEN

Mitch and Donna were taking a chance, moving in daylight, but the group was fast running out of alternatives. With the local food supply drying up, they were having to look further afield for rations, but straying onto rival gangs' territory brought its own dangers. They had lost half a dozen of their number to other humans protecting their stashes – Michael, the ex-teacher, had been the last casualty, shot through the neck with some kind of bladed projectile just over a month ago – and the zombs too were increasing their patrols, making a concerted sweep of all known haunts of the living. The general consensus amongst the survivors was that the larders of the dead were empty too, and they were processing fresh meat in greater quantities. This overriding feeling of desperation between both parties made the streets the last place anyone in their right mind would want to be.

But Mitch knew they had little choice. Liz and the others could barely stand so ferocious was their hunger. Their physical weakness, the lack of protein and vitamins, had made them susceptible to infection, and with no easy access to clean water they had had to sup from whatever rainwater they could collect in drainage pipes. Sickness was rife, unsurprisingly, and the rudimentary medicines they had stored were not enough to treat it. Mitch himself was not immune to illness. He was quick to lose his breath, and the dizzy spells and headaches that descended with a frightening force suggested that his blood was becoming perilously thin, but he had disguised his ailments sufficiently to convince his colleagues that he was fit enough to make this trip. They had looked sceptical, but he knew secretly that they had been praying someone would volunteer, too embarrassed to voice their selfish needs above others' suffering.

He had been aware of the risks well enough, and had to bury his own fears, lest the group fretted that he was not up to the task. He wanted to prove that they could rely on him, Donna especially. He wanted her to accept him as a useful part of the enclave, that he had a role to play, and wasn't merely another frightened survivor tagging along with whatever set of humans he could find and leeching off their supplies. Others had done that, over the years, with little sign of gratitude, then sloping off if they sniffed out a bigger trough to stick their snouts in. Liz meanwhile had been instrumental in bringing their band of survivors together, or at least reinforcing their need to look after one another. She maintained that it was those that separated from the main body of the group that were likely to fall victim to the Returners. They were like lions stalking their prey, she once said, zeroing in on the straggler that had fallen behind, or who had broken free from the herd. If they worked as one, however, they could present a united front.

Previously, he had always thought of himself as peripheral to the group, younger than most of them and not privy to the decision-making process, grudgingly content to go along with the final outcome, whether it was moving their settlement further from the zombs' patrol lines or dividing up rations. But recently it was his very youth that ensured his strength had endured while others had weakened, to the point where they had come increasingly to rely upon him aiding them in scouting enemy positions, fixing meals and tending to the wounded. The responsibility had brought a rush of personal pride that he had never experienced before, and rather than tire of it, he longed for more. He enjoyed them asking his opinion, listening to his views and taking it on board. He realised he was having an influence. It was a unique sensation that he quickly grew addicted to.

Hence his precarious position right now on the streets of Eltham. While their food situation was undeniably desperate, and someone was needed to replenish their stock otherwise they were going to starve, at the same time he felt his newfound sense of responsibility was being pushed to the limit. His nerves jangled, his skin prickling with unease, as the two of them sneaked along the pavement, their backs to the privet hedges of the silent council-estate houses that lined the thoroughfares, looking anxiously left and right for any signs of life (or, rather, the *absence* of it). Donna had insisted on accompanying him, arguing it was unsafe for anyone to go alone, and he certainly wasn't going to begrudge her presence. She had been one of the first of the group to befriend him, and had a deeply humane streak that he admired. She was a fierce fighter too; a passionate and dedicated twenty-five year old.

Even so, he couldn't stop his hackles rising. He was deep in the heart of south London suburbia, an area he'd been familiar with since his childhood, and whose environs he'd explored with his friends, but it had never looked so alien as it did now. Gone were the comforting, reliable reminders of family – cars being washed in their driveways, the sound of lawnmowers drifting on the breeze together with the smell of cut grass, children circling the roads on bicycles, their younger siblings toddling after on tricycles – to be replaced with a grey slate of emptiness. Nothing moved, nothing made a sound. Even the sky was featureless, a dirty squall of cloud hanging low and heavy over the landscape.

Despite the quiet, Mitch walked as if he was on a tightrope, holding his breath, rucksack bumping against his shoulders. He felt dangerously exposed out here, constantly under the impression that his progress was being monitored, and that any moment an alarm would be raised, the dead pouring from the buildings on either side to drag them within. It was not possible, he was sure; these houses had been sacked by the various bands of humans in the area, scoured for what little foodstuff they contained. Any ghouls that they would've encountered would've been quickly disposed of, and were no doubt now lying decaying in basements or back gardens. The houses were nothing more than shells, abandoned crypts gathering mould. Yet his imagination conjured all manner of tenants still lurking on the other side of the walls, awakening from dusty sleep at their presence.

If truth be told, the threat lay not in some rotting pusbag shambling into their path – these braindead stiffs were becoming increasingly rare, subject to the same laws of entropy as everything else – but the intelligent zombs and their organised meat purges. It was a phenomenon that few could have predicted; that the dead would start thinking for themselves and form an opposing faction against the living. When Mitch had first heard the rumours that deadfucks were starting to talk and going after their victims in consolidated attacks, he'd been in his teens and dismissed it as someone attempting to wind him up. Even when reports came back with greater insistence that the resurrected were not just randomly devouring warm flesh but collecting it for storage and processing in their self-styled 'body shops', he refused to accept the notion that the zombie was anything but a staggering cadaver with infantile reasoning power, that could be put down with a bullet to the head.

It wasn't until he finally witnessed one of their assaults – winkling out a small knot of survivors that had holed up in a decrepit garage in Deptford, senses as keen as a bloodhound's, moving quickly and purposefully, without the typical drunken zombie gait that he'd become accustomed to – that he realised the things were evolving. They were getting smarter and, in their coldly methodical way of gathering sustenance, more vicious. They seemed to have somehow halted their decomposition too, as if they were clawing their way back to being halfway human; or perhaps something else entirely. But they hadn't lost their appetite for the living, and didn't appear to be in any hurry to grow out of it. They revelled in their tyranny, enjoying the terror they instilled in what pockets of resistance they could uncover. They didn't seem to see their meals as anything more than a species below them on the food chain, farming them like cattle; in fact, the only thing they considered less than humanity was their cadaverous dim-witted cousins, whom they treated with utter disdain, often casually splitting their skulls with an arrogant brutality.

Mitch didn't understand how some of the Returners had reached this higher state of consciousness while others remained rooted in their initial resurrection condition. It had to be something to do with the virus that had brought the dead back in the first place, but his knowledge of such matters was limited. He had vague childhood memories of the news coverage, of the shaky camera footage of a ghoul staggering through a field being tracked by armed policemen, of the unnerving, panicky tone that had crept into the newsreader's voice, but no one in his family could help explain what had caused the outbreak. Even after he lost his parents and sisters, and had joined up with Donna, Liz and the rest, they had no scientists amongst their number to clarify the situation. They knew the basics – the dead want to eat you – and that seemed good enough. But he couldn't shake the feeling that the world was changing around them, and that the intelligent stiffs were a crucial signifier of that; the living were being forced to acknowledge that their time was over, and something new was coming to take their place. A next phase in evolution was just around the corner, and these ruthless inheritors of the earth were preparing to embrace it.

If he was sure of anything, it was that he didn't want to be taken in the meat purges. He had a small sharpened shiv tucked into his back pocket which he'd become adept at driving through the soft parts of a deadfuck's head – he had chalked up eight confirmed kills at the last count – and he had resolved that if he was ever seized by those smart maggoty bastards then he would thrust it into his jugular at the first opportunity. Naturally, no one who had been rounded up and transported to the body shops had returned, so his ideas of what fate awaited him were based on the flimsy rumours that filtered back through the human camps. A few brave souls had tried to observe the processing plants from a nominally safe vantage point, but little information could be gleaned other than that the Returners wanted their food initially kept alive. It had been mooted that rather than slaughterhouses, the body shops were more akin to battery farms, the livestock permanently tethered and used as a source of warm flesh until their hearts finally gave out and the skin went cold. Quite how the stiffs had developed the technology to establish these factories was another mystery, but there was some agreement that there was a directing force behind it all, a guiding superior hand that they were working for – a King Zombie. Some big-brain ghoul had made plans and organised his brethren into a formidable army. If there was one thing worse than the creatures that walked the streets of the city, it was the possibility of some super-intelligent entity lurking at the black, rotting centre of it all.

Liz had suggested that they ought to try to capture one of the talking dead and interrogate the thing, gain some kind of knowledge of what they wanted other than to fill their bellies, how they operated, and the details of their set-up. But it would prove an impossible task. The smart ones moved in squads, just as the humans did, and none of the survivors were skilled enough in combat to tackle a group of the cadavers head-on. They moved surprisingly fast, and had picked up the principles of wielding weapons, so now they were twice as lethal as well as being virtually indestructible. It was a fight they couldn't win. The zombs were gaining ground all the time while the number of humans dwindled proportionately. Mitch wondered if his comrades' continued battle to exist – their perpetual quest for food, and struggle to overcome illness – was not a touch pointless in the face of such overwhelming odds; it was only a matter of time before the dead found them or they succumbed to sickness. Why keep trying when the future was as bleak as the grey slate sky above him? With little hope in a change in their circumstances, were they kidding themselves that this was any kind of life at all?

But he had made a promise, he told himself, as he and Donna reached the corner of the estate and peered down a side road, checking that the coast was clear. He had wanted to prove that he could be useful, and right now that was the most important matter at hand; giving up would simply be selfish, an act that aided no one but merely absolved him of all responsibility. And anyway, he didn't want to roll over for those deadfucks. As Donna had encouraged him to believe, while the living still had breath in their lungs, why shouldn't they carry on? They had every right to exist too, didn't they? Why make the stiffs' genocidal designs any easier?

Glancing around him, this was the part of town he'd suggested to Donna they check out. Although the area they were hurrying through had been considered looted empty, he knew enough about it from his past to believe there was a spot that might have been missed. It was a lock-up that was hidden from sight down a narrow alley, which backed on to a short parade of shops, one of which was a convenience store. The store itself had been gutted, stripped of everything that wasn't nailed to the walls, but Mitch was hoping that few were aware that the proprietor used the storage space to hold excess stock. Back in the day, he and his friends had watched the man carry jars and cardboard boxes into it before locking the shutter with a heavy padlock. They had held a certain childish romantic ideal between them about what the lock-up might contain, as if to step within was to be whisked to another world, but their crude attempts to force entry did not get them very far. Now, he thought, he might have the strength and tools to complete the job.

He spotted the entrance to the alley and scurried across the road, disappearing into its shadows, Donna behind him. He turned to her, wordlessly indicating with his head for them to continue, then strode towards the courtyard at the other end. The alley opened into an enclosed area, on one side of which was a fence separating the nearby houses' gardens and on the other a block of five garages, their once white exteriors scrawled with graffiti. A couple of the shutters had been wrenched open, and assorted bric-a-brac – an exercise bike, an old refrigerator, lawn furniture; possessions that had no possible value anymore – were visibly scattered within the darkness, filmed with grime and mildew. But his garage seemed still intact.

Mitch crouched and hefted the padlock. It was substantial, and not a little rusty, but apparently hadn't been tampered with.

"Can you keep an eye out?" he whispered. "This might make some noise."

"Sure." Donna unslung a baseball bat from her backpack. "Be quick."

"I'll try. It looks like it could be hard work."

He slipped his own rucksack from his back and unzipped it, pulling from it a hacksaw, hammer and pliers. He placed the hacksaw blade against the padlock and began.

It was as difficult as he feared, and noisier than he had expected, the metal squeal causing him to wince. And that was before he set about it with the hammer, the dull thrumming resounding off the surrounding walls, his arms aching from the vibration. Sweat glued his shirt to his back, and his hands were red and sore, but he did not stop, confident that the lock was twisting in its housing. At last it bent and snapped, and he let out a restrained whoop of triumph. Donna slapped him on the back. He kicked it free, then yanked on the shutter, straining to push it upwards; unused for over a decade, it resisted and he and Donna had to put all their weight behind it to get it to move even a few inches. After rising a foot and a half, it wouldn't open any further, so Mitch dropped to his knees, retrieved a slender flashlight from his bag and shone it into the blackness. The beam illuminated the outlines of crates stacked on top of each other, and glimmered against glass bottles lining makeshift shelves.

"Reckon we've hit the jackpot," he said, casting an eye to a smiling Donna. "Stacks of stuff in there. I'm going to take a closer look."

"You can't carry it all by yourself," she protested, moving closer to help.

"I'm just going to see what's usable. I'd feel happier if you stayed out here, in case the shutter's unsafe. We don't want to be both trapped in there."

"OK. But be—"

"—quick, I know." He grinned and squeezed her arm.

He put the torch between his teeth and slid onto his stomach, wriggling his way into the garage, the lip of the shutter pressing against his back; as an afterthought, he reached round and wedged the hammer into the gap as an extra precaution.

Once inside, he stood and surveyed the contents of the lock-up, sweeping the torch before him. Seconds later, the smell of rotting vegetation hit him as he caught glimpses of pallets of liquefying tomatoes and deflated apples. Muttering under his breath and covering his mouth and nose with his sleeve, he moved closer, his mood lightening when he saw the stacks of tins. He picked a selection up: potatoes, beans, peas, soup. The contents were several years past their sell-by date, and their labels were encrusted with dirt and dangling with spider husks, but they were the most edible things he'd seen for the best part of a month. He caught sight too of a pack of bottled water, the liquid inside cloudy with age but nevertheless clearer than the rainwater they'd become accustomed to drinking.

"Some great stuff here, Donna," he called. "I'll bring some out. We could fill both bags, I reckon. Might even need extra trips."

There was no reply. Assuming that she couldn't hear

him through the shutter, he began to place as many cans and bottles inside his rucksack as he could physically carry. He smiled to himself; he was already picturing Liz's face when she saw his haul, and then her grin broadening even further when he told her there was more to collect. He liked the feeling he got when he was the bearer of good news for a change.

He pushed the bulging bag through the gap beneath the shutter, then squeezed his way after it, squinting in the daylight after the building's gloom and wiping the cobweb strands from his face.

"Donna? You want to take a look in there yourself?" He got to his knees, looked up and froze.

Four Returners were standing at the mouth of the alley watching him. They were smart ones; evolvers. Although not as visibly putrescent as their brainless kin, their skin was still tight and brittle where it had shrunk, and one's mortal wound – a huge rent in its neck – was readily apparent. Also unlike the average zomb (who usually looked like they'd crawled out of a grave backwards), they took a certain pride in their appearance, evidently swiping off-the-peg suits from the remains of department stores; no doubt behaviour stirred by latent memories. What immediately separated them from deadfucks, though, was the fact that they could see a human, rather than sensing them through their warmth. The four of them cast a baleful gaze over Mitch, flicking their milky-white stare for a second to the lock-up, before returning to settle on him.

A fifth stood behind them, its hand clamped over Donna's mouth, her arms twisted behind her back. Her eyes bulged in fear, and silently pleaded to Mitch for help. Her bat lay in two pieces on the other side of the courtyard.

As one, the Returners started to walk forward, their stride stiff but purposeful, and without instruction slowly began to fan out around the width of the enclosed space. The one in centre nearest Mitch unhooked a truncheon from its hip and gripped it in its bony fist.

Getting to his feet, Mitch cursed the noise he must've made shattering the padlock, imagining the echoes drifting down the still streets, pricking the ears of a passing patrol. It had been risky, he knew, but he'd hoped they would be gone before the alarm was raised.

"You come with us," the stiff in front of him said, the words not so much spoken as falling from its wrinkled lips. There was no inflection, the dead language carried like wind whistling through its voice box. It was the first time he'd been addressed by the resurrected, and it was as chilling to hear as he'd thought it would be. "You come now," it reiterated.

Mitch couldn't reply, his mouth dry, and stepped backwards. The other ghouls to either side of him also drew blunt weapons – they wanted he and Donna alive, he reasoned, but they were willing to break a few bones to make them more manageable – and closed in. His hand went to his back pocket and unsheathed his knife, remembering the vow he'd made; it would be easy enough to open his throat before they even got within grabbing distance, and he'd be useless to them. Bleeding like a stuck pig, they would only be able to watch helplessly as the life they coveted drained out of his body. He brought the blade up behind him, steeling himself. If he went deep enough, it was possible he could sever his spinal column and stop himself from returning. From becoming like *them*.

But one look at Donna, struggling in the clutches of the dead, forced him to dispel the notion. He wasn't going to leave her in their hands.

"Come now," it said again. "Or we take you by force."

Mitch glared back at it, hate swelling up inside him, loathing these creatures and the atrocity they had wrought, the millions that had died to feed their insatiable hunger. He felt blood trickle down his palm as he clutched the knife even tighter. He wasn't going to give these fucking maggots anything.

With a speed that surprised even him, he lashed out and powered the shiv into the nearest Returner's left eye, the three-inch blade burying itself into its socket. The orb popped like a balloon, vitreous liquid sprinkling his hand. The momentum of the attack carried Mitch forward and he tumbled over the stiff as it collapsed to the ground. He lost his grip on the knife and it remained rooted in the thing's head, just half an inch of the handle protruding below its brow. But it had seemingly penetrated far enough to reach the brain because the zombie lay motionless, blood trickling from its nose and ruptured eye to form a widening pool on the flagstones.

The other ghouls were moving, though, advancing on him quickly. He rolled, seeking out a weapon, and his gaze settled on the hammer. Tugging it free from beneath the garage door, which crashed shut behind him, he swung round to face his enemies. One of them caught his wrist with its club and pain juddered up his arm, knocking him sideways; it stalked closer, and bounced the truncheon off his temple, forcing him onto his knees. His vision swam and his head throbbed. He fell onto his back, stars exploding behind his eyes, as the Returner towered above him, drawing back to administer a final blow. Before it could make contact, however, he ducked and swerved, smashing the hammer down on its ankle, which splintered with an audible crack. The ghoul tottered, lost its balance then fell, its shinbone shearing off completely.

Mitch crawled over to it, struggling to right itself like an upturned beetle, and slammed the hammer down into the middle of its face, the thin tissue caving in with a wet crunch. He hit it again and again, with as much strength as he could muster, unaware of the yell of rage and frustration that he was emitting, punctuating each cry with another strike, until its skull had all but disintegrated, pink globules of brain matter squeezing between the shards. He would've carried on, had the air not caught in his throat when another of the stiffs yanked its cudgel under his chin and pulled him away, the weapon held hard against his windpipe. He fought to breathe, dropping the hammer and bringing both hands up to wrest it free. Meanwhile, the fourth creature circled in front of him and delivered savage blows to his ribcage and belly, Mitch barely able to fill his lungs to scream. He felt unconsciousness seeping into him, and his legs grew heavy.

"Good," the zomb before him said between strikes, its mouth spread wide into a rictus grin. "I like meat tender."

"You watch us strip flesh from your bones," the one standing behind him added, its thin, emotionless voice filling his ear. "You watch us eat you alive."

"Go to hell," he whispered, coughing the words free, tears beading at the corners of his eyes.

The first one lowered its club, took a step forward and wrenched open Mitch's lower jaw, taking the tip of his tongue between forefinger and thumb in a tight pinch. "Think we have a taste first. Tired of hearing it whine." It glanced at its partner. "Keep it still." It looked back at the Returner holding Donna. "Take that one back. We be along shortly."

Mitch moaned, watching in horror as Donna was frogmarched down the alley and out of sight, her muffled cries diminishing. He wrestled against his captors, but they held him firm. The Returner grasped his tongue and put its other hand against his forehead, to brace itself. He squeezed his eyes shut, tasting the ghoul's graveyard residue in his mouth, waiting for the inevitable sharp stab of agony to blossom alongside it.

It didn't. Rather, there was release.

Suddenly, the pressure around his neck was gone, and he dropped to the floor, sucking in air, aware that his tongue was still intact. He wiped his face with a shaking hand, and gazed around him. The head of the zombie that had been restraining him lay close by, face expressing a note of surprise; its body was several feet away, slumped against the lock-up.

Mitch scooted backwards, uncomprehending, and let out a shout of startled surprise when its colleague hit the ground like a felled tree to his right, a machete embedded in its scalp. He looked it straight in the eyes as the life dimmed from them and a watery dribble of blood spilled from its lips. He was still staring at it when a hand reached down and ripped the machete free. At last, he glanced up at the figure standing over him.

It was another Returner, wiping the crimson streaks off the blade with its jacket sleeve before sliding the weapon into its sheath. The creature made a gesture to help haul him up.

"Come on," it said. "Not going to hurt you."

Mitch feverishly shook his head, tried to scrabble to his feet and promptly fainted dead away.

CHAPTER FIFTEEN

Mitch became aware of something soft enveloping him before he fully returned to consciousness; he was sinking back into it, his hands sliding across its surface, his head rolling unsupported. It was vaguely comforting but it unsettled him too. There was a distasteful smell that he couldn't turn his face from, and the material beneath his touch was firm but yielded a greasy residue. As he slowly opened his eyes, colours swirled before them, muted reds and greens fading to black. When the images finally coalesced into a pattern that his fuzzy brain could make sense of, he realised he was looking at a bank of entwined roses, their petals seemingly smeared with ash. He blinked and wiped the grit from his lashes, then refocused: it was a sofa design, he ascertained at last, repeated across the cushions and arms, and the grey dusting was grime, as if the piece of furniture had been left undisturbed in a locked room for a very long time. He was sitting up, his head slumped to one side, cheek resting on his shoulder. The stench was coming from the sofa too, dampness mixed with neglect, and in a bid to escape it he leaned forward and put his elbows on his knees, massaging his temples with his fingers, trying to recollect what had happened.

"You're awake," a voice said somewhere in the gloom.

Mitch's senses instantly came alive. His head snapped up and he peered about him. The room was in shadow, but his eyes were becoming accustomed to the darkness, aided by the thin shards of light that pierced the curtains pulled shut across the windows. It was a lounge, but one that hadn't seen life within it for quite some time. The TV in the corner and the Welsh dresser against the far wall were similarly bedecked with cobwebs, framed family photographs hanging above the mantelpiece turned almost opaque with dirt. From what he could see, he didn't recognise the faces smiling out at him. There was a wooden dining chair standing conspicuously in the centre of the carpet, and upon it was seated an unmoving figure, evidently watching him, even though at the moment it was just an outline from which it was impossible to discern any features.

He heard breathing close by, heavy and ragged, only to realise that it was his own. He held it for a second, and in the silence that followed came to the conclusion that he was the only living thing in the immediate vicinity. Then he remembered the Returner that had offered its hand, and the way that it had wiped its gore-streaked machete blade across its jacket sleeve. He must've blacked out, because everything after that was a haze.

"How are you feeling?" it asked. "Are you hurt?"

The rush of questions that had surfaced in his mind upon awakening had superseded any physical pain, but as he considered the query he was aware the he was indeed in some considerable discomfort. His right forearm throbbed where he had been struck, and when he put a hand to his chest he winced at its tenderness. No wonder his breathing sounded so strained, he thought. It was possible that several of his ribs had been fractured and were pressing on his lungs. He felt like a mass of bruises, in which each new movement would lead to a fresh ache. Despite its mildewy stink, right now he didn't have the energy or the inclination to leave the sofa. If he was in danger, then so be it, he had little left to defend himself with. But he guessed he was safe from harm for the moment; he would've been carved up like a Sunday roast long ago if all this thing wanted of him was a snack.

He didn't know how or why it was acting differently to the others, but he couldn't pretend he wasn't grateful.

Mitch cleared his throat. "How... long have I been out?"

"Few hours. Thought you might be concussed." It paused, then added: "You can understand what I'm saying?"

He nodded. "I'm OK. At least, I think I am. No impairment up here, anyway." He tapped his forehead. "Bit battered elsewhere, but I'll live." He bit his tongue, wondering if the creature would regard that as a sly dig, then admonished himself for worrying about insulting a stiff. In any other circumstances, he wouldn't hesitate in trying to ram a spike through its brain. "I... I guess I've got you to thank for that. I'm not sure I'd be in one piece if you hadn't come along."

It didn't reply for a moment, then said: "You put up quite a fight."

There was something slightly sinister about its declaration, as if it were making a grudging statement of approval about the liveliness of its prey. But it didn't elaborate any further. Suddenly, the image of Donna's frightened eyes sprang into his mind, a zombie's hand clamped over her mouth. "Shit, Donna—" He tried to stand, and regretted it, his legs wobbly beneath him. "Is she OK? Did you get her back?"

The figure shook its head. "They had gone."

"Hell, we gotta go after her. They'll have taken her to be processed."

"I know. They've adapted a school near here, St Jude's, into one of their body shops. That's where she'll be taken."

"So let's *go!*"

It shook its head. "There'll be too many of them for

the two of us to handle. We'll go after your friend soon enough, but we'll need back-up."

"But in the meantime she could be torn apart."

"They'll want to keep her alive for as along as possible. There's still time. But we should lie low for a while, wait until dark. There's no reason why our handiwork won't be found for days, but in my experience it pays to be careful."

Mitch sat in silence, a mixture of frustration and fatigue gnawing at him. Eventually, he asked: "Where are we?"

"One of the houses nearby. They're all deserted round here."

"You carried me?"

"You weren't going to waltz in by yourself."

Although he should've been appreciative of its actions, Mitch couldn't help feeling prickly at the thought of the dead thing touching him. It triggered the ingrained hatred he had against Returners and he sensed himself becoming more defensive. "You're one of them, aren't you? One of the flesh-eaters."

It said nothing.

"Why did you save me? Why attack your own kind?"

Again, there was no reply. But instead the silhouette stood and stepped towards him. As it moved closer, Mitch could gain a better appreciation of its features: it looked remarkably fresh for a ghoul, the pinched, tight texture of its skin the most visible sign that it had resurrected. There was a blackened patch on its chest, and its shirt was stained with similar dark areas, but there was a looseness to its posture and gait that was unlike even the smart zombs. It didn't stagger or jerk, and the eyes still had some spark of humanity behind them. It had been a man in his early thirties when it had died, and it was as if a tiny fragment of his former life had stayed trapped in that shell when the virus had worked its magic. It leaned over him, one hand on the back of the sofa, and put its face close to his.

"They're not my kind," it said, an eerie lack of breath behind its words. "So consider yourself fortunate I got to you first. If you're worried I'm going to eat you, relax. I didn't bring you here for a picnic."

Mitch leaned back, aware there was nowhere he could retreat to. "How can I trust you?"

It cast an eye over each shoulder before turning back to look at him, shrugging; a disarmingly human gesture. "You have a choice?"

Mitch found himself relaxing, despite himself. This thing was far too eloquent, far too self-aware, for a stiff. "What are you? You're like no Returner I've seen before."

It straightened, walked back to its chair, picked it up and brought it closer to the sofa, then sat down. "I am what I am. I can offer no other explanation than that."

"You are undead, though? You've resurrected?"

It nodded.

"Can you remember who you were? Do you have a name?"

"My name is Gabriel, and I can remember everything. As far as I am concerned, there is little difference between my states of being, pre- and post-death. Perhaps I notice the chill more these days, that's all."

"But you're a deadhead. You don't breathe, your heart doesn't beat..."

"You get used to it."

"And the flesh-eating? You get used to that to?"

It looked away. When it replied, its voice was low and steady. "It can be controlled."

Mitch was incredulous. The creature was right, in

a way; conversing like this, there was little difference between it and a living being. It was just one shade away from human. But even so, it was still on the other side of the divide, and thus couldn't be entirely trusted. For all its apparent intelligence, it surely must have dangerous urges that he should be wary of. "How long have you been like this?"

"A decade, perhaps more. Time loses all meaning." It looked down at itself. "I'm... not changing. I'm growing no older, like I'm frozen."

"What happened to you? I mean, what killed you?"

It parted its jacket and gestured to the dark circular patch on its chest, a hole ripped in the material of the shirt. "Shot," it said simply. It fingered the entry point sadly.

"By whom?"

"By someone who is due a reckoning."

Gabe had made sure he was on his very best behaviour, talking to the human. Mitch needed to be convinced that Gabe wasn't a threat to him or his friends, if they were to be any use, and so he swallowed the raging hunger that clawed his hollow belly and diligently answered his questions. Mostly, he told the truth. He told him that he had worked for a criminal called Harry Flowers, and that his employer had believed he'd turned traitor and had him executed. He told him that he'd been bitten by a ghoul and taken a bullet in the heart, and that for what seemed the briefest time he'd floated through darkness, pulled inexorably towards a destination he couldn't visualise. Only when he thought he'd arrived did he open his eyes and stare at the cold light of day. His body had been slung beyond the boundaries of Resurrection Alley, and he was lying amidst the shambling crowds of the dead, who battered disinterestedly against him. All life had long since left him, and therefore he had little to offer them.

Gabe had stood, on the day of his resurrection, conscious of the stillness of his pulse and the sour taste of his final breaths at the back of his throat, and realised he had some semblance of his wits about him. At first, he'd wondered if was truly dead; that somehow he hadn't passed over, impossible as that was to believe, since his mind was so clear and precise. But his skin was icy to the touch, and when he ran his hand over his chest wound his fingers came away coated crimson. The zombs ignored him too, obviously regarding him as one of their own. There could be little doubt that he had joined the ranks of the undead. Shock hit him like a tsunami, and he had staggered away to some private corner to come to terms with his new cadaverous state in his own way.

But his body had stopped working, and he could no longer weep, try though he might. Inside his head, he howled and cried, but nothing would emerge from the dead shell he was shackled to. It was like trying to shout in a vast, echoing room. When he had regained his mental composure, he struggled to recollect everything that had brought him to this point, and he was amazed to discover that he could focus on it all: Flowers, Anna, Hewitt, Vassily's undead father, everything. He could even remember his own name. He could think for himself, make free associations, memorise faces from the past. This was not what being a Returner was meant to be. Surely he should be a mindless stiff, driven by the need for warm flesh?

At that moment, two things happened: he became aware

of a scratchy sensation in the pit of his stomach that had somehow always been there but he had not considered; and the civil servant Fletchley's words floated back to him about how the ghouls were learning, that the virus was working on their brains. The scratch became an ache, and Gabe knew that he had not escaped the full state of zombiehood, despite his clearly advanced status. He had a hunger that was growing with intensity all the time, and it could not be dismissed.

It was around this element that Gabe deviated from what was strictly true. He had told Mitch that his craving for warm meat was an addiction that could be controlled, and while he managed to keep the stabbing pains in his belly fairly low-level, they would not be denied for ever. In the years since he'd resurrected, he'd managed to assuage the need when it became too great by feasting on what vermin and stray pets he could catch, the thin, bitter flesh just keeping a lid on his hunger. It was a frustrating and demeaning position to find himself in, his self-awareness pointedly reminding him of the levels he was stooping to: chasing half-starved, diseased animals for their scraggly hide. He almost envied the rank-and-file ghouls and their mindless consumption. But that very intelligence he possessed ensured he could not devour the humans, no matter how strong the cravings became. He told himself that he would not sink that low, that there was still some vestige of the man he'd once been inside the Returner he'd become. Even so, close proximity to the living awakened an appetite that verged on the carnal, and it was this that he would have to keep in check around the kid's colleagues. It was unlikely that he'd snap and rip a chunk out of someone's throat, but he might get distracted, which could be dangerous for all of them. And if they got wind of the fact he was looking at them like they were his next meal, they were going to stave in his head at the first opportunity.

So he had assured Mitch that his diet was not a problem, and the kid seemed to believe him; or said he did, at least. Gabe knew he'd have to cross that bridge when he came to it: working with humans was always going to be tricky, even without the ceaseless demands of his stomach.

Having waited several hours for night to fall, Mitch was leading him back to his group's hideout in a deserted pub on the outskirts of Blackheath, the two of them carrying what they could snaffle from the lock-up. Gabe's assistance had gone some way to soothing the younger man's fears and cementing an element of trust, to the point where he was willing to take the Returner to meet his friends. There would be some explaining to do, Gabe envisioned, and more than a few threats to suffer. But he'd outlined a little of his plan to Mitch, who'd been anxious to volunteer his services, and by proxy that of his fellow humans, if only to rescue his friend, Donna, whom Gabe believed Mitch was more than a little sweet on. When he'd told him that he believed Harry Flowers was now the power at the centre of the city, that it was he all the organised zombies reported to, and that the living were being farmed on his orders – and that Gabe was determined to take the grizzled old fuck down – Mitch had thrown his full weight behind the scheme. Gabe got the impression that the kid reckoned that by taking out the ganglord, things would return to normal. He wasn't going to dissuade him if it guaranteed his help, but as far as he was concerned normality was a very long way away indeed.

"You mind if I ask you something?" Mitch asked as they hurried through the moonlit streets. He had gained some degree of confidence being in Gabe's company, feeling protected from the other stiffs by walking alongside one.

"Go ahead."

"How did you learn to talk? You said that when you resurrected you were trapped in a dead shell. Was it something you remembered from your past life?"

"Partly. I understood the language as much as I did before I died; it was just a matter of getting my mouth and tongue to coordinate once more. I listened to tapes and practised until the sounds that emerged from my throat were formed into words. It wasn't easy. We're talking a period of five years or more."

"You could hear too, then?"

Gabe nodded. "It was like the senses were all there, I simply needed to retune them to a different frequency."

"Are the other smart Returners – the ones that work for Flowers – like that? Have they learnt like you?"

He was amused by the kid's insistent interrogation. He supposed it was the first time a survivor, who'd spent a good portion of his life battling an enemy he couldn't reason or empathise with, had gained inside information on what made them tick. The zombies' basic carnivorous motivation was pretty straightforward, but there were always the questions that nobody had yet found an answer to: why did they continually want to eat, especially when their bellies were incapable of processing the nourishment? Why were some regaining their pre-death motor skills? What did they plan to do when they had devoured everything on the planet? The ghouls were a species mankind had yet to fathom. Even Gabe was at a loss to explain what the virus was doing inside his head, what primal functions it was adapting for its own end. And indeed, what end was that? That bacteria had brought the dead back to life and given them cannibalistic tendencies, a goal it had achieved quite spectacularly; but what was the next step? What would it progress to next? How would it develop?

"I suspect so," he told Mitch. "But their learning seems rudimentary, like they've just mastered the basics. You've heard them talk?"

"Yeah. They're kinda slow."

"I think their brains aren't quite as knitted together as mine. They're taking longer to pick things up."

"But why you? How did you get so to be advanced?"

Gabe shook his head. "Your guess is as good as mine. Maybe the virus found a natural home in my physiology to take hold. But I can tell you that I'm not alone – there're others like me, in similar states, with more growing all the time."

Mitch stopped dead and turned to him. "More like you?"

"A veritable Dirty Dozen. Or a Filthy Five, at least." Gabe tapped him on the shoulder and indicated that they should continue. "But we need more recruits."

As expected, Mitch's friends came within a hair's breadth of putting a bullet between Gabe's eyes on first introduction. The zombie had had guns thrust in his face before, and he had become accustomed to staying calm looking down the length of a shotgun barrel, but that didn't mean he didn't tire of it eventually. As an act of conciliation, he had removed the machete from his belt and laid it on the ground, his hands held up to show he meant no harm. But it seemed to cut little ice with the humans, who regarded him with open hatred. Their attention was divided between keeping the Returner securely in their sights, and arguing with the kid for bringing it to their door and being naive enough to trust it.

Gabe's patience was wearing thin, and he was getting nervous that someone's trigger finger was going to twitch. They were a sorry-looking bunch, skinny and unhealthy, a few cold months away from death's door, and dressed like refugees; typical of the many batches of humans scratching a living among the ruins. Not counting Mitch, there was eight of them in total – four men, three women and a young girl, hunched up on a chair, pale and painfully frail – and it seemed one of the women was nominally in charge; or at least the others looked to her for a decision. Liz, she was called; broadly built and in her early forties, she had the air of a well-heeled PA about her, someone who once presided over a tidy, efficiently managed office. Despite the dirt-smeared jeans and shapeless T-shirt she wore, she exuded an unmistakable corporate attitude. The kid had breathlessly explained the evening's events, insisting they mount a rescue mission to save Donna, and pulling open the bags they'd brought with them and displaying the booty, which earned more than a few murmurs of appreciation from the others. Liz had nodded and listened, refreshingly cool-headed, despite casting the occasional sour glance Gabe's way.

"It's a deadfuck," the guy with the twin-bore snarled, the tip of the weapon no more than a couple of inches from Gabe's nose. "They never change."

"I think you'll find they're changing all the time," Gabe replied. "Or hadn't you noticed?"

"I say you could talk, maggotbrain?"

"Easy, John," Liz said. "It's not any threat at the moment. And you've got to admit, we've never come across one like this before. It's clearly of a different stripe to the collectors."

"Collectors?" Gabe raised any eyebrow at Mitch.

"The smart zombs that patrol the streets, rounding up what living they can find. They collect them in trucks and ship them off to the nearest body shop. The ones that took Donna."

The Returner nodded slowly. "I know."

Liz studied him distastefully. "You were part of them? Part of that... organisation?"

"No, I've merely observed them." Gabe returned her gaze. "I've been out on the streets for over half a decade, trying to find out more about who is behind it all, who's marshalling these undead troops."

"This is bullshit—" John snapped, but was silenced by a glare from the woman.

"What do you know?" she asked.

"The processed humans are being used to feed the intelligent dead, I guess you've assumed that much," Gabe told them. "But the majority of the living are being delivered to the brains behind the organisation – his name is Harry Flowers. He's taken over Resurrection Alley – his cronies are responsible for the human entertainment that goes on there – and he's got a safe house on the outskirts of the city. Basically, any patrols you see on the streets report to him. For the past five years, he's been tightening his grip around London, bringing it within his power."

"This Flowers guy is a Returner?"

"Yes. And if I thought he was threatening in life, I had no idea just how dangerous he could be in death."

"Wait," Liz said, her brow furrowing. "You're saying you knew him before he died?"

"*Knew* him?" Gabe gave a little shake of the head. "I think it was me that killed him."

The group of survivors exchanged glances, John adjusting his grip on his shotgun. Mitch looked anxious, as if he was wondering if he'd just made a colossal mistake. Liz merely indicated with her hand for Gabe to elaborate.

"I worked for Flowers. In life, I mean," he continued. "He was a... a gangster, I suppose you'd call him. On the surface he was a legitimate businessman, owned clubs and bars in the capital, but he was involved in a number of shady deals, and wasn't averse to intimidation to get what he wanted. I was part of his workforce, but I was just his driver. I was never privy to the sharp end of his transactions. That sounds like a weak excuse but it's the truth: for the most part I was never involved in the criminal side of his business. That ended when the shit came down."

"The outbreak," Liz said.

Gabe nodded. "When everything fell apart, it became clear there was safety in numbers. It made sense to stay with Flowers' outfit. Plus, I don't think I could've walked away, even I had wanted to. I'd become... involved." He paused, head bowed. "The authorities lost control, and Harry seemed to know what to do to fill the vacuum, to take advantage of the crisis. We became thieves and hijackers, consolidating our strength. The world changed and I changed with it. I embraced my place in the new scheme of things, because there seemed no way back to the old one. The boss promised order and rule – under his terms, naturally – and I signed up for it, played my part in ushering it along."

"And you killed him...?" Liz asked.

"Things got fucked up. Flowers thought I sold him out, and had me executed. But before I died, I stabbed him with a syringe full of the virus sample. I'm guessing here, but I think it killed him. Not only that, but it may have accelerated his post-death development, to the point where he can coordinate the other smart zombs for his own uses..." He shrugged. "I don't know, I'm not one of the boffins that engineered the thing, but it seems feasible. Something's been motivating the dead over the past few years, getting them to work together."

There was silence as the humans all regarded him warily. He couldn't blame their reluctance to trust him – he certainly wouldn't, if the situation were reversed – but he hoped that they could see past their reservations to recognise that he was offering them their first real chance at striking back at the ghouls. The dead had been an inscrutable enemy up to this point, but through him they could assimilate an attack plan.

"Why are you doing this?" a rat-faced man with shoulder-length hair and round glasses asked, stepping forward from the group. They turned to listen to him speak. "What's it to you that we don't all fall victim to this Flowers?"

"Revenge, pure and simple," Gabe replied flatly. "I want to bring him down." And save someone too, he mentally added. "I need your help to do that. But either way, we both get what we want by having him removed. Plus, I can help you save your friend." He pointedly looked at Mitch.

"And what's to say you won't turn on us the same way you've sold him out?" John remarked. The others murmured their assent.

"Because once this is over – one way or another – you won't ever see me again. Beyond that, you'll just have to take my offer at face value. The choice is yours. If you're not interested, I'll go find another bunch of humans willing to take the risk."

Liz reached out and placed her hand on the top of John's shotgun, gently lowering it. He threw her a questioning look, but she gave a reassuring nod.

She turned her attention to Gabe. "I still don't understand – where do we fit into the plan? What do you need *us* for?"

He gave the approximation of a smile. "You're still warm flesh, aren't you?"

CHAPTER SIXTEEN

They spotted the human immediately, rooting amidst the rubble, seemingly oblivious to the danger that he was in. He was working his way through a short parade of blackened shops, pulling away soot-stained planks of wood and charred furniture to find something worth salvaging. The stores themselves had been nothing of note before they'd been put to the torch – a downmarket carpet warehouse, a bookmaker's, a laundrette, a newsagent and a Chinese takeaway, situated on a sombre stretch of dual carriageway and bracketed by a pair of high-rise flats – and it appeared unlikely on first inspection that anyone would find anything of value within their crumbling walls. Indeed, there was an air of desperation to the figure as he tossed debris over his shoulder, scrabbling on hands and knees sifting the ash, and hammering at the warped filing cabinets and desk drawers in a bid to open them. He was so intent on his task, and taking so little care in attracting attention through the noise he was making, that they wondered if the balance of his mind was disturbed. Maybe one of these buildings had been a business of his and he was trying to restore what was once his. Surely no one sane would continue with such a fruitless endeavour?

Still, loss of wits or not, he possessed a beating heart and warm, rich blood flowing through pulsing veins, and that was enough for them to stop. The din he was creating was enough to cover the sound of the truck coming to a halt, and they stepped down from the cab, pausing to glance at each other. The human had not looked up from his toil, utterly focused on the detritus surrounding him. Each blow of the hammer resounded down the empty thoroughfare like a distress signal, almost as if he was willingly provoking interest. As one, they walked towards him, unsheathing their truncheons from their belts; this would not take a great deal of effort. Stragglers such as these – the mad, those cast out from their human communities, the foolhardy – were easy pickings.

As they approached, still he did not turn. Only when they were within a couple of feet of him, their shadows stretching either side of him like a pair of dark jaws, did he cock his head to one side as if he had finally sensed he was not alone. He gazed up at the two Returners grinning fixedly down at him, seeming strangely unperturbed at their arrival, as if he'd been expecting them.

"Come with us," one of them said, brandishing its weapon. "Or else, trouble."

The human appraised them for a moment. "I don't think so," he replied finally.

They glanced at one another again, bemused. They had never encountered one so unconcerned by their presence; most would beg for mercy, or attempt to flee. "Come now," the first ghoul reiterated, reaching out to grab the young man by the shoulder.

But before he could make contact, the human lashed out and grasped its wrist tightly, pulling himself up to eye level. They locked stares for a second, his palm still wrapped around its forearm, refusing to relinquish it. "No," he said simply. "Not any more." With that, he released his grip and nodded over its shoulder.

The two Returners were too confused by this sudden display of defiance to fully acknowledge what happened next. They half turned to see what was behind them and were battered in the faces with machete blades. The first swing opened a rift in the nearest's forehead from brow to cheek, the knife lodging in the skull for a second before wrenching free with an audible crack. The next blow was brought down on the second zombie's cranium with enough force to cave in the left-hand side of its head entirely. It crumpled under the power of the strike, its features flattened. The first was still standing somehow, raising its baton in a half-hearted attempt at a counter-attack, its right eyeball poking comically at ninety degrees to the rest of its face. Gabe strode up to it while it was trying to get its bearings and rammed his blade up under its chin till the tip broke the surface of its scalp. The two halves of its head parted like a flower opening its petals to the rays of the sun.

Mitch watched Gabe yank the machete free, a little taken aback by the brutality of the assault. "When they said destroy the brain, you weren't going to take any chances, were you?" he remarked.

"Pays not to use half measures when you're dealing with the undead," he answered. "Nature of the beast means you're never sure when the damn things are down and out."

Mitch guessed that made sense, but he couldn't help but detect something personal in the vicious glee with which the zombies had been dispatched. He wondered if Gabe loathed them more than humans did; indeed, whether there was some self-hatred in those explosions of violence, a disgust at what he had become directed towards his cousins. Maybe there was an element of catharsis too. Whatever, Mitch was glad the full brunt of it was coming the deadheads' way, and not his.

"Success?" Liz asked as she and the five other members of the group (one of the older women had stayed behind to look after Rosa, the little girl) emerged from their hiding place on the other side of the road to meet them. They were carrying between them every weapon they had been able to lay their hands upon – knives, cudgels, baseball bats – and looked every inch the ragtag army. They were no soldiers, certainly, and seemed ill equipped for what lay ahead of them; but their grim, determined faces gave some indication of the spark that still resided inside them, despite the gaunt features and frail bodies. They congregated around the truck parked in the centre of the dual carriageway.

"The old bait and switch," Gabe replied. "Whether the mark's dead or alive, it's a reliable standby."

"The voice of experience," Liz said sardonically, folding her arms.

"You're talking to someone who spent five years of his life hijacking shipments. Be grateful it's an area of expertise, 'cause it's going to be our way in."

Mitch swung up into the cab and cast an eye over the interior. "Been simplified," he called down to them. "Looks like it runs off a battery, like a milk float."

"Like I said," Gabe told him, "the smart zombs have only learnt the basics. Flowers has probably taught them just enough so they can get themselves around in these things, and transport livestock."

"Can't have much power, either."

"Doesn't need to. We're going through the front door, not smashing our way in."

"What if we need to make a quick getaway?"

"In which case, you're better off scattering on foot. Give them multiple targets to go after. But listen," Gabe looked around at the group, "I'm not going to lie to you: chances are, we don't pull this off, we're not going to have the opportunity to escape. We go in, we go in with one intention, and that's destroying every Returner in there. Anything less than that and we're going to fail. Understand?"

The humans nodded slowly.

"OK." Gabe pulled down the tailgate at the back of the truck. "Climb aboard. Let's move out."

Standing face to face on the truck bed, the humans held onto each other for support as it rattled its way through the fringes of the city. The back of the vehicle was roofed by a tarpaulin and wooden slats ran the length of the sides, so they only got brief glimpses of the landscape outside. Mitch had put an eye to a gap to get a better view, and had seen other intelligent zombs watching the truck move past with expressions of hungry expectation. He knew he had imagined them licking their thin, dry lips, but the image stayed in his head nevertheless, and he turned away from the world outside, preferring to wait in the dark like an animal anticipating its trip to the slaughterhouse. The others stared at their feet, swaying with the motion of the vehicle, deep in contemplation.

The truck hit a pothole and all seven of the survivors clattered into one another, breaking the reverie. The longhair, Phillips, slammed his hand against the wall separating the bed from the cab, and looked round at the others, adjusting his glasses.

"We must be mad trusting this... thing," he hissed.

"None of us trust him," Liz said, then corrected herself. "*It.*" She glanced at each of her colleagues in turn. "But we all know this is a chance we can't afford not to take. Imagine the repercussions if we can pull this off. Imagine what could be possible. We're talking about finally fighting back against the dead, about having the chance to reclaim our lives."

"That's a pretty bloody big 'if'," Phillips sneered. "For

all you know, it could be offering us up on a plate. You heard its story: it's an ex-criminal who fell out of favour with its boss. Who's to say that it's not using us as an opportunity to curry favour with this Flowers guy? Deliver some fresh meat into the body shops as a means to weasel his way back into the old man's good books."

"That's enough," another member of the group said sternly. Tendry was a former theatre actor in his fifties. "There's no need for such talk."

"All the same, I agree with him," John remarked. "This thing – Gabriel – was prepared to sell out its boss. It pretty much said so itself. It won't think twice about betraying us if it suits it." He swept his arms either side of him. "It took the weapons off us, stored them in the cab. We're defenceless. If the pusbags come for us, we won't have a chance."

"It was just a precaution," Mitch piped up. "Just in case any of the stiffs check the back of the truck."

Liz turned to him. "You've spent the most amount of time with it, Mitch. What do you make of it?"

"I know that Gabe saved me, and would've done the same for Donna if he'd been able to. Everything he's said so far has been straight down the line. I think we've got to give him the benefit of the doubt. There's only so far you can get without trusting anyone."

"*He?*" Phillips barked a laugh. "I think you better remind yourself exactly what this thing is, before you start forgetting what side of the grave it's on."

"He's more human that some I could mention." Mitch turned back to Liz. "I genuinely think he wants to bring Flowers down, with our help. He's got his own agenda, and his own axe to grind, but I don't think it's in his interests to turn on us." He paused. "But that doesn't mean I'm not wary of him. There was something I sensed on our return trip; he tried to hide it, tried to act like it wasn't there, but all the same... There're some elements of his undead nature that he's still subject to."

"What do you mean?"

Mitch sighed. "He's still highly carnivorous. You can see it sometimes in his eyes – he's still got the hunger."

"Christ," John breathed. "And we're putting our lives in the hands of this fucking flesh-eater?"

Nobody answered, and the rest of the journey was spent in silence.

With a bump the truck came to a halt, and seconds later the tailgate was opened, the humans squinting in the daylight at Gabe standing below them. He motioned for them to stay quiet, and looked off to the side, beckoning to someone out of sight. Mitch craned his head around the edge of the vehicle and saw half a dozen Returners emerge from a side alley. Like Gabe they bore little signs of their zombie status – they could walk at a steady pace, and few carried extravagant wounds, though one was missing an arm and another had had his jaw wrenched at an odd angle – but they were unmistakably dead. Common to them all was the greenish, stretched complexion of their skin, the milky cast to their eyes, and the slow, almost languorous manner with which they regarded the living. Mitch had seen more repellent stiffs in his time, but few were as creepy as this bunch; it was their collected awareness of their own cadaverous state that gave them a chilling air of poised menace.

"OK, I've rounded up these guys on my travels," Gabe said. "They've pledged to help us." It was unclear which group he was specifically referring to.

"This the bait?" asked one of the Returners, a tall blond woman with a livid scar running from her ear to her chin.

"They're going to help us get in, yes."

"You think they're up to it?"

"Don't worry about us," John replied, the disdain undisguised in his voice. "We'll be ready to fight, as long as our weapons are returned." He glanced at Gabe.

"You'll get them back once we're through the gates and they're not expecting trouble. They," Gabe indicated the other ghouls, "are going to be providing support. The important thing is we get inside without arousing suspicion, OK? To that end, I need one of you humans to walk alongside the truck, acting as a sample. Flowers' dead are quite picky about the meat they consume, and they like to approve what enters their body shops." There were murmurs of disapproval, but he added: "That's just the way they do things. We need this to look like a regular shipment."

Mitch moved forward to volunteer, but Liz held him back. "I'll go." She jumped down onto the road before anyone could argue.

"Factory is just about half a mile away," Gabe told them, raising the tailgate. "So get ready." He turned to the blond zombie. "Alice, can you drive? I'll be escorting Liz here."

The Returners formed an arrowhead around the truck as it rumbled onwards, Liz trudging alongside with Gabe's hand on the small of her back. She knew it was for appearances' sake only, but still she bristled, feeling uncomfortably exposed and unhappy at having to trust these stiffs. She'd taught herself to hate the things, to paint a clear delineation between the living and the dead; in the early days, it had been simple, you were either one or the other, and if you stank of tomb-rot then you deserved nothing more than a bullet in the brain. But despite the straightforward battle-lines, it hadn't made the fight against them any easier, and the truth of the matter was that the dead were winning. Before this self-aware ghoul had turned up at their door, she had been fast losing hope, although she had said nothing to the group. She couldn't see how they could've survived much longer. Now, though, there was a slim chance they could change the situation; it was unbelievably risky, but it was one more chance than they had a few days before. And it was through trusting the enemy, the one thing she imagined she would never do.

"So who are they? Your friends, I mean," she asked Gabe.

"Other dead souls that I came across on my wanderings, of a similar level to me. They were just the same: frightened at what they'd become, still human enough to want to stop the mass extinction of the living, but ultimately undead and therefore now another species. In the eyes of groups like yours, at least."

"Can you blame us? We've spent years fighting the zombs. It was them or us. That kind of mentality is hard to shake, even if you wanted to."

"Things are a bit more complicated now."

"Tell me about it." She looked at the Returners either side of her. "How did this happen? How are you able to retain so much of your life and personality? Why you?"

Gabe shrugged. "I guess you could call us the next generation. There seems to be no rhyme or reason why any of these people –" he gestured to the others – "should've resurrected differently, and yet here we are, the anomalies. I'm sure there're others still, all over the country, growing in number. It must be the virus, I'm convinced of that. It's almost like it's developed into an entirely different strain over the course of the past decade."

"All over the country," Liz mused quietly. "You think this thing is everywhere?"

"Don't doubt it. This isn't confined to London. I've heard rumours that it's global." He turned to her. "You lost family too?"

She shook her head. "No one close. My folks were living up in Newcastle, and I haven't heard from them since the outbreak. But I must be one of the few that hasn't got a spouse or kids to worry about – guess that was why I could take charge of this bunch; I wasn't quite as shell-shocked as the others. Used to just doing things, I suppose."

"They've survived, thanks to you."

"I got them this far. Nothing's guaranteed, though, is it? Not these days."

They came within sight of the body shop, the requisitioned school. The high brick walls concealed much of what was going on behind them, but there were at least eight Returners on sentry duty, guarding the short driveway into the car park. They spotted the truck and its entourage heading towards them, and several peeled off from the main group and strode out to meet it.

"Flesh?" the lead ghoul asked Gabe, peering past him at the vehicle.

"Yes. Resistance humans," he replied, modulating his speech to that of the typical collector stiff. "More in truck like this one." He pinched Liz's upper arm and held it up for the creature to see. She winced, holding her breath.

It looked her over and ran its bony fingers through her hair. It made a noise of approval. "How many?"

"Another six in back."

It nodded at a pair of its colleagues, who sauntered round to the rear of the truck. Then it turned its attention back to Gabe. "Don't recognise you. Where all come from?"

"Across the river. Heard foodstocks running low. That true?"

"Boss demanding more, but living scarce. Avoiding patrols. Can't make quota."

"We might be able to help food situation. Bring in more like this, work for boss?"

The zomb narrowed its eyes. "What makes you think you can find humans?"

"Got this flesh to talk," Gabe replied, motioning to Liz. "Knows where we can find more. Bring them in for processing?"

The two deadheads came back from inspecting the truck. "Good batch," one said.

The leader nodded. "OK. Bring them in," he called, and stepped back to allow the procession to pass by. "Show them where to take the meat," it added to its assistants.

They entered the car park, and brought the truck to a stop by a line of similar vehicles standing empty. It looked like there hadn't been a delivery for a while. The humans were ordered to leave the truck bed and hustled into a tight knot, Returners on each side. Over to the left was a large green expanse of playing fields, netted goal posts strung at either end, and a fenced-off cricket strip next to them. Further away was a cement yard, with a trio of outbuildings circling it. As ever, it was eerily quiet; given the setting, it was especially unnerving. Once upon a time there would've been thousands of young voices echoing across this area, but now it was as silent as a tomb.

"Processing in main hall," one of the body shop's guards told Gabe. "Follow us."

"Got their weapons," Alice said, emerging from the cab, a set of canvas bags in her hands.

"Bring them to armoury on way," it answered.

They marched down some steps and into the school's quadrangle, heading towards a pair of double doors. Once inside, they gestured for them to continue down a corridor lined with lockers. Despite the silence outside, now they were within the building's walls they could hear cries drifting in the distance. They grew louder with each step they took.

"The sound of flesh," one of the ghouls said, grinning.

Gabe didn't reply, merely cast an eye over his shoulder. There was no one else in the corridor; it seemed as good a place as any. He nonchalantly stuck his foot in front of Liz and gave her a gentle push, sending her sprawling. The group splintered as she fell, the two stiff escorts looking back in confusion. Gabe drew his machete. "She trying to escape," he warned.

As they moved forwards to grab hold of her, he beheaded one with a swift swing of his blade. Before the disembodied skull had even hit the parquet floor, he speared the other one through the mouth, the machete tip embedding itself in a locker door; it hung there, an expression of surprise etched on its features. He yanked his weapon free, allowing the zomb to fall to the ground.

Alice opened the bags and tossed the humans and the other Returners their weapons. John greedily snatched his shotgun, and thumbed in some shells that he had stowed in his pockets. Gabe leaned down and offered his hand to Liz, who looked up at him with a mixture of fury and mistrust; but she grasped his palm and allowed him to pull her up.

"Sorry about that," he said. "Needed a diversion." He handed her a knife.

She took it. "Let's just get this done."

"Kill every deadhead in here," Gabe called as the group hurried up the corridor, the groans from the hall luring them forward. "No mercy."

Mitch hefted the baseball bat in his hand, slippery with sweat. He prayed they were in time to save Donna. He passed a classroom and glanced in, noting the overturned desks, trampled books and bloody footprints. He could feel anger building up inside him, for everything the zombs had done to them. He felt like smashing skulls for every ounce of hurt they had been responsible for.

The doorway to the hall opened and a stiff wandered out, a scream bellowing in its wake, cut short as the door flapped shut behind it. It glanced up, uncomprehending, at the group of figures charging towards it. A second later there was an explosion of fire as John discharged his shotgun, catching it in the belly, severing it in two; its lower half stood stationary while its upper torso flailed around in a mess of entrails, trying to squirm its way back to where it had come from. Gabe shouted a caution, but John ignored it. He quickly chambered another round and put the barrels to the back of its head, blasting a hole in it the size of his fist.

"You were saying?" John asked Gabe.

"Guess there goes our element of surprise," the Returner muttered in answer. He glanced at the group, nodded, then pulled open the door to the hall.

"Christ," Mitch whispered as he crossed the threshold, shock at what he saw bringing him to a standstill.

CHAPTER SEVENTEEN

It was an atrocity, a waking nightmare. The living were strapped to beds and gurneys haphazardly lining the length of the cavernous hall, more than two dozen of them in number; a violent splash of white linen and crimson rags. Drips and saline sacs stood attendant by each stretcher, tubes running into the arms of the prone humans, feeding them nutrients, keeping them alive while strips of their flesh were removed from their deathly pale, still-warm frames. They were being farmed for their meat, but the ghouls had no appetite for cold cuts – the skin and muscle had to be drawn from the bodies of the breathing, rich with oxygenated blood, and so food parcels were being carved from their thighs and buttocks while they were kept in a sustained state of awareness. They clearly felt every incision of the knife, every tear of tissue, as their pained cries filled the room, shrieks of agony rebounding off the high walls. Some had yet to be touched or were missing just small squares of body fat; others had been ripped raw, limbs amputated, sinew stolen in vast swathes to the point where they resembled scarlet plastic dummies, with little clue offered to the casual observer as to whether they were once men or women. Yet despite the damage wrought upon their person, incredibly even these unfortunates still clung on to life, their veins weakly pulsing.

The pounds of flesh torn from the living were being stored in an adjacent area, evidently what were once the school kitchens. Somehow they had to be transported from here to Flowers' mansion, and still retain their freshness. Mitch saw wheeled containers stacked with ice and guessed the set-up: joints were being kept frozen for the journey, ensuring that the meat didn't spoil or lose its tenderness. It was a huge butcher's operation, slaughter on a massive scale, but without any notion of limiting the suffering of those being farmed. Indeed, the Returners seemed to relish each wail of distress that emanated from the humans writhing beneath their knives, as if it added texture to the soft tissue. However, the zombs' satisfied expressions as they went about their bloody business abruptly changed once they looked round and realised they had company.

For a moment, as they took in the full extent of the hall's horror, there was only stunned silence, punctuated by the moans of the humans tied to the gurneys. Mitch, Liz and the rest had scarcely wanted to imagine what dread deeds were being perpetrated in the stiffs' body shops, and now, face to face with it, the shocking reality was breathtaking. Yet even in the presence of its barbarity, they still wanted to shy away from the full truth: they shuddered to think how long some of these poor wretches had been tortured here, slowly consumed in segments, or what had become of their minds in the process. It was too awful to contemplate.

It was the image of Donna, a victim of this abattoir, that kick-started Mitch into action. With a yell, he charged forward and clobbered the nearest zomb in the head with his baseball bat, powering it into the hard tiled floor. The shout of defiance acted as a catalyst, snapping the others into focus; they let rip as if fired from a cannon.

"Bastards!" John roared, and blew another away with both barrels.

The Returners seemed taken aback by this sudden invasion, but were quick to regain their senses, lurching forward in a stumbling half-run to engage the enemy, wielding whatever instruments came to hand: scalpels, meathooks, tenderisers. The humans initially took the advantage, spraying their opponents with the few semi-automatic weapons they had at their disposal, but their lack of skill with them quickly became apparent – too many shots went wide, or slotted the ghouls in their arms and midriffs – and they began to panic, unnerved at the speed with which the resurrected were moving towards them, shrugging off the rapid impacts of the bullets. Occasionally, the back of a zomb's head would explode as a missile found its target, but such hits were seldom, and the humans watched the gap between them and the flesh-eaters rapidly decrease.

Phillips' revolver clicked empty at just the wrong moment, and the instant he dug into his pocket for some spare rounds, a hook embedded in his skull. Pulled off his feet, he was dragged into the throng of advancing ghouls, who fell upon him hungrily. His stomach punctured, loops of intestine were tugged from his belly, and his shrieks were only cut short when his tongue was wrenched free.

One stiff flung a carving knife, and it glanced off Liz's cheek, knocking her backwards; she staggered, dizzy, a hand held to her face to stem the flow of blood that streamed down her jaw, and her legs collapsed under her. The zomb pressed home its attack, and leapt upon her, pushing up her head to fix its teeth on her throat. She got a hand to the side of its skull and tried to force it away, her fingers curling away from its bared incisors, but it was too strong and too determined. It shook itself free like a tangled animal and resumed its attempt to savage her neck. She screwed up her eyes, hoping it would be quick.

Then there was a rush of movement, and the deadhead was gone, pulled off her and thrown to the side. She looked up to see Gabe stalking towards it, kicking it onto its back and stamping hard on its face so that its features disappeared into a craggy hole. He turned back and helped Liz to her feet.

"Did it bite you?" he asked matter of factly, studying her wounds.

"No... no, I don't think so," she replied, gingerly running her hand over her throat. It was sticky with blood, but there were no teeth marks.

"That's quite a cut you've got there. You're going to grow faint, you keep losing blood like that."

"Don't see I've got much choice. I can't sit this one out."

"Here." Gabe took hold of her T-shirt and tore it along the bottom. She stiffened as he tied it around her head as a makeshift bandage. "What it lacks in grace, it'll at least keep your brains in."

"Thanks." She touched it; it felt tight and secure.

"Give support where you can," he told her. "We're taking over, and things are about to get a little crazy."

Gabe instructed the surviving gun-wielders to cease fire and take a step back, while he and his band of Returners moved in front of what remained of the body shop's ghouls.

"Out of the way, dead things," one of the zombs snarled at Gabe. "Why not consuming this flesh? Why siding with them?"

"Because they're us," Gabe replied. "And you were them once, only you've forgotten that you used to be human. How does it feel, eating your own kind to extinction?"

It frowned, confused. "Not our kind. *Never* our kind."

"No. You've gone too far to remember, haven't you?"

With that, Gabe lashed out and slammed his fist into the creature's face, its nose crumpling and its forehead buckling, as if the bone had grown supple beneath the skin. It keeled over backwards, and with a yell of fury Gabe jolted his elbow into the next one's throat, leaping upon it and ripping open the top of its scalp with his teeth. The others followed suit, tearing their way through the undead horde like wolves, biting and scratching, all sense of civilised restraint lost in the melee. Liz looked on, both appalled and fascinated, as Gabe and the other Returners became whirling dervishes of destruction, punching and gouging, seemingly ignoring the jaws snapping at their own flesh. If they felt any kind of pain then they showed no sign. It was a depraved, bestial display, Gabe annihilating all those within his grasp; his machete flashed and a pair of severed heads tumbled across the floor.

"Liz!" It was Mitch, beckoning her over. She ran towards him. "I've found Donna. I think... I think she might be OK. Help me get her free." She nodded, and turned to tell the others to start trying to loosen the restraints on those that were still capable of walking out of the building.

He led her to one of the beds, upon which the girl was tied. She was conscious, moaning softly, and had lost a couple of fingers on each hand, but the rest of her body was virtually untouched. She did, however, have a cotton pad taped over her left eye. Liz and Mitch exchanged glances; then the woman leant across and lifted the material, exposing the dark red abscess beneath.

"Mother of God," she murmured.

"Fuckers," Mitch rasped, spinning away in anger.

"She's still alive, though," Liz asserted. "Be thankful for that, at least."

They eased Donna upright, Mitch whispering platitudes in her ear and stroking her hair, though whether the girl heard or felt anything was another matter. She was shivering uncontrollably, and wouldn't open her remaining eye to look at either of them, continuing instead to merely murmur to herself. Liz tore her gaze from Donna's trembling figure and regarded the rest of the hall: attempts were being made to cut the living loose but with mixed results. Some were all too eager to leap from the gurneys, tearing out the drip feeds from their arms and sobbing with relief; others didn't move, even if they still had the limbs to do so. They stared up at the ceiling, their expressions blank and unreadable, sanity probably having long deserted them.

The last of the zombies were being despatched by Gabe and his small undead army; their speed and strength had eventually overwhelmed Flowers' Returners, who had looked distinctly creaky in comparison. Even so, Gabe's team had suffered a couple of casualties – one of them was struggling on the ground, its back broken, another was lying in pieces, scattered over a wide area; still animated, but unsalvageable. There was something brutal about the aftermath of the fight between the dead factions, Liz thought, surveying the scene. It reminded her of nature documentaries she'd seen back in her old life, of the uncompromising attacks that insects perpetrated on each other, and the twitching, quartered corpses that they'd leave in their wake. Gabe himself was wiping blood and other fluids off his clothes, but it was clear he'd taken some hits too: he had deep scratches across his face, and a chunk of flesh from the nape of his neck was missing. His bottom lip was drooping lower than it used to, and he held a hand across his torso, as if he was pushing something back in that had been rent open. He appeared to pay them no mind, though; he was dead meat, and surely incapable of feeling any sensation. As long as the brain remained intact, he could keep on going, even if bit by bit he was slowly falling apart.

Gabe shambled over towards her. "Is she OK?" he asked, nodding towards Donna.

"I don't know," Liz answered with a sigh, shaking her head. "She's lost an eye and several fingers, and I think she's in an advanced state of shock. She's going to need medical attention, though God knows how we're going to treat her. As for her mental state... it's impossible to guess what she's been through."

Mitch looked up, his expression grim, and pulled the girl closer, holding her head against his. "I'll take care of her."

"We all will," Liz said, "but it's going to take time."

"There's going to be no shortage of casualties," Gabe remarked, gesturing to the other humans pulling themselves free from the gurneys. "You're going to have to look out for each other. Some will probably need putting out of their misery." He shrugged when they glanced sharply at him. "Be the kindest act you can do; they've suffered enough. Just make sure you put them down so they don't get back up again."

"Does that go the same for your friends?" Liz asked, pointing at the two Returners still jerking spasmodically amongst the necrotic remains.

"I'll deal with them."

"So what now?" Mitch wanted to know. "How do we get nearer to Flowers?"

"*We* nothing, son. You and the rest of the humans' part in this is done. We're going to commandeer a shipment," Gabe replied, hooking a thumb over at the wheeled containers filled with ice and body parts. "Make it look like we're delivering a regular supply of sweetmeats. Once inside, it's payback time."

"You think you can go up against the might of your old boss? Just you and your undead pals?"

"You got a better idea?"

"I reckon you need all the help you can get."

"I thought your place was with Donna." When the kid didn't answer, Gabe continued: "I appreciate your offer, but this is going to be no place for the living. I'm not sure I'm going to come out of there in one piece, and I've got certain... advantages. I said at the beginning, you wouldn't see me again after we did this, and it still stands. Whatever happens, whether I take down Harry or not, I'm gone."

"I want my revenge too," Mitch said quietly.

"You already have, son. You've helped save these people, and now you have to look after them. Show the deadfucks that they've lost." Gabe reached out and placed a hand on his shoulder. "I couldn't have got this far without you, you know that, don't you?"

Mitch nodded grudgingly and gave a tight smile, hugging Donna to his chest.

"I'll get some guys together," Liz said. "Help you load up."

"First, we need to do a complete sweep of this place," Gabe replied. "Wipe out any ghouls still left in the building. I don't want any word getting back to Flowers and having him waiting for us. Once the area's secure," he turned to Liz, raising his eyebrows, "then it's time to pay the old man a visit."

Gabe sat behind the wheel of the truck, guiding it out of the city, aware that he was possibly leaving it for the final time. Beside him, Alice was staring out the passenger window with unblinking eyes, while in the back, standing over five crates of fresh meat, were two others: Adam and Beth. It had been grisly work for the living to have handled these containers – the guards at the mansion would be checking the vehicle's contents, so there was no question that they had to carry them if they were to get inside the house's perimeter – but it had been equally hard for the Returners, controlling their hunger in the face of such temptations. After the battle, having sunk his teeth into rotten carcasses, the thought of devouring these succulent morsels was overwhelming; but the human Gabe that still resided in his resurrected body nixed that notion before it could take hold.

He often felt there were two sides within him fighting for control: the man that he used to be, and the wretched graveyard creature, lusting after the flesh of the living. He was ashamed, and a little scared, to admit that he had succumbed entirely to the latter when he had launched himself at the stiffs in the body shop, revelling in the slaughter, reverting back to his primal instincts. Certainly, he was aware he was no longer a human being when that element was to the fore. He was more akin to a force of nature, an amoral carnivore driven by the centre of his brain that the virus had reawakened. He had had no desire to eat the zombs' putrescent tissue – it was warm skin and bone that he craved – but taking apart the things with his teeth had been a gloriously atavistic act.

There had been a similar sense of satisfaction as they wiped out every one of Flowers' zombies that were still remaining in the school. Their look of uncomprehending shock as their factory-farmed food rose up and smashed their brains out, the ones standing guard at the main gate repeatedly rammed with purloined trucks until they resembled nothing more than greasy smears on the tarmac. For so long the body shops had been places to fear, casting a long shadow over the area; now one had been disabled, its evil vanquished, and that had given the living hope. Other humans could be saved, the tyrannical rule of the deadheads could be shattered. When Gabe had said goodbye to Liz, she had shook his hand and for the first time had looked him in the eye without a wrinkle of distaste souring her expression. She and Mitch and the others already appeared stronger, despite what they had been through, and although he didn't know where they would take the battle next – it was something they still had to decide for themselves – he guessed that they were more than ready.

Maybe the air of revolution had gone to his head, but he thought he could discern a vulnerability amongst the stiffs as they passed them through Greater London's streets: a sense that their time was passing. Change had always been Harry's ally, the belief that things couldn't stay the same. It had served him well, certainly since the outbreak all those years ago, and it had eventually brought him the city he'd dreamed of possessing. Now, however, events seemed to be undergoing another shift; Flowers' ghouls looked tired and clumsy and slow, and they were losing their grip on what remained of the human populace. Their generation was coming to an end, and something else was emerging to take their place. Was it him, Gabe wondered; he and others like him that were undead but progressing back to their former selves. Were they the next stage in the virus's evolution? And if he toppled Flowers as the dark ruler of this corrupt kingdom, was he fated to take his place?

Gabe saw the glinting metal strung across the road too late; they weren't travelling at speed – the refitted trucks could barely reach more than twenty miles per hour, so he could've avoided it if he'd spotted it early enough – but the spikes were hidden beneath a layer of debris strung across the width of the thoroughfare, with only the jagged tops visible. He knew as soon as he stamped on the brake pedal that he wasn't going to miss them, and sure enough there was a shudder and a low rumble as the tyres were punctured.

"Shit, what was that?" Alice asked as the tremor passed through the vehicle.

"Homemade stingers," Gabe replied, wrestling with the wheel. "Somebody's set a trap for us."

"Humans?"

"Must be. They're gonna be thinking that we're taking Flowers his next three-course meal."

"Hell." The truck started to skew to the side, and Gabe realised that it was pointless to try to progress any further; he pulled on the handbrake to bring it to a halt. "What are we going to do?"

"Do what we usually do," he said, pushing open the driver's door. "Talk our way out of it."

He walked round to the back, opened the doors and told the pair inside what had happened, and warned them to keep their wits about them. As he did so, he saw figures emerging from the derelict office buildings on either side. *Can't believe it*, he thought ruefully, *never thought I'd be on the wrong end of a carjacking.*

But there was something odd about the way these humans were moving, and as they came closer their shuffling gait was explained: they were deadheads, and ones in a particularly bad way. They looked like they were rotting right before his eyes, their bodies stick-thin, their skin almost translucent. They carried no weapons either, as if they didn't have the strength in their arms to lift anything. Instead, they merely stared at Gabe and the truck hungrily, a faint groan issuing from the group.

They're pusbags, he thought, frowning at Alice, who

came out to join him. *They're not capable of setting anything like this up. Someone else has to be behind them.*

"Can you talk?" Gabe asked them. "Can you understand me?"

In answer, they parted and allowed another figure to step through. He was a zomb too, but more sprightly; a short guy with a sprig of unruly dark hair atop his heavily lacerated face. He gazed at Gabe uncertainly, hefting a small revolver in his hand.

"You're not one of Flowers'," he said, a Scottish lilt to his voice still audible despite the slightly slurring quality of its timbre. It was a statement, rather than a question.

"No."

"But you're Returners? Fully cognitive resurrected?"

They both nodded.

"My God. I'd heard there were more, I knew your numbers were growing, but trying to track any of you down..." He seemed genuinely excited. "My theories were right. You're the living – well, undead – proof of that."

"Theories?" Gabe repeated. "Who are you?"

"Gannon," he said, holstering the gun and extending his hand in greeting. "Doctor Robert Gannon. Welcome to my world."

CHAPTER EIGHTEEN

On a clear day, the view was magnificent. Standing at the upstairs picture window of his mansion, binoculars held to his atrophied eyes, Harry Flowers surveyed his kingdom spread before him with approval; it was everything he could've asked for, everything he'd strived for. From his vantage point, London curled into the distance, a grey mass choked of life. At this time of the morning, just after dawn, a mist rose off the iron waters of the Thames, seeping past the office blocks standing silent sentinel on its banks. The dance of those few wisps, chased from the surface of the river by a stiff wind, was the only movement that he could see; the metropolis was inert, a desiccated corpse the colour and vibrancy of cold embers. A few pockets of resistance still remained, he knew; a few parasites still clung to its rotting hide. But he was slowly, inexorably, consuming the city, gradually absorbing it into his domain; and the best thing was this was only the beginning. Once the capital fell utterly under his command, then he could extend his reach – send out his men to the peripheral settlements that he knew to exist in the satellite towns and stamp his mark even further. He saw it as spinning a web, casting the strands wider and wider until the entire country was his to control; and with him naturally at the centre, at the hub. He never wanted to be anywhere else.

He lowered the binoculars, studying the grounds nearer to home. He had ordered the woods that had backed on to the house to be cleared completely, so he could obtain just such an unobstructed view of the city that was now his. There wasn't a day that went past when he didn't like to gaze upon it and marvel. Elsewhere, the gardens had been allowed to grow wild, his interest in keeping them manicured and healthy having waned over the years. It was an odd sensation, one that he hadn't expected come his resurrection: his appreciation of beauty had diminished, to the point where he found the still, bare qualities of the barren landscape more appealing. He had allowed the weeds to choke the roses and the rhododendron, the nettles to encroach from the edges of the paths to virtually engulf them, and the potted plants to wither and die. There was nothing of colour out there now, just decay and those feeding upon it, and yet he felt unmoved by this loss. It seemed to suit his mood, and the empire he was building – a bleak, desolate land fit only for the dead, and the man (or what was once a man) that ruled it. Instead, in place of the flora that had once ringed his mansion, he had devised more fortifications: fences, sentry posts, anti-personnel weaponry, to keep him safe from those that would do him harm.

He turned away from the window, placing the binoculars on the sill. A familiar gnawing ache resounded in his empty belly, and he reached out and grasped the back of a nearby chair to steady himself, waiting for the moment to pass. It was taking longer these days, and he gritted his teeth, the pain blossoming. Despite his dead nerve-endings, the need to feed still brought with it its own singular sting. It was the one reminder of his undead status, the one link to the pusbags that staggered through the city streets, and he could not rid himself of it. All that he had accomplished post-death – an organised militia, enforcing his rule, a London paralysed by fear and ripe for the taking – and yet still his body was slave to the demands of his zombiehood.

At the start, it had been easy satiate his hunger. Warm flesh was readily available, and once the pangs took hold he had no trouble feeding. In the interim, as he and his troops established the body shops that enabled the living to be distributed in convenient, pre-packed states, he fought to lessen the control his stomach had over him; as far as he was concerned, he called the shots, not the virus squatting in his brain. Sheer strength of will enabled him to gain the upper hand, and he found he could manage and maintain his belly's insistent need for sustenance, not requiring living meat more than once a week or so. Such a diet was soon an act of necessity as much of choice as the regular deliveries from the processing stations were beginning to dry up, and humans became increasingly difficult to find. Others lesser than him took to stumbling about the mansion grounds, groaning, not much better than the rotting deadheads they themselves looked down upon. But not he. He had not been dictated to in life, and he certainly would not become a mere puppet at the whim of his own body post-death.

But in his heart, he knew it could not be denied, no matter how much he fought it. The hunger, the lust to feed, was his nature, and it was impossible to resist. It had to be at least a fortnight now since he'd properly feasted, and the throbbing pain that swelled from his gut was a wake-up call, an intestinal nudge to suggest it wasn't going to go away. However, unless the situation changed, he didn't know how he could face the eternity stretching ahead of him, a victim to cravings he couldn't satisfy. What good was it to rule over an empire, when there was nothing left to consume? And what would become of him if his belly's desires were not met?

Despite Flowers' instructions to his resident boffins many years ago (just how long was it, he wondered; time seemed to slip past him with little relevance) to find a way of tweaking the virus's demand for flesh, they had come up with few results. Given its stubborn refusal to be adapted by artificial means, he suspected the best he could hope for was that the bacteria would continue to evolve along a similar path that it had taken so far; but that process could take decades, if not centuries. He hated being at the mercy of elements he could not manipulate to his own ends. It left him helpless, and that was a state of being that had previously been an anathema to him.

The ache in his belly gradually subsided, and he straightened. Perhaps he should investigate the pantry and see what supplies remained, he pondered, loathing the junkie-like caving of his willpower. He left the room and crossed the landing, noting the disrepair the house had fallen into; the wallpaper was streaked with dirt, the carpet frayed and stained. How long had it looked like this, he wondered. How many months had the mansion slowly slid into decay without him being aware of it? It felt cadaverous itself, a crumbling, hollow shell. He realised with a sudden stab of amazement that he hadn't ventured beyond these walls for over three years, too wrapped up inside his own addiction to see it falling apart around him.

He padded to the first floor, then paused in his descent. He glanced across at the closed door to his right, hesitated, but finally rapped upon it and stepped across the threshold without waiting for an answer. As ever, the room was silent save the ticking of the clock on the mantelpiece, and the rising sun cast the chair in front of the window in silhouette, an aura of light haloing the figure seated upon it. He squinted as he strode towards the window, casting an eye to the woman staring at the landscape beyond the glass. He pulled a curtain across the view, lengthening the chamber's shadows. She blinked and stirred, conscious of the gloom that had settled upon her.

Flowers pulled up a chair and sat beside her. "Anna," he said. "Have you slept at all?"

"Like the light," she replied in a tiny voice, fidgeting in her seat.

"It's too bright. You shouldn't sit so close to the window."

"S-scared of dark. Scared of what's t-there. Want to close eyes, but scared."

"You need rest."

"Don't tell me w-what I need," she muttered. "And s-since when have you cared?"

"I'm still your father."

She looked at him for a second, then laughed, an eerie sound as dry as kindling. "You? You're n-not even human."

He studied her, a mixture of sadness and frustration and self-hatred churning in his chest. That he had cut himself adrift from his daughter like this hurt him as deeply as a knife to the heart; or at least when he was still capable of feeling such a wound. His resurrection might've brought him a lack of physical sensation, but the mental anguish at what he'd done all those years ago was sharp as ever. He had selfishly hoped that he could slough off the trappings of his former life upon coming back as a Returner, his sins fading like the memory of breath in his lungs. But it was not to be, his torments were as fresh as they ever were in life and they were here in front of him, represented by the young woman that had once been his kin. But now... now she was the past that he would not allow himself to forget. Her condition, her indifference towards him, the future that she had been denied, was all his fault, and every time he came to visit, it was to reaffirm his guilt – a confessional not to absolve his failings as a parent but to refresh them anew.

She was regressing, and he didn't know how to stop it; indeed, wasn't even sure whether halting it was the correct thing to do. Where once she had been trapped between life and death, the moment of her passing held in stasis by the virus, now it was as if the reanimation bacteria was struggling to stay in control, losing its grip on her central cortex. While he had witnessed other undead growing more intelligent over the years, she was the first to take the backward path. Her speech and sense of balance were becoming unstable, she was increasingly unresponsive, and she was losing her ability to comprehend those around her. He didn't know why it was happening, or where her decline would take her. Towards a true death? Or to become one of the shambling hordes? He could not accept that, yet he had no good reason why he shouldn't just let her go. She had lived this half-life for over a decade, ever since he had shot through her to prove his strength of will to Goran Vassily, and had hovered on the cusp of mortality, a prisoner inside her own skin. The kindest act would be to finish it, to set her free, to lead her into the weed-ridden gardens and place a gun to the back of her head. But he was too much of a coward for that, he could not bear the weight of that responsibility; and in truth, he did not want to lose her, because once she was gone, nothing would stop his transformation into a monster. Her presence reminded him of his past deeds, of what terrible crimes he had committed, a wound that he would never allow to heal. If she was gone, then all would be consumed – identity, history, love and regrets – in the pursuit of power, and he would no longer recognise his own reflection.

"I've always cared for you, Anna," he said, reaching out and stroking her hair. She flinched at his touch. "If I could do anything to bring you back to me, I would."

"Just let me g-go," she whispered, her head bowed.

"What?"

She looked up at him, her eyes glistening. "I'm t-trying s-so hard to leave, to end this. S-scared of dark, don't want to close eyes, but I know it's only w-way of escape."

Flowers knelt quickly, placing a hand on her knee, the fingertips of the other holding her chin. She was as cold as porcelain. "What are you saying? That you're bringing on this decline yourself?"

"Only way... to escape you. I w-won't be held here anymore."

"No, please, Anna, don't do this. I need you here—"

"I want... to go..."

"Anna—"

It was then that the first of the explosions rocked the mansion, and the alarms started to wail.

Twenty-four hours earlier

"Give me one good reason why I shouldn't just rip your fucking throat out," Gabe rasped, holding Gannon by the lapels. "Tell me why I wouldn't be doing the human race a huge favour."

"And you think that will change anything?" the former scientist replied. "You think that's going to magic the world back into what it was fifteen, twenty years ago?"

"It would make *me* feel better."

"And once that feeling had passed, what would you be left with? Just another corpse on the floor, and a host of unanswered questions. Killing me will solve nothing."

Gabe considered this, then released the man. They were

standing in Gannon's makeshift laboratory, a collection of tables and rudimentary scientific equipment that he'd looted from various sources and collected together in a long-abandoned back room of a chemist's. His jottings and diagrams were tacked to the walls and covered the work surfaces, while a few works in progress were evident, scattered about the space: a severed ghoul's head was held in a clamp, it's brain exposed, another was wired up to a car battery. Everything looked crude, filthy and incapable of bringing usable results.

"Some sense at last," Gannon muttered.

"Pal, there would be a queue of people from here to the Watford Gap trying to get hold of you, if they knew where you were. In fact, a few survivors that I met recently probably wouldn't mind five minutes alone with the man who destroyed their lives."

"We've all suffered, believe me."

"Yeah? So what happened to you?"

He shrugged. "I was called to my superior's office in London once the outbreak hit, part of an MoD convoy that got caught in a riot. I managed to make it to a government station, and was working on containing the crisis. Unfortunately, the safety of the outpost was compromised."

"Compromised?"

"The infection got inside and spread like wildfire. I was bitten, end of story."

"Well, not quite. You're standing here talking like me, completely self-aware and an evolutionary step up from those deadheads outside. That doesn't sound like the end of the story to me." The stiffs that had initially appeared with Gannon had remained on the street, watching over the vehicle while Alice and the rest had made some attempt to repair the damage done to the tyres. Gabe had had to give a brief explanation of why they were travelling in one of Flowers' trucks, and their business of infiltrating his mansion.

"True," the scientist said, nodding. "HS-03 has developed beyond all my expectations. If it keeps growing at this rate, we could have a new species of human being in the next thirty years." He studied Gabe, his eyes roving over him with clinical dispassion. "Your strength and intelligence makes me wonder if it did have military applications after all..."

"I'm not one of your test subjects, Gannon."

"Don't you see, you're the next generation. The mindless carnivores were just the first stage. HS-03 is constantly evolving the dead to an incredible degree."

"You must be very proud." Gabe gestured to the experiments dotted about the room. "So what are you doing here? Trying to replicate it?"

"I've got some advanced cultures, yes. But I'm also trying to control the Returners, make them reasonably docile and open to instruction. I was working on something similar before the outbreak. As you've seen from the little band outside, I've had some partial success."

"They'll do what you tell them to?"

"Up to a point. Interesting thing is, even they are growing quite territorial – they're recognising that those trucks you came in are removing all the warm flesh from the area. They're conscious that the ruling elite is getting all the food, while they are being left to rot. It's a simple animal deduction, but they're smart enough to have laid the stinger trap."

"My God."

"Like I say, that's HS-03's evolutionary power." He chuckled to himself. "The dead aren't taking it lying down anymore."

"So the zombs are no fans of Harry Flowers either."

"Few are. They're as much under the cosh as the humans."

Alice entered, her expression grim. "Wheels are screwed, Gabe. Too shredded to be repaired."

"Damn," he murmured. "We've just lost our way in." He slumped against a table. "No way we're going to be able to get past Flowers' security, not without some kind of cover..." He looked up suddenly and grabbed Gannon by the arm. "Wait a minute – Doctor, you want to go some way to compensating for the shitstorm you landed everybody in? You want to claw back a few brownie points? And your undead friends out there want to grab a piece of the action they're being denied?"

The scientist blinked, bemused.

"You think you could you could control more of them – a regular army?"

Gannon nodded. "If we could round them up."

Gabe smiled. "Then I think I might have a solution."

"Which is?" Alice asked.

"We're going to do this the Harry Flowers way. We're going to storm that fucking mansion head on."

CHAPTER NINETEEN

"What the hell is going on?" Flowers roared as another explosion rent the air. He clattered down the stairs, drawn like the rest of his men racing across the hallway towards the open main doors by the pulsating warble of the perimeter alarms. To his ears, it could only mean one thing: the fences had been breached, and the detonations were the landmines grouped sporadically within the mansion grounds being triggered. The rattle of gunfire drifted in, short bursts at the edge of the gardens. The enemy was at the gates, he thought. But who would dare take him on?

He heard his name called, and saw Hewitt pushing his way through the throng heading outside and making his way towards him. The kid had an Uzi held down at his side, and he looked harried: his grey face was etched in a grimace, anger and perhaps a touch of concern visible in his eyes. He met Flowers at the foot of the staircase.

"Who is it?" the older man demanded.

"We're not sure," Hewitt replied. "At least, not yet." If Flowers didn't know better, it was almost as if the kid was breathless. He couldn't possibly experience exhaustion, yet here he was, looking for all the world like he was about to keel over. He kept glancing back towards the grounds and fingering the weapon in his hand nervously. "There's an army of deadheads massing at the fences; I mean, a *lot*. Where they've come from, we have no fucking idea."

"But the defences are holding?" Flowers asked impatiently, if a tad relieved that he'd been premature in assuming that what he could hear were the sounds of intruders entering the gardens.

"Yeah, at the moment. They're just hitting the electrified perimeter fences and going up like fucking rockets. But they keep on coming, hundreds of them, and we're worried that the sheer weight of numbers is going to put a strain on the gate. Plus the burning bodies could end up short-circuiting the security system."

"So there's a chance they could get in?"

"I can't see them getting even near the house. If they get past the gates, they've got the tripwires to deal with, and *us*." He held up the Uzi. "But why should they want to get in here anyway? We've got nothing a pusbag would want. Even if they could sense the meat we've got in the stores, it wouldn't bring them in droves like this."

"Somebody's behind them."

Hewitt nodded. "This isn't some wandering bunch of zombs that have stumbled onto our land; they were directed here and instructed to attack. But why? What can they hope to achieve? The fucking things are just destroying themselves."

"It's to wear us down. Like you say, sheer weight of numbers to put a strain on our defences. Somebody wants in, and is using the stiffs as both barrier and distraction."

"Humans, you think?"

"Seems to be on too grand a scale for a bunch of shit-scared survivors," Flowers mused. "They wouldn't be able to get deadheads to do what they want anyway. No, this has the fingerprints of a Returner all over it. A new rival, deciding to piss on my territory." He turned to Hewitt. "Let's take a look at them."

"Are you sure, Harry? I mean, I don't think we're in any danger, but all the same, it would make sense for you to stay in the house."

"I'm not cowering from uninvited guests," Flowers said

sternly, already walking towards the doors. He beckoned to one of his men. "Tate, ensure that the entire perimeter is monitored. I don't want anyone sneaking in under the radar while we're dealing with the frontal attack. Oh, and see if you can reset the alarm, it's doing my head in." The man nodded, and jogged away around the side of the mansion, a pair of his colleagues following.

Hewitt scurried to keep up with his boss as the old man strode down the drive, feet scrunching on the gravel, and stopped at the edge of the lawn, raising a hand over his eyes to shield them from the glare of the rising sun. Nice touch, Flowers thought, initiating an assault at dawn. Several metres away, a knot of his men were spraying the fence with automatic fire, though it was difficult to see the targets they were aiming for; the invading zombies were turning into a charcoal morass, impossible to determine one from another. Immediately beyond the gate was a row of blackened cadavers, fusing to the metal as they melted from the high voltage running through it. A few were on fire, hair crisping, bones popping, as they jerked and danced from each power surge. Behind them, more ghouls still came, stumbling blithely into the fence – those that could actually get near it – and exploding as they brushed against the wire. Flowers watched one's ribcage flung open like shutter doors, the organs sizzling as they plopped onto the grass.

Christ, they're disintegrating, he thought, studying the figures with grim fascination. *The things are burning up before my eyes.*

"Cease fire," he yelled. The gunshots dribbled to a halt. Glancing at the kid beside him, he added: "Pointless to try to hit them through that barbeque. Just a waste of ammo."

"What do you want to do?"

"Give me contact with the watchtowers." He held out his hand, and Hewitt passed him a walkie-talkie. Flowers lifted it to his lips. "Simmons, what's the news?"

"Not good, sir," a tinny voice replied in his ear. "Got maybe three hundred flesh-eaters backed up against the wire, and the system is not looking healthy. It's showing signs of overload. Could start to spark any minute."

"You see anything else apart from the deadheads? Someone controlling them?"

"Nope, just wave after wave of brainless maggotdicks. They're relentless, coming right across the fields, straight for the house."

"Roger that." Flowers clicked off the two-way. "They're coming out of London, I'm sure of that," he said to Hewitt.

"London? Who's left that we know could—"

The old man held up a hand for silence, and pondered for a few moments. Then he raised the walkie-talkie once more. "Simmons, shut off the power to the fence."

"You sure?"

"If it blows, we could risk losing the power to the whole mansion. Or fire could spread across the gardens. Turn it off."

"Wilco." Seconds later there was a buzz followed by a whine, and the microwaved dead ceased their convulsions. In its stead, the early-morning air was filled with the groans of the ghouls, the jangle of the gate as many bodies incessantly pressed against it, and the crackle of burning flesh, pungent smoke drifting into the sky.

"Double the guard on the perimeter," Flowers told Hewitt. "Keep an eye out for any breaches in the fences, any weak spots. Also be prepared to move back to the house if need be, to defend that." He turned and headed back towards the front doors. "This was just the beginning.

Whoever's behind this will be making a move – be ready for it."

"Right," Hewitt acknowledged, then coughed. He frowned and rubbed his throat, then coughed again, as if trying to rid himself of an irritation lodged there.

Flowers halted, and turned around to study the kid. Their eyes locked in puzzlement. Then they heard retching coming from across the grounds.

"They've turned off the power to the fence."

"So we make a move?" Alice asked.

"Not yet," Gannon replied. "Give it a few more minutes for the agent to disperse. No point going in there and suffering the ill effects ourselves. Wait for it to take hold."

They were crouching in the peripheral scrubland to the left of the mansion, hidden enough to not be discernable from the watchtowers but at a vantage point from which they could monitor the situation. Fortunately, Flowers' guards were preoccupied with the stiffs accumulating at the front gate, spraying those that were still alight – and those they could reach through the tangle of limbs and charcoal skeletons – with extinguishers. The zombs that hadn't been fried continued to tug at the fence, the wire rattling wildly. Evidently, the triggermen had been ordered not to fire upon the dead, as the battering went unchecked, those inside the mansion grounds watching the assault impassively. More guards were being deployed at regular intervals along the perimeter, all hefting semi-automatics.

"They're increasing the security," Gabe said. "They know we're coming."

"They know *someone's* coming," Gannon corrected. "They don't know exactly who they're expecting."

"Are they all Returners?" Beth enquired. "Flowers' soldiers, I mean."

"Yeah. He made his workforce turn after he resurrected," Gabe murmured. "Always likes to be in control, does Harry... He wouldn't have humans alongside him – considers them beneath him now. Only one place for the living and that's on his dining table."

"Aren't we kind of adopting the same position?" Alice said, nodding to the zombs hammering against the fence. "We're using deadheads 'cause we think they're expendable, and a lesser species than ourselves. We've got more in common with them than the humans."

"They're test animals," Gannon answered bluntly. "Mindless automatons to be directed as we instruct. We've got no more in common with them as we would a lab rat."

"You told *them* that?"

Gannon frowned. "Meaning what?"

"Meaning how do you know what's going on inside their heads? You think they're happy being used like this?"

"They're barely aware of where they are, of what they're doing. There's no cognitive reasoning in their brains at all, just what they've been told."

"Only because you've tampered with them–"

"Can we have this argument another time?" Gabe interjected, silencing the pair. "I have to say, I'm not happy about using them as mobile dirty bombs, but if it knocks Flowers' outfit onto the back foot, then I say we take the advantage." He turned to Gannon. "Must admit, doctor, they've worked like clockwork. It's almost as if you've rewired their internal circuitry."

The scientist shrugged. "I've been studying HS-03 for over ten years, had experience of it at first hand. I know now how to modify it, how to get it to work on certain urges and act upon it. The corpses are vehicles driven by the virus, nothing more." He looked off towards the stiffs slamming against the fence, and sighed. "This would've been my army, this is what I was working towards. If only I'd had more time, I could've perfected it..."

"Wait," Alice said, indicating towards the mansion. "I think the agent's doing its stuff."

They all turned their attention towards the house and watched the guards begin to exhibit signs of infection. The sound of coughing reached even their hiding place, drowning out the mournful wailing of the dead. Some were bent double, their guns shouldered, spluttering into the lawns. Others scratched at their pallid faces and arms, shavings of cold flesh fluttering to their feet, fistfuls of hair pulled out in clumps.

"So it's going through the skin?" Gabe asked.

Gannon nodded. "They wouldn't breathe it in, now that their respiratory systems are dormant. But it's entering the epidermis, the necrosis attacking the cells, decaying them from the inside out. What they're coughing up is matter dislodging into their windpipes."

"Nasty."

"It's like bacterial acid. Once it gets under the skin, it'll eat through to the bone."

"And you created this?"

"Not long after the outbreak, the MoD asked me to come up with a way of neutralising the zombie threat over a wide area, but it never got past the prototype stage. I've been tinkering with it ever since. Thought it might be handy to have a little weapon of mass destruction all of my very own."

"Bet your masters never thought you'd be using deadheads as carriers for it. You could do a hell of a lot of damage, you know, across the whole city."

"No," Gannon replied, shaking his head. "It's only got a limited dispersal field, and a short lifespan, which is why we'll be able to go down there any second without it affecting us. In fact, it'll probably burn itself out before it's entirely disabled Flowers' goons. They'll still be on their feet – just – but should be compromised enough for us to get past them without too much trouble."

Gabe stood. "Well, I'm getting a hankering to wreak some bloody vengeance. Care to join me?"

They picked a point at the perimeter fence at which security was the most lax: a pair of guards were on their hands and knees, the flesh of their hands and forearms almost liquescent, white bone emerging from the grey puddle where their skin used to be. They barely noticed the newcomers, whimpering and pawing the earth like sick dogs, shrunken facial features disappearing into their skulls, and didn't have the time to recognise the fact that intruders were snipping the wire free before a figure snuck through and beheaded them both with a single sweep of his machete. Gabe stooped and passed one of the guns to Alice, who was next through the fence. Adam and Beth followed, leaving Gannon on the other side of the wire, looking ill at ease now he was so close to Flowers' domain.

"You sure you don't want to come with us?" Gabe asked him.

"I've done my part, I've got you in," the scientist replied. "The rest I'll leave up to you."

"Stay close by."

"I will. Good luck."

The four of them headed off, gluing themselves to the curving shadow of the house, avoiding confrontation where they could. For the most part, Flowers' enforcers were struggling to purge their bodies of the agent that was devouring them, and paid little heed to the knot of Returners that were skulking past. A few caught sight of them and tried to raise the alarm, but found no sound would emerge from their ravaged throats other than a soupy gurgle, and when they attempted to hoist their rifles the strength left their arms, the limbs putrefying. Those they were close to reached out or made an effort to block them, but Gabe either ran them through with his blade – their skulls now the consistency of mud – or Alice took them out with a discreet burst from her semi. The bullets shredded them like paper; it was as if they were vanishing, losing all sense of corporeality.

They threaded their way through the grounds, Gabe's memory of the layout leading them, and they reached the main doors of the mansion. He turned to the other three. "I want to create maximum chaos, keep them all occupied. Adam, Beth – can you see if you can get the front gate open, let the remaining deadheads in? That should cause enough confusion to keep Flowers' goons away from the house. Once that's done, make a start on the other matter."

The pair nodded, and sprinted off down the drive. He glanced at Alice and motioned that they should enter, stepping out of the light and into the cool dark of the hallway. He could feel the vaguest tingle of the bacteria in the air, despite Gannon's assurance that his bio-weapon had a finite exposure time. His skin prickled slightly, but he seemed to be suffering none of the symptoms Harry's lot were displaying. In fact, the further they moved into the building, the more the sensation eased, as if it couldn't permeate brick and mortar. If that was the case, then the ganglord was probably unaffected, hiding away within the structure's bowels, waiting for whoever was coming for him.

The design of the house hadn't changed much since Gabe was last here, he noted, but he was surprised to see it go to rack and ruin; dirt and debris were collecting on the tiled floor, and huge cobwebs dangled like gossamer nets from the ceiling. It was becoming derelict, as much subject to entropy as its residents. It looked ready to collapse. They reached the foot of the staircase, scanning left and right for signs of movement. Now they were far from the cries of the dead, it had fallen uncomfortably quiet. He hoped that much of the security had been placed outside to protect the perimeter, leaving a minimal staff within the building itself.

"We need to make for the first floor," he whispered.

"How do you know that's where Flowers will be?"

"I don't. But there's someone up there I need to see." He paused. "To save."

Alice studied him for a second. "OK. But be ready – this isn't going to be easy."

As if in answer, there was the roar of a sub-machine gun opening up and the plaster near their heads exploded as bullets raked across the hall. The pair of them dived behind the banister, splinters following in their wake. The shooter was at the top of the first flight of stairs, and was moving down, punctuating each footfall with a five-second burst. The wood around them cracked with each impact. Alice rolled into space, placed the barrel of the rifle between stairposts and fired up, catching the figure in the legs; it grunted and stumbled, pausing in its descent. She took advantage of the momentary lull, jumped to her feet, and squeezed off another blast, ripping through its neck and head. The shooter toppled onto its back, and slid down the remainder of the stairs, the remains of its skull bumping against the steps. Gabe joined her, standing over the body.

"Recognise him?" she asked, poking the cadaver's side with her barrel.

"Not any more." It was one of Harry's mob, but not much was left intact above the chin.

They started to ascend cautiously, and made it to the first landing. Gabe silently pointed to the next set of stairs they needed to take, then grimaced as a bullet powered through his arm; a second and third followed in quick succession, catching him in the thigh and chest. He didn't feel any pain, but the shock fleetingly paralysed him.

"Fuck!"

They crouched and ran, bullets zipping into the carpet at their feet or ricocheting off the light fittings: they were being fired on from above again. Gabe hooked a pistol free from his belt, and shot off several rounds blindly as they sought the safety of an alcove.

"Can you see where they are?" he breathed, curiously examining the new holes in his torso and limbs.

"Leaning over the railing, I think," Alice said, looking up. "They're going to get us pinned down."

"What do you reckon?"

She glanced around her, wiping a finger in the dust on a vase. "State of this place, you think it's got woodworm?" She smiled at him, then stood up from her hiding place, and put her semi to her shoulder, sighting it upwards on the banister above. Shots immediately rained down on her, and she took hits to the neck, arms and belly, but seemingly ignored them as she raked her fire on the structure itself, splintering the wood of the railing until it all but disintegrated. There was loud snap and it came apart, the whole balcony splitting in half. Alice dove back against the wall. As shards of debris plummeted, so they were followed by two bodies spiralling to the floor, hitting the hallway tiles with a sharp smack. Their necks twisted sideways, neither of them stirred.

Gabe whistled. "Nice shootin', Tex." He caught sight of the extent of her wounds, blood seeping from a gouge that had removed a good portion of her left cheek. "You OK?"

Alice shrugged. "A few more leaks, nothing I won't grow used to. Come on, let's keep moving, use the noise as cover."

They speedily climbed the rest of the stairs, shrouded in the clouds of grey dust that hung in the air. Gabe spotted the door that led to Anna's room and strode towards it, not knowing what he was going to do or say once he crossed the threshold, or indeed what would be waiting for him on the other side. He had laid his hand on the handle when he heard the voice.

"Just like old times, eh, O'Connell?"

Hewitt emerged from the shadows of the corridor, the silhouettes of two other figures behind him. They were all armed.

"Never thought I'd get to kill you twice."

CHAPTER TWENTY

"Drop your weapons," Hewitt ordered. They did as they were told, metal hitting the floorboards with a dry thump.

The kid looked terrible. The youth was still evident in his face – his resurrection had halted any ageing process, freezing him in that early twenties self-regard that Gabe had been so familiar with a decade earlier – but he hadn't escaped the effects of Gannon's chemical agent. Half of Hewitt's features were sagging on the right side, his eye, eyebrow, cheek and the corner of his mouth dripping like melted wax, the flesh hanging from his jaw in a grey dewlap. His hands too were pinkish claws, the skin stripped from the layers of muscle, and he gripped the shotgun in an insectile manner, white bone and knotted tendons visibly jutting between his knuckles. When he spoke, his words were slurred and apparently difficult to form, spilling from his mouth in a weary monotone.

"Why am I not surprised?" he said. "Somehow I had a feeling you'd be back."

"We all come back these days," Gabe replied.

"True." He contemplated this. "Y'know, I should've shot you in the head. Thought there'd be more indignity in seeing you staggering around with the rest of the deadfucks. Can't even rely on that now. Even the maggotdicks are pulling themselves out of their tombs, dusting themselves down and pretending to be civilised."

"They're evolving."

"Towards what? You think you're more human than dead, O'Connell? Have you seen your reflection lately?"

"Look who's talking."

Hewitt made a guttural croak, which Gabe assumed was

his nearest approximation of a laugh. "Yeah, you fucked us up. What the hell have you done to us, anyway?" He held up his contorted limbs in wonder.

"It's an airborne flesh-eating agent that was injected into those stiffs currently crisping up at the gate. Once the voltage hit them and they exploded, it was released."

Hewitt chuckled again. "Well, you got your revenge. Harry threw you out as his favourite son, and you wanted a little payback. That don't mean you're about to join the ranks of the living."

"That was never my intention," Gabe replied. "I'm just here to bring things to a close." He studied Hewitt curiously. "Talking of the old man, how's that working out for you, being his second in command? The position everything you hoped it would be? I know how much you wanted it."

"Fuck you, traitor."

"'Cause I also know it was you that shot me that night on Westminster Bridge, as I tried to escape. Shot me in the leg, for either the zombs or the army to get me. Either way, I was a dead man, and you were just the person to fill that vacancy."

The two Returners standing sentinel either side of the kid glanced at their colleague sharply.

Hewitt raised the shotgun, pumping the slide. "Guess this is third-time lucky–"

Gabe's eyes slid to one of the other figures. "Hey, Hendricks – how are the dogs?"

"Long gone." He had similarly suffered from the agent, his hair missing in clumps, the pigmentation of his skin almost boiled white. His voice was a low rumble. "Once Harry insisted we resurrect, the dogs couldn't stay. They wouldn't be comfortable around us. So he told me I had to kill them, every one. And I did."

"Hewitt here used to hate the stiffs with a passion," Gabe said. "Wanted to wipe them all from the face of the earth. Now he's a zomb himself. It's funny what we're prepared to do on the instructions of our masters."

"Enough." Hewitt strode forward, the shotgun held to his shoulder. "We've heard enough of your fucking bullshit." He swung the weapon towards Alice. "You thought you were going to help him overthrow Harry? Did he talk you into it? Talk up the revolution?" His grip tightened on the barrel. "You know what? It was for nothing. Because nothing changes. *Ever.*"

At point-blank range, he discharged the shotgun into Alice face, and her head disappeared in a wet explosion of crimson skull shards, a red spray hitting the wall behind her. The body beneath crumpled in a swirl of dust and gunsmoke. The ear-splitting retort blasted Gabe into a momentary daze, but the second her lifeless corpse hit the ground at his feet, he snapped back into focus. With a yell he lunged at Hewitt, and tried to grab him around the neck, but the kid was too fast. He weaved out of Gabe's reach, then brought up the gun butt and slammed it into his temple, dropping him to his knees.

"You were a fool to come back," Hewitt snarled, standing over him. "You should've disappeared when you had the chance, grateful at your resurrection. Instead, you throw it all away on some petty pissant attempt at retribution." He straightened, withdrawing more shells from his pocket, chambering them into the shotgun. "I don't know what your problem is, O'Connell. You seem to go out of your way to make trouble for yourself."

"I was doing the right thing," Gabe murmured.

Hewitt snorted, mucus thick in his throat. "Like that means anything. Not so long ago, you thought being part of Harry's outfit was the right thing to do." He leaned in closer again. "Right and wrong have no place in this world anymore. It's just circumstances, and what you can get out of them. Isn't that what the old man taught you?"

"That's always been Flowers' way, but it's no longer mine."

"You're a weak, naive fucking idiot," Hewitt rasped and placed the shotgun to Gabe's head. "How many times have I got to put a bullet in you to make my point?"

Gabe rolled at the moment Hewitt's finger tightened on the trigger, knocking the barrel with his hand a fraction to the left just as he fired. He felt the shot scrape the side of cheek and singe his hair as the shell powered into the skirting board. Again the roar deafened him, but he was moving despite the stars dancing before his eyes. He grappled with Hewitt for control of the gun, which was gripped upwards between them.

"Fucking shoot him!" Hewitt yelled at his comrades, but they hesitated, seemingly unsure of what action to take.

Wrenching the shotgun to one side, Gabe seized the advantage and drove his forehead into the bridge of Hewitt's nose, already rendered shapeless by the chemical agent. It burst like a grape, and he staggered backwards. Gabe wrested the shotgun from him, spinning around in time to see one of the pair – the enforcer he didn't recognise – finally advancing towards him. Gabe put two shots through him, blowing him across the landing to tumble down the stairs.

He swung back to Hewitt, grabbed him by the collar and stuck the gun under his chin. "You know what your problem is, pal? You underestimate people." He fired, detonating the top of Hewitt's head; brain matter exited in a purple stream and twisted itself around the chandeliers like a Christmas decoration. He threw the remains of the kid's body over the balcony. Then he turned back to face Hendricks, who remained motionless a few feet away.

"I don't want to have to do this," Gabe warned. Hendricks nodded and held up his hands in surrender, letting go of his semi-automatic. "Get out of here," he continued. "Don't waste any more of your... life... protecting him." He made a sideways motion of the head towards the door. Hendricks nodded again, and cautiously backed down the stairs until he vanished from sight.

Gabe leaned back against the wall, putting a hand to the side of his face that had taken a portion of the shotgun blast; his fingers disappeared into a rent in his cheek and brushed against his teeth and gumline. It had been closer than he thought, and had disintegrated a considerable section of flesh. Touching his scalp, there were deep bald grooves where it had seared past. Christ, how much of him was going to be left? He felt as if he was strung together by the flimsiest of threads.

He glanced sadly at Alice's headless cadaver, reasoning that at least she was at some kind of peace, free from the limitations of this fragile shell. He'd known little about her pre-death, and she hadn't been willing to reveal the human she'd once been. The other Returners that had pledged to help him had been the same. It was as if it was too painful to remember their past lives, of what they had once been. But now there would be no more resurrections, no more hunger, no more shuddering awareness of the creature that she – that all of them – had become. It was an end, final and complete.

"Won't be long before I'll join you," he whispered. Then he turned back to the door, yanked down on the handle and entered.

The room was just as he remembered it from all those

years ago. It was as if by crossing the threshold he had stepped back in time by a decade or more. Unlike the decay that had tainted the rest of the building, this room – Anna's room – remained strangely untouched by the ravages of the passing months. The clock still ticked somnolently on the mantelpiece, the bare walls still tracked the progress of the passing sun, the chair still stood before the window, the curtains pulled back to reveal the expanse of the gardens, and the occupant of the chair was still seated upon it, facing the glass. On this occasion, however, there was someone else in the room. He was knelt on the carpet beside the chair, his hands perched on the arm, his head bowed. Gabe closed the door quietly behind him, and walked towards the pair, the shotgun hanging loosely at his side. He stopped no more than a couple of feet from the prone figure.

"Harry."

Flowers looked up, age and pain prominent in his eyes before recognition flooded in to join them. "Gabriel, my boy. To what do I owe this pleasure?" He didn't seem surprised at his presence.

"I've come to kill you. To tear all this down."

"Just you?"

"No. I've brought some others with me. If you look out the window, you'll see them."

Flowers swivelled and peered into the grounds. Somehow, Beth and Adam had succeeded in breaking open the gates – or at least a section of them – and the walking dead were stumbling through. The sporadic *thwump* of a landmine being triggered could be intermittently heard, and the glass shook in its frame with each explosion. But there were enough of them to easily swamp the defences.

"They've come to reclaim what's theirs," Gabe said.

The old man turned back to face him. "And you? You've come for my daughter?"

"Just to set her free."

Flowers laughed. "She doesn't need you for that, son. She's quite capable of doing it for herself."

"What do you mean?"

"Meaning," he reached out and placed a hand on hers, though she remained motionless, "I'm losing her with every passing second."

"You lost her a long time ago." He paused, studying his former boss. "Tell me something, Harry – you feel all this was worth it? Your acquisition of power. Was it worth the expense? What it cost you?"

Flowers withdrew his hand and stood. "I've hated myself for what I've had to do over the years. But somebody needed to take control, you must know that. You saw it when you joined my organisation – you were unused to the kind of work myself and my boys deal with, but you stuck around, especially after the outbreak. Why? Because for all that you might've despised me, you recognised there was somebody making decisions, formulating plans. A position like that is a beacon around which others gather, an anchor in uncertain times. But it requires sacrifices."

"Don't play the fucking martyr," Gabe snapped. "Everything you did, you did for your own benefit."

"Maybe. But don't kid yourself that you coming here is some kind of noble gesture. You're assuaging your own guilt too, for the mess you left behind."

"I always told her I'd be here for her. That's why I continued to work for you, and that's why I'm here right now. To try to bring her back."

"Well, you're too late," Flowers murmured. "She's lost to us both."

"What you mean is that the wound you inflicted a decade or more ago has finally reached her heart," Gabe snarled. "And now you can put her in the ground where she won't be a problem any longer."

Flowers' eyes flamed with anger. "I was protecting her, like any father would."

"Yeah? That what you told her infant son, as you held him for the final time?"

The older man let a bellow of rage and backhanded Gabe across the face. The impact knocked him back but he barely felt it. He swung the shotgun into Flowers' midriff, doubling him up, then delivered a powerful blow across the back of his head, a strike so hard it splintered the wooden stock of the weapon. He discarded the gun, grabbed Flowers by the throat and lifted him up against the wall, his fingers digging into the cold skin of his neck.

"You think... you're any better than me, O'Connell?" Flowers hissed, blood and drool dribbling from his mouth. "We're just two creatures... from the grave, who... should've died a long time ago."

"Difference is, I tried everything I could to stop becoming the monster, whereas you embraced it. But you know what? For you, I'll make the exception." Gabe pushed the old man's head back, exposing a tract of flesh. But just as he leaned in to take a bite, he felt a hand on his shoulder. He cast a quizzical glance over his shoulder, and saw Anna standing behind him. He relaxed his hold on Flowers, and stepped back; she was looking at her father, eyes full of shadow, her features composed in a death mask.

"Anna?" Flowers whispered.

"Dad." Her voice didn't seem to come as much from her lips as from *within* her, vast and emotionless.

"I'm so sorry."

His words were barely audible, but even so she shushed him quiet, placing a hand on his cheek, stroking it, moving down to his throat. She held it there, then tightened and squeezed and tugged, wrenching open her father's windpipe, which came free with a moist sluicing sound. He gargled, the rotten tissue of his neck collapsing without the support. Anna planted two hands on either side of his head and twisted it like a screw-cap, decapitating him with one swift motion. She studied her father's head for a moment, kissed it lightly before dropping it to the floor, then stepped back beside the window. Gabe moved forward, and took her crimson-stained hand in his.

"I'm not going to become like you," she said quietly, her gaze roving over the world beyond the glass.

"I know."

"I'm not going to stay."

"Me neither."

Anna lay her head on Gabe's shoulder, and they stood there in silence, framed against the light.

They found Gannon not far from where they'd left him, crouched among the scrub. He raised his eyebrows that it was just the two of them.

"Gabe was never coming back," Beth said, before the question could be voiced.

"But the charges have been lit?"

Adam nodded. "With the deadheads providing the distraction, it wasn't difficult to start the fire."

The three of them watched as smoke began to billow from Harry Flowers' mansion, windows shattering from the heat, flames greedily swallowing timbers, dark black clouds massing above the roof. The dead that had poured through into the grounds stopped and circled the conflagration, like pilgrims to a great mystical vision. Beth wondered briefly if it was her imagination, or whether she actually saw a couple intertwined at an upstairs room, unconcerned by the encroaching fire, gazing back out at their audience; but in an instant they were gone, hidden by the roiling, thick smoke.

They watched until the house was no more than a blackened skeleton, a husk, confident that it wouldn't rise again. Then they turned and started back towards the city.

EPILOGUE

The Quiet Earth

I lingered round them, under that benign sky: watched the moths fluttering among the heath and hare-bells; listened to the soft wind breathing through the grass; and wondered how any one could ever imagine unquiet slumbers for the sleepers in that quiet earth.

Emily Brontë,
Wuthering Heights

22 MAY 1992
Foothills North of Srebrenica,
Bosnia-Herzegovina

Bird cry echoes through the valleys, sharp and distant and mournful, like a parent calling for a lost child, and the black shadows of great wheeling shapes, wings outspread, circle the verdant slopes of the lowlands. A wind ruffles through the landscape, long grass dipping with the same tremulous undulation as the rhythmic pulse of a sea tide, and he stands with his face to the breeze, allowing himself to be buffeted by it. His skin is pocked with grit, his eyes watering from the flecks of dirt blown into them, yet he refuses to turn away. He feels like he's composed of shifting sand, subject to the whims of the elements; or maybe one of the skeletal trees perched upon the outcroppings, clinging tenaciously to life as it's stripped and scoured by an unstoppable eroding force. The chill in the air numbs his ears, dries his lips, and causes his nose to run – he wipes it on his sleeve – but the sky is the colour of sapphire and nothing can diminish the unblemished beauty of the vast canopy above him. It is a glorious spring morning, one in which the blood rushes a little faster and the hair tingles in syncopation with the new season budding around it.

He likes to take at least one moment a day to appreciate the country in this way, which has otherwise been disfigured by conflict. It serves as a reminder that time and nature will prevail, despite his species' best interests; that the planet keeps turning, that the sun continues to bestow its nourishing rays upon the surface, teasing seed into bloom, oblivious to the rampant designs of his kind. This land has seen enough hate wrought upon it to deface it permanently, the scars running deep below root and rock to leave it irrevocably changed, yet it refuses to be battered into ugliness: it continues, unbowed, to exist while all around it death tries to spread its taint.

It's a small moment of marvel, and one that he never

grows tired of experiencing. He flicks the last of his ash off the end of his cigarette, and drops the butt into the mud, grinding it out with his heel. Breathing in that fresh-dew smell, swelling his chest with cool mountain air, he reaches for his shovel and hums as he begins to dig, dark soil turning beneath his blade. For two long hours he toils, producing a pit several feet square, work so professionally accomplished that he barely gives it a second glance, rarely stops to consider its size; he knows from instinct that its dimensions are correct. He's dug many more like it, and the procedure has the touch of routine about it, his labour accompanied constantly by quiet and tuneless melodies, as if he's unaware he's even making a sound. His movements are swift and unhampered by doubt, aware that he cannot afford to linger too long; this will not be the only hole he will have to dig before the day is done.

Hoisting himself out of the pit, he tosses the spade aside and grabs the nearest of the bodies by the legs, dragging it towards its makeshift grave. All the corpses have been wrapped in linen and tightly bound, and he is relieved that at least he does not have to look them in the face when he showers the dirt down upon them; but even so he can tell by the size and weight of this cadaver that it was a child, no more than a teenager. It is not the first he has buried, but that doesn't make it easier, to feel its lightness as he hefts it in his arms for a moment before allowing it to tumble into the ground. He hopes that the bodies that will be following it are the child's family – it makes little sense in the scheme of things, but provides some crumb of comfort that they will have each other's company beneath the soil – yet there is no way for sure of knowing. There are too many dead requiring his attention, and the niceties of a civilised grave have been foregone in the interests of speed and sheer quantity. Entire villages have been decimated, carcasses line the roads, and he has been charged with their disposal. So he retrieves the next and the one after that, filling his pit with these human-shaped parcels, humming in that cracked voice, stopping to pile the dirt back in once it is full before starting to dig again. He coughs, sniffs, wipes back tears, and continues, knowing he has no time to dawdle; and knowing too that this job will never be finished, not by him nor his successors. It is an insurmountable task, and yet one that he has accepted and one he will endeavour to complete while there is still breath left in his lungs.

The birds cry to one another as they skate low across the windswept hills, their shadows playing on the heaped mound of bodies that extends around the base of the valley: there are thousands of them, with no markers to distinguish each swaddled corpse from its neighbour. The dead congregate patiently as they await their return to the quiet earth, now gratefully far from the words of their roaring.

Matthew Smith was employed as a desk editor for Pan Macmillan book publishers for three years before joining *2000 AD* as assistant editor in July 2000 to work on a comic he had read religiously since 1985. He became editor of the Galaxy's Greatest in December 2001, and then editor-in-chief of the *2000 AD* titles in January 2006. He has written one other novel, *Judge Dredd: The Final Cut,* and lives in Oxford.

coming
October
2007...

Now read the first chapter from the third book in
the chilling *Tomes of The Dead* collection...

TOMES OF THE DEAD

THE DEVIL'S PLAGUE

Mark Beynon

COMING OCTOBER 2007 (UK)
DECEMBER 2007 (US)

ISBN 13: 978-1-905437-41-2
ISBN 10: 1-905437-41-2

£6.99 (UK)/ $7.99 (US)

WWW.ABADDONBOOKS.COM

CHAPTER ONE

The Battle of Worcester
3rd September, 1651

The battlefield was stained a dark reddish brown and the once lush green meadows were littered with corpses. Blood coursed through the Rivers Severn and Teme whilst the aptly named Red Hill was just that.

Oliver Cromwell surveyed the carnage in front of him with a wry smile. It was whispered from the narrowest street in London to the vastest field in Edinburgh that Cromwell was the anti-Christ and that his Generals were his minions. Closer inspection of the battlefield would only add credence to such rumour-mongering. None of those lying dead and decapitated wore red. The Puritans' colour. Cromwell's colour. Instead, almost four thousand Royalist Scots lay lifeless and inert, eight hundred of which came from the Clan MacLeod.

One would have been forgiven for believing that Cromwell had single-handedly slayed his enemy as none of his soldiers were in sight, just a handful of his Generals who had the painstakingly unenviable task of sifting through the dead Scots in search of one man.

"Have you found him?" Cromwell yelled out in the direction of Thomas Harrison, a runtish Major General, aiding those sieving through the nearby body parts.

"No sign of him yet, sir." Harrison hadn't the heart to tell him that those lying dead were so badly mutilated they were virtually indistinguishable from one another.

"Have your men help you."

"My men are sleeping, sir. I fear the scent and sight of blood would set them off again." Harrison spoke with a faint sign of trepidation in his voice. Was he scared of his own men?

"Quite right, Harrison," replied Cromwell reassuringly.

Even though his pact with the Devil had cost him his friendship with his dear friend Thomas Fairfax, Cromwell's leadership and authority were no longer in question. He was a far cry from the once obscure and inexperienced Cambridgeshire MP – he was now one of the power-brokers in Parliament. Cromwell had played a decisive role in the revolution during the winter of 1649, which saw the trial and execution of King Charles I and the abolition of the Monarchy and the House of Lords.

It was often rumoured in the darkest corners of the darkest taverns that Cromwell must have sold his soul to the Devil in order to find the gall to execute a King. They would say that in return, the Devil covered Cromwell's body in warts.

Those drunken sots would never know how right they were.

"I'VE FOUND HIM, SIR!" Harrison could barely contain his excitement. He stood triumphantly over an unrecognisable bloodied heap strewn across the turf, seemingly identical to thousands of other bloodied heaps. Cromwell flicked the reigns on his horse, prompting it into a smart gallop. He marvelled at the thought of being the man responsible for the deaths of two Kings, father and son. That would send those Royalist bastards back to Edinburgh without a monarch!

As he dismounted, he examined the evidence – the

Royal coat of arms engraved on the man's chest plate. *This had to be Charles*. The arms of England and France were placed in the first and fourth quarters, the arms of Scotland were placed in the second quarter and the arms of Ireland in the third quarter. The same coat of arms had belonged to his father, Cromwell noted.

"Well done, Harrison. Well done indeed. We have our man. Send word to the committees that Charles Stuart is dead and the war is over."

However, Cromwell had underestimated his adversary. Little did he know that just prior to the battle, Charles had switched his armour with a decoy. He had fought side by side with the common man, not leading from the front as a King would. And little did Cromwell know that hiding up in the branches of a nearby oak tree with the Scottish soldier John Middleton, was none other than Charles Stuart, King of Scotland and rightful heir to the throne of England.

By the time the last of Cromwell's Generals had left the battlefield, a deep trench had been dug and the dead bodies hurled into the dark void. A vulgar burial. The sun was setting in the red sky, mirroring the earth below. It would take months, maybe years for the stains of battle to be washed away.

In the deepest part of the trench, something moved. A twitch at first, the merest of spasms. The dead man lay motionless, like his four thousand comrades piled high and wide of him. Yet in him seemed to linger a vivid spark of vitality, some faint sign of consciousness in his malevolent eyes. And then he blinked.

And so did the dead man next to him...

The Mug House, Bewdley
6ᵗʰ September, 1651

Little Cave Underhill shivered as the biting Autumnal wind gripped his young bones. He rubbed his hands together furiously in a vain attempt to provide further warmth as the brisk wind blew his thick tousled hair over his eyes. Although only twelve years of age, Underhill's demeanour suggested he was a good deal older. He could hear the performance from within; several inaudible lines of dialogue followed by a groan of audience disapproval. They were performing *Salmacida Spolia* tonight, one of William Davenant's own poems, notoriously despised by audiences of rich and poor alike.

Underhill took comfort in the fact that one day he'd be an actor and then some other poor bastard could freeze to death as sentry. Yet he knew his place and he owed his life to Davenant for rescuing him from the Fleet Street poorhouse; the stinking, diseased, rotting hellhole it was. As an orphan, Davenant was the closest thing to a father he'd ever had. He never knew his parents, although he later discovered that his mother had sent him to the poorhouse as a weak and helpless two year old. He was forced to work as soon as he could walk, thus he grew up very quickly.

He smiled contently; it might have been bitterly cold, but keeping watch outside the tavern was paradise in comparison to his previous job. As a Saltpetre Boy he had had to break into premises or dig up latrines to collect as much urine as possible for the manufacture of saltpetre, which in turn was used to make gunpowder. The Saltpetre Company's slogan – 'We're taking the piss' – caused much hilarity amongst the actors, but it was breaking into Davenant's house that had changed Underhill's life. Davenant had found him trying to escape through his loft, took pity on the poor wretch and offered him a job within his troupe of players. He had to endure frequent jibes and keeping guard wasn't much of a job, but he had found a family, and all the while Cromwell and his Puritan hordes insisted on banning theatre, someone had to keep a look out.

It was ironic, he thought. Why would a man like Cromwell, a man rumoured to have a close affiliation with the Devil himself, want to close down the theatre which had long been known as Satan's chapel, or dens of vice and immorality, and the actors the spawn of Lucifer? He drew his blanket closer and admired the fine architecture of the building overlooking him. A smart, modest tavern which dominated the narrow street. The theatre might have been abolished, but these buildings left a proud legacy. Intricate carvings depicting bear baiting and cock fighting were embossed in the wooden beams. Cromwell had dispensed with those frivolities too, along with 'lewd and heathen' maypole dancing. And Christmas! From the perspective of a child, there was no greater sin. A real killjoy, he thought.

"The rich make full of avarice as pride."

William Davenant stood alone upon a crudely built stage within the tavern's dingy cellar. The willowy flames of a rough torch hung in an iron bracket revealed the grime and residue clinging to the two-hundred year old stone. The stench of rank ale and sweat was almost too much for Davenant to bear, yet he continued to perform with admirable vigour. His ruggedly handsome quality was well hidden underneath his vulgar, ill-fitted costume and ludicrously garish makeup.

"Like graves, or swallowing seas, unsatisfied."

He gestured flamboyantly much to the ridicule of his audience, comprised solely of drunken revellers huddled together in a darkened corner.

"Call yourself an actor? You're bloody 'opeless," bellowed one of the revellers.

Davenant ignored the goading and carried on regardless. "From poor men's fortunes, never from their own."

"We want Shakespeare!" The outspoken reveller had pushed his way to the front, swaying drunkenly from side to side. His taunt drew one or two sniggers from his fellow dwellers.

"Well you can't have him," hissed Davenant, breaking temporarily out of character. He turned pleadingly to Thomas Betterton, a fellow actor stood at the side of the stage. Betterton was young, brash and carried himself with an air of complacency. He shrugged his shoulders nonchalantly, much to Davenant's annoyance.

Davenant had discovered Betterton's precocious talent on the London stage. He was playing Claudio in his company's underground presentation of *Much Ado About Nothing*. The show was abysmal but Davenant had seen sufficient potential in his performance to offer him a place within the players. When the majority of Betterton's company were conveniently arrested and imprisoned in The Tower after Cromwell's men had received a tip-off from a vagrant, he leapt at the chance of working with Davenant, a real name on the circuit. However, Davenant's insistence on performing his own plays and poems coupled with the ensuing heckling had begun to take its toll on Betterton. He wanted Shakespeare too! And he wasn't afraid to let Davenant know it.

Underhill blew warm air into his freezing hands. He could hear the muffled bickering emanating from the cellar. Indeed, he was used to such an occurrence. The previous week in Ipswich, Davenant had called the landlord of some boisterous watering hole a 'toothless simpleton.' It had sparked a small riot in which Davenant and his fellow players were forced to escape through a small priest hole hidden within the chimney. He ignored the quarrelling and proceeded to sit on his hands. He'd rather they were numb than icy cold.

A faint pounding resonated along the narrow street. Underhill ignored it at first, thinking that it was probably just a horse-drawn carriage. It became louder, closer. Underhill got to his feet gingerly. He craned his neck to peer down the street. Five or six mounted shadows moved furtively, yet rapidly towards him. As the shadows drew closer, the noise became louder – a distinct pounding of hooves clattering along the stones followed by a high pitched hissing between razor-sharp teeth.

Cromwell's men. *The Kryfangan.*

Davenant had always told Underhill that the play was not to be disturbed 'unless it was of the utmost importance.' Well this was of the utmost importance. The Kryfangan had been trailing Davenant for months and Cromwell had even gone as far as to offer a reward for his capture. Underhill could imagine numerous members of tonight's audience willing to make themselves a fast shilling.

He wasted no time in bounding inside the tavern and descending the rickety wooden steps that led down into the cellar. He could see that the play was in disarray. Davenant was appealing for calm whilst Betterton was seemingly egging the revellers on.

"CROMWELL'S MEN! THEY'RE OUTSIDE!" Underhill was surprised to find his shrill appeal generating such a silence, as he was far more used to being ignored and overlooked completely. In an instant, every man within the cellar had turned to face him, unsure of their next move. "Well don't just stand there! They're coming!"

En masse, the revellers pushed past Underhill, who fell awkwardly and got trampled underfoot.

Davenant and Betterton hurriedly gathered together their belongings, although in the confusion a solitary silver costume was clumsily left behind. Underhill was hoisted to his feet by Davenant, wincing as they clambered up the staircase. Once in the tavern, Davenant slammed the cellar hatch down, dislodging dust and grime as it bounced off the timber floor.

After joining the melee outside, they darted through the cool night air, along the cobblestone and into the pool of darkness that enveloped the end of the street. Davenant looked back only once. Once was enough. He could just make out the dull red eyes belonging to the Kryfangan as they mercilessly smashed open the tavern door.

Charles Fleetwood, Cromwell's Major General, strode inside. Fleetwood was in his thirties, tall, imposing. His cropped red hair complemented his notoriously fiery temperament. His fellow Generals, Lambert and Desborough, followed closely behind. Giving the distinct impression of being the hired help, they stood menacingly on either side of Fleetwood. All three men were dressed head to toe in their black Puritan robes, hats, jerkins and boots – a look that had become synonymous with evil.

Fleetwood scowled as he inspected the ageing tavern. The Kryfangan had already torn it to pieces. Broken glass littered the floor. Wooden furniture was turned upside down.

"Actors! The stench of vanity is overwhelming." Fleetwood spat his words out venomously. His eyes wandered around the room until they fell on the cellar hatch in the corner, dust hanging above it like fog. "The cellar."

Fleetwood marched over to the hatch and tore it open, shards of glass shattering underneath his heavy boots. He clambered down the rickety staircase, a cascade of moonlight pursuing him. Desborough followed, handing Fleetwood a lantern which he duly held aloft. He waved it around, illuminating the makeshift stage.

Fleetwood turned sharply to Lambert who was half way down the staircase. "Have your men scour the area. They can't have got far."

Lambert nodded in acknowledgement before hauling himself back up. Fleetwood and Desborough paced onto the stage. The silver costume glistened in the lantern light, catching Fleetwood's attention immediately. He knelt down to pick it up before thrusting it in Desborough's direction – a half-smirk crossing his lips.

"*Davenant!*"

Davenant, Betterton and Underhill emerged from the end of a narrow alleyway, fighting their way through the thick withes and strands of ivy that covered the entrance like a giant spider's web. They walked briskly, like the criminals they were, inconspicuously fleeing the scene of the crime.

Davenant, still dressed in his ridiculous costume, panted from the exertion. "I've had it with these tavern dwellers," he said, in between breaths.

"Well, if you gave them what they wanted," replied Betterton, typically antagonistic.

Davenant stopped dead in his tracks. He turned to face Betterton, carrying a face like thunder. "I've told you a thousand times! We will not perform Shakespeare in *my* company."

Betterton sneered at the remark. It was hard to take a man seriously when he was dressed up like a workhouse whore. "What about us? Don't we at least have a say in the matter?"

"You forget it is I who pays your wage and you'll do as I say. Now, if we're done with arguing?" Davenant strode off, Underhill followed close behind.

"We'd perform Shakespeare with Killigrew!"

Davenant stopped and faced Betterton once more. This time he'd *really* struck a chord. "That is because Killigrew is a fat, illiterate windbag. You're far better off performing *my* plays and learning your craft with *me*." Davenant was incandescent, even behind a thick layer of white stage makeup. "Besides, Killigrew couldn't write a lurid limerick if his life depended on it!"

Betterton shot Underhill a glance. They both grinned.

Davenant hated Thomas Killigrew more than he hated the lowly tavern dwellers. In the reign of Charles I, Davenant and Killigrew had vied for the King's patronage. After much mudslinging and bad tempered poetry, Davenant was rewarded with the office of poet-laureate and was subsequently knighted by the King. And then the Civil War broke out, ruining the aspirations of playwrights and actors across the country.

A despondent donkey, attached to a rickety old cart,

sat conspicuously at the side of a woodland path, whilst a stout, middle-aged gentleman kept guard.

"Over 'ere! Mister Davenant, sir!" The gentleman, George Turnbull, was Davenant's trusted manservant. Davenant put his finger to his lips, appealing for silence. Turnbull was a simpleton and his behaviour somewhat childlike; a stark contrast to his formidable bulk. It was a marvel he hadn't caught the pox in his hedonistic days. Davenant had found him loitering outside a house of ill repute. On this occasion, he'd got himself into trouble with money, so Davenant generously settled his bill. In return, Turnbull pledged his allegiance and remained his dogsbody a decade later. Davenant knew only too well what happened when someone crossed Turnbull, with many an unruly theatre goer having paid the price for heckling. On more than one occasion he'd had to haul Turnbull off a drunkard before he beat him to death.

Turnbull proceeded to wave his arms in the air in an effort to catch Davenant's attention.

"Yes, I can see you, you great lump," said Davenant under his breath. He turned to Betterton and Underhill who were ambling idly behind him. "Not a word of our narrow escape to the others." There was a marked sincerity in his voice, seemingly reserved for times of importance.

As they reached the mule and cart, a striking young girl emerged from the darkness. Her long auburn hair ran all the way to the small of her back. Her legs were as long as paradise and her bosom the prize for having made the voyage. She had a kind, caring face of chiselled perfection, coupled with a sumptuous beauty.

"So? How did it go?" Elizabeth Davenant had a genuine interest in her father's well-being.

"As well as could be expected. The Mug House is hardly

the Globe," replied Davenant, trying to loosen his ill-fitted costume.

"You should have given them Shakespeare," said Elizabeth innocently. Betterton let out a sly cackle.

"Elizabeth, my dear, could you pass me my clothes?"

"Either give them Shakespeare, or let us girls on the stage." Elizabeth handed Davenant's extravagant doublet to him. It had been a long time since he was able to afford one of these. It explained its shabby appearance; the elbows had faded to a matt sheen where they had rested on the tables in so many inns.

"The last thing we need is the fairer sex treading the boards," replied Davenant, disappearing behind a nearby tree to get changed.

Betterton waited until Davenant was out of sight before sidling up to Elizabeth. "I missed you tonight," he said, running his hand gently down the silk of her skirt.

"Not here. Not now." She pushed him away, conscious of her father's gaze. Davenant had caught them together before in a deserted barn on the outskirts of Lowestoft. On that occasion Elizabeth had to plead with him not to fire Betterton, yet she could understand her father's controlling nature. Davenant's wife had died shortly after giving birth to Elizabeth and although he had resented his daugher at first, he soon became the devoted father, not least because of her startling resemblance to her mother.

Although he rated Betterton as a young actor, the thought of him courting Elizabeth made him feel sick to his stomach. She was far too pretty, far too perfect for a young upstart like him. In Davenant's eyes, she belonged to a Prince – or someone with vast sums of money to keep him in his dotage.

The Kryfangan approached stealthily on horseback. They'd got the scent from the silver costume and had picked up the trail not far from the riverbank. They had the taste for blood now – as if the flesh from the four thousand Scots hadn't abated their appetite. Their faces were concealed, sunk deep into their hooded cloaks, although one of the Kryfangan was revealed by the stark moonlight as his horse strayed momentarily off course. Two little pip-like eyes lurked in the depths of the dark, vacant sockets. They glowed red. Puritan red. Several jagged, thin teeth, like those of a rat, overlaid its withered lower lip.

It pulled sharply on its horses reigns, almost snapping its neck. The horse duly obeyed and cantered back onto the concealed path.

The Kryfangan hissed.

It began to rain. Davenant wanted to get back on the road and as far away from Bewdley as possible. He could have sworn he heard a shrill hissing when he was getting changed behind the tree and was mindful that Cromwell's men were on the lookout for him. Davenant had no idea who the red-eyed hooded horsemen were or how dangerous they might be, but he had no intention of finding out tonight. Those eyes had scared him, not for the first time.

"Let's move out," he commanded.

Turnbull sprung into action, gathering together the few belongings scattered across the path; a lantern, Davenant's gaudy costume, several wooden platters and a spare jerkin. Underhill urinated into a nearby bush. He had been needing that for hours.

Suddenly, a branch snapped close by.

Davenant snatched the lantern from Turnbull and waved it around, lighting up the immediate vicinity. Nothing, no-one.

Elizabeth sought refuge in the unsteady wooden cart. Betterton followed. Underhill didn't move a muscle. They'd rehearsed a rough drill to prepare themselves for times like these. Underhill cursed his luck – the drill never involved him pissing into close at hand foliage.

Another branch snapped. This time Davenant was able to pinpoint its location – it came from above. He reluctantly shone the lantern upwards, half terrified of what he'd find prowling in the treetops.

To his surprise, he found two men staring back at him. One of them was a King.

For more information on this
and other titles visit...

Abaddon
Books

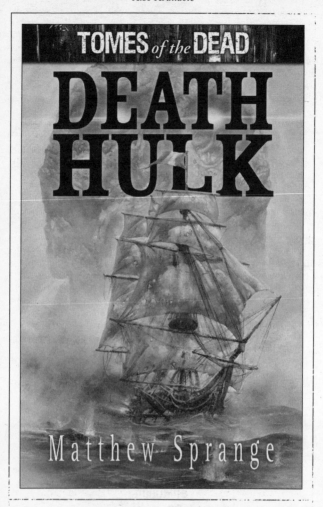

TOMES *of the* DEAD

DEATH HULK

Matthew Sprange

Price: £6.99 ★ ISBN: 1-905437-03X

Price: $7.99 ★ ISBN 13: 978-1-905437-03-0

TOMES *of the* DEAD

THE DEVIL'S PLAGUE

Mark Beynon

Price: £6.99 ★ ISBN: 1-905437-41-2

Price: $7.99 ★ ISBN 13: 978-1-905437-41-2

THE AFTERBLIGHT CHRONICLES

The CULLED

Simon Spurrier

Price: £6.99 ★ ISBN: 1-905437-01-3

Price: $7.99 ★ ISBN 13: 978-1-905437-01-6

THE AFTERBLIGHT CHRONICLES

KILL OR CURE

Rebecca Levene

Price: £6.99 ★ ISBN: 1-905437-32-3

Price: $7.99 ★ ISBN 13: 978-1-905437-32-0

THE AFTERBLIGHT CHRONICLES

SCHOOL'S OUT

Scott Andrews

Price: £6.99 ★ ISBN: 1-905437-40-4

Price: $7.99 ★ ISBN 13: 978-1-905437-40-5

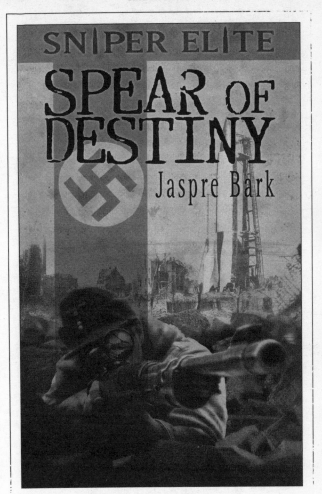

Price: £6.99 ★ ISBN: 1-905437-04-8

Price: $7.99 ★ ISBN 13: 978-1-905437-04-7

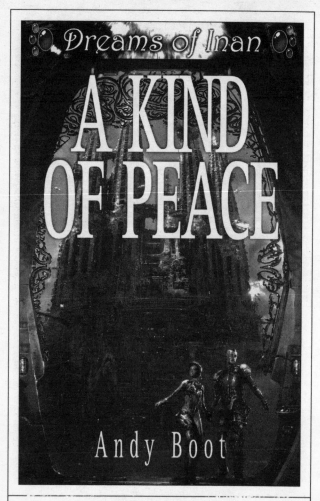

Dreams of Inan

A KIND OF PEACE

Andy Boot

Price: £6.99 ★ ISBN: 1-905437-12-9

Price: $7.99 ★ ISBN 13: 978-1-905437-12-2

Dreams of Inan

STEALING LIFE

Antony Johnston

Price: £6.99 ★ ISBN: 1-905437-12-9

Price: $7.99 ★ ISBN 13: 978-1-905437-12-2

PAX BRITANNIA

UNNATURAL
HISTORY

Jonathan Green

Price: £6.99 ★ ISBN: 1-905437-10-2

Price: $7.99 ★ ISBN 13: 978-1-905437-10-8

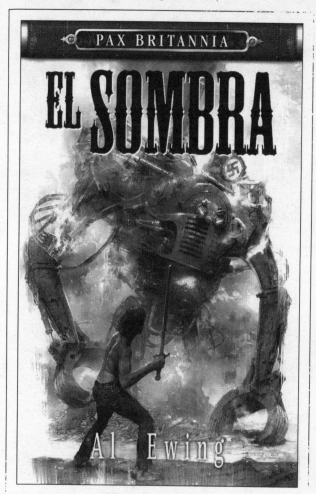

PAX BRITANNIA

EL SOMBRA

Al Ewing

Price: £6.99 ★ ISBN: 1-905437-34-X

Price: $7.99 ★ ISBN 13: 978-1-905437-34-4

Abaddon Books